I0642920

Time Gate
Crossing

Time Gate Crossing

Ted Tillotson

Time Gate Crossing

Published by Dragon Lair Books

Avenal, California

http://www.tedtillotsondragonlairbooks.com

Book design by Lord Dragon

ISBN 978-0615486833

Printed in the United States of America

Cover photo – courtesy of:

NASA/JPL-Caltech/UCLA

Also By Ted Tillotson

Available on Amazon.com and other retail outlets

Deathmaker – a dark psychological thriller

**Published by Omega Publications
Palm Springs, CA**

* * * *

***The Magic Meadow*
Kayla's fantasy**

**Published by
Dragon Lair Books**

Avenal, California

* * * *

Thorns of the Rose

* * * *

* * * *

Many thanks to my editor,

Norma Howell

She was tough, and usually right.

* * * *

I can't forget

James Callahan

**He helped solve many
Science issues**

* * * *

Philosophy of space and time

Theories of time travel are riddled with questions about causality and paradoxes. Compared to other fundamental concepts in modern physics, time is still not understood very well.

Philosophers have been theorizing about the nature of time since the era of the ancient Greek philosophers and earlier. Some philosophers and physicists who study the nature of time also study the possibility of time travel and its logical implications. The probability of paradoxes and their possible solutions are often considered.

Prologue

TIME TRAVEL ENFORCEMENT COMMISSION 12:00 pm Thursday, 7/15/2498

*P*hil Khrismann, head of TTEC, came out of his office just as his chief supervisor, Tim Carey, signaled a second-stage alert. Phil crossed the main control room and leaned against the console. "What've we got?" They both stared at the huge computer screen.

Tim keyed three digits. "Looks like an intrusion." The computer enlarged a section of the gate simulation. The two men looked at each other and smiled.

Phil said, "Scramble Zebra and get HRC online immediately!" He gripped Tim's shoulder. "Sonofabitch--we got a crossing!" Phil's excitement caught the other half-dozen technicians in the room. The entire E/C staff had worked *Time Gate* crossings *into* the past. None had experienced a crossing *from* the past—not in their lifetime.

Prologue II

Tim said, "HRC's on-line and tracking." A red square flashed on and off in the lower right corner of the big screen. "Zebra's on the grid, sir."

"Give Zebra-leader *Code Blue* until otherwise ordered." Phil stood away from the console. "I'm headed for the Command Center. Alert General Mackendrick. Just give him a *yellow.* I don't want him crashing in here with his ass on fire until we know more."

A green light flashed at the upper-left corner of Tim's screen. "There's HRC's report." He keyed a six-letter sequence.

The rest of the people in the control room gathered behind Phil and Tim. The History Research Commission's report filled Tim's monitor.

CROSSING INTRUSION CONFIRMED DESIGNATION: COMMERCIAL JET: HEAVY, 747-D 230 PASSENGERS & CREW: TIME PERIOD: TWENTIETH CENTURY: 1998: HRC DATA-SEARCH IN PROGRESS:
END REPORT

Tim said, "Zebra's locked on."

Phil Khrismann leaned on the control console and stared at the screen. "Order Zee-Leader to bring them down. I'll alert the chairman myself."

PART ONE

Present Time:

*I*t is fundamentally impossible
to create a time gate.

Within the time and space continuum,
tens of thousands of time gates already exist.

* * * *

Chapter One
The Chosen Five
Re-entry – 7/15/98

*C*ongressman Alan Franklin checked his watch again as the 747 jetliner flew across the United States. In less than sixty minutes the plane would crash. Alan, his wife and three others were set up to survive. They were the keys to the future.

Laura, Alan's wife, stopped writing and leaned toward him from the aisle seat. She clutched his arm and whispered, "I'm scared to death."

"In all my fifty three years, I haven't felt as excited as I do right now." The tall congressman shifted his two-hundred-ten pounds and managed a smile. He patted Laura's hand. "We'll be all right."

"It's impossible for me to really understand what happened, but I'm certain our lives will never be the same."

"Politically, yes," he lied. Alan had been shown every important event in the rest of his life. Including the circumstances of his own death. That is where he made the bargain. An agreement that may prove immoral. "As for us," he continued, "we'll be fine." He touched her soft face. His big hands were gentle and warm against her skin. She loved his touch on her face and in her soft, brown hair. She needed it now more than ever.

"I don't want to know any more." Laura's eyes widened, straightening her smile. "I can't believe what I already know." She shuddered again.

"Don't think about it. We're okay. All of us." He kissed her on the forehead. "Chairman Fisher assured us. I trust him more than the others." He kissed her again, on the lips. The soft loving took her back to snow-covered Iowa fields, balmy summer hayrides and dangerously sensual petting, which brought them together in marriage.

"When it's time, hold me." She looked into her husband's eyes deeply and shivered.

"You bet, beautiful lady ... I have to." When Alan embraced his wife he glanced at the small tablet on the fold down tray. The words were clear. Laura's handwriting stood out on the yellow paper like art work. Dear Robbie, topped the page in black, 'Fine-Point', fiber pen. Below the nickname of their twenty seven year old son, Robert, the unfinished message sent icy fingers through the hair on the back of his neck.

The letter read as if she were saying goodbye forever.

The Congressman pulled away and smiled. "We're going to make it, Honey ... we already know that." He wasn't dealing with matters of government at that moment. He was handling the complex human fiber that weaves long-shared lives into one. The sting of what appeared to be a farewell letter to their son, pricked the walls of his heart. He would keep it there. He understood Laura's fear.

"I'm sorry, Sweetheart," said Mrs. Franklin. She blinked her tears away. She swallowed the gravel in her throat and a word came part way out, then melted into a long sigh.

"What?" Alan said and scanned Laura's forty-eight-year-old face, which looked ten years younger.

She touched the firm chin of her big husband. He kissed her fingers and her forehead and leaned back.

"Do you remember the first time you did

that, Congressman Franklin?"

"It was over thirty years ago."

"And?" Laura's devilish smile filled her eyes as the memory played across the back of her mind.

"And I knew I was in love and would be for the rest of my life."

"That's corny." She touched the remains of his hairline with the first and second fingers of her right hand. A rush of fresh tears flooded into Laura's eyes, she smiled as they spilled onto her face. "I loved it ... you were so shy. I love it even more now." Her voice wavered. Mrs. Franklin pushed her face into Alan's chest and hugged him desperately.

He held her like he would a little girl who'd been lost at a county fair, then found again.

Alan fought his own tears as the old memory marched through his head. "I love you, Laura," he whispered. The heat of that long-gone August afternoon covered him. He held his wife tighter. The tastes of corn harvesting fell out of his mind and filled his dry mouth. "I love you ...."

* * * *

Laura! Keep your hands away from there!
The last three words echoed in Alan's head.
That old summer day focused and drew him into

into the past.

* * * *

She had just turned eighteen. Alan was a proud, strong twenty three and knew farming wouldn't be in his future.

Laura had come with her mom and dad to help Alan's widowed father harvest more than fifty acres of corn. Alan's mother had died suddenly when he was barely sixteen.

A haunting look filled his father's eyes. It held the knowledge that Alan would soon be gone like a bastard, wet spring that delayed the planting.

Spring had passed—that was the summer of his son's leaving.

* * * *

IOWA - THIRTY YEARS EARLIER:

"Why are you shouting, Alan?" Laura's long, brown ponytail flew over her right shoulder as she jerked her head to the left. She pulled her hand away from the machine and looked back at the sharp blades spinning in the noon sun.

"Laura, how long have you helped at

harvest time with your parents?"

"Since I was ten."

"I'm surprised you haven't lost at least one arm and a leg!"

"Do you care?"

"A lot, young lady. I care a lot."

* * * *

The congressman gripped his wife harder and let out a long breath.

Dr. Hal Jordon, a forty two year old black Physics Professor at U.C.L.A. had left his seat in coach and headed up the aisle toward the Franklins in first class.

* * * *

Hal pushed the dividing curtain aside. The congressman's memory-movie faded away.

* * * *

Alan looked up and nodded to Dr. Jordan.

The professor glanced around the first class cabin shaking his head. He touched Laura's shoulder. "Are you okay?"

She smiled. "Yes ... thank you." She gripped his hand briefly then returned to the letter in front of her.

"How are you doing, Hal?" Alan was pleased that Dr. Jordan was among the chosen few who were allowed to return.

After a moment of serious eye contact, a grand smile ran from ear-to-ear on the professor's confident face. "Fine, I'm fine. It'd be easier if Virginia were here. On the other hand— I'm damn glad she's not." The smile fell away. Dr. Jordan stood in the aisle and looked around the cabin again. He sat in the empty seat behind Laura and leaned toward Alan. "Do they bother you?" He tilted his head toward the rest of the passengers.

"Yes, they do." The congressman rose up and looked forward in the huge plane and across the center section to his right. First class was nearly full. He sat back and turned to face Dr. Jordan. "How are the Sternfelds?"

"Okay, I guess. The three of us are talking a lot." Jordan smiled again, but not as broad as before. "They're scared ... just like we are." He patted the side of the congressman's seat back. "Under the circumstances, I think they're doing great."

"Good ...." Alan looked away in a moment of thought and watched Laura work her pen along another carefully written line. He turned back to Jordan and whispered, "I can't help wonder about Mrs. Sternfeld's unborn baby."

"That baby is the very reason her and her husband are going back with us."

"That's true." Alan let his seat recline. He lowered his whisper and continued, "My concern is with what the baby knows now."

Several seconds passed between them as Franklin's comment filtered through the logic files of the physics professor's mind.

"I never considered that." Dr. Jordan looked away, blinked and turned back to Alan. "Is it possible?"

The congressman hesitated. "From what we've discovered on this trip, anything is possible.

"Amen ...." He slapped the seat again and stood up. The 747 banked slightly, throwing Jordan off balance. He bumped against the passenger seated across the aisle. "Sorry."

Nothing. No response.

Laura turned to see the female passenger settle slightly in the seat. A chill crawled up her back. She shuddered and looked away.

Jordan stared down at the figure in the seat then glanced toward Alan. "Are they Aware of anything at all?"

"I think they have enough consciousness to remain seated. Nothing more."

Laura continued writing.

Jordan moved away from the seat. "Not counting us, eventful Tran's International flight two-eighty is carrying two-hundred-twenty-five zombies."

"Correction Doctor. Lifeless, clones ... without souls, to be specific."

Laura shivered and stared out the window.

"Yeah," offered Jordan. "I'm seated with most of them." He turned and left the first class cabin.

Chapter 2
Silent Passengers

*J*ordan pulled the dividing curtain closed to give Laura and Alan some privacy.

Without souls.

Franklin's words echoed twice in Hal's head before slipping into another of his many mental files. The meaning of the thought would be analyzed and kept for future reference.

Were they really?

He remembered a paper he'd read at U.C.L.A. while his students were taking finals. *The cloned cell is identical to the parent cell.* The information hung in the center of his brain like hot, humid air.

The professor stood in the far left aisle of the jumbo jet looking over the rows of passengers *clones* in the first section of coach. There wasn't any sound except for the hum of the huge jet engines. No conversation. No movement, just relative silence.

Enough consciousness to remain seated. Not much more.

He pulled his tie loose and unbuttoned his shirt at the neck. A pressure closed around him. He shifted his glance from left to right. He looked to the rear and across the front of the section. His eyes stopped on individual faces. A moment here. A second there. Some he recognized, but they weren't the same people they were *copies.*

Each face had color. Hair moved in the flow of air conditioning. They were all breathing. They were all blinking.

Breathing—blinking—color! Alive!

The meaning of the words gripped Dr. Jordan deep in his guts. "Dammit! I can't deal with this!" His loud voice fell on, apparently, deaf ears. He thought about that too, somewhere in his frantic disbelief.

* * * *

Michael and Linda Sternfeld did *hear* the professor's outburst. They were seated together further back in the plane. A service wall stood between their section and where Hal Jordan was.

"That's Dr. Jordan," said Michael, and got out of his seat.

"Mike. Don't leave me alone." A chill ran through the young mother-to-be as she considered the *other passengers.*

"I'll be right back, sweetheart; I have to see what's wrong." He touched his wife's hand and moved quickly up the aisle.

Linda sat stiff. Her husband disappeared into the forward section.

* * * *

Michael entered the area on the opposite side of where Professor Jordan had been standing. At first he didn't see him. Then he spotted him. Hal Jordan was on one knee in the aisle talking to a clone.

"Dr. Jordan, are you all right?"

"I'm okay." The doctor gestured. "Come over here."

When the younger man came around the front row of center seats he saw the passenger Professor Jordan was talking to. "I heard you shout." He watched the black man pat the soft hand of a pretty little girl about ten years old.

"I shouted ... I may scream next."

"I was afraid Linda might. Not you."

"Do you recognize this child, Michael?"

"Yes, and about half the others on this plane, *whatever* they are."

Professor Jordan brushed the girl's hair and turned his head from side to side. "They have every detail. Right down to the I.D. badge the airline clips on minors traveling alone." Hal turned the laminated plastic rectangle in his fingers. He rubbed his big thumb across the one-and-a-half by two inch photograph. "Carol Hollinger," he whispered, and blinked several times. "You're not going to make it to Los Angeles, Carol ...."

The expression on the small face held the hint of a smile, as if its owner were lost in a pleasant dream.

"It isn't her, Dr. Jordan."

"No, it's not." The professor let the badge rest against the blue, Ship & Shore blouse and held the clone's tiny hand in both of his, covering it completely.

"The little girl who entertained us on the flight from New York is with the other two-hundred-twenty-five People who occupied these seats." Dr. Jordan's voice was loud again.

"They're all okay, and we will be too!"

"I know that." Jordan let go of the clone's hand and looked up at the young man. "Carol's mother doesn't know it. She never will!"

"The friends and relatives of the others won't either—we can't change that." He stepped around Dr. Jordan and looked into the rear section. "Linda."

She turned from the window.

"We'll just be a minute, honey."

Mrs. Sternfeld nodded and smiled.

He sat on the arm of an empty seat near Jordan.

"What about this child, Michael?" The professor stood and brushed strands of the clone's fine, blonde hair away from its face. He looked Michael square in the eyes. "What about all of them?" He waved out across the cabin.

"Doctor, I operate a camera store in Troy, New York. You're a Professor of Physics at U.C.L.A. Thank God we can continue doing those things. How ever all this came to be, including *them* is so far beyond my comprehension I'm afraid to think about it." He shrugged. "You tell me."

"Forget the rest of it Michael. Just think about your unborn son and what you now know he'll accomplish in his life."

The younger man's eyes flashed. He stood and turned away. "I don't want to think about it." He shuddered. "It scares the hell out of me. I can't think about it."

"And Linda?" Dr. Jordan leaned against the seat in front of the little girl.

Michael shifted his position so he could see his wife in the rear of the cabin. He sat down again on the arm of the empty seat. "We've decided to let it take its course, one day-at-a-time." He looked over at the copy of Carol Hollinger and shook his head.

Jordan took a deep breath. "Your son will be, in this case, partly responsible for *them.* That should make you wonder."

"Linda and I have all we can handle just knowing our son's whole life *before* he's born." Michael looked up at Dr. Jordan and laughed. "When we got on this plane at Kennedy, we didn't know she was pregnant!" He shook his head, and then lowered his voice. "Another thing, we're dealing with," he cleared his throat and looked down at his shoes, "Linda's not just pregnant. She's three months pregnant!" Michael's eyes shifted across the aisle to the small clone, then he looked at Professor Jordan again. "It's a good thing she's a small woman. She doesn't show. That's a blessing."

Dr. Jordan looked away and remembered the third month of his wife's first pregnancy. Tears welled in his eyes as he felt the pain again—they lost that child. Nothing in the world meant anything to them at that time. Nothing except each other. "I'm sorry, Michael. I shouldn't have said what I did regarding your son." He reached across the aisle and gripped Michael's shoulder. "We all have *enough* to consider." He pulled his hand away and stroked the small clone's soft hair once more. "I'm just concerned about what *they* are." He turned back to Michael with a grave expression on his educated face. "I'm frightened for them."

Michael focused his thoughts on the final briefing in 2498. "We were told these clones are just plastic copies of the other passengers who couldn't return."

Dr. Jordan leaned forward lifted the clone's left hand and held it. "Touch her, Michael. Hold her hand like I am."

Young Sternfeld shook his head and stood.

The professor continued in a deliberate, serious manner. "This little hand is soft and warm." He swallowed, making a *clicking* sound in his throat.

"It's just a copy. An advanced copy." Michael shivered at the thought of such a thing.

"She has a pulse, Mike ... so do the others."

"Why aren't they moving and talking?"

"I don't know." The professor looked into the girl's eyes. "It has to do with consciousness. There's something missing."

"Feelings, doctor—they have none. They're not human. That was all explained to us."

Dr. Jordan dropped the child's hand into her lap. He *slapped* her across the face. The blow was fast and hard. The small head *snapped* to the right. Carol's body fell against the armrest. Strands of blonde hair cascaded over the left side of the child's forehead and face.

"What the hell'd you do that for?"

"Michael!" Linda's startled voice came from the rear of the section.

"It's all right, honey. I'll be there in a minute." He started toward the clone. "Are you crazy?" Michael was reacting to a child being struck by a grown man.

The professor held him back. Both men stared at the rag-doll shape slumped to the right of its seat.

Michael moved forward. Jordan held out his big hand without taking his eyes off the clone.

"Dammit, Jordan!"

"Wait," whispered the professor.

Linda entered the section at the opposite side of the cabin. She could only see her husband and Hal Jordan bending over what appeared to be an empty seat on the far aisle. "Is everything all right?"

Michael waved toward her. "Stay there, Linda, please."

Congressman Franklin pushed the curtain aside and headed up the aisle toward the other two men.

Laura stood beside the drawn curtain and looked toward Mrs. Sternfeld.

"What's happened?" Alan came up behind Michael and Hal.

Dr. Jordan held up his hand. "You'll see."

Silence.

The small child raised her left arm and brushed strands of hair from her face. Her slender fingers touched the red mark left by Jordan's slap.

The three men stepped back.

"Jesus!" Michael caught a short breath.

Carol Hollinger straightened and looked directly into Dr. Jordan's eyes.

"God forgive us." The professor swallowed and shook his head. "God forgive us all ...."

The clone turned away. Small tears fell over her pale cheeks. She shifted into the position she had before the slap and held a hurt expression in silence.

Hal touched the fading red marks on the clone's face. "I'm sorry, Carol." He pushed several strands of her fine, blonde hair back over her shoulder.

"What happened?" The Congressman looked from Michael to Jordan.

The professor stared out the window. He watched thick clouds pass far below. He couldn't tell where they were. It didn't matter. Without turning around he answered the question. "I slapped her to prove a point ... and I proved it."

Michael crossed through a row of empty seats to his wife. "Let's sit down."

"I want you to tell me why you and Dr. Jordan were arguing."

"There wasn't any argument. I'll explain it as well as I can." He looked at Linda for a moment and kissed her. "I love you."

Linda glanced across the cabin at Laura and their eyes met. "Mrs. Franklin, would you come and sit with us for a few minutes? I'd like to talk to you."

"I would enjoy that very much."

Laura and her husband had been married longer than the Sternfelds had been alive. Michael was twenty-five, Linda recently turned twenty-three. Before flight 280 and the time gate crossing their lives would never have touched. Now, they were bonded for the rest of their lives.

The three of them walked to the rear section of the middle of the plane.

"Hal, sit down please." Congressman Franklin rested his big hand on the professor's shoulder.

Dr. Jordan looked into Alan's sincere face and felt understanding. He let out a long sigh and settled himself into an aisle seat.

Franklin sat across from him directly in front of Carol Hollinger.

Hal turned to look at her again. The tears had dried and the red marks on her face were gone. Her eyes were still wet. The child blinked and stared straight ahead.

Alan turned back to look at Carol then met Jordan's eyes across the aisle. "Tell me about your concern for these, *silent passengers,* Hal."

"Concern?" Dr. Jordan shook his head. He pulled both hands over his face, as if to gather himself and focus his thoughts.

"What were you trying to prove by slapping the clone?" Alan rested his head against the back of the seat and took a deep breath.

"That they're *alive* and I did." Jordan smacked the arm of his seat. "They won't be when this is over!" He leaned toward the Congressman. "When this plane plows into the ground two-hundred-twenty-five *living* beings will die!"

"You're right." Alan squeezed his eyes shut for a moment. He glanced around at the other *silent* passengers. "So will two-hundred-twenty-five beef cattle, turkeys, chickens, pheasant, ducks and lambs." He stared at the blank movie screen where a first-run film would be playing on a five-and-a-half hour flight from New York to Los Angeles. How many had he seen without really seeing? An odd thought under existing circumstances.

"What?" Dr. Jordan looked across the aisle puzzled.

"We slaughter more than that number of living creatures every day so we can enjoy great meals."

Jordan stiffened. "I can't believe you said that. You're comparing human life with livestock?"

Franklin leaned across the aisle to face the professor. "Yes, I am. These creatures are no more than a chicken or a cow." His expression intensified. "Smack a young lamb across the snout. It'll react just like this young clone here." He caught a quick breath. "They're not human, Hal, they're just living tissue."

Dr. Jordan looked away from the Congressman. A memory ran across his mind. He saw a dead kitten. His five-year-old daughter, Angela was holding it and crying.

"Fluffy's dead, Daddy." The child hugged the lifeless animal.

"It's all right, Angie." He had petted the dead kitten. *"Fluffy's gone to a special place."*

He held little Carol's hand. "I'm sure you'll go someplace special too."

Chapter 3
Dr. Hal Jordan

$\mathscr{P}$rofessor Jordan sat across from Carol Hollinger's clone for some time. Congressman Franklin had gone back to be with the Sternfelds and Laura.

I think you're more than living tissue or cattle, Carol, Hal thought. He stared at the child again, stood and brushed at her hair once more. *There's something involved here beyond my understanding—we're tampering with creation.* The thought of it chilled him. He straightened the collar of the girl's blouse. "There will come a time of reckoning, I'm *sure* of that." He spoke to the silent clone convinced it heard and understood. After a moment he walked forward to a stewardess service area. He opened several stainless steel drawers until he located the stash of liquor.

"Cutty Sark," he mumbled. "That's the ticket." Hal took out two of the miniature green bottles. "I'll fix a nice double. As a matter of fact, I'll have two doubles." He removed two more bottles from the drawer. He found what he needed for the set ups and returned to his seat across from Carol's clone.

Franklin entered the section on the far side. "Are you all right?"

"Fine." He lifted the tiny green bottle. "I'll be even better in a few minutes."

"How about joining the rest of us."

"Maybe later. I need to be alone for a while."

"Hal ... I didn't mean to be harsh. I just wanted you to understand the truth."

"I do, Congressman—believe me, I do." He twisted off the cap on the Cutty bottle and poured its contents over the ice in the plastic cup. "Cheers, our time has come."

"Yeah ... I think it has." Alan turned and walked back into the rear section again.

Hal opened the second bottle and added it to the cup. "Not much room left for soda," he smiled, adding a small amount of mix to the liquor. He stirred the mixture and raised his drink in toast, nodding first toward the clone of Carol Hollinger. "To you, my child ... and may God be with us all." He sipped, shuddered and raised his cup again.

"And to the rest of you." The cold bite of the strong Cutty ran through him. "We've come a long way— a long, long way!" Hal downed his drink in three gulps. He set the cup on the tray in front of him and contemplated the wet, melting ice. "Virginia," he whispered. "I love you. You have no idea how much." He remembered his wife's insistence that he take this trip.

* * * *

Hal Jordan! Virginia's sharp voice rang in his head. He smiled when she planted her fists on her round, full hips and bent toward him. *You tell that committee you'll be there with bells on!*

* * * *

What a sight she was. He chuckled at the image as he fixed another double Cutty Sark. Virginia was just two years younger than Hal and smart as a whip. If she chose to, she could command his full attention. She had done just that. He smiled and sipped the Cutty. The memory continued.

* * * *

Virginia's long, soft ebony hair fell forward covering part of her exotic black face. She could've been a model, even after two children, close together. She had the figure of a Peter Gowan nude. *Adjusting our camping vacation is of little consideration compared to the contacts you'll make. And don't forget, Lover, the points you gain with the University.* Virginia was right of course, Hal knew that. She had been the strength of his whole life since they first met. He swallowed another sip from the smooth Cutty and slipped further into the past.

* * * *

Hal focused on a cold, windy night along San Diego's Mission Bay. He and Virginia had met during classes at San Diego State College two months earlier—they fell in love immediately.
Yes, I love you—very much. The wind had tossed her hair and flapped the tails of her long leather coat against her legs. The memory was all in slow motion as it unfolded.

* * * *

But, I won't marry you until you've got your degree and you're teaching.

A stiff, icy shiver ran through him, just as it did that night so long ago. He made a commitment and kept it.

For you, wonderful lady, I will meet that demand. He remembered the look of strength in her expression, he realized then, as he has known everyday since, there was no other woman on earth for him except Virginia. Whatever she needed him to be, he would become.

If I didn't know you could do it Hal, I wouldn't ask.

I know—and because of you ... I will.

* * * *

The memory swam through his brain as he gulped another swallow of Liquor.

Do it, Hal Jordan, and I'll be there for you, every day, for the rest of your life. She has been— and because of her, Hal Jordan made it—he became a professor at U.C.L.A. Because of her, he was on this trip. Thanks to Virginia, Hal Jordan's existence has meaning.

His wife and children were more important to him now than ever before. Everything in life was more important, and had nothing to do with the college professor's convention in New York.
Another gulp of Cutty—another shudder.

Someone else would become part of Dr. Jordan's life. A student named Stephen Russell, whom the professor wouldn't meet until next semester. He shook his head in wonder and swallowed more scotch.

Hal, you're an instrument of the future. The confident, quiet voice of Chairman Robert Fisher echoed through the professor's recent memory. He felt another chill crawl around his neck as he remembered clearly.

* * * *

Your teaching will give young Russell the basics he'll need to develop the self-supporting energy source we now have.

He rolled the cold cup across his forehead. The memory played on in his mental VCR.

The student, and the work you'll accomplish together, are the sole reasons you're being allowed to return to nineteen-ninety-eight.

* * * *

"Unbelievable," said Professor Jordan, to the clones. "I'm going home to teach a young man I won't meet until next year." He sipped his drink. "And my future has been laid out before me by a man of great power. A man who won't be born for another four-hundred and forty-five years!"

* * * *

On the flight deck of the giant 747, The Pilot switched on the aircraft's PA system.

"This is Captain Ballard." The voice was *unnatural and stilted.* "We are approximately twenty-five minutes away from the time gate. Please be in your assigned seats five-minutes prior to re-entry. Be sure you're buckled in securely. Thank you."

* * * *

Dr. Jordan returned to the service bar for another Cutty.

Chapter 4
The Sternfelds

*Y*oung Michael adjusted the flow of cold air from the blower above Linda. He pulled the light blanket higher around her shoulders and gently kissed her soft cheek. She slept peacefully for the first time in several weeks.

"I love you, Sweetheart," he whispered. Linda nestled her head deeper into the small airline pillow. He looked up and smiled.

Congressman Franklin had returned from first class with coffee for both of them. "Is she okay?" He handed Michael a steaming cup and sat in the seat across the aisle.

"Yeah, thanks. How's Mrs. Franklin?"

"Good. She's writing a letter to our daughter." He sipped his coffee and looked over at Michael. "Did you hear the message?"

"Yes. Less than twenty minutes and we re-enter the time gate." Michael thought a moment then shivered slightly. "Are we in nineteen-ninety-eight or twenty-four-ninety-eight?"

"Actually, we're in a state of transition—guided by some control system."

Michael stared into his coffee, took a sip, then glanced at his wife again. "They told you and Dr. Jordan a lot more, didn't they?" He shifted his eyes to the congressman.

"According to Chairman Fisher, this ... limbo stage is necessary to line everything up—"

"You aren't answering my question, Congressman."

"We were each told what we needed to know relative to our role in the complete picture."

Michael laughed. "It's true what they say about politicians."

"Which is?"

"You've all attended bullshit school—you're masters at avoiding questions!"

Alan Franklin took a deep breath then sipped his coffee twice. "Michael, this flight has been a strain on all of us."

"Especially for over two-hundred of us who'll never see their families again!"

"That was explained to them—and they've accepted it!"

Michael grinned without humor and nodded.

"This whole thing was an accident and we must deal with the consequences!" The congressman's words had a sharp edge.

"Part of it was explained to me too," offered Michael in a harsh tone, as quietly as he could manage. "That doesn't stop the nagging questions or the frightening reality of it."

"I don't doubt that for a minute."

"My wife is on the edge of her sanity dealing with a three month pregnancy she didn't know she had when we boarded this Goddamn flight in New York!"

"I understand ...."

"Shit, you understand ... I don't understand." He drank all his coffee then looked at Linda again. "This whole damn thing is beyond understanding—it's beyond God—it's a nightmare!" He shook his head in frustrated anger.

"Yes! It is a nightmare." The congressman cleared his throat. "And your unborn child is your salvation, son. Your baby will make a mark on the future of life itself. What caused our side-trip to twenty-four-ninety-eight is of the least concern—it happened. The results, in our case, are positive. That's what we have to hang onto—nothing else."

"My son will contribute to a process that created the *other passengers* on this plane."

Michael's eyes flashed. The pricking fingers of anger scraped their way up his spine.

"For some odd reason, the thought of all that makes me feel sick!" He slapped the armrest.

Linda stirred and opened her eyes. "Michael," she said in a foggy voice.

"It's okay, honey." He smoothed her hair with trembling fingers. She kissed his hand and closed her eyes.

Michael somehow appeared older

The two men looked at each other for a long moment.

The congressman said, "I'm going back to be with Laura. We're almost there." He stood and smiled.

"Congressman, I'm—"

"It's all right, son ... I understand." Alan gripped the young man's shoulder then moved up the aisle into first class.

Michael stared into the empty space where Alan Franklin had been. *I'm a merchant—a clerk in a camera store. How can I deal with this?* He shivered at the thought. "Dammit!"

"Michael?" Linda had been awake.

"Sorry, I didn't mean to disturb you."

"I heard you and the Congressman talking. You sounded angry."

"It's frustration more than anger. There's so much I don't understand."

Linda's voice wavered. "Michael, I love you more than ever."

"Me too." He put his arms around his wife and held her tight. "I always will."

"We know our love will last for life. We've been given a gift. Something other couples can only guess at. We know the future—we've been there. We've seen our whole lives together." Linda pulled her head from her husband's chest and smiled. She looked at him for a moment. "Michael, we know who our son will be! We've seen his accomplishments as a man." She shook her head and swallowed hard. "We know our son's wife." Linda shuddered. "Her parents won't be married for four more years! We know our boy's children—our grandchildren." She pushed further away and looked up at him. "My God, Michael. Think of it."

He watched Linda's eyes widen with each word. He kissed her forehead and held her against his chest again. "I'm afraid, Linda ... I'm so afraid ...."

"Michael," she whispered into her husband's shirt.

"What?"

"Thank you for our son ...."

"I'm scared to death of what we know he's going to do."

"So am I."

"It seems ... unholy, Linda." Michael shivered again.

"It's meant to be. Maybe in the eyes of God it's right."

They held each other for a long moment. The meaning of what they had shared sifted through their limited understanding. They were an integral part of a future time they had experienced. A time beyond their own lives.

* * * *

The voice of Chairman Robert Fisher came over the jetliner's P/A system.

"This is Chairman Fisher I'm in the Command Center where we are tracking your flight. I wanted to speak to all of you myself. In Just five more minutes your plane will begin re-entry into the time gate."

Congressman Franklin held both of Laura's trembling hands. "Everything's going to be all right." He thought he knew what the Chairman was about to say.

Linda clung to her husband with all the strength she had. "Michael, I'm frightened.

"I am too, honey."

In coach, Dr. Jordan swallowed the last of another scotch. "Good God in heaven." He gripped Carol Hollinger's arm. "It'll be okay, sweetheart."

Chairman Fisher continued in a comforting tone. "Each of you has an important mission which must be completed. At this time it is my responsibility to inform you." He hesitated. "There has been a change in the program."

Little Carol Hollinger turned and looked at Hal. "Professor Jordan, why did you slap me?"

Chapter 5
The First Encounter

God be with you.

Congressman Franklin let the Chairman's farewell linger in his mind. He shook as the thought settled. The change in the program had been unexpected. *Why hadn't Fisher explained it to me before?*

Laura gripped his hand. "Alan?" Her voice sounded tense and her hand felt cold. She took a deep breath and pointed a shaking finger toward the window. "It's started, Alan—the light!"

He glanced at his watch, shaded his eyes, and turned toward the window. *Eight minutes. In just eight minutes of our time we've gone five-hundred years into the future and stayed three months.*

Billions of tiny stars shot out of space and

engulfed the giant 747.

Eight minutes..... The fact of time displayed itself in Alan's mind, over and over, like multi-colored computer graphics.   Congressman Franklin did, indeed, feel the suspension promised by Chairman Fisher. It felt wonderful—fluid—warm. He drifted back to when they first encountered the *Time Gate.*

* * * *

JULY 15 MID AFTERNOON 1998:

Some of the passengers aboard Flight 280 were in panic. They grabbed the oxygen masks dangling in front of them. A few simply stared into space, afraid to breathe at all.

Laura pulled the yellow mask to her face and began inhaling rapidly. Her eyes opened wide and frantic.

"You don't need it!" Congressman Franklin took a breath, exhaled. "It's all right. You can breathe." He nodded.

Laura hesitated then slowly removed the ugly mask from her face. She held her breath and stared at her husband. "Alan, what happened?"

"I don't know ... but we're okay."

* * * *

Captain Raymond Ballard, a twenty year veteran airline pilot, held the yoke steady with both hands. The vibration had stopped and the aircraft was stable. He turned to his copilot, Tom Parrish, who sat in the right seat. "We're stabilized."

The copilot glanced over his shoulder to the flight engineer, K.W. Soo, who faced his instrument panel. He shifted his glance from the copilot to Captain Ballard. "Don't look at me; I don't know what the hell it was." He gestured toward the captain. "Take a look below. We're over dense cloud cover that doesn't show on the radar."

The chief stewardess entered the flight deck nearly in shock and tried to find an answer on the faces of the three men flying the jumbo jet. "Captain?" her hand shook in its grasp of the small door handle.

"Its okay, Cindy. I'll talk to them." He lifted the cabin P/A mike and winked.

"Thank you, sir ...." Cindy left the flight deck and closed the door. A trained, professional smile painted itself on her face. She motioned for the other crew members to come forward.

* * * *

The captain cleared his throat, keyed the P/A mike and spoke to his passengers. "This is Captain Ballard. May I have your attention please? We've experienced an undetected, turbulent weather system. I apologize for any discomfort you may have experienced. At the moment we're safe and stable. Please remain seated with your seatbelts fastened. Drinks on the house when we clear the storm. Thank you." He clicked off the mike and returned it to its holder. "Get Kansas City control, we'll take her in." He met eyes with Tom and then K.W. Their, faces were pale.

Tom said, "The radio's out."

"Back up?"

"Same," replied K.W.

* * * *

"Alan!" Laura pointed toward the window. The sky around them burst into blazing stars.

"My god, what is it!"

* * * *

"Jesus! Ballard gripped the controls.

The blinding light gave way to dense blackness.

Billions of tiny stars filled the void, gathered in clusters and enveloped the huge aircraft.

* * * *

Voices rose among the passengers. "We're going to crash!" It was a widow from White Plains, New York. "I knew I shouldn't get on this plane."

Powerful streaks of lightening flashed in the blackness around the jumbo jet.

An intense thunder clap vibrated the aircraft.

* * * *

"Mother of god!" The captain fought for control.

Thunder and lightening ceased. Instantly the sky above cleared. The star-storm ceased.

The 747 leveled off at two-eight-thousand.

Contact.

Captain Ballard, Tom, and K.W. jumped when the radio came to life.

"This is Zebra leader to Tran's International, over."

Tom and the captain looked at each other.

"What the hell's a Zebra leader?" asked K.W. from behind Tom.

"Sounds military," added Ballard, and pulled on his headset. "This is Captain Raymond Ballard, over."

The radio *squawked.* "Report your destination, mission and origin immediately."

"We are, Tran's. International, flight two-eight-zero heavy. We're carrying passengers from Kennedy to LAX." He glanced at Tom and continued. "Zebra leader, we've experienced unusual turbulence that may have caused damage. I'm requesting a priority landing at K.C. or Denver, over."

More static through their headsets.

"Your aircraft shows no apparent damage captain. Maintain altitude and present course, over."

Ballard glanced at Tom. "The flight recorder?"

"I switched it on when we hit the storm."

"How the hell can he see us?"

"I don't know, but it better be good." The captain keyed his mike. "Zebra leader, I'm repeating my request for priority landing and demanding your identification, over."

"T.I. two eight zero, you have entered an unauthorized time zone. You are now in restricted military air space. Do you read?"

The radio scratched.

K.W. had started scanning other frequencies for contact with Denver or Kansas City.

"Anything," asked Tom.

"Not diddly squat."

Captain Ballard answered. "I read you loud and clear, Zebra leader. What you say is impossible. You're in violation of F.A.A. and F.C.C. rules, good buddy. I suggest you get off the air!"

Tom cleared his throat and offered input. "What if he's right, Ray?"

"Bullshit! The only air space we're guilty of violating is being below our assigned altitude—and we're about to take her back up."

K.W. said, "Why not play it out, Captain? We're still headed toward Denver. If this clown *is* a radio pirate, he can't block all the frequencies—"

Tom cut in. "I guess you guys didn't get my drift." He shifted his glance from K.W. to Ballard. "None of us has ever seen a storm like we just flew through—and no severe weather system comes out of a clear sky, then vanishes." The three men stared at each other, digesting Tom's observation.

"You're suggesting the time-zone crap is real."

"Suppose it is ...."

A slow chill walked up the back of Ballard's neck and settled in behind his ears. "Forget it. We're dealing with a crazy asshole and nothing more." The Captain shook his head and scanned the instrument panel. Everything was all in order. Air speed, cabin pressure, hydraulics, engine temperatures, and back up systems. "If this fruitcake's for real, where the hell is he? Have either of you seen anything?" He looked at his crew.

"No," answered Tom. He glanced out and down through the right window. "The cloud cover is right under our belly and that's impossible."

"I haven't seen anything either. Ray— you're right. Ignore the sonofabitch and let's get this big mother back up to thirty-eight before we run into real trouble." K.W. swiveled himself around to face his console and started plotting a course to Stapleton International.

"Take her up."

"Yes, sir ...." Reluctantly, Tom took the yoke, and slowly advanced the throttles. The giant engines responded instantly.

Captain Ballard reached for the P/A mike to announce the unscheduled Denver stop just as the radio squawked to life again.

"Flight two eight zero, this is Zebra leader."

"Up yours, Zebra." Ray laughed at his own

comment and flipped off the space in front of him.

Tom smiled.

"Right on!" added K.W. from the background.

The Captain keyed his radio mike and answered Zebra leader. "Hey, Zebra—we're outta here!"

"Captain!" Tom's voice cracked. "She won't climb!" The knuckles on Tom's left hand were white. He pulled back on the yoke with three times the force necessary to lift the 747. The altimeter read twenty-eight-thousand. The jetliner remained in level flight.

"I'll take her." Ballard resumed control and eased the throttles forward.

"Captain, we're losing altitude!"

The altimeter read: twenty-seven-thousand-five-hundred. Twenty-six-five and stopped at twenty-six-thousand feet.

* * * *

Frightened passengers grabbed for swinging oxygen masks they didn't need. The widow from White Plains fainted.

* * * *

Cindy entered the flight deck, closed the door and leaned against the right bulkhead alongside K.W. "What is it?" She looked at the three men who held over two-hundred lives in their *fallible* hands.

"We don't have a clue," said K.W., "We're going into Denver on emergency."

Tom turned to see Cindy's fear. "We're okay. We'll make it." He nodded. "Tell them we're landing at Stapleton for a safety inspection. Do not mention the word *emergency.*"

"Tom?" The young woman's heart raced.

"Tell them, Cindy—now!"

She left the flight deck and walked into the first class galley. "Dear God, give me strength," she whispered and clicked on the P/A mike.

Chapter 6
Military Escort

JULY 15 MID DAY 2498

"*D*enver approach, this is Trans International, two eighty." Tom adjusted the volume on his headset. "We're heading west, northwest at twenty six thousand." He paused, not sure he was being received at all. "We've come through extreme turbulence with unknown structural damage. We can't climb to assigned altitude. I repeat. We are unable to reach assigned altitude, over."

Static scratched through the crew's headsets.

"Zebra leader to Captain Ballard, over."

Tom Parrish glanced left as the Captain adjusted the tiny mike attached to his headset.

"This is gonna be a good one," mumbled K.W. waiting for the Captain's response.

"I hear you Zebra leader." Captain Ballard drew a slow, deep breath. "I'll try to make this as clear and calm as I can. You are endangering the lives of over two hundred people. I have a damaged aircraft under an unassigned altitude. At any second we could explode in a violent mid-air collision. Now get-the-hell-off-my-radio!" His voice rose one word at a time until the last one blasted out of his mouth to fill the cockpit with human thunder.

"Stand by Captain," responded Zebra leader.

Instantly a slight pressure and low level hum poured through the 747 like thick, warm liquid.

The space around the huge jet shimmered.

The crew looked out dumbfounded. They saw what appeared to be wavering, glassy reflections bouncing off the sky.

****

Just as the frightened air travelers were about to panic, again, a mild ringing worked its way into every bone and brain simultaneously.

All as one, the passengers and cabin crew fell into a delicious slumber.

* * * *

On the flight deck, the crew watched the forward reflection being replaced by a military fighter one-third the size of the 747.

"Zebra leader to Captain Ballard, over."

"I see it, Zebra."

"There are four of us, captain. I'm off your port wing."

Ballard looked. He swallowed hard. "The other two?"

Tom pointed toward the right window.

"Zebra three is off your starboard wing. Zebra four is above and aft of your tail."

"Roger that, Zebra one. We understand." Tiny rivulets of sweat trickled down Ballard's temples. He clicked off his mike and spoke to Tom. "They're ours! What are the other markings?" He switched the mike back on. "I'm here, Zebra. Just checking with my crew."

"We are not hostile, Captain. You can see the flag. Rest easy."

"I have to be sure, Zebra one."

"Understood, captain. Maintain present course until otherwise instructed."

"Roger, Zebra one."

Tom waved at the captain. "Standard ID numbers, I guess and the letters, U.W.M.F. — whatever that means." He gestured toward the fighter off the starboard wing.

"I see it." Ballard switched on his mike. "Zebra leader, why the military escort?"

"You're in restricted military air space, captain."

"What the hell is U.W.M.C.?"

"That's who we answer to."

"And that is?"

"United World Military Council and they're monitoring us as we speak."

"Holy shit!" K.W. Soo shook from head to toe.

Tom Parrish swallowed a lump in his throat that felt like hot sand. "Dear Jesus ... what now?"

Captain Ballard clutched the control in both hands. He stared at the aircraft in front of the 747. He shifted his eyes to the instrument panel. Air speed: four-hundred-eighty knots. *Insane!* The word stood out in his mind in bright red neon. He thought he could hear the *hissing* that comes from the gas-filled tubes of such a sign. It burned hot, and smoke rose from the mental image as the neon word flashed white. On and off—blinding white. It was the strobe on the lead fighter.

"They've been there all along, and they're

Goddamn well armed!"

"Easy Parrish," Ballard responded. "They're also ours. I don't think we shoot down civilian jets."

"Zebra leader to Captain Ballard. Over."

What now, sonofabitch! He thought, before answering. "This is Ballard, over."

"Your passengers and cabin crew are safe and your aircraft is undamaged. You have two choices. Follow us down without resistance or we'll force you down. Which will it be, over?"

Ray glanced at his flight crew and in an instant he knew the answer. "I cannot comply without clarification of your authority, over." The radio scratched.

"Our authority is absolute, captain. Your violation of the time gate makes it so, over."

"We have no idea what you're talking about. Clarify."

The radio sputtered and *squawked* in the collective headsets.

"We know that, otherwise your aircraft would have ceased to exist on contact. Listen carefully. I've been authorized to give you basic information."

"I'm listening." *And it better be good,* he thought. He studied the markings on the fighter.

U.W.M.F.

"You accidentally entered the time gate with no hostile intention. That was ascertained upon detection. It is my duty to guide or force you to the UWC Command

Center immediately. Do you accept the voluntary procedure? Over."

Captain Ballard caught the expression on the faces of his crew. The answer was obvious. "I respect your position and accept voluntary procedure. What do I have to do? Over."

"Follow us in captain. Welcome to the twenty fifth century."

A *time gate.* Impossible. Yet Captain Raymond Ballard Submitted his ship, passengers and crew to the commands of what could be a hostile force.

FUTURE/PAST

[Definition]

*Time is finite or earthly duration
as distinguished from infinity
or eternity.*

[The New Lexicon: Webster]

Chapter 7
A MATTER OF PRIORITY

UNITED WORLD COUNCIL HEADQUARTERS, NEVADA DESERT,
(12:30pm, July 15th, 2498)

$\mathcal{T}$he UWC is a Democratic/Socialist organization governing peaceful co-existence between Superpowers. The United States Delegation convened in an emergency session within ten minutes of the Time Gate intrusion.

* * * *

Councilman Larry Cross had the floor:

"The number of people in this crossing makes it a major threat. They can't be absorbed and they cannot be sent back!"

Chairman Fisher adjusted his glasses and leaned back. "You've made your point, Larry ... sit down." The emergency meeting was being held in a top-secret, priority-one conference room, five stories underground. That alone dictated the seriousness of the issue. Fisher grinned.

"Threat? So far they're just tourists."

Chairman Fisher's term expires in two years. If all other electives *except Cross* had their way, Fisher would head UWC for life.

"What you're suggesting is that we eliminate Two-hundred-thirty people, and their airplane. Poof! No problem." Fisher glared at Cross, sat forward and raised his chin.

Larry Cross, a tough conservative, was next in line for Fisher's chairmanship said, *"Threat,* Mr. Chairman, is the only consideration until we know otherwise." In his mind he said, *You're beyond your time Bobby-boy; soft.* "My concerns are for the society as a whole. We must after all, consider the negative impact of returning any of these people to their own time. I'm sure you're aware of the potential disaster that could very well become reality."

"There are other alternatives, Mr. Cross."

Councilwoman, Kathy Simmons said, "Sir ,may I?" She was a Humanist with a Ph.D. in Holistic Science, and assistant director of the History/Research Commission.

Fisher said, "Something from HRC?"

"Yes, Mr. Chairman." She glared across the wide conference table at Larry Cross then softened her expression as she addressed the Chair. Ms. Simmons removed a sheaf of papers from a blue file-folder. "These people," she said, and cast an ugly glance toward Cross, "are from a time of incredible development." She passed three pages of information to each council member then entered an access code into the keyboard in front of her.

Each position around the table had a terminal linked to the mainframe of specific departments.

Three giant screens, one on each of the room's three walls, lit up and displayed the HRC logo. Under it, in yellow letters, appeared the words: LOADING FILES.

"They're five-hundred years behind us, Simmons," chortled Councilman Cross.

"Yes," added Kathy. "From what we've learned so far, six of them play a significant role in our time. Two of the six are spouses and must be given the same priority." She glared at Cross again. "Further research is underway, as you'll see."

Fisher grinned in approval.

All council members watched information from HRC fill the computer screens.

The History/Research Commission served as an independent advisory board, which supplied information for, and answered directly to, UWC. HRC was formed soon after the discovery of the *Time gate.* Its purpose is to chart the course of any mission through the gate, all of which are top secret.

Special androids: Time Agents, T.A.s, are sent through the time gate to alter the course of particular events. The T.A.s appear human in every detail. They're given complete backgrounds and blend perfectly into whatever time they're programmed for.

Kathy Simmons programs the T.A.s and plots the course of their assignments.

* * * *

The big computer screens displayed the names of the six key passengers from flight two-eighty in order of importance, after each name a file code and research status was listed.

* * * *

CONGRESSMAN ALAN FRANKLIN (D): F# 1340 (INCOMPLETE)

LAURA FRANKLIN (WIFE OF ALAN): F# 1341 (INCOMPLETE)
HAL JORDAN (PROFFESSOR-PHYSICS Ph.D.): F# 1342 (INCOMPLETE)
LINDA STERNFELD (PREGNANT): F# 1343 (INCOMPLETE)
WILLIAM STERNFELD (EMBRYO): F# 1344 (INCOMPLETE)
MICHAEL STERNFELD (FATHER): F# 1345 (INCOMPLETE)
ESTIMATED DATA COMPLETION: 1500HRS
(END REQUESTED INFORMATION)
(ACCESS DATA IN PROGRESS-Y/N?)

* * * *

"Chairman Fisher?" Kathy waited.

"Hang on a minute, Kathy." Fisher drummed the fingers of his left hand on the table and rubbed his chin, with the other. Without taking his eyes off the screen he spoke. "Steve .... How much do you think we have on the embryo file at this point?"

* * * *

Steve Palmer forty-two, six feet one, two-hundred pounds, liberal views, Masters Degree in world history and director of HRC.

* * * *

"About twenty percent on each file, sir." He smiled at Kathy then looked toward the Chairman. Flight two-eighty was the first incident of forward travel, by people of the past, into the twenty-third century for decades. He knew he would be involved in the making of major decisions.

"Good," nodded Fisher. "Kathy, bring up what we have on the embryo ... that interests me." He turned back to the nearest screen and adjusted his glasses again.

She keyed (Y) and the words *ENTER F#* appeared on the screen. She typed: F-#-I-3-4-4, which also appeared, followed by the H.R.C. logo and a, *PLEASE WAIT* message.

* * * *

"Mr. Chairman," said Larry Cross. The others in the room looked at him. "This is all academic. Once we have the necessary information on these people, and their accomplishments, we replace them with high-intellect clones. There's simply too much risk otherwise." He raised his hand to the council. Chairman Fisher regarded him with a frown. Cross continued. "I move that we—"

* * * *

The computer screen displayed the facts collected, to that moment, about file number 1344.

* * * *

(2k% COMPLETE & STORING)

WILLIAM STERNFELD (EMBRYO): H.R.C. REFERENCE CODE: (GENETICS LOG) PRIORITY LISTING, # 96-(A)-RED MAJORS IN GENETIC RESEARCH AND DEVELOPS BASIC (CL-15) PROCESS NECESSARY FOR RAPID CLONING OF HUMAN CELLS. WITHOUT (CL-15) INTELLEGENT ACCELLERATED CLONING CANNOT BE ACCOMPLISHED.

URGENT: WILLIAM STERNFELD REQUIRES T.A. MONITORING AFTER (CL-15) PROCESS IS PERFECTED. LOWER PRIORITY INFORMATION ON THIS FILE IS BEING STORED. ACCESS-(Y/N?)

* * * *

The giant cursor blinked amber light on the faces of the council.

For a long moment, the distinguished members of the council sat in silence.

* * * *

* * * *

"Another file, Mr. Chairman?" Steven broke the tension.

"No," responded Fisher. He turned to Kathy. "Bring up the original screen."

She keyed the command and the names appeared.

"Fellow council members, we are faced with a matter for serious consideration." He removed his glasses and placed them on the table.

For another long moment, the council sat in silence.

"Chairman Fisher, please."

"Yes, Larry. You have the floor–again." Fisher drew an irritated breath, the others shifted in their seats. They were equally troubled by the Larry Cross method of dealing with the issue.

"Gentlemen." He nodded toward Kathy and grinned. "And, of course, ladies." He waved his hand toward the nearest screen. "I know, Mr. Palmer will correct me if I'm wrong, but Surely, we must consider our power over the current situation." He sat back and tapped his chin with his pen. "All we have to do, in the case of the embryo here, is move ahead in it's life, observe the CL-fifteen procedure, document it and–"

"Mr. Chairman." Stephen hesitated.

Kathy smiled. She anticipated the logical argument her boss and friend was about to shove down the throat of Larry Cross.

"Go ahead," approved Chairman Fisher, glad that someone had countered the suggestion of Mr. Cross.

"We are only able to observe the results of any individual development in progress. There's no way of knowing the mental steps to bring it about, and thank God we can't." He shuddered when the name, *God* passed his lips.

"That, Mr. Palmer is personal opinion. I'll thank you to keep it out of this discussion." Chairman Fisher regarded Stephen with cold eyes.

"I'm sorry, Sir."

* * * *

The name, *God,* or any such religious reference was forbidden at any meeting of governmental proceedings.

* * * *

"What are you saying, Palmer?" Cross sat back, obviously irritated.

"We must consider allowing these six people to return to their own time." He looked around the conference room, there were mixed emotions.

"I'm absolutely opposed." Cross looked at the screen again, unable to meet Stephen's eyes.

"Your opposition is noted, Councilman. And I hope, all facts considered, it will be defeated by the majority."

Stephen held in the contempt he was ready to express in reference to Councilman Cross.

"Ladies and gentlemen, we'll wait for a full report before making any final decision."

Chairman Fisher addressed Councilman Phil Khrismann, head of the Time Travel Enforcement Commission. "Phil, what's the E.T.A. on flight two-eighty?"

"Twenty five minutes, sir, at the outside."

* * * *

Time Travel Enforcement Commission (T.T.E.C.) this governing body controls the Time Gate. Special operatives and T.A.s, exclusively, are allowed through. Any other attempt to enter the gate is met with serious military force. A highly-trained, elite corps of agents enforces the rules.

* * * *

"Mr. Chairman," continued Phil. "The arrival is taking longer because of the target aircraft."

Fisher nodded. "I'm aware of that. Thank you." He studied the screen again, focusing his attention on Congressman Franklin's name. "It's a seven-forty-seven, isn't it?" He turned to Phil.

"Yes, it is, sir." The Councilman pulled himself closer to the table. "I've entered primary information into the TTEC computer. With your permission, I can cross-reference G.S.A. and find out how the aircraft got through."

"Excuse me, Councilman, the plane didn't *get* through. It accidentally *slipped* into our time." The Chairman put his glasses on again and met Phil's eyes. "I'm sensing a collective idea here that most of you are approaching this matter as some kind of *hostile* breach of the time Gate."

Phil looked down at the small monitor in front of him.

Councilman Cross cleared his throat and sat forward. "It is a consideration, Mr. Chairman."

"Is it now?"

Phil spoke up. "There is that chance, Sir."

"Of course there is." Fisher pushed his chair back and stood. "Councilman, your department has a lot of power." He started to walk around the table. "Sometimes ... a little too much," added the Chairman. "TTEC is a lethal weapon in a *basically* peaceful world." He stopped and extended his arms to lean on the back of an empty chair. Fisher faced the small group with his back to the list of names on the large screen.

"Sir, I only meant—"

"I know what you meant." The Chairman's eyes flashed behind his glasses. "I'm raising a question about TTEC because it holds a cocked and loaded high caliber gun." He slapped the chair's back rest with his right hand.

His audience jumped.

Chairman Robert Fisher was a soft-spoken, easy man when it came to U.W.C. business. If he were to raise his voice it would be for good reason.

All present listened.

Chapter 8
CODE RED

TOP SECRET OPERATION PRIORITY ONE:

"*Z*ebra leader, this is C/C, over."

"Go ahead, center."

"We have your ETA at thirteen hundred hours. Is that correct?"

"On the money, Center. We're at six-hundred knots."

"Copy that Zebra leader. Wrap your package. You're on code red."

"Cloaking now, Center."

"Roger, Zebra leader. Bring her in on E.L. five-two. Ground control will take her from there."

"Copy, Center. We're easing back to four-hundred."

"Any resistance?"

"Some, Center. We're okay now. Captain Ballard and crew are good people."

"Great job, Zebra leader. She's all yours, bring her on home."

"Roger that, Center. We're on final. Zebra leader out."

* * * *

U.W.C. HEADQUARTERS:
12:35 PM July 15, 2498

Emergency session Cont'd:

Phil Khrismann would rather have heard the boss make an example of another department, regardless of the lesson to learn. He sat nearly at attention pretending that being singled out didn't bother him. It did.

"Why did Phil use the words, *get* through, and, *target,* aircraft?" Chairman Fisher gripped the back of the chair. "Because," he continued, "Mr. Khrismann and his people are trained to *defend* the gate." He crossed his arms behind his back and moved further around the table. All heads, and eventually, all bodies turned to follow Fisher's serious stroll.

"Mr. Chairman, it's—"

"Quiet, Larry!" Fisher and Councilman Cross met eyes. "You, Mr. Cross, need to wake up to what I'm saying as much as anybody. Maybe more." Robert Fisher had walked to the opposite side of the conference table. He continued toward his own seat. "Where did I leave off, Sophy?"

"At, defend the gate." Sophy had been Fisher's personal and private secretary all of his public life.

Neither had ever married, they hadn't slept together, though the thought did cross their minds. Their relationship was however, more emotional and intimate than some couples married fifty years.

"Thank you, dear." Chairman Fisher often used the term in reference to Sophy and everyone accepted it for what it was, deep affection. "Yes, *defend* the gate. That word, by itself, puts pressure on the hair-trigger of the big-gun I spoke of." He shook his head when he reached his chair then turned to look at the others in the room. "The people and crew on board this airplane from the past are here by reason of accident. I want that understood by *all* departments and I want it made clear to the full International Council when the representatives convene for final disposition of this matter." He adjusted his glasses and slowly scanned the room. "That, ladies and gentlemen, is an executive order." Fisher turned to Kathy Simmons. "Ms. Simmons."

"Yes, sir?"

"I want the full file on Congressman Alan Franklin as soon as it's complete. I don't want to wait until three o'clock."

"You'll have it, Mr. Chairman." She looked at Steve, he nodded.

"Councilman Khrismann."

"Sir?" Phil responded in a tactful military attitude.

"I'm counting on you to keep what we know out of the G.S.A. computer until we're ready to learn how the plane crossed the time gate."

"You have my word, sir." Phil shuddered at the thought that he nearly accessed the Global Space Administration mainframe on his own—without U.W.C. clearance.

"And Phil," added Fisher.

"Sir?" He swallowed hard and continued to sit at attention.

"Make absolutely sure the arrival of flight two-eighty is conducted under the utmost of security procedures."

"Mr. Chairman, they're under code red now. I'll handle the actual arrival personally." He stood and pushed his chair up to the table. "I need to get to area fifty-two right away, sir."

"You're excused, Councilman. Get to it." Fisher sat at the head of the table. "This session is adjourned." He gestured toward Steve Palmer.

"Steve, I'll need the Franklin file as soon as it's available."

"You'll have it, sir."

Kathy gathered her folders. "I'll be in my lab if you need me, sir." She headed toward the door.

"We're all going to need each other before this matter is finished." He smiled at young Palmer. "We're going to be working close together on this. Thank God we trust each other."

"Pardon me, sir ...." The younger man flushed.

Chairman Fisher met Palmer's eyes. "Yes, I said thank *God.*" He smiled. "I owe you an apology." He gripped Steve's right arm.

"You owe me nothing, sir ... I'm honored to be in your company." Steve glanced around the room to see that the others had left. Especially Larry Cross. "May I ask you something—off the record?"

"You may."

"Why the special interest in the congressman?"

"For three reasons." Fisher leaned forward and waved his hand in a half circle. "Your H.R.C. computer gives the congressman top billing. That's important. Secondly, the man's a politician. That interests me. And third, the name, Franklin rings a bell." The chairman sat back and tented his fingers. "I believe this man has a major involvement with what, in his time, was called NASA."

Palmer smiled and looked at the nearest screen then back to Fisher. "The Global Space Administration?"

"Exactly. And I think we'll find our congressman connected to another significant development."

"Which would be?"

"A project set in motion five-hundred years ago, the *Ground-Based Interceptor System.* It's the foundation of today's worldwide defense. Without Franklin's efforts life would be a lot different."

"Another question, Mr. Chairman." Steven cleared his throat.

"Of course."

"Do you want Ms. Simmons involved beyond the initial files?"

"Is her input necessary?"

"Absolutely. Kathy's work in plotting T.A.s will be useful."

"Good." Fisher paused. "One word of caution."

"Yes?"

"For security reasons, make sure there's a *priority need to know* before anyone else in H.R.C. has access to the files."

"I'll handle it personally and have a list of

names and numbers of everyone involved in the project."

"Excellent." Fisher pushed back from the table and stood. He patted the jacket of his suit.

"You put your glasses in your breast pocket, sir."

"So I did," he smiled, resting a firm hand on Palmer's shoulder. "Steven," he added. "I don't have to tell you how important it is that this, *Time Gate,* incident remain top secret."

"I understand, sir." He stood and shook the chairman's hand. "We've managed to keep knowledge of the gate itself secret so far."

Fisher took one last look at the large screens and shook his head. "I'm not convinced we have altogether." He keyed his panel and the big screens cleared.

"Is there a leak?"

Fisher looked up at the taller Palmer and patted him on the arm. "Suffice it to say, there are factions within the system that have narrow, self-serving ambition." They started toward the electronic doors of the conference room. "It's a sensitive situation, Steven. And it's a calculated risk." They stopped in front of the passageway leading to the metal doors where the chairman continued in a lower voice. "This current turn of events could make a noise loud enough to be heard by too many wrong ears."

"How do you mean?" They stepped into the ten foot passage.

"At the moment, we're only looking at the surface. The six files your computer is developing is just page one."

"And there are quite a few more to come." Steve looked up at the security camera mounted above the thick, metal doors. "Steven Palmer. Red one, H.R.C."

Fisher did the same. "Robert Fisher, Chairman. Red one, U.W.C."

A blue curtain of light fell over the two men. Fisher blinked and rubbed his eyes. "Every time I go through here, I'm afraid the door will open on Saturn and I'll instantly choke to death."

Young Palmer laughed. "It reminds me of an old science fiction movie one of our T.A.s brought back. "It was called, *Dune,* I think."

"I saw that ... I liked the giant worms."

The metal doors opened into an elevator the size of a small waiting room and closed behind them without a sound. "Level one, please." Fisher's voice activated the lift and it rose swiftly toward the main floor of the complex. He studied Steven for a moment. "What I started to say before is serious. I didn't really think about it until the meeting was nearly over."

"The files we have to run?"

"That's my point exactly." Fisher glanced up at the illuminated numeral one above the elevator doors. "Hold please," he ordered, and the word, *wait* flashed by the floor number. "Do you remember what Cross and I were discussing before Kathy displayed the files?"

"You were talking about ... about the others ...." Steven's arms crawled with goose bumps.

"Yes, Mr. Palmer. The other two-hundred-twenty-five souls on board flight two-eighty." He turned away and pinched his forehead. "If we don't eliminate them, what *do* we do with them?" He looked back at Steven with an expression of grave concern. "How do we blend them into a society five-hundred years ahead of their own time?"

"Jesus!" He caught himself. "Sorry, sir."

"My feelings exactly." He shook his head. "We're ready, thank you." The "wait" light blinked off and the doors opened into a high-security area of the first floor. "Get me the Franklin file as soon as you can, we have a lot of work to do."

"Yes, sir. It should be ready by now."

"I want nothing but red clearance on this. Understood?"

Palmer nodded with a stern look in his eyes. "Perfectly." He watched Chairman Fisher walk past a security monitor.

"Good afternoon, Chairman Fisher," greeted a synthesized human voice from an unseen source.

"Same to you, Tillie," answered Fisher, as he entered his executive office and closed the door.

"How are you, Councilman Palmer?" asked the same security monitor, some twenty feet away.

"I'm fine ... I'm just-fine." Steven turned and walked out of one high-security area into another. His mind was filled with more concern than he'd known in his entire young life.

$\mathcal{P}$ART TWO
ARRIVAL

Chapter 9
FINAL APPROACH
Phase One

"Zebra leader to T.I. two-eighty, over."

"Go ahead Zebra, this is Captain Ballard."

"We're eighty miles out and closing. Reduce air speed and descend to ten-thousand. I'll have further instructions when we're on final, over."

"Roger, Zebra leader. Where are we headed, Vegas?"

"A Little further northeast. Las Vegas, as you know it, doesn't exist. Zebra leader out."

Tom Parrish reduced the throttles and deployed the slats by two percent.

"What the hell does he mean, *Vegas as we know it?*"

Ballard chuckled. "Maybe the whole place has become one huge brothel."

The big engines changed pitch when the thrust eased off. The extension of the slats altered the aerodynamics of the wings and the seven-forty-seven began its descent.

K.W. stepped onto the flight deck from the cabin and closed the door. "They're sleeping like babies, Captain. How that's possible, I have no idea."

"Is the crew secured?"

"Yes, sir. I buckled them in myself."

The copilot turned around. "Is Cindy okay?"

"They all are." He sat at his console and snapped on his harness. "Does it seem strange to either of you guys that a cabin full of people could be zonked out all at once?" He put on his headset.

Tom said, "I'm wondering why they didn't zap us and take the Goddamn plane down without our help. They have enough control to keep us from climbing."

"Speaking of altitude, why are we losing it?" K.W. scanned his instruments and adjusted radio frequencies as he would have on any other flight.

"We've been given orders to descend to ten-thousand," answered Tom.

"Where we going, the Sands?"

"That was my question," said the Captain. "They told me Vegas doesn't exist as we know it."

"Great," responded K.W. "We're gonna land this mother in the middle of the Nevada desert, at a place unknown. And I'm sure we won't want to stay there after we arrive."

"To answer your earlier question," offered Captain Ballard. He turned to Tom. "They didn't zap us because I don't think they can actually control our aircraft—"

The slats extended full. The seven-forty-seven went into a dive.

"Jesus!" Tom Parrish pulled back on the yoke—the plane kept diving. After five-hundred feet it leveled off.

"I've got it!" shouted Captain Ballard. The landing gears went down and locked.

"Holy-mother-of-God!" yelled K.W., hanging on to his table. All three lurched forward with the sudden drag on the aircraft.

Ballard's face turned ashen. The huge jetliner went into a steep left bank. He knew what was happening.

After losing another five-hundred feet the jet leveled off again, the wheels went back up. The slats retracted back to two percent and the seven-forty-seven resumed its previous, controlled descent.

"Zebra leader to Captain Ballard, over."

"I know, Zebra." Raymond Ballard's hands shook. He gripped the controls.

Tom Parrish and K.W. sat stiff and wide-eyed listening to their hearts pounding.

"Just a small demonstration, Captain. Try not to be so sure of yourself in the future." The radio *squawked*. "Do you want to bring her in, or shall we? Over."

"I'll make the landing, Zebra."

"Much better, Captain. We're ten miles out and on final approach. Stand by."

Tom whispered, "They've heard every damn word we've said."

"Right. Don't say anything we don't want them to hear."

"Prepare your aircraft for landing, Captain, and listen carefully to my instructions, over."

"I'm all ears, Zebra leader."

K.W. punched up radio frequencies rapidly, trying to get a fix on the unknown approach control. He received nothing. "Captain, I can't find any approach control!"

"I don't think it matters, just listen to Zebra—he's in charge."

"Correct, Captain. I'll be the voice of approach control." The escort spread its formation and flew above the jumbo jet.

The cloud cover that had obscured the

ground vanished.

What looked like a large city appeared in the distance.

"The complex ahead is headquarters for the United World Council and the command center for the United World Military Force. That's where we come from, captain."

U.W.M.F., thought Ballard. *A global military?* The idea was only a dream in the twentieth century. It was something for candidates to rant about during election campaigns. A chill raised the hair on the back of his neck and arms. *What cost had there been to bring about a world council and a world military?*

"You'll land from the east on V.F.R., into a fifteen knot wind. Ground temperature is one-zero-seven. Use runway EL-five-two. After you touch down, taxi to the waiting ground-escort vehicles. No one on the ground can see your aircraft or us, Captain, except the escort crew. We're *cloaked.* Copy that?"

"Zebra leader, what the hell are you talking about?"

Tom grinned. "We're in an episode of *Star Trek.*"

"I don't know what your co-pilot means, Captain, but I assure you your aircraft is invisible for security reasons, and you're perfectly safe."

"Thanks for sharing, Zebra. At this

point, I'll believe anything you say."

"Copy that. Follow the escort to a designated gate. You'll be told what to do from there. All understood, captain?"

"Understood, Zebra."

"We'll be above you until contact with ground-escort."

"Roger, Zebra."

"For your information, captain. You're landing at a restricted, high-security, code-red, base. Do whatever you're told and don't ask questions. You won't get answers anyway. Stand by."

"Roger." Captain Ballard glanced at Tom. "Put 'em down."

"Gears coming down, sir." Tom pulled the lever.

"Let me have flaps."

"Flaps deployed, captain."

The seven-forty-seven banked easy to the left and slipped down to two-thousand feet. Captain Ballard straightened his approach as Tom Parrish pulled back on the throttles.

The complex before them was awesome. Tom stared forward. "That building is at least fifty stories high!" He shook his head. "It's in the shape of a star."

Captain Ballard said, "It's three-times the size of the Pentagon."

Tom said, "The building's smack in the center of the development."

Captain Ballard pointed forward. "The place is bigger than Dallas and Fort Worth together."

Tom looked off the starboard wing. "I can see a high wall that appears to surround the whole place."

"Zebra leader, over."

"Go ahead Zebra leader."

"Take her in, captain, she's all yours."

"Affirmative, Zebra, I see EL-five-two." He brought the nose up and passed over the flashing markers of the runway.

"K.W. said, "Kiss my butt on Sunset Boulevard—this strip must be five miles long!"

"Yeah, and it looks like our welcoming committee knows we don't need all of it to land."

Two Intimidating military vehicles pulled up at opposite sides of the runway. They waited less than ten yards from where the big jet would come to a stop.

Ballard set the aircraft down and kept his eyes on the military trucks. He rolled the seven-forty-seven to a halt with her nose between the two vehicles. He looked down from his three story window. Nothing moved but the flashing amber lights on top of each vehicle.

"Zebra leader to Captain Ballard, over."

"Yes, Zebra, go ahead."

"The escort on your port side will take you to the gate. The other one will bring up your tail. Over."

"Roger, Zebra. Where are you?"

"One flight up."

Ballard, Parrish and Soo looked up at the same time. Above, and to the left, hovered the four fighters. The engines of the jumbo jet were louder than the collective sound of the fighter formation.

Zebra leader moved down to cockpit level and waved at Ballard. The pilot's face was covered by his helmet and sun visor. He nodded. "Nice flying with you, captain. Zebra leader out."

A roar of air, filled with a dull thunder, rocked the jetliner. In less time than it takes to crack an egg, the four fighters climbed straight up, shot across the complex, and were gone.

The radio *crackled.* "This is ground escort one. You will follow me immediately." The port vehicle came to life, pulled up in front of the jetliner and drove forward ahead of the 747.

Captain Ballard released the brakes and followed along behind.

* * * *

The jumbo jet followed the lead vehicle to the gaping mouth of the largest hangar he had ever seen.

"This is ground escort one. Shut her down, Captain, you've arrived. Ground escort one out."

"Where in the hell are we?" Tom shook his head, still dazzled by the departure of the fighters.

"We've reached the end of the line. Wherever the hell that is." He pulled off his headset and ran his hands through his thinning hair.

* * * *

The last thing he heard was the down-whine of the big engines—and a ringing in his ears—his head—his entire body....

Chapter 10
ARRIVAL
Phase 2

$\mathcal{P}$hil Khrismann stood at a window of the main U.W.M.F. security building. He was on the third floor looking straight into the windshield of the Tran's International seven-forty-seven. Below, a team of service droids secured the wheels of the jumbo jet. Eight armed guards were in position around the aircraft. Their squad leader walked casually under the belly of the old bird, inspecting it with great interest.

How many more people would know of this incident before the file could be closed? He weighed the question and thought, *there are too many already.*

An attractive young woman in a white and

gray uniform stepped into the hallway behind Phil. "He'll see you now."

He came out of his thoughts and turned to the woman. "So soon? I thought I'd have to wait an hour."

"Not on this one," she added, "He's just finished a long, high-level, chat with Fisher."

"What's his mood?"

"Let's see." She tilted her head back and rolled her sparkling, deep green eyes. "I'd put it somewhere between a budget refusal and having to attend a full U.W.C. conference."

"Terrific. Why wasn't he at the priority session today?"

"He was knee-deep in the Poland thing. Be glad." She laughed. "He'd be in blacker spirits if he had been there."

Phil shook his head. "Does he know what we've got here?"

"Of course. He reviewed the meeting from his terminal." She laughed again and clutched Phil's arm. "Some of his comments were actually funny."

"How so?"

She shook her head and grinned. "He suggested that Larry Cross be sent back to the twentieth century on a one-way ride." They both laughed and held eye contact for a moment.

"Jennifer ... I wanted to see you—"

He turned away and took a deep breath.

"It's all right, Phil. I understand."

"No, you don't—not really." He faced her again and touched her thick, black hair. She tilted her head and kissed the back of his hand. "Kerry made the divorce hell on earth."

"I'm sorry."

"Yeah." Phil touched Jennifer's cheek then stroked her hair again. "In the middle of that, I had to deal with the reorganization of my department." He paused and smiled. "That's when you took up with Trevor."

"Trevor's history." Jennifer took Phil's hand and pressed it against her face. "He had Global Security so far up his ass he couldn't think of anything else."

"My job's demanding too, Jennifer. I've got this gate thing now. And for some reason I think it's heavy—really heavy."

"You still have to eat, right?"

"So?" Phil knew what was coming and he welcomed it.

"You'll have dinner with me, at my place tonight."

"I don't know ... there's a lot involved here."

"You do get time for meals—don't you?" She couldn't stop the feelings that rose up and ran into the corners of her eyes.

"Yes, we get to eat."

"Good!" Her voice fluttered. "You'll eat with me even if it's only fifteen minutes." She swallowed hard and looked up at him. "I need to hear you say yes."

"If I do ... it starts again. You know that?" He looked up and a flash of their last time together raced through him.

"Yes. Yes—dammit—yes! We'll deal with it."

"Okay." Phil lowered his voice to a whisper. "After I meet with the man, we'll set a time."

Jennifer hugged him and pressed her face against his chest. "I've missed you so much."

More flashes of his relationship with her danced across his mind. He parted from her and smiled. "By the way, Jen dear. How come you're not answering my *official* calls?"

"I've moved up in the world. I'm now *his* private secretary. I'm in on all of it." She smiled. "I'm going to the ladies room. You go on in. He's waiting." She gave him another quick hug then started down the hall.

"Jennifer."

She stopped and turned back. "Yes?"

"I love you."

Her face brightened. "I know, I love you too."

Phil watched her walk away and turn right toward another corridor twenty yards away. She looked back and playfully blew him a kiss. He smiled and felt more of the old memories tugging at his heart.

Theirs had been a special relationship. It was born during hours of working together and grew on the sharp edge of, draining, top secret matters. The same situation existed now.

Khrismann knew the excitement of the time gate incident would dig into both of them. They'd be drawn back together as before. This time however, they were involved in matters concerning the lives of two-hundred-thirty people from another time. Six of them would have to live. The others may have to be eliminated.

Chapter 11
A Matter of Concern
Disposition

COMMANDING GENERAL'S OFFICE 1:35 PM.

"*I*s he ready?" Phil showed his I.D. badge to the General's new, young, receptionist.

She glanced at the small picture and at the man standing in front of her.

"He's impatiently ready. Go right in, Mr. Khrismann."

"Thanks." Phil let himself into the C.G.'s office to find it empty of the man in charge of the entire operation of the United World Military Force. "Mack! It's Khrismann." The private conference room door was open.

"I'm in here—waiting." The gruff, superior voice of Commanding General, Charles *Mack* Mackendrick boomed out of the adjoining room.

Phil entered and saw the C.G. standing in front of his large computer screen. He was studying the completed file on Congressman Alan Franklin. "The other files will be ready in an hour according to Palmer."

Mack kept his back to Phil and continued to stare at the displayed information. "This one concerns me the most," he said, in an abrupt manner. "I don't give a shit about the rest of the crap these people got themselves into." He turned around with obvious military bearing. "Sit down, Khrismann. What the fuck are we dealing with?" He clasped his hands behind his back and paced in front of the screen.

"You talked with Fisher?"

The C.G. glared at Phil. "I did. I heard his story. Now I want yours." Mack held his stare. "He's an appointed official. You're at least half military. You and Fisher see things from a different point of view. Give it to me from where you stand."

"Our job is mainly security. The full council will decide what to do with them." Phil Khrismann's position was basically equal to the C.G.'s as far as their respective departments were concerned, but Phil couldn't help feel subordinate to Mackendrick.

"We have to baby sit these people and keep a lid on the whole issue." Charles was, in military slang, a *lifer.* He joined up at eighteen and had served thirty years. He carried his hundred-ninety-five pound bulk on a six foot one inch frame. He stood straight and tall. If anyone was born to be in charge, it was Mack.

His wide-set, steel-gray, eyes were an asset to his position, commanding respect over the harshness of his rigid personality.

Mackendrick favored hard booze. He loved a filthy joke, and a good fight. He was difficult to get close to. Mack lived alone. His job was his life. "Sitting on this sonofabitch could be an exercise in futility, Khrismann. It's a goddamned pointless nightmare."

"This situation isn't any more difficult than keeping a lid on the gate."

Mack waved toward the screen and paced in front of it. "We have a different situation here."

"A little more complicated."

"Two-hundred-thirty flapping mouths, that's a lot of complication!"

"If they're separated and spread out, the risk is reduced."

"*If* they're spread out?" countered Mack.

"They have to be. The alternatives are limited." He leaned on the table with both hands and glared into Phil's eyes. "The Larry Cross solution will *not* be considered under any circumstances whatsoever."

Phil pushed his chair out and casually crossed his legs. "Not by us, Mack—"

"Not by anybody!" He turned and started pacing again.

Khrismann drummed his fingers on the glossy conference table. He knew his and the Mackendrick machine would be more involved in the flight-two-eighty matter than routine security. For a brief moment he *did* consider the Larry Cross solution. "All possibilities have to be examined, Mack. You damn well know it."

The commanding general snapped around, as he had earlier, holding his hands behind his back. "Not that one!" The General moved quickly to Phil's side of the table. He sat on the edge of it, close to the Time Travel Enforcement Commission Director and leaned toward him. "What the fuck's the matter with you? Push elimination and our departments become death squads!"

Phil got out of his chair and walked away from the table. "I'm not talking about killing them, General." He glanced at the screen, which continued to display Congressman Franklin's file.

"What then?"

Khrismann kept his back to the C.G. when

he answered. "Having superior authority, in matters of security, we present a preconceived plan to the full council."

Mack pulled a small tube of *paralayne* compound from the inside pocket of his uniform blouse and fumbled with the safety cap. "Which is?"

Phil turned back to Mack with a face full of confidence. His smile fell away. He watched Mackendrick squeeze two drops of paralayne into his mouth. "I thought you quit,"

"I did ... for three months." Mack held the tube toward Phil and nodded.

"No, I haven't touched it for a year and I feel a hell of a lot better. Besides, it costs too much."

Mack replaced the cap and stuffed the narcotic back into his breast pocket. "It gives me an edge. "So, what's this great plan?" He blinked several times and cleared his throat.

* * * *

Paralayne had replaced cocaine, heroine and pot more than one-hundred years earlier. It was considered medicinal. Mack had a medical permit to use the substance. Anyone in his position could buy it for a thousand-dollars a tube.

* * * *

"The plan isn't great—it's simply effective."

"I'm listening."

Phil approached Mack and sat on the edge of the table. He leaned forward. "We send the key people back through the time gate and scatter the rest around the globe." He stood up and waved his arms in front of the C.G. "If they tell the whole goddamned story, nobody'll believe it."

"According to my estimate, close to a hundred people already know about this problem."

"Within two hours you can add another fifty or more."

Mackendrick puzzled a moment then shook his head. "Are you serious? What about the two-hundred-twenty-five people who don't go back?" He hesitated. "Phil, you're not thinking. They all have to return."

"They can't, Mack. That's the problem!"

"There's a better solution. I should've realized it earlier." He stood and walked quickly toward the head of the conference table.

"What?" Phil narrowed his eyes and slid himself off the table.

Mack pushed a button on the console next to his computer keyboard. He directed an order through the intercom. "I want a red-priority line to Fisher ASAP!"

"Yes, sir."

"Mack, what are you up to?" Phil's question painted a smile across the C.G.'s face.

"We've been sitting on our goddamned thumbs since you came in here."

"What are you talking about?"

"Khrismann, sometimes I think you're on the moon or Mars for Christ's sake!"

Phil flinched at the remark. He was an equal to this pillar of military authority. "No! I'm right here, in this conference room. Now what's your solution?" Hot blood shot into Phil's ears, burning the back of his neck and flushing his cheeks.

"Don't you see it? We were just about to miss the boat!" The Commanding General laughed and sat in his chair at the head of the table.

"Enlighten me, Mack."

Chapter 12
The General's Plan

*M*ackendrick leaned on his elbows, laced his fingers and propped up his chin. "Our two-hundred-thirty security risks are asleep. They're in never-never land." He chuckled.

Khrismann thought a moment. "They are now, but forty-eight hours is MAX." Phil looked at the Franklin file displayed on the screen then at Mack. "What?"

"We'll get the whole goddamned mess out of here before it becomes a problem. Send them all back now."

"We can't!"

"Why?"

"The gate's closing. It's unpredictable!"

"It's a calculated risk." Mack stared at the screen with a confident expression. "Everything about that *time gate* is risky."

Phil paced. "At the moment, I could use a hit of paralayne."

Mack reached inside his blouse. "Be my guest."

"I'm just thinking out loud." He rubbed the back of his neck. "What you're proposing is one step away from the Cross solution." He moved between Mackendrick and the screen. "First of all, we never use the gate when it's unstable."

Mack stood abruptly. He didn't like anybody towering over him. "It's become necessary."

"Let me finish." Phil paused. "Secondly, there isn't enough time to plot a crossing of this type. And finally, the decision is not ours to make."

Mackendrick shoved his empty chair in place with a muffled thud. "That's exactly why I ordered a priority-red call to Fisher."

Phil held his ground. "He can't rule on a matter like this without the approval of the full council."

"Once we convince him, he'll get the goddamned approval!" Mack's eyes flared. "I want this problem *handled* and my solution is the most efficient.

"Fisher won't buy it."

"He supports us in all matters of security!"

"Not at the risk of innocent lives." Khrismann turned and waved at the computer screen. "Have you forgotten *him* and the other key people at issue here?"

"No. I haven't!" Mack pulled the paralayne out of his pocket and pointed the tube at the Franklin file. "Especially *him!*" He removed the cap from the tube and squeezed two drops into his mouth. "I know one hell of a lot more about the congressman's role in this than you do!" He cleared his throat and raised his voice. "If that man doesn't accomplish the shit recorded in the file. Our lives will be altered to a degree you don't want to hear about." He snapped the cap on the paralayne.

Phil glanced at the screen then back to Mackendrick. "And you're willing to risk a dangerous crossing?"

"Think about it, Phil. If you transport them today or at the next cycle. The risk is the same."

"No—it's less with a stable time-window and accurate plotting."

The General keyed a print code into the computer. "It's a trade-off, Phil." He twisted the paralayne tube in his fingers and watched the silent light-printer produce ten, neatly stacked, pale blue pages of hard copy. "Send these people back now and the security problem will vanish with them." He slipped the tube into his pants pocket and looked at Khrismann through a narrow stare. "Wait for your damn stable time-window and another problem falls right in our lap."

Phil sat on the edge of the table and leaned toward the sheaf of blue paper. "The security factor will be minimized by global separation, as I told you." He turned the stack of papers around so he could see them. "We'll have no trouble selling Fisher, and the council, on that idea." Phil looked at the screen. "Franklin here and the other key four can be sent back home when the gate recycles in three months."

Mackendrick keyed another command into the computer and the large screen went black. He chuckled under his breath, and pulled a red file folder from a drawer under the head of the table. "TA's, Phil. Give it some thought." Mack slipped the blue pages of the Franklin file into the folder and slapped it down hard on the table.

Phil flinched and looked up to meet the C.G.'s eyes. "Time Agents are standard procedure with every mission. So what?"

"Nothing important, just a little fact to consider." Mackendrick tapped his fingers on the red folder. "According to the information on these, *key* people, as we call them, you'll be dealing with a T.A. situation every day for the rest of your career. What's that—another ten—fifteen years?"

"No mission takes that long." He shook his head and walked away from the head of the table. "Alteration circumstances take a few days—a week at the most. And that's in past-time. In real-time, the duration factor is eight minutes." Phil brushed his hand through his hair. "It's less complicated than it sounds."

Mackendrick stood tall to affect a superior attitude between himself and Khrismann. "Let these people wake up and return to their own time with knowledge of where they've been, and the role they play in the future, and you'll have a massive problem." Mack rubbed his chin and walked in front of the black screen. He turned and faced Khrismann with confidence and power. "You'll be dealing with enough daily monitoring reports and T.A. control programs to fry your brain." He leaned on the back of his chair confident he'd made his point and won his way.

Phil made his position clear. "If it comes to what you say, we'll find a way to make it work. Whatever it takes." He choked down a swallow that felt like hot copper shavings. "I will not however, support a dangerous time-transport to make my job, or yours, any easier." He held Mack's eyes. "Is that understood?"

"Perfectly."

A red light flashed on the intercom in front of Mackendrick. Without looking away from Phil's defiant stare, Mack triggered the response key. "Yes?"

"I have Chairman Fisher on priority-red, sir." The voice of Mack's secretary grated the air in the room like blown sand across a hot desert canyon.

"Consider it further," added Mack.

"Not on your life, or theirs."

"I'm going to suggest the idea to Fisher."

"That's your call. I'll fight it."

"You're being an asshole Phil!"

"We'll see who that turns out to be, General."

Mackendrick glared for a moment then responded to the intercom. "Put Fisher through." He left the speaker on and leaned on the back of his chair.

Fisher's voice filled the room through the console. "What is it, Mack?"

"Councilman Khrismann and I are requesting an emergency meeting with you prior to link-up with the full council." Mack's eyes followed Phil as he walked to the far end of the table and sat down. "We may have a way to dilute the current problem immediately. You need to know the details before any other solution is considered. It's top priority, sir."

Fisher's voice echoed. "Is the situation stable?"

Mack took his eyes off Phil and stood up again. "The subjects are in the medical wing of security block nine."

"Are they all right?"

"Sleeping peacefully, sir."

"I'll meet you there in one hour."

Mackendrick smiled across the table. "We'll be waiting, Chairman. Thank you." He reached forward and buzzed his receptionist again.

"Yes, sir?"

Mack's grin filled with arrogance. He answered the woman. "Have Taylor bring my craft up to level three and leave it. I'll be driving."

"Right away, General."

"We got our meeting." He crossed his arms behind his back and regarded Khrismann with a pleased grin.

"Fisher will listen, he always does, but he won't agree with you."

Mack picked up the file folder. "I don't need

this shit right now!" He slapped the folder hard against his thigh. "Let's go. We have an important meeting to attend."

The two men walked back into Mack's office just as Jennifer entered the room from the reception area. "Hi," she said, and looked at Phil. "Major Normand and Scott Price are waiting at hangar twenty-four. It's secure and ready."

Mackendrick said, "About goddamn time." He placed the file folder on his desk and reached for the red phone.

Phil glared at the C.G. "How the hell did Price get involved?" He glanced at Jennifer, she shrugged.

"I authorized it," said Mack. He punched three numbers on the keypad of the red phone.

"Jesus!" Phil shook his head and looked around the room in frustration.

"This is Mackendrick, put sergeant Wygant on the line." He cupped his left hand over the receiver's mouthpiece. "You disapprove?"

Phil leaned on a corner of Mack's desk. "I was ordered to keep GSA out of this for—"

Mack held up his hand. "Wygant. Move the plane to twenty-four." He met Phil's eyes and felt the anger he was intended to feel. "Yeah, and Major Normand calls the shots when you get it there. Good. Immediately, Sergeant."

Jennifer had gone to her small office area at the far end of the room. She returned with phone messages in her hand. Mackendrick turned away from Phil's stare and took the slips of paper from Jennifer. "I think," she said, "both of you should see the top message."

"What about, Price?" insisted Phil. he moved back from the desk.

Mack studied the green slip of paper and smiled. "Here," he said, and handed the message to Phil. "Don't get hot about Price. GSA had to know sooner or later. I chose *sooner!*"

"I *am* hot, Goddammit!" He held the message, but didn't look at it. His glare was fixed on the C.G. "You should've consulted me first."

"There wasn't time. Anyway, I brought him in before Fisher suggested otherwise." He took his uniform hat off a tall file cabinet and winked at Jennifer.

She returned a faint smile.

Phil shook his head. "Son-of-a-bitch!" He tossed the phone message on Mack's desk and looked, first at Jennifer then at Mackendrick. "Did you call him in?"

Mack frowned as he adjusted his hat to a perfect military tilt and exactly two fingers off his nose. "You know better," he said. "Frank Tanner's like any other member of the media. He pokes around just to keep us on our toes."

"My ass!"

Mack laughed and came around his desk. "What about your ass, Phil?"

"It's got a large pain in it called security leak!"

The commanding general tapped his right temple with his index finger. "That's what I call a headache. We'll have to rename our pains if we hope to understand each other." He winked at Jennifer again. "Jen-girl," he added. *She hated the phrase.* "Get me hard copies of the other happy time-traveler files from the HRC computer." He stepped closer to Phil and gripped his shoulder firmly. "All of them, Jen-girl. If Fisher agrees with your boyfriend here, I want to know everything there is on each of these people."

"Yes, sir." Jennifer blushed. *He had to say that, the bastard!* She noticed a flush on Phil's face.

Khrismann grinned in an effort to minimize Jennifer's embarrassment. "I'll call you."

"Let's move," ordered Mackendrick, and lead the way through the outer office. He swept passed the front desk, entered the hall, stopped short and regarded Phil with hard, cold eyes. "Jennifer's in a sensitive position, Khrismann. Don't let your pecker compromise her. Got it?"

Phil's neck and ears turned red. "What

Jennifer and I do outside your office is our own *fucking* business. Got that?"

Mack smiled. *"Fucking* her would be nice business. I'm not. You are, and it forges a weak link. That *is* my business. Keep your brains in your head and out of your pants."

"You're an asshole, Mackendrick."

"And a clever one at that."

Phil shook his head and wondered how Mack could be so intelligent and stupid at the same time. "What about Tanner?"

"He's not a problem. We'll feed him false information."

* * * *

Mack's favorite hover-craft waited at the entrance to level three.

Chapter 13
The Medical Wing

*M*ackendrick and Khrismann entered security block nine through an electronic surveillance system. They walked to the center of a large, circular foyer and stopped in front of a floor-mounted, translucent directory. Each division of the vast complex was shown on the huge display screen. A bright red light blinked on and off in the center of the display showing their current location. Mack touched the screen on a small square marked, *M-3(B)*

A synthesized female voice filled the foyer in pleasant, soft tones. "Enter code at access way, *M-3(B)*."

Phil and Mack moved to the medical wing entrance and punched in their code numbers.

Phil: 3-7-6-5

Mack: 8-4-5-1

The female voice responded. "Body scan complete, you are cleared to enter. This is a code-red medical research department. Any information gathered here will have a classified designation."

Click.

The electronic lock disengaged. Mack and Phil entered.

The door closed and sealed behind them.

Mack looked up and smiled. "There's no way to get in here in a hurry."

A ceiling-mounted camera recorded the two men and the time and date of their entrance.

Phil winked at the lens. "Research takes time, General."

"Yeah, and most of it turns out to be crap anyway."

* * * *

On the surface, *M-3(B)* appears to be nothing more than a busy, metropolitan hospital. It is, in fact, *much more.* Each room is electronically secured and can not be entered without a special numerical code. The second And third floors house recombinant-DNA research laboratories. The labs are linked to a massive computer center on the fourth floor. The main-frame of the comp-center is isolated from all other computer systems in the complex.

The fifth floor is devoted *entirely* to android and cloning projects. Access to anything on that floor is restricted to research scientists, department heads and UWC Chairman, Robert Fisher.

* * * *

Mackendrick and Khrismann approached the white counter set off to one side of the *M-3(B)* entrance area.

A plump brunette, in her early forties, looked up from behind the counter and smiled. "Who do you wish to see?"

"Doctor Rankin," barked the commanding general. "Tell him, Mackendrick and Khrismann are here."

"Yes, sir." She pressed three numbers on the panel in front of her. "They're here, Doctor." She looked at Mack and Phil, "I'll tell them." She touched another key on her communication panel. "Doctor Rankin will meet you by lift three."

"Thanks," offered Mack, and stepped away from the counter. Phil followed him to elevators at the end of a long stark-white corridor. Mack took another hit from his tube of *Paralayne.*

In less than a minute the doors of elevator three opened and Dr. Gregory Rankin stepped into the hallway.   "Gentlemen." He shook hands with Mack then Phil. "Fisher's in my office. We'll talk there."

The General straightened his blouse. "He's early."

The doctor smiled. "As always."

Dr. Rankin looked, dressed and acted more like a corporate executive than a research scientist.   He was in his mid-thirties, lean and stood about five-eleven.

"Is everything under control?" Phil, met Rankin's eyes.

"Everything." He lead the way toward his office.

"How much longer can you keep them asleep?"

"Less than forty-eight hours, Mack ... if you want them alive." Dr. Rankin stopped at a door marked, GENETIC RESEARCH, and punched a code into the key-pad above the knob. He held the door open for Mack and Phil.

"Of course I want them alive," said Mackendrick.

"Then there's no time to waste. After you, general." He gestured toward the interior of his office. "The Chairman is waiting."

Phil entered first and shook hands with Fisher. "Chairman, thank you for seeing us so quickly."

"It's an urgent matter." Fisher reached out to Mackendrick and pumped his arm. "Let's get to it gentlemen."

"In my conference room, offered Rankin, "we'll be more comfortable."

The four men seated themselves around the table in the modest-sized room. It didn't have large computer screens on the walls, nor individual terminals in front of each seat. There was just one transparent screen and keyboard at the head of the table, now occupied by Chairman Fisher. "Dr. Rankin," he said, "I need to hear from you first."

Mack reached for a hit of Paralayne. *Not in front of the chairman.*

Fisher continued. "In terms of life support, what's the bottom line with our guests right now?"

Gregory Rankin sat back and stroked his ID badge. "We have two-hundred-thirty people in an induced state of deep sleep. At the outside, they can remain so another forty-six hours." He leaned forward. "To be absolutely safe, we should bring them out within thirty-six hours." Rankin glanced at Mackendrick.

Fisher leaned on his elbows, clasped his

hands and tapped his thumbs against his chin. "If we wait?" He looked at the doctor from under a wrinkled brow.

"One, maybe two out of five may not come out of it."

Chairman Fisher unfolded his hands and nodded toward General Mackendrick. "Mack, you have a solution, what is it?"

The general leaned forward and announced his answer with confidence. "Send them back now." He turned to Khrismann, then back to Fisher. "They won't know where the hell they've been and the *special* five, I mean six, will go on to accomplish what they're destined to."

Fisher tensed then addressed Phil. "I need to hear from you."

Khrismann pushed back from the table and stood. He rubbed his hands over his face and let what he knew page through his mind once more. He turned, leaned on the table and stared directly into Fisher's eyes. "The time gate is unstable, sir. If it closes during re-entry we lose them all—and what they're supposed to do." He stood and spoke in a lower tone. "I'm dead against it." He shifted his glance to Mackendrick and met his eyes.

"Mr. Chairman," asserted Mack, spreading his arms and holding his palms up. "Consider the alternatives. The risk is worth taking."

"The alternatives," offered Fisher, "are heavy security and more work for you. That's your job. We cannot risk the lives of two-hundred-thirty innocent people!" He pushed back from the table. "We damn well can't live, as we do now, if the *key* group doesn't complete what has to be done." The chairman stood.

The others did the same.

"Phil," said Fisher, "when is the time gate active and stable again?"

"Ninety days, sir." He looked toward the general, then back to the chairman. "I can assure a safe crossing at that time."

Robert Fisher let out a slow breath and addressed Dr. Rankin. "Greg, can you and your people start reviving our guests in twenty-four hours?" He cocked his head to the right and waited for the answer.

"Yes, Mr. Chairman, and without risk."

"Do it—and start with the five priority people." Fisher rubbed his chin thoughtfully and turned his glance to Mackendrick. "Mack, you take the necessary steps to double security on that aircraft."

He looked away then slammed his hands on the back of the chair in front of him. "Sir! I'm up to my ass in the Poland situation right now—"

Fisher responded in sharp terms. "Forget Poland! I want double security underway by fifteen-thirty hours–that's an order!"

"Yes, sir."

"Good. Get your people ready right away, Phil."

Khrismann looked down and smiled, then turned to catch the anger in Mack's eyes. "Yes, Sir."

Fisher started out of the room and the others followed. As an after-thought the chairman gripped Dr. Rankin's arm. "When you revive the key people, inform me immediately." He nodded. "I would like to see the congressman as soon as possible."

"You'll know the minute they come around, sir."

Chairman Fisher faced the others before entering the doctor's office. "In one way or another, gentlemen, our decisions will touch the lives of everyone on this planet." He glanced again at Mackendrick. "Until this matter is settled it is to be given *top* priority."

Obviously irritated, Mackendrick put on his hat and adjusted it sharply. "As you ordered, sir."

"There will be a meeting of the full council tomorrow morning," added Fisher. "What we've decided here, will be explained to the council as orders in progress. The other nations will be on-line for a full report." He smiled. "You're good people. I expect the best from each of you."

Dr. Rankin stepped aside and gestured toward his office. "Let me give you a close look at our visitors from the past."

Chapter 14
Frank Tanner

THE NEVADA SUN: *History:*

*M*ost of its readers consider the Nevada Sun the best newspaper in the state. The paper sprang up during the first decade of the twenty-third century. Six, serious-minded, reporters founded the tabloid as, *The Advocate.* Early editions were published twice a week on a modest budget. The funding came from supporting business people who bought ads and out of the pockets of the paper's founders.

* * * *

From 2305 to 2310, the power of the *United World Council* grew rapidly, diluting the strength of the presidency. During those years a giant central complex was established on a former nuclear test site in the Nevada desert. The complex houses the headquarters for: UWC, GSA, UWMF, TTEC *(secret),* and HRC *(secret).*

* * * *

The Advocate is based in Carson City, an hour away from the headquarters complex, which soon became a daily beat for Advocate reporters.

Bold *Advocate* editorials forced UWC to open a public information/media center for television, radio and print reporters. Within a few months, *The Advocate* gained national attention with a series of articles regarding a secret project called, *Time Gate.* The stories concerned eight research scientists who were, allegedly, sent into the future and lost. Follow up features insisted subjects referred to as, *Time Agents,* were being transported backward in time to alter the future.

The Information Office released reports that the *Time Gate* was a classified aero-science project to study a recurring depletion of the ozone layer above Antarctica. It was called, *Time Gate,* because of its semi-annual occurrence.

* * * *

Eight months later The Advocate was purchased by a massive conglomerate known as, Garrett Publishing.

The Advocate became, The Nevada Sun, a new Editor-in-Chief was named and Time Gate stories were retracted.

"A FABRICATION!" proclaimed the first banner headline of the Sun.

"FICTION FOR PROFIT!" was the top story of the next day's edition.

"TIME GATE/NON EXISTENT!" led the third front page of the Nevada Sun.

Within two weeks the newspaper published pictures of a dejected-looking man named, Harry Fellin. He was said to be the reporter who distorted the facts of the Time Gate project to bring attention to himself. Under his picture the caption read, HARRY FELLIN: FIRED BY SUN.

The story claimed Fellin's job had been on the line for several weeks and he colored the Time Gate story to save his position. The Editor-in-Chief added a comment to the piece, "It's a sad day when the integrity of responsible reporting is reduced to fiction. Harry Fellin made a serious blunder. The Nevada Sun will give you the straight, unaltered, facts. Should you be concerned about the research scientists named in Mr. Fellin's fictionalized report, I assure you, they and their families are pleased to know the truth has been made public."

A few weeks later the story of the *Time Gate* was brought to the level of a political joke.

Harry Fellin was never seen or heard from again. Thanks to the power of a well connected, rich press.

* * * *

Frank Tanner joined the Nevada Sun with a Masters Degree in Political Science and World History. He was twenty-five and eager to make his mark in journalism. Within two years he became a highly respected, *special reporter.* At thirty-five, Frank remains single and dedicated to his work. His column, The *Tanner File,* has helped the Sun's circulation grow to five-hundred-thousand.

A phone message from Frank Tanner is not taken lightly by any government or military official. Over the last eight years his accurate commentary has made and broken political careers.

The owners of the Nevada Sun have mixed feelings regarding Mr. Tanner's ability to stir public opinion. It weakens their power over him.

* * * *

"Has Mackendrick called yet?" The voice on the phone was the same one that had told Frank about a strange aircraft being brought in by military escort.

"No, he hasn't," replied Tanner, from his office at the Sun. He leaned back in his chair and looked out at the cloudless Nevada sky.

"Well, add this to your notes, Mr. Tanner." The filtered voice continued. "The plane is five-hundred years old and it's now in hangar twenty-four under security-red conditions."

"Look, I deal in issues of government and politics, not old airplanes." Frank thumbed through other messages on his desk and shook his head. "I left word with Mack this morning. If there's anything worth reporting we'll get it to the right department." He leaned forward and prepared to hang up.

"Listen to me, Tanner. Do you know what TTEC means?"

"It has *ring* to it."

"Be sure to mention those letters to Mackendrick when you talk to him."

CLICK

"Hello ... Hello." The call was terminated. Frank looked at the receiver for a moment, then hung up. He stared at the letters, TTEC, on his note pad then read them to himself. "T-T-E-C?" He pulled a thick directory off the cluttered shelf behind him. It was a listing and synopsis of every department housed in the UWC Command Center. He leafed through the back pages of the huge volume and part of what the voice on the phone had said echoed in his head. *security-red—five-hundred-years old—* "TTEC," he whispered. "Teck?" Frank spoke louder. "Tee-eck?" He was trying to verbalize an acronym for the letters, *TTEC.* He started to say the letters again. "Tee-Tee ... wait a minute." Frank raised his voice. "Five-hundred years old—past—time." He shook his head and glanced at the note book again. "Tee-tee! Time travel!" Instantly, the words, *TIME GATE* shot out of a dark corner of his memory and lit up like a bright red, neon sign.

Frank spun around and faced the terminal beside him. He keyed the paper's research files.

ENTER ACCESS CODE prompted the computer screen.

51-56, keyed Frank.

PLEASE WAIT

The computer could be voice activated, but when used in that mode, it responded by voice. Frank hated the sound of it. He preferred hands-on access.

(H)EADLINE/(I)SSUE/(S)TORY/(D)ATE? SELECT

Frank typed: (S).

TITLE & SUBJECT? Displayed the computer.

TIME GATE: AERO-SCIENCE PROJECT

In a moment the computer responded.

SEARCHING FILES

Frank looked at the note book again. "Sonofabitch."

ACCESS DENIED came on the screen.

"Bullshit!" He typed: (I)

The computer displayed: (M)AST-HEAD/(Y)EAR? SELECT

THE ADVOCATE 2310

REFERENCE CODE? By selecting various numerical sequences, an authorized reporter could communicate with the computer, in a specific file, by typing direct questions.

Frank entered: (1)2310-900. With that code, the computer would extract any information requested from any issue published in 2310 under the banner, *The Advocate.* He could locate and print an article, story, entire issue or single ad by simply asking for it as if he were talking to a human librarian.

READY. The word appeared above the blinking cursor on Frank's screen.

He typed: DISPLAY ALL HEADLINES & ISSUE DATES REGARDING THE TIME GATE PROJECT

PLEASE WAIT (SEARCHING DATA BANKS)

He watched the screen and thought, *Harry Fellin went down this road and disappeared. Tread easy, Tanner—you can be replaced.* A cold sting ran up the back of Frank's neck when he remembered just how completely Harry Fellin had vanished.

The words, STATUS 00, appeared on the screen. Status zero-zero meant no such headline existed.

Frank knew the *Time Gate* stories were published, and Harry Fellin wrote them. He typed: GIVE ME EVERY STORY WITH THE HARRY FELLIN BYLINE FOR THE YEAR 2310

SEARCHING (PLEASE WAIT)

While he waited, Frank paged through the directory. TTEC wasn't listed. "I didn't think so," he muttered.

The word, SENDING, flashed on Frank's computer screen followed by forty-six headlines above the Harry Fellin byline. Not one of them had anything to do with *Time Gate.* "Shit!" He entered a final question: IS THERE ANY REFERENCE TO TIME GATE IN YOUR FILES?

The computer answered: PLEASE WAIT

"There better be! I damn well know it sold a pile of Hologram-Disks and Port-Pods."

One by one the headlines stacked up on Frank's screen.

A FABRICATION / FICTION / NOT FACT!
TIME GATE: NON-EXISTANT!

* * * *

The editorial content of each story followed. Before the third story cleared, Frank keyed: RUN/STOP.

"What a crock of shit!"

BREAK appeared on the screen then: ANY FURTHER ACCESS REQUESTED? The cursor blinked under the question.

Frank typed: None.

The screen filled with the newspaper's logo.

He settled back in his chair and turned to the note book again. "What the hell does E-C mean?"

Chapter 15
The Waking of The
The Flight Crew and
The key- Five

MEDICAL WING – LEVEL FIVE:

*C*aptain Raymond Ballard, his crewmen, Tom Parrish and K.W. Soo had been taken to a doctor's lounge on the fifth floor of the medical wing.

They were escorted by Dr. Gregory Rankin, who immediately tried to make them comfortable. "Relax gentlemen. Chairman Fisher and two important people are on their way here. They'll fill you in on a few more details."

Captain Ballard studied Rankin with a stern expression. "I'm still sifting this crazy nightmare through my mind, Doctor." He glanced at Tom and K.W. and read the uneasiness in their eyes. "There are a lot of questions in need of answers." He sharpened the edge of his voice. "So far you haven't told us much at all!"

Tom added, "What happened to our cabin crew? That's a good place to start." Tom was selfishly concerned about Cindy.

"And our passengers too, Doc.," said K.W. "Not to mention our Goddamn airplane!"

Dr. Rankin sat on a corner of a reading table in the center of the large room. "Your passengers, plane and crew are safe and sound." His manner was deliberately easy. He wanted to reduce the tension feeding off the emotions of his three guests. "Every question will be answered in detail when Chairman Fisher arrives." He waved his right hand and smiled. "My responsibility in this matter is your welfare." He stood and walked to the back of the room. "I assure you, I'm tending to that with the best my department can offer."

He faced a row of futuristic vending machines and pressed a lighted panel. "Coffee? It's still popular in the twenty-third century."

Ballard, Parrish and K.W. looked at one

another and smiled. "Put three fingers of brandy in it," said Raymond.

"I can get it."

"Coffee black will do."

Dr. Rankin handed rich brew to each of the men. He gestured toward a circle of chairs around a low table. The hostility tapered off.

Captain Ballard, Tom and K.W. sat down.

Rankin joined them and relaxed. He held his cup in both hands. "I can understand how you must feel. I don't think the magnitude of what's happened has been comprehended by any of us."

Ballard sipped his coffee. "From our point of view, it's frightening." He looked at K.W. and Tom. "I'm sure I speak for the three of us when I say, we feel threatened, and I'm not comfortable with it."

"Amen to that," added K.W.

Rankin looked into his cup and turned it several times. "An accidental crossing of the time gate is the curse of the beast." He glanced up and, one-by-one met the eyes of the three men. "Now you're here ... we exist in this moment. Yet, we live five-hundred years apart."

Silence.

All four men drank their brew. They shared a slice of time impossible to conceive.

* * * *

Gathered, on the same floor, in another lounge, the five *key* passengers from flight 280 met Steve Palmer.

"As Kathy told you," he said. "I'm the director of the History Research Commission. She and I will answer all your questions and assist you in any way we can."

Kathy added, "What you've gone through already, and the things you were told in the ward, are frightening enough. Our job now is to help you comprehend what has happened and guide you through events to come."

Congressman Franklin stood up abruptly, nearly toppling his chair. He reached deep within himself for a handful of clarity and logic. "Young lady!" His face flushed and a faint dizziness hung at the edge of his balance. "The five of us have come through some kind of hell!" Alan glanced at the pale faces of his fellow passengers and gripped the edge of the table for support. "Frightening? Dear lady, the word doesn't come close. Tell us the truth about the other two-hundred some-odd people who were on the plane!"

His wife, Laura, patted his hand and looked from her husband to Ms. Simmons.

Alan continued. "What in God's name are

you people up to?"

Steve and Kathy looked at each other. Emotional reactions and outbursts had been expected and prepared for. Not altogether from a man like Alan Franklin. It had come. They had to deal with it.

Steve said, "Congressman, please. As hostile as it may seem, I assure you there's nothing to be afraid of."

Kathy glanced at him. She stepped forward and leaned against the table Alan used for support. "Everyone, please understand, you are in no danger here. Your fellow passengers are safe and no harm will come to them."

The Congressman pushed away from the table and paced behind the others.

Dr. Jordan stood up. He was angry but in full control of himself. "Mr. Palmer ... excuse my French, but I think you, and the young lady are full of crap!" He nodded at the Sternfelds and continued. "Now let's have the bottom line. "Why was our plane hijacked? And where in hell are we? Don't give us the nonsense we were told in the hospital ward. Tell the truth."

Steve rubbed his chin and met Kathy's eyes. "Congressman ... Professor. Please, sit down." He drew his hand across his face and Leaned on the table between him and the others.

Alan and Hal sat down.

Kathy took a clipboard and file-folder from the counter behind her and stood beside Steve. She studied Linda Sternfeld for a moment and made a check mark beside the woman's name on page one in the file-folder. She smiled—Linda did not.

Michael Sternfeld added, "Why are we here an' the others aren't?"

Steve nodded. "The six of you are vital to the future." He stood and gestured toward Kathy.

Laura Franklin looked at Steve and Kathy and the others. "The six of us?"

Kathy smiled at Mrs. Sternfeld again. "Linda, you and Michael are going to have a baby."

* * * *

Chairman Fisher came into the other fifth floor lounge first. He grinned and approached Raymond Ballard. "Captain, I'm pleased to meet you, I'm Robert Fisher."

Ballard grasped the Chairman's hand and shook it. "Mr. Chairman."

General Mackendrick entered next and nodded at those present.

Phil Khrismann closed the door behind him.

Dr. Rankin introduced Mack and Phil.

All present glanced at one another uncomfortably.

Chairman Fisher met eyes with the flight crew then addressed Dr. Rankin. "Can you get something stronger than coffee?"

"Brandy?" asked Rankin.

"Good, Doctor ... we'll need it." He smiled and took a seat at the table in the middle of the room.

Mackendrick and Khrismann stood beside him like guards.

The chairman looked up at one then the other. "Will you two sit down? We're on their side." He glanced at the doctor. "Rankin."

"I'm ordering, sir."

"Excellent."

Rankin went about the process of getting liquor and food sent up to the lounge.

Fisher leaned back in his chair and removed his glasses, which he wiped with a tissue from his suit-coat pocket.

Captain Ballard spoke first. "With all respects, chairman, why the hell are we here?"

Mack answered. "You violated military air space that's why. Consider yourself under arrest!"

"Bullshit!" responded Ballard.

Chairman Fisher continued wiping his glasses and held a calm expression.

Khrismann cut in. "Protective custody—not arrest." He glared at Mackendrick.

Ballard yelled, "You have no right to hold us in either case, Goddammit!"

Soo and Tom remained silent.

Chairman Fisher checked the lenses of his glasses and calmly stated the facts, "No one is under arrest and no one is being held in protective custody." He slipped his glasses on. "Mack ... Phil, these men aren't guilty of anything and will be treated accordingly. Is that understood?"

Mack reached for his Paralayne and thought better of it. "Yes, sir."

Phil added, "Understood, Mr. Chairman."

Fisher studied the faces of the men across from him. "Gentleman, what happened was an accident. You are now in the twenty-third century and we intend to get you, your passengers and crew back into 1998 safely."

Captain Ballard said, "I'm not ready to buy into this 2498 story." He glanced at Tom and K.W. "I think we got caught in some above ground test and it almost cost our lives."

Chairman Fisher glanced at Khrismann. "Phil, this is your department. Tell Captain Ballard exactly what happened."

Mackendrick shifted in his chair and shook his head.

"I *thought* it–I didn't *say* it!"

"Exactly, Captain. You *thought* it and we documented that thought."

"I don't believe any of this! I must've said something out loud. I know you heard all of our communications."

"Right again. Zebra Leader gave you a little demonstration."

Ballard looked at his crew and shook his head. "This is all unreal."

Phil went on. "In your time, yes, it would be, but not in 2498."

General Mackendrick couldn't keep still. "Ballard, you flew through a *Time Gate.* You're five-hundred years ahead of your time. Now you're a problem we have to deal with."

Chairman Fisher stood. "Keep it to yourself, Mack." To Captain Ballard he said, "None of this is easy. Please accept our concern. You, your crew, the 747 and all your passengers are safe and will be cared for."

Ballard pushed back his chair, stood and faced the Chairman. "How is any of this even possible?"

Phil answered. "It is. Within a few days, you'll know all the answers."

Ballard turned to Phil. "A few days?"

Mackendrick spoke up again. "You'll be a sore on our ass for the next ninety-days!"

Tom said, "Three-months! What the hell for?"

The Captain glared at Mackendrick. "We're off the radar *now.*" He addressed the Chairman. "Good God, Fisher we're considered down!"

Phil cut in. "Easy. Flight 280 hasn't even been missed. Denver is tracking you at thirty-five-thousand right now."

Frustrated, Ballard looked around the room. He caught the startled expressions on the faces of his flight crew. "What the hell are you talking about?"

Chairman Fisher responded. "You assumed your flight was being diverted and Denver knew it. That's why it didn't occur to you until now. The illusion was created for you." Fisher smiled. "Your plane is not off the radar."

Ballard sat down. "I can't understand any of this."

Phil patted the Captain's shoulder. "You will, Ray. I'll make sure you and your crew understands everything completely."

Tom leaned back in his chair. "I sure as hell hope you do."

Dr. Rankin had been taking notes from his position at the far end of the room.

The Captain raised his voice. "Why can't we go back now?"

Phil answered. "The gate's unstable. If we shot you through it now it could be fatal. That's the reason."

Chairman Fisher interrupted. "I made the decision for the sake of you, your crew and passengers. The risk is too great."

Mackendrick added, "In the meantime, gentlemen, you're considered a high security risk. The *Time-Gate* is top secret, you already know more than the mass population. You have four priorities, listen, learn, understand and keep your mouths shut."

Chairman Fisher added. "I'll leave you with Mack and Phil. When you've learned what you need to know, we'll meet in my office." He leaned on the back of his chair. "We're not your enemies, you need to know that."

A uniformed guard let a young man in kitchen-whites into the lounge. Lunch was being served and a wet-bar was part of the order.

Mack said, "About Goddamn time." He got up and headed toward the portable steam table.

Phil gestured in the same direction. "Gentlemen, our treat."

Fisher paused at the door. "You're welcome here, and you'll be well cared for." He smiled and left the lounge.

Ballard, Soo and Parrish looked at each other.

Parrish leaned back in his chair and said, "Sonofabitch."

Chapter 16
Human Cells
Moral considerations

$\mathcal{D}$r. Gregory Rankin entered the main genetic research lab and found Jerry Zanster at his desk. He was studying a small twenty-inch, high resolution hologram monitor.   "How's it going?"

Dr. Zanster, Science Advisor on the United World Council, didn't answer immediately. He rubbed his beard and adjusted his special glasses.

Rankin watched him jot down a few notes and waited.

Jerry had a fourth level Ph.D. in genetic engineering and research and was in charge of all cloning operations and development. He was a brooding man, often lost in thought.

Without looking away from his monitor he responded. "You're looking at the substance of a man named K.W. Soo, an Oriental. His parents were born in Korea—and died there in 1961. K.W. was brought to the United States by Master Sergeant Paul Kessin. He and his wife, Beverley raised K.W. as their own son. The boy was given the best they could offer, including military school, a college education and financial assistance to get him through aviation training.

Mr. and Mrs. Kessin were proud of K.W. when he landed the flight engineer's job with Tran's International Airlines.

Fly—that's all K.W. wanted to do. Just to be part of a crew on a massive jetliner. K.W. loves charting a course from New York to Los Angeles. He loves keeping tabs on fuel consumption, whatever. Mr. Soo didn't have the slightest idea he'd fly into the twenty-third century—and die." Dr. Zanster turned to look at Greg.

"None of them knew. Jesus, Jerry, they're not going to die!"

"To those in their own time they are. Paul and Beverley Kessin will attend K.W.'s funeral. So will the families of some two-hundred-twenty-five others. That comes down to dead, Greg. Stone, cold, dead."

"We can't be concerned with that—"

"Can't we? I sure as hell am."

"Jerry, you've done this a thousand times—what's the problem now?"

"I've cloned a few for productive purposes and research, not hundreds for deception. Not the way we're doing it here!"

"Nothing like this has ever happened. It has to be done for the good of the whole."

"Perhaps, Greg ... nevertheless, there's something immoral in what we're doing."

"You're not regressing are you, Jerry?"

"Maybe a little ... just a little."

"What about the others, the passengers?"

Dr. Zanster glanced at the hologram again and answered. "Done. The cells have all been cataloged and frozen until they're needed."

"What about the rest of the flight crew?"

"Like K.W. here, they're being processed for full development. They should be ready for phase one by tomorrow."

"Excellent. Jerry, are you okay?"

"Right now, no—but I will be."

"Good. I'll report to Fisher."

"When you do, tell him I'll look for him Sunday."

"What?"

"Just tell him. He'll know what it means."

Dr. Zanster didn't pay any attention to Greg's leaving. He studied the image and smiled. What he saw in the genetic structure of K.W. Soo's cell reminded him of all the other passengers.

To Zanster those two-hundred-twenty-five souls could be a *congregation*. They were a group of people who still believed in a God. Those who didn't could easily be enlightened.

Such superstitions were no longer entertained in the year 2498. Religion and church services had become part of a dead past. Jerry's father, the Reverend Lowell Zanster was one of the last to fade into extinction. Jerry was ten, and remembered his father as a man of faith.

He chuckled as his mother's voice came to mind. *Sister Carol* his father called her. Several times after the reverend's death his mother would say, *The Lord took your father to be part of a higher order. He gave his life to a dying cause. Pray, Son. Pray to God that a spark of that faith stays alive in your heart.*

Two years after Reverend Zanster passed on, Sister Carol picked up a laser knife and cooked her brains to cinder-ash.

That spark of faith *did* stay alive in Jerry's heart.

Now, when he thought of living souls from a time long dead, the spark burst into flame.

"Tell him I'll look for him Sunday," he heard himself say.

Dr. Zanster laughed.

Chapter 17
Future/Past
The chosen few

U.W.C. HEADQUARTERS:

$\mathcal{T}$he five *key* passengers from flight 280 had been taken to the main conference room at U.W.C. headquarters. Steve Palmer was with them and doing his best to answer questions.

Congressman Franklin swung from irritation to frustration to anger.

Dr. Hal Jordan tried to understand the situation scientifically.

Laura Franklin sat at the huge conference table in a kind of numb trance. Her thoughts were focused on her children and oddly, her rose garden.

Linda Sternfeld kept holding her stomach and drifting from tears to soft, sniffing chuckles.

Her husband Michael repeated himself as he held his wife in his arms. "A baby. Honey, we're having a baby." Each time he said it, Linda would slip into quiet sobs. Michael couldn't tell if she was happy or sad.

Kathy Simmons hadn't told Linda the child was a boy. That news was yet to come. Want to or not, the Sternfelds would have to know. The baby had a major role to play in the future.

Ms. Simmons was with Chairman Fisher in his office, one room away from the conference chambers.

Fisher said, "I don't really want to separate them. I think it would have a negative result."

"I agree, but we must separate the interviews. Their situations are completely individual."

Fisher tapped his upper lip and leaned back in his chair. He glanced at his faithful secretary. "Sophy, would you mind ordering a fantastic luncheon for the nine of us?"

She looked at him from her desk across the room. She pushed her glasses back on her nose. "Nine?"

"Yes, our five guests, Steve, Kathy, you and me."

"Robert, sometimes you amaze me." She grinned, shook her head and began leafing through a desk file. "We're up to our hips in a red-hot security matter and you want to order food."

"We have to eat, Sophy."

Kathy chuckled to herself as she observed a deep respectful, relationship work between two exceptional people. She knew, in her heart-of-hearts, Robert Fisher was the *right* man to have the current crisis under his control. If there was anyone more caring and human, she didn't know who that could be.

The chairman smiled at her across his desk. "The fastest way to a man's heart is through his stomach and there are three men in the next room who need to be reached."

Kathy grinned, "Mr. Chairman, you're a special kind of person."

"No, Kathy, I'm just an old man who happens to believe in people."

"Much more than that, sir—much more."

Fisher stood and gathered a sheaf of papers into a file folder. "Let's try this," he said. "I'll address them as a group. We'll all enjoy lunch, during which I'll plan separate sessions with each of them individually."

"Split the couples as well?"

"You bet. There are things in the

congressman's future his wife may not want to know. Likewise for Alan regarding Laura. And the same applies to the Sternfelds."

"You mean—"

"Yes." He tapped the file folder. "We have sensitive information here. Facts an individual must decide to learn on his or her own."

Ms. Simmons took a breath and stiffened. "You're talking about the circumstances and time of death?"

"Among other things, yes."

"I've tried to avoid that information."

"Of course you have."

"I'm sorry ...."

"Don't be. There are right and wrong ways. Let's try to do this as right as possible."

"I understand." Kathy stared down at her clipboard and notes. She realized how much she did know about five innocent people who played a major role in her own future—her very existence. "This gets more serious by the minute, doesn't it?"

"It does, now let's try to make it as easy as we can." Fisher glanced at his secretary. "Sophy?"

"Lunch will be served in thirty minutes."

"Excellent. Shall we?" Fisher gestured toward the door.

Ms. Simmons led the way into the huge

conference room. All heads turned. Chairman Fisher, Kathy and Sophy entered.

Steve Palmer and the guests were seated at a *horseshoe* shaped conference table. There were twenty-four chairs around the table and one at the head. Each place had an inlaid keyboard and a small transparent monitor.

Steve stood up immediately, almost coming to attention. Clearing his throat he said, "Ladies and gentlemen, may I present Chairman Robert Fisher, head of the United World Council."

Congressman Franklin, also on his feet, spoke up. "Now we're getting somewhere. Mr. Chairman—"

"Congressman Franklin, I'm honored to make your acquaintance." He stepped around the head of the table and shook Alan's hand vigorously. "I think between you and me, we'll have this situation by the ass in no time." He smiled toward the women. "Excuse the language ladies. I'm quite excited to be in the congressman's company and finally have a chance to meet you all."

Steve and Kathy shared a quick glance and grinned.

Indeed, Chairman Fisher was in control. Everyone knew it, even irritated, frustrated Congressman Franklin.

Steve, Kathy and Sophy took seats toward

the head of the table.

Sophy opened her note book and keyed the terminal in front of her.

The U.W.C. logo appeared on a huge screen at the far end of the room.

Fisher released the congressman's hand and smiled. "Take a seat, Alan. We'll start slow, have a great lunch then work up to running speed."

The chairman stood behind his chair at the head of the table. He put down the file folder Sophy had handed him and addressed the group. "Whatever questions you have will be answered in complete detail. You people are special and shall be treated as such." He faced the group. "You have my absolute word on that."

Franklin cut in. "Chairman, I admire your diplomacy, but on behalf of this group, I demand more than the vague, half-explanations we've been given—"

"You have every right to make demands and they shall be met." He Stepped closer to the table. "Congressman, I know more about your life than you do." He pointed to the folder at the head of the table. "That file goes beyond your present years. It contains the outcome of projects you haven't thought of yet."

Alan said, "That's impossible."

"Is it?" Fisher spoke with authority. He walked over to Hal Jordan and gripped the professor's shoulders. "This intelligent tutor here has an important student in his career who will be taking his physics classes in the fall of 1999."

"Dear God," said Dr. Jordan and stiffened in his seat.

The chairman patted Hal's shoulder then smiled at Linda. "Mrs. Sternfeld, your coming child will be responsible for part of the process that makes it possible to send you and your husband back to your own time." He stepped away from Hal, who sat in thought. Fisher walked back toward his chair at the head of the table. He said, "Steve, did I leave anything out?"

Palmer stood and faced Laura Franklin. "Mrs. Franklin, the influence you have on your husband will effect his political decisions in the years ahead."

Laura stared and blinked. No words came, just a deep sigh. Alan put his arm around her and shuddered in his chair.

To Mr. Sternfeld, Steve said, "Michael, the father role you play will have a useful and strong effect on the development of your child. That relationship is an important factor in your future and ours."

Linda Sternfeld asserted herself. "Child, baby—it! What are you talking about? Will I have a boy or a girl?"

Kathy went to Linda. A tight lump formed in her throat. Kathy knew what the child would be. That information was not for a room full of people. It was private, something Linda had to hear alone—if she wanted to. One of them *had* to know, Michael most likely, but that had not been decided either. It could not be said just then, only in private.

Linda broke and sobbed.

Kathy held her and glanced at Michael. He nodded and let Kathy have control.

She said, "Not now, Linda. We'll talk alone. If you want to know, I'll tell you then, but only if you want to, okay?"

Linda shuddered. "Okay." She was frightened out of her wits. The impact of information was too much all at once—for everyone.

Chairman Fisher knew it. He said, "We want to talk with each of you individually. There are private things to deal with and we respect that."

Congressman Franklin got up.

Fisher added, "Alan, you and I have a lot to talk about. Let's do it after lunch." He lowered his voice. "It's private."

Franklin took a slow breath and let the heat in his neck and ears drain away. "All right, Fisher. I can wait."

Three young men in kitchen-whites entered the conference chamber pushing two portable steam tables and a tempting dessert-bar.

Sophy stood up and took charge. "Over there, boys, right in front of the screen."

Fisher smiled at Alan. "I know you're upset. Just give me a chance to explain."

Alan whispered, "Not one Goddamn bit of this makes sense."

The chairman nodded. "It will, I promise you. It will."

Both men studied each other for a long moment.

Congressman Franklin spoke first. "It had better, chairman. That is my promise."

Though Franklin had no way of knowing his situation, Fisher let the statement rest as it was, a valiant effort to defend himself and the others. The chairman smiled and added, "For the benefit of everyone, you and I need to talk at length."

Alan added, "Yes, we do."

Sophy said, "Food's on and you'll love it."

Steve gestured toward the steam tables. "Ladies, after you."

* * * *

A moment later, the *special* people walked to the tables and began filling their plates with a great lunch.

Chapter 18
The Tanner File
A reporter's hunch

THE NEVADA SUN – FRANK'S OFFICE:

Tanner had filled two sheets of paper with possible phrases and words to spell out the acronym TTEC. Nothing made sense until he wrote and circled the words, *Time Travel Enforcement Commission.* The word *enforcement* was underlined several times.

"I'll be damned," he muttered. "That's it, *enforcement.* I'll bet my ass it's military." He accessed his computer and requested any and all information regarding TTEC.

As advanced as it was, the computer displayed the *Nevada Sun* logo and the word, **STANDBY.**

Frank bristled. "C'mon!"

A moment later the screen cleared and displayed the words, FILES NOT FOUND.

Tanner shook his head. "Bullshit!" He grabbed his UWC directory again and leafed to the listing of the council's various committees. Nothing even close to TTEC was shown.

"Crap!" He reached for the phone and punched number four on the keypad.

A female voice came on the line. "Councilman Cross's office, may I help you?"

"Yeah, Carol, this is Frank Tanner. Is Larry available?"

"He's in. Let me see if he's taking calls."

The letters, T-T-E-C swam around in Frank's head. He underlined *enforcement* three more times.

Larry Cross came on. "Frank, what's up?"

"That's my question, Councilman. Urgent voices out of nowhere are telling me you're on red alert over there."

Silence.

"We do have drills, Frank."

"Is that what it is?"

"Jesus, Tanner. Call the media center. If there's an alert, they'll know about it. Better yet, get in touch with Mack."

"I have a call in to Mackendrick. He's not responding."

"He's a busy man. Why are you so testy about a possible alert?"

"My voices tell me there's a five-hundred year old aircraft involved. Apparently, the plane landed under military escort."

"You sound like a fiction writer, Frank, not a reporter. Did you run out of hard news?"

"How does the *Time Gate* angle sound? Or does that bring up a bad memory, Mr. Cross?"

Silence.

Click

Frank said, "Secure and recording, right Larry?"

Cross answered. "Look, you know damn well loose shit like you're saying can cause problems. I have to record it."

"Yes, you do. To cover your own ass."

"Whatever. Listen to me, Tanner. The Time Gate issue evaporated a long time ago. So did the reporter who stirred the stew."

"That would be, Harry Fellin, correct?"

"Yes, Harry Fellin." Cross hesitated then added, "Is any of this getting through?"

"Loud and clear. Since you're recording this conversation instead of just hanging up, I think there might be something to it."

"I'm being polite. We do have to work together occasionally."

"Then try this on. What is TTEC?"

"Nothing, Frank. I never heard of such a commission."

"Commission? Why did you call it a commission?"

"I have nothing further to say to you. I'm terminating this call."

Click

To the dead line, Frank muttered, "Goodbye, Councilman Cross." He hung up.

A bright light flashed in the back of Frank's mind. *Enforcement commission.* The two words repeated themselves in his head until they had substance.

Frank turned to his keyboard and typed, ENFORCEMENT COMMISSION

A moment later the computer screen displayed a queer menu:
ENFORCEMENT COMMISSIONS:
Government
United World Council
military-Air Force
military-Ground Force
Police-nation-wide
Police-state-wide
Police-local
SELECT

As if the computer could hear him, which it could, if he chose that function, Frank said, "I'm not sure." He keyed voice activation. "List them."

A cold, but very human-sounding, female voice came on. That was the real reason Frank preferred manual access. Voice activation was faster however.

"Please wait."

He nodded. The computer could not respond to that.

The cold voice came back, "Sending."

Tanner studied the screen as it presented the information requested:

ENFORCEMENT COMMISSIONS:
GVT. SECRET SERVICE (CLASSIFIED)
TAX-COMM: (CLASSIFIED)
UWC GLOBAL NET COMM: (CLASSIFIED)
MAF ELITE AIR COMM: (CLASSIFIED)
MGF .... (NONE)
PNW .... (NONE)
PSW STATE EVENTS COMM: (ACCESS 0-3)
PL PARALAYNE COMM: (CLASSIFIED)
ACCESS REQUEST (Y)? (N)?

Frank knew of every commission displayed, but not as *enforcement* operations. To the computer he said, "Yes."

The electronic voice answered and displayed information simultaneously.

SELECT FILE

Frank said, "Elite Air Commission."

FILE INACCESSIBLE FROM THIS TERMINAL
WITHOUT UWC (CODE RED) SEQUENCE DATA:

FETCH NEXT FILE? (Y)? (N)?

Frank switched off voice activation and typed: NO: PRINT CURRENT SCREEN

In less than ten seconds a hard copy of the screen information slipped silently from the light printer.

Frank circled *MAF* ELITE AIR COMMISSION. He added the word, *enforcement* and underlined it in red.

He tapped his pen on the paper and mumbled, "I'll bet my shorts and my old man's bionic arm, TTEC and Time Gate are hidden behind this Elite Air Commission bullshit."

He rubbed his chin and remembered Harry Fellin, who once was and is no more.

A chill crawled up Frank's back. He thought, *If the Time Gate exists, why the hell is it so secret?*

"Commission?" He said it out loud. "Cross identified TTEC as a commission the moment I mentioned it. Dammit—the Time Gate *is* a reality!"

Frank put another call through to Mackendrick's office. Mack wasn't in. He wouldn't be available until the next day.

* * * *

MINDEN, NEVADA-THAT SAME HOUR:

Nevil Garrett opened the front door of his small, but well-kept, wood frame, modular home. The bright afternoon sun pushed the shadows back from the cool interior.

Garrett was in the company of Janice Breslaw again, a topless dancer from old Vegas. Her *professional* name was, *Candy Topps.* She entered first, well acquainted with Nevil's nest and headed straight for the efficient, cozy kitchen. "Is there a fresh bottle?"

Nevil closed and locked the door. "Third shelf, untouched."

Candy opened the booze cupboard and took down a brand new bottle of *Hailey's* gin. "Tonic?" She grabbed two tall glasses.

The blinking red light on his com-machine caught Nevil's eye. "In the fridge."

Candy said, "I love it when you're uptight. Somehow you're better." She pursed her lips and made a smacking sound. She crossed the short distance to the refrigerator, saw the blinking light and grinned. "Better take that call, hon. I did the deed big-time to get the information you wanted."

"Yeah, in a second." Nevil wrung his hands and felt his heart-rate increase.

Candy always acted stupid. She wanted it

that way. It made a better show. Fat-bellied, sweating men tipped a sensuous, stupid broad with big tits. They would have been offended by who she really was. She could be intelligent, challenging, sensitive, graceful and warm. However, the sophisticated elegance didn't pay the bills. The grating, down and dirty moves of Candy Topps paid off big. She was about five-thousand bucks away from telling the whole world to *BUZZ OFF!*

The payday for the information waiting on Nevil's phone was worth ten-grand. Goodbye Nevil, goodbye the *dumb broad* act. Hello independence! This was the first day of her new life.

Nevil picked up the handset. "This is N.G 858." He listened and jotted down the information he was hearing. "Got it." He hung up and wiped the sweat off his face with a dish towel. "You did it, baby–you did it!" He crossed the room and hugged her."

"Easy, darling." She kissed him. You're shaking all over."

Nevil let out a long breath. "Yeah. Now we're set. Two-hundred-thousand solves a lot of problems."

"Now *you* have to deliver. Make the call, hon. Then we can get busy with an afternoon delight."

Candy didn't love Nevil, but she would never say so. *Be what he wants, girl. When you are you're alive. The rest is horse shit.*

She opened a bottle of tonic and made two stiff drinks. Candy stuck her well manicured finger into the cold liquid of one glass and sucked off the wetness. "Perfect, Nevil. It'll knock your ass off." She shook her head and let long locks of rich brown hair fall over her shoulders. She licked her index again and added, "Nevil, Candy wants your body." She smiled and sucked on a piece of ice.

Nevil grinned and picked up the phone.

Candy reached into her purse on the kitchen counter. "Remember to repeat the code when he hangs up."

"That's 33 star zero, right?"

"You got it, sweetheart." She sipped from her drink and activated the small device in her purse.

Nevil dialed the Nevada Sun. As he waited for the connection he said, "There's no woman like you on earth, you know that?"

Candy licked her finger again and swallowed another gulp of gin and tonic.

Nevil held up his hand. "Frank Tanner please." He studied the woman in the doorway and nodded. "The bedroom—an' be ready for me."

Candy smiled and slipped away. Four minutes after Nevil's call and she would never have to be *Candy* again.

Into the phone, Nevil said, "Frank, Just listen. TTEC is in the main UWC computer as MAF-SR1-(A)*T/G. The password is, Devil2025B. Key it exactly that way and you're in. Got it?"

Frank said, "What does it mean? Who are you?"

Nevil chuckled. "Have a great life, Tanner. Key the sequence and watch your ass." He hung up, gulped a breath of air and shook his head. "Jesus, that's it! Two-hundred grand. We're out of it free and clear." He lifted the receiver again and punched 3-3-star zero. A tone followed. Nevil whispered, "Red three is history." He hung up and walked to the bedroom doorway. He stopped, unbuttoned his shirt and studied Candy.

She tipped her glass toward him and whispered, "I have to go out to the Zephyr and get something special."

"Hurry, I want to celebrate!"

Candy kissed him and started for the kitchen. "Back in a flash, hon." They told her she had four minutes to get out. She grabbed her purse off the counter.

The red light on Nevil's console blinked twice.

The explosion destroyed Garrett's house, and everything in it, including him and Candy.

* * * *

UWC – THE OFFICE OF COUNCILMAN LARRY CROSS:

Larry's secretary buzzed him.
"Yes?"
"You have a call on red-three, sir."
"Thank you." He picked up. "This is Cross." He grinned. "I'm sorry to hear that, I liked Candy."

The wrath of Cross
has just begun.

Chapter 19
FISHER & SOPHY

$\mathcal{T}$hey entered Chairman Fisher's fifth-level office. Steve Palmer took Congressman Franklin into the UWC chambers.

Fisher paused by the desk and waited for Sophy to finish a call. When she hung up he asked, "Was that Mack?"

Sophy shook her head. "Mr. Khrismann. He and General Mackendrick are escorting Captain Ballard and his crew to the airplane."

"Good." Fisher turned toward the council room.

"Robert."

The chairman stopped. "Yes?"

"Phil's worried about security."

"We all are, Sophy."

"He's concerned about a leak."

"From what department?"

Sophy glanced around the office as if someone might be listening. "He mentioned the paper."

"The Sun?"

"Yes."

"Tanner?"

"Exactly."

"Does he think Frank knows anything?"

She nodded.

"Get Tanner through his private message system." He started away then turned back. "I'll talk to him on my red-security line tomorrow morning at eight sharp. You monitor the call. I want every word taken down—by hand, Sophy, along with electronics."

She smiled. "I'll see to it immediately."

Fisher grinned. "You're a gem."

"I know it."

"We're in for some overtime tonight. Do you mind having supper here with these people?"

She grinned, "Not as long as you eat a good meal."

He shook his head and sighed. "What would I do without you?"

"You'd die of malnutrition." She laughed.

"No," he said, "I think loneliness would kill me first."

They held each other's eyes for a long, moment.

Sophy said, "I'll call food service."

"A good, lean roast beef would be nice."

"How about a couple of choices?"

Fisher leaned toward her. "Pull that off and you'll get a bonus."

"I'll hold you to that."

Fisher became instantly serious. "I want this session, and the others, piped directly into your computer. Scramble the data and code it for executive access only."

"Suspicions?"

"More than that."

Sophy stiffened and cupped her chin. "How bad is this?"

Chairman Fisher stared into her eyes. "Bad enough to change life as we know it."

"I understand." They shared a silent, private moment. Sophy said, "Get going, they're waiting."

"Thank you ... thank you for putting up with me for all these years."

She blushed. "Now get a move on." She watched him enter the conference room and swallowed hard. There was an audible click in her throat. She thought, *I love you, Robert Fisher. Though you don't want to hear it, God bless you, and may he help us all.*

Chapter 20
A Question of Faith

CONGRESSMAN ALAN FRANKLIN:

*C*hairman Fisher stood just inside the commission chambers and listened to Steve pleading with Congressman Franklin. Steve said, "I understand how you feel, sir and I want you to know you have nothing to worry about. Mrs. Franklin is in good hands—I assure you." He caught Fisher out of the corner of his eye.

The congressman said, "Fisher. Dammit! Why have I been separated from my wife?" His eyes flared and he leaned on the back of one of the chairs.

Robert's responding grin was shallow. He still sifted the conversation with Sophy through his mind. He gestured toward the huge computer screen and glanced at Steve. "Bring up the file." He walked to the head of the table. "Let's relax," he said, and faced Franklin. He pulled his chair away from the table and spoke to the congressman. "Please, sit down, Alan."

Steve keyed the computer from a keyboard on the opposite side of the conference table and the giant screen came to life.

Alan looked and took a seat at the far end of the table. He sighed deeply as the computer displayed his personal file. It cleared and centered his name.

ALAN FRANKLIN
U.S. CONGRESSMAN (D) CA
FILE # AF/280
PRIORITY RED
READY

Franklin mumbled, "I'm a *priority* now."

Chairman Fisher addressed Palmer. "What about the others with Ms. Simmons and Dr. Rankin. Are they okay?"

"They're excellent, sir."

"And the Flight crew and passengers?"

Steve glanced at Alan and answered.

"According to our medical supervisors, isolation and distribution can begin sometime tomorrow."

Fisher thought a moment and added, "Are they aware of the priority."

"Yes, sir, the importance of family units has been made clear."

"What about those without the company of family?"

"A group of my best people is arranging their placement. For now it's national. After the world conference I think we'll have to go global."

"We don't want to move too fast. There's a hell a lot to consider before we start any placement program"

"I agree, sir." He lowered his voice. "Dr Rankin needs to know when he should start waking the general passengers. You did indicate twenty-four hours."

"Have him hold off on that until I give the order. Certain issues need attention before hand. I understand the risk, but it's necessary."

Franklin stood, leaned on the table and raised his voice. "What the hell are you two talking about?"

Fisher sat down and motioned at Steve to do the same. "Congressman, your anger is understandable—would you please sit down and try to relax?"

"Relax?"

"Exactly. Try to take it easy."

Franklin looked at Palmer then the chairman. He waved toward the big screen and   sank into a chair at the far end of the table. He laced his fingers. "What about My wife and the others? Where are they?"

Fisher cleared his throat and leaned back. "As we told you, they're fine. Everything's under control."

The congressman leaned forward. "Get to the point right now." He caught a breath. "I'm tired of the bullshit. I want answers!"

Fisher raised his right hand and pointed toward the giant screen. "Before we run the balance of that file, you need to answer a few questions."

Franklin demanded, "My wife?"

Fisher addressed Steve. "Bring up Kathy please."

"Yes Sir." He keyed three numbers into the keyboard and a moment later Kathy Simmons appeared on the monitor.

"What is it, Steve?"

"We   need   a   Status   report   for   the congressman."

"Take a look." Kathy stepped aside and Laura Franklin appeared.

"Alan?" She leaned closer to the camera. "Are you all right?"

He spoke to the image of his wife. "Yes, are you?"

"We're all just fine. Ms. Simmons is explaining everything."

A wider view showed Hal Jordan and the Sternfelds. Hal waved, Michael smiled and Linda nodded.

Laura said, "We'll see you soon."

Kathy came back into view. "Is there a problem?"

Palmer turned to Alan. "Any problem, congressman?"

"No, no problem."

Fisher said, "Thank you. I think we're all right now."

Kathy said, "We'll all get together later."

Steve entered a code into the computer and Congressman Franklin's file came back on. He studied the screen. "What are your questions?"

The chairman said, "Excuse me a second." He addressed Palmer. "Would you have Sophy get us a pot of coffee and a half-dozen of those filled pastries I like?"
He glanced at the congressman. "Alan?"

"Yes and make it strong."

Steve said, "Right away, sir."

Fisher sat back and tented his fingers as was his habit. "Alan, before we see your file, I need to know what you're thinking ... how you're feeling right now?"

"Direct to the point, Mr. Chairman. Like a prisoner with privileges."

Fisher laughed. "I assure you, that's not the case." He leaned forward and rested his elbows on the table. "How do you feel about knowing your own future?"

"Give me an example."

"The accomplishments of your political career. Why not start there?"

The congressman held Fisher's eyes for a long moment then glanced at the big screen again. "I think it would scare the hell out of me." He smiled, but his eyes did not. "However, on occasion, I've wanted to do just that." The thought of it lingered at the back of his mind.

Fisher whispered, "So have I." He studied Alan's strange look. "I'm in *your* future, not mine."

Franklin pressed his fingers against his temples. "I've considered myself an intelligent man. At the moment, I feel about as dumb as a congressional aide on his first day in the house." He looked up when Steve came back with the coffee and everything to go with it.

Palmer said, "Hot and fresh."

Chairman Fisher nodded. To Alan he said, "Mr. Palmer and I have a pretty good idea how you must feel. At the moment, the situation seems

Incomprehensible, unbelievable."

"Frustrating—add that."

Steve said, "Anger too, I suppose?"

Alan watched him pour coffee. "A lot of anger, Mr. Palmer—and on top of it, one hell of a measure of old fashion fear." He sat back and glanced from one man to the other. "Should I be afraid, gentlemen?"

Fisher said, "Of us, no. Of yourself, yes."

"Why?"

"Go back to my first question."

"Seeing my future?"

"Precisely. There are some things you must know. The rest ... you decide."

Franklin slapped the table. "For God's sake, get specific!"

Steve jumped.

Chairman Fisher took a breath. "As I told you on the way up here, Steve is head of the History Research Commission. He knows everything there is to know about the twentieth century."

Alan glared at Fisher. "Vague. I said specific!"

Fisher hesitated. "Steve."

Palmer took a sip from his coffee. "Congressman, I mean no offense in what I'm going to tell you. We know the result of every move you'll make for the rest of your life. The same applies to every other soul on your plane."

"That's impossible!"

"On the contrary, sir. It's as simple as adding a column of two digit figures."

The chairman added, "He's absolutely right. Listen and please try to understand."

Franklin stiffened. For an instant he was offended by young Palmer for what he felt was arrogance.

Steve continued. "Congressman, the entire United World Council is on your side. Believe me. Our future depends on you and the other four." He hesitated and added, "You can thank God for that." He glanced at Fisher and cleared his throat.

The chairman glared at him.

Alan leaned forward and waved his right hand. "Just a minute. Time out!"

Steve said, "Sir?"

The congressman stood and shook his head. "Every damn time someone has said, *Christ, God. Jesus* or made any reference to religious names, you people get your back up!" He stared at Fisher, then Palmer. "Now, what the hell is that all about?"

Without looking at him, Steve said, "Chairman, would you answer?"

"Religion, as known in your time, is no longer practiced in any solid, organized way in the twenty-third century. There are faithful groups, but nothing like there were in 1998. Our government didn't *outlaw* religious organizations. The people split from the various sects all on their own. Non-secular, community churches developed rapidly over the last two centuries and many are still going strong."

Franklin cut in. "Why do you cringe when God is mentioned?"

Steve answered. "We enforce a ruling you should be quite familiar with. The *separation* of church and state. Religious terms are restricted from any activities conducted within the walls of this entire complex."

Alan grinned. "They slip in though, don't they?"

Fisher chuckled. "It's just human nature."

Palmer added. "Does that answer your question?"

Alan sipped some coffee. "To a degree. Yes, it does."

The chairman said, "We are not without faith. In this century the people of the world, most of them anyway, believe in each other, in mankind itself. In universal intelligence, if you will, but not a bearded god on a golden throne."

The congressman grinned. "I stopped believing in that image when I was about eighteen."

Fisher sat back and gestured with open arms. "There you have it. I've always felt the same way."

Palmer cleared his throat. "With all respect, sir, I think we're drifting away from the objectives."

To Palmer the congressman said, "Young man, I tend to like you, at least what I know of you. Something tells me I need to trust both you and Fisher. On the other hand, you irritate the hell out of me with this touch of arrogance you send out now and then."

Steve turned around, straight-faced and tight-lipped. "Congressman, I'm—"

"I have the floor, Mr. Palmer. If politics has evolved along with everything else I've seen, then I'll finish my piece. I'll thank you to keep your mouth shut until I do." He shot a glance to Fisher, then to the red-faced Steve.

"Please continue, sir," said Steve, just above a whisper.

Franklin went on. "Apparently the four people with Ms. Simmons, and myself, are important ingredients in whatever stew you've got cooking here."

Fisher nodded. "You're absolutely right, Alan."

Chapter 21
Questions & Answers

$\mathcal{P}$almer sat on the edge of the table and let out a long slow, irritated breath.

Franklin stood and started around the table toward the screen. He stopped at the far end and addressed both men. "Gentlemen, until you've answered a few questions, you can take your plans and shove them straight up your collective asses."

Fisher leaned back and laughed. He crossed his legs and tried to shake away the full-faced grin that brightened his eyes. "Congressman, I wish you were staying on here." The grin slipped away.

"Excuse me?"

Steve said, "That fits in with our objectives, sir. It will be covered."

Without blinking, Franklin and Palmer glared at each other for a long moment.

Chairman Fisher stood and leaned on the huge table and spoke softly. "Stephen, Alan. Put away your swords. Hostility has no place here. All of us are involved in a most delicate situation—and not a single one of us asked for it." He studied both men and went on. "Alan, if I have to repeat it a hundred times then I shall. We are not your enemy. You are not on the floor of Congress in nineteen-ninety-eight." He lifted his right hand made a fist and slammed it down on the table. He stared straight into Franklin's eyes. "Congressman, you have come five hundred years into the future and the situation is serious! This whole damn complex is on red alert. My dear man, you and every person on flight two-eighty are top secret of the highest priority!"

Franklin and Palmer glanced at each other and let a small measure of tension roll away.

Steve said, "Sorry, sir ...."

Fisher held his serious expression.

Alan added, "I need answers."

"Of course you do and we'll provide them. Now please, both of you sit down." They did, Fisher began to pace slowly before the big screen. "Organize your thoughts, Alan, and ask your questions."

Steve cut in. "Congressman, I need you to

know, I mean no offense."

"I understand."

Fisher cleaned his glasses again. "Let me tell you a few things that will be hard to believe."

Alan said, "This entire situation is unbelievable."

The chairman looked up at the screen and gestured toward the title of the congressman's file. "I knew something about you before this *accident of time* took place." He walked toward the table and leaned on it. He smiled, a little and shook his head. "Don't have a heart attack, but what I was looking into, you haven't done yet." Fisher hesitated. "Not in your own time you haven't"

Franklin shivered and leaned back in his chair. "I've been dying for a cigar ever since our flight left Kennedy." He looked at Palmer and Fisher. "Would you mind?" He drew a slim aluminum tube from the breast pocket of his suit jacket and watched the expression on the two other faces.

Palmer sat back abruptly. "Tobacco is illegal!"

Fisher added, "It can be purchased if you know the wrong people."

Franklin started to put the expensive cigar away. "I'm sorry."

Fisher said, "No—go ahead. Former smokers use *Paralayne*. It's one of the few drugs allowed.

The congressman slipped the cigar from its tube and took out his chrome cigar cutter.

Fisher and Palmer watched him snip the end of the Havana. He grinned. "These are supposed to stay in Cuba."

Steve grabbed an extra cup from the coffee service and placed it before Alan. It would be an ashtray.

Franklin torched the end of his smoke with a cigar lighter and sat back. Plumes of blue smoke drifted up from the tip of the Havana.

Fisher leaned toward the congressman. "Do you have an extra one of those?"

"Sure." He reached into his vest pocket and produced a second tube. "Should I set it for you?"

"No," said Fisher. "I'd like to keep it, if I may."

"Certainly, a token of brotherhood, I guess." Franklin smiled.

"Yes, it will be ours."

Steve said, "About seven or eight-hundred years ago, north American Indians smoked peyote in what they called peace pipes. They did so around a fire during tribal meetings."

"True," added Alan with a wide grin. "Isn't this a Powwow?"

Palmer said, "It could be called that."

Alan enjoyed a long puff on his cigar. "Let's call it a peace-meeting of sorts?"

Steve thought a moment. "It is, exactly."

Chairman Fisher took in the aroma of the Havana and cleared his throat. "In 1995, you launched a project for the advancement of space travel. When this Time-Gate business came up, I took the liberty of tracing your history." He glanced at Steve. "I couldn't have done it without the History Research Commission."

Franklin puffed his cigar and smiled. "My comprehension is muddy at the moment, I'm listening."

Steve nodded. "Under the circumstances, you're light years ahead of what I would've expected."

"Hold that thought—go on, Mr. Fisher."

"The Space Plane, Alan?"

"It's locked up in committee—no funding." It dawned on him all at once. He was talking in present terms, 1998. Fisher was speaking of the future, 2498—he knew the outcome of a project that had been put on hold. Alan coughed and studied the two men intently. He rubbed his chin and squeezed his temples. "Holy Hanna!"

Fisher said, "Yes, Alan, there will be funding. The Space Plane will become a reality through your efforts. Understand that. You make it happen."

Congressman Franklin said, "Judas Priest!" The words seeped from his mouth on a cloud of smoke.

Fisher touched Alan's arm. "Without your work we wouldn't be as far as we are today."

"My God ...." Alan stared at his hands, his cigar and blinked rapidly. "The space plane made it—sonofabitch!"

Steve said, "Will make it, sir."

Fisher added, "It hasn't happened in your time yet, that's why it's important for all of us that you return to 1998 and do what you have to."

Franklin looked at the two men. "How does the Space Plane project have an effect on 2498?"

The Chairman nodded to Steve.

Palmer left the table to get fresh coffee. "Your concept evolved, Alan. We have fleets of Space Planes positioned around the world. Now they have another designation. We call them, *Shadow Trackers.*"

Alan grinned, "Shadow Trackers, I like the sound of it." He took a draw on his cigar. "Are they military spy planes?"

Palmer returned with more coffee. He had heard the question. "They're strictly scientific. A *Shadow Tracker* is twice the size of one of your Space shuttles and carries a crew of ten." He began pouring coffee. "An important feature is long-term space missions." He filled Alan's cup. "They're armed as well."

Franklin sipped his coffee. "Gentlemen, I am baffled." He put out his cigar.

Fisher got up to stretch his legs. "You have more work ahead, Alan. In 2005 you'll become the key figure in the development of a flawless, state-of-the-art, national defense system. It will be fully operational on September eleven, 2010."

Alan waved his right hand. "Wait, I've toyed with the defense idea for a couple of years, but the technology isn't there."

Fisher smiled. "It will be by 2005 and you'll make it happen."

"There's a glitch in your history system. I may not get re-elected."

Steve said, "You'll be in office, congressman. On that issue we can say no more—don't ask, please."

Frustrated, Franklin added, "Such a project takes Presidential and Congressional approval."

The chairman spoke up. "You will have both and your project will be well funded and praised by the voters."

Alan thought a moment. "Why September eleven? Things don't click that smoothly with any government project."

Fisher and Palmer glanced at each other. Steve said, "It's just a date, but the system will go active on that day.

The congressman took another sip of coffee. "Is there something you're not telling me?"

Robert sat in his chair. "Yes, there's a lot we

can't tell you. Try to understand the gravity of this whole situation." He leaned forward and looked at Franklin. "You're destined to do what we've explained. Knowing it in advance is as dangerous as a lighted fuse."

Palmer cut in. "Excuse me, sir." He addressed the congressman. "You only need to know what you must do. Alan, as we sit here in 2498 it's already been done." He sat on the edge of the table closer to the congressman who was still standing. "Would you change something in your life if you could?"

"You bet your ass I would!"

"That's my point. If you changed just one thing everything after that would be altered. It's critical, sir. You can only know what you must know."

"Just the facts, right?"

"I'm afraid so."

"Then why the hell didn't your people keep us asleep and send us right back through the—whatever it is?"

Fisher finished his coffee. "That was the first thing we wanted to do. However, the Time Gate is closing and it's unstable. The risk is too great. If it fluctuated or closed while your aircraft was inside you'd all be lost in oblivion."

Alan looked from one man to the other. "When will it be safe?"

Steve took a long breath. "In three months."

"Ninety-days! Are you two nuts? They'll be looking for us all over the damn map!"

Fisher pushed his chair back. "When you return you will have been gone only eight minutes of your time."

"What the hell are you talking about?"

Steve said, "Congressman, it's late. You've been through a lot. Let's get you back with your wife. We'll deal with the rest of it in the morning."

"Listen, young man, staying here for three months is out of the question!"

"You'll be gone just eight minutes, congressman. By the way, I'm forty two."

"You look to be about twenty two."

Fisher smiled. "He looks good for his age. I'll be eighty seven the second of next month." He chuckled.

Alan stared at Fisher. "Eighty seven? I don't believe it."

"It's true. The average life expectancy has increased to one-hundred-sixty-years."

Chapter 22
Mackendrick & Tanner

9:15 AM July 16, 2498
THE GARRETT CONNECTION:

$\mathcal{F}$rank's intercom beeped three times before he answered. "I'm in the middle of something, Farrah." He stared at his computer screen.

"It's Mack on two-five."

"I'll get back. Take a message, whatever." He shook his head and continued saving data. He had successfully accessed the UWC mainframe and opened the TTEC file.

The intercom beeped again. He ignored it. A moment later Farrah stepped into his office and shut the door. "Mackendrick won't go away, Frank. He said, *Tell that boss of yours to pick up now or I'll have his ass hauled in by military escort!* Those are his exact words."

Frank looked away from the computer and studied his secretary for a moment. For some, odd, reason he remembered the last time they slept together. "I'll take the call. Record it." He smiled and added, "Are you free this weekend?"

"No, but I'll give you a good price."

He laughed. "That's trite and petty, Ms. Walters."

"Yeah, but you love it. Talk to the general before he has a heart attack."

"This is Tanner."

Mack was hot. "Listen, Mr. Newspaper—you're a goddamn dime holding up a dollar!"

"Easy, I called you first, remember?"

"Hell with that. "

"Watch your language, General, you're going on disk."

"Cut it. No notes! I don't want any record at all. You're in deep shit. I'm calling to avoid a public incident, but I'll wave that risk if you fight me."

"I haven't the slightest idea what you're yelling about."

"You will, Tanner. Tell your, sex-a-tarry, to kill the disk and get off the line--now!"

"You heard the man, Farrah."

Click
"Okay, Tanner, if one word of what I say next gets documented in any form, you'll spend a long time in *Gray Plan.* Are we clear on that?"

A sharp sting shot from the end of Frank Tanner's spine to the base of his skull.

* * * *

Gray Plan is a UWC rehabilitation center built on the moon. Ninety-five percent of its inmates never come back. Those who do would never cause any trouble for the rest of their lives. In fact, they would never cause anything at all. Those who know anything about Gray Plan refer to it as Gray Hell.

* * * *

Frank didn't think Mackendrick could make good on his threat, but the mere thought of it chilled him to the marrow of his bones. He said, "Farrah, make damn sure that disk is voided, and stay off the line."

"It's done, sir. I'm gone."

Frank demanded, "What's the horse shit, General?"

"Now who's getting testy?"

"You've insulted my secretary and made a serious threat to me. You bet your high-level military ass I'm pissed!"

"Sack it, Frank. Yelling at each other isn't going to help. Just listen and memorize what I'm telling you." He cleared his throat and lowered his voice. "Don't even think of processing it."

"I've just broken my pencil and ripped up my notebook. I'm listening. Stop the military-secret crap and tell me what you're up to."

"You know the *New Star* on highway fifty?"

"Yeah, a dive southeast of Fallen."

"It's a private club. I'm a charter member."

"I'm impressed. Is it black tie or casual?"

"Comics work in Old Vegas and Reno, smart-mouth. Be there at eight-thirty tonight. Khrismann and I will be waiting in a private room. Ask the doorman for Mack. Got it?"

"Where does Khrismann fit in? He's a working stiff, like me."

"He fits. Be there or I'll have your ass."

"It's close to twenty-five miles."

"We have to drive sixty, so don't bitch."

"Is there a story in this?"

Mackendrick laughed. "Story? You think this is material for your goddamned column? Let me tell you something, Mr. Newspaper. I'm asking the questions on this one. You're giving the answers. For the moment, the three of us are keeping things unofficial."

"Mack, get serious. How many times have you seen off-the-record information shoved down somebody's throat?"

"Didn't you hear me mention, *Gray plan?* It wasn't a joke." He hesitated. "You're involved in a major security leak here. Take my word for it. Your ass is on the line. If word gets out and you force the issue. The Nevada Sun will shit-can you faster than last week's headlines."

"General, differences aside. I honestly have no idea what you're talking about!"

"Does the name, Harry Fellin, ring a bell?"

"Yes."

"Then you know what I'm talking about."

"The Time Gate?"

Mackendrick lowered his voice. "Shut the hell up, Tanner."

"Jesus."

"Be there on time."

"I'll be there."

"You damn-well better be."

The general hung up with a slam.

Frank studied the computer screen. He knew good and well what Mack was getting at. *The source of the access code to TTEC.* "Something's happened ... what ?"

Farrah stepped into the office. "Are you okay?"

Tanner glanced up. "You listened?"

"I heard all of it."

"Dammit, Farrah, they'll nail your ass to the wall just for an example! I said get off the line—why the hell didn't you?"

"It's big, too big. If push comes to shove, you'll need someone on your side and I'm it!"

"We're dealing with more than a political story here. The way Mack put it, I'm into something dangerous."

"And I'm in it with you."

"There's no need—"

"Shut up--I want it that way."

"You're a gem."

"I give good love."

"Stop it. You're more to me than that."

"I am?"

"You bet you are."

"Then my butt's on the line with yours." She crossed the room and came toward him.

"Farrah, think about what you're doing."

"I have. I also recorded everything Mack said on sub-system."

Frank came out from behind his desk. "I thought you might try that."

They met in the middle of the room. Frank took her by the shoulders. "Go back to your desk and scratch that file completely."

"No." She pushed his arms aside and hugged him, resting her head into his chest. "I can't."

He pulled away and looked at her. "You sent the data to my coded file?"

"Yes."

"It might come back and kill you."

"Then I'll deal with it. We're taking the risk together."

Tanner held her and pressed his face into her thick rich black hair. "I should've fired you the minute I started liking you."

"Can't now, I know too much. Besides, nobody else would put up with you."

"You're out on a limb for me again—"

"I am because I want to be. I'm nuts enough to think you're worth it."

"There's a lot at stake here, lady."

"Go to Fallon, tell Mack what he wants to know. You don't owe the council anything. I don't want you to be another Harry."

"You know about him?"

"Everything I need to. I'm your sex-a-tarry, remember?"

"How could I forget? You're a lot more than a secretary. Have you heard the phrase, *behind every successful man there's a woman?*"

"It's true." She started to leave. "I almost forgot. Jeff Blake called while you were talking to the high an' mighty general. He wants you to call him. He said it's urgent."

"Isn't He one of our reporters?"

Yeah, he said something about a fatal explosion out in Minden, Mendon wherever that is. You want me to get him?"

"Okay, I'll talk to him." Frank thought a moment. "Put him through on my private com-link."

* * * *

"Hi, Jeff, why should an explosion interest me?"

"Mr. Tanner. We need to talk."

"I'm listening."

"In person. I can't talk on any com-system or company line."

"You have my word, this is a clear link."

"In person, Mr. Tanner, please."

"You work for the paper. Come up to my office."

"Not even there." He took a short breath. "I drive a red Falcon X-300. It will be parked at rest stop fifty six off route 632. I'll be in the coffee shop. I'm wearing a dark blue cap with the *Sun* logo and a red jacket."

"Is all this necessary?"

"Believe me, Mr. Tanner, it's absolutely necessary. I'm buying lunch."

"I could never turn down a free lunch."

"Great, meet me in one hour."

"I'll be there." He cleared the private link. "Farrah, pull up whatever you can on Jeff Blake." He got up, put on his suit jacket and checked his recording device."

Farrah stepped into his office. "Already done, sir." She handed him a four-page print out. "I thought you'd rather read it than listen to it in your over-priced Eagle-670-Z." She grinned. "But, I made a disk anyway."

"You're so damned efficient. Hey, you love the *zee.*"

"Yes, I do. Especially when you shove it into hover-mode and we fly across the desert at night going over two-hundred-eighty. Yeah, that's a major turn-on."

"Maybe we'll do that again soon." He kissed her. "Sometimes you excite me so much I've considered getting serious."

"Really?" She kissed him back. "You, getting serious?"

"Who else would have me?"

She slapped him playfully. "You're a shit, Tanner."

"And you love it."

Farrah adjusted the lapels on his coat. "Yes ... I do."

he smiled. "I'm going to meet Blake. It might be important. The way he tells it he's got information regarding the end of the world."

"You be careful." She studied his eyes. "I mean it."

"Always, love. When I'm finished with Jeff, I'll head out to meet Mack. I'll call you when that's done."

Farrah folded the papers on Jeff Blake and slipped them and the disk into the right side pocket of Frank's suit coat. "I'll be waiting at your place. If I haven't heard from you by midnight, I'll make more noise than this paper has ever heard."

"Farrah ... I'd never make it without you."

"Don't try, Mr. Newspaper."

"Shut your pretty little mouth, woman."

She kissed him. "Hit the road, Tiger."

Chapter 23
The Franklin File

**COUNCIL CHAMBERS: UWC HEADQUARTERS:
10:00 AM July 16, 2498**

$\mathcal{R}$obert Fisher stood behind his chair and nodded toward Palmer. "Clear the screen, Steve." To Congressman Franklin he said, "You're a brave man, Alan. I'm not sure I could look at my whole life like that."

Franklin watched the huge computer screen blink away the last page of his file and replace it with the UWC logo. "I needed to know," he whispered, more to himself than the other two men. "Now, I do ...." He glanced down at his laced fingers and realized how hard he was squeezing. His knuckles and the tips of his fingers had gone bloodless-white. "After our session last night, I didn't think there could be any more surprises." He looked up at Fisher and Palmer. "I think I'm ready to go on now."

The chairman said, "Would you mind a personal question?"

Alan laughed softly. "You already know everything there is."

"I don't know how you feel right now. I have an idea, but I'd like to hear it from you."

He rubbed his hands and smiled at the younger man. "Steve, what do you suspect I feel?" The congressman absently twisted his wedding band on his ring-finger.

Palmer cleared his throat and walked to the opposite end of the table. "I believe what you learned about your son, Robbie had the most impact."

"You're absolutely right." Franklin shook his head and snapped his fingers. "That kid—a young man now, has rocked between blessing and curse since he was ten." Alan cut off the next word to swallow the tightness in his throat. He drew a quick breath. "He'll be all right though ... he'll get where he's going after all." He blinked rapidly and lowered his voice. "I'm glad ...."

Fisher sat down and leaned toward the congressman. "In a sense of the word, Alan, you've been given a gift. However, it comes with a high price."

He nodded. "I know. I can't do anything that would alter the course of events."

"Exactly," whispered Fisher. "To do so would be most dangerous."

"In my heart, I love him more than I would have ... I think he'll feel that."

The chairman said, "Be careful of it, Alan, more than you will about anything you know, especially in regard to our profound agreement."

"You have my word, Robert, my absolute word."

* * * *

THE OTHER FOUR:

$\mathcal{K}$athy Simmons had finished explaining the situation to the others when Sophy stepped into the room.

Kathy said, "Excuse me a minute." She met Fisher's secretary at the door.

Sophy whispered, "He wants to see Dr. Jordan now. I'll escort him to the office."

"What about the congressman?"

"Steve is bringing him here right now."

"Okay, thanks."

Sophy waited.

Kathy went to her desk and pulled Jordan's file. "Dr. Jordan, Chairman Fisher will see you now."

"I've been ready for this one since yesterday."

Laura Franklin asked, "Where's Alan?"

Kathy smiled. "He's on his way right now." To Hal she said, "Doctor, you'll find the chairman very pleasant." She nodded toward Fisher's secretary. "Sophy will show you the way." She handed her the file.

Hal stood and grinned at the others. "I hope the chairman finds me equally pleasant."

Michael Sternfeld added, "Name, rank and serial number, Hal. Nothing more." He smiled. His wife remained expressionless. She said nothing.

Hal chuckled and left the room with Sophy.

To the others, Kathy said, "As soon as the Congressman arrives you can return to your quarters and rest before lunch."

Michael said, "Doesn't Fisher want to see us?"

"This evening he'll meet with us as a group." Looking at Mrs. Sternfeld, Kathy added, "Linda, I'd like to see you alone later, if I may."

Linda hesitated then whispered, "Okay ... I want to talk to you too."

With a measure of irritation, Michael said,

"There are still a few more questions I'd like answered."

Kathy responded. "We respect that. After lunch, you'll have time with Steve and me. We'll give you all the answers you want."

"Thank you." He gripped Linda's hand and whispered, "We'll be all right, honey. Just one-step-at-a-time."

* * * *

CHAIRMAN FISHER'S OFFICE:
10:45 AM SAME DAY:

S ophy tapped a lighted keypad on her desk.

The chairman responded. "Do we have the pleasure of Dr. Jordan's company?"

"We do, sir, but first you need to talk with Councilman Khrismann on red-five."

"Show Dr. Jordan into the council room. I'll be there in a minute."

"Yes, sir."

Fisher picked up on red-5. "What've you got, Phil?"

"I'm not positive, but I think something's up regarding our current issue."

"Such as?"

"It may be nothing. However, Mackendrick has asked, actually, ordered me to a private meeting with him and Frank Tanner."

Fisher pushed a green button. The call would be scrambled and recorded in code. The chairman and Sophy had the only access.

Robert said, "Mack throws Tanner a bone every now and again just to keep him friendly."

"That may be all it is, sir, but Mack was pretty adamant about my being there."

"Where is the meeting taking place?"

"At the *New Star* on highway fifty. It's a private club."

"What did Mack say that makes you nervous enough to call me?"

"These are his words, sir. *It's a matter of the highest security.* He wouldn't say any more."

"When will you meet?"

"Eight-thirty this evening."

"All right, Phil. I appreciate the information. If it amounts to anything call me in the morning."

"I will, sir, thank you."

The chairman closed the line and secured the coded file. He got up from his desk and started toward the conference room. "What the hell's Mack up to?"

Chapter 24
Tanner & Blake

THE COFFEE SHOP:
11:15 AM ROUTE 632, REST STOP #56

$\mathcal{F}$rank spotted Blake in a corner booth as far back in the place as he could get.

Jeff recognized him and waved.

"Jeff?"

"Yeah, thanks for coming."

They shook hands. Tanner sat down. "You've been with the *sun* for eight years, graduated, with honors, in 2490 from UWU and specialize in regional crime reporting."

"Yes, sir and I'm still learning." He waved at a passing waitress. "Fresh coffee please." He looked at Frank. "Lunch is on me, Mr. Tanner."

"I accept, the name's Frank, okay?"

"Right. It's just that I'm on the ground floor, you're way upstairs."

"It takes time."

Jeff looked out into the parking lot and adjusted his cap. "I'd like to get my own column."

"It took me ten years." He slipped off his jacket.

The waitress, a young redhead, smiled at Frank and poured coffee. "Ready to order, honey?"

Tanner glanced at the menu. "How's number two with herbs?"

The woman leaned closer. "It's on special today for twenty-five cents."

Frank grinned. "How much is it every other day?"

"Fifty cents. How you want it, hon?"

"Hot, steamed and open-face."

"You got it." She entered the order on her keypad and turned to Jeff. "And you, young man?"

"I'll do the same. Make it without the herbs."

"Be comin' right up, gents." She winked at Frank.

Tanner studied the young reporter. "What've you got? You didn't cover an explosion and call me unless there's a lot more to it." He spooned sweetener into his coffee and added refined cream. "According to your file, you're assigned to the homicide division."

"Yeah, it's homicide, narcotics and security, HNS." Jeff stirred his coffee and whispered, "I have reason to believe I've found something bigger." He looked out the window again.

The waitress returned with their order. "Here we are gentlemen." She served Frank first. "Anything else just shout."

Tanner grinned. "We're okay, thanks." He hesitated until the redhead left. "Why are you so interested in the parking lot?"

Blake leaned forward. "I may be a subject of interest to the WCI."

"If they're on your ass you have a major problem." Frank seasoned his food. "What the hell are you into?"

The young reporter reached into his jacket pocket and produced a paralayne tube. He shook his head. "That's not what it is." He held up his hand and lowered his voice. "I got to the scene of the blast with an HNS team before the smoke cleared. "It was no accident." He pushed the tube toward Tanner. "I know what

CN/X-10 smells like. And I know what it can do."

Frank swallowed some food. "That's military fireworks, Jeff. Are you sure?"

"The whole scene reeked with the acrid odor of CN/X-10. Every shrub, bush and tree within fifty feet was burned to a black crisp."

"How many casualties?"

"The heat was so intense none of us could get close enough to see." Jeff took a bite of his food. "That's when the World Council investigators arrived."

Frank stopped eating. "WCI shows up at a house fire?" He sat back. "Are you sure?"

"They had ID, and they damn-well flashed it." He pointed to the paralayne tube. "Inside that tube you'll find an XP/20 data vault. I spent all yesterday afternoon and most of the night documenting everything at the scene. That includes pictures I took before the big-guns got there."

"They knew you were a reporter?"

"My badge was shinning in the bright, Nevada sun."

"How did you get out of there with pictures?"

"Good question." Jeff grinned wide. "I've altered my equipment to hold two chips. The agent in charge demanded my pictures, I gave him a chip. I hope he likes my work."

"I suppose you did the same with your voice recorder?"

"You suppose right. Nobody knows but you and me."

Tanner slipped the tube into his inside pocket. "What else is in the data vault that makes all of this so urgent?"

"Okay, all the homes in the area of the incident are built on five or six acre parcels. No other places were damaged. However, a nosy neighbor was on the scene and I talked to him."

"The agents didn't stop you?"

"They were too busy with the NHS guys." Jeff took a sip of coffee. "The neighbor, Tim Moran, said a man named Garrett lived there. He didn't know his first name. He told me he saw Garrett and a woman go in the house about forty-minutes before the explosion. He was positive." Blake looked into the parking lot again.

Frank took the last bite of his lunch and pushed the plate away. "There had to be a vehicle somewhere."

"There were two. One was a dark green Zephyr-360 and the other was a black Laren-500. Both vehicles were destroyed by the blast."

Frank flagged the waitress. She came right over.

"Could you heat up my coffee?"

"I'll heat your coffee any time darlin'" She filled Tanner's cup.

"Thank you."

She glanced at Jeff. "You want some?"

"I'll pass thanks."

Frank stirred in fresh cream. "Is that it?"

"Not quite. I tapped a source at UWC and found out that Garrett had worked for Councilman Larry Cross. There was a nasty disagreement and Cross fired him. Garrett promised to get even."

Tanner leaned back. "Cross. He's not a man you want to piss off." He hesitated. "Anything on the woman?"

"Actually, yes. She went by the name of Candy Topps. She was a former dancer in Old Vegas. Oddly enough, Ms. Topps also worked for Councilman Cross, with benefits. By the way, my source tells me Candy owned a dark green Zephyr."

Frank finished his coffee. "Okay, all this boils down to what appears to be a conspiracy to snuff out two people who had sensitive connections with Larry Cross and the workings of UWC."

Jeff adjusted his cap and relaxed a little. "That's why I called you." He put his elbows on the table. "Something's going on at UWC

Command Center to put it on red alert. I think my story has a connection."

Tanner thought a moment. "I know something big is going on and it all started yesterday." He studied Jeff's expression. "Have you secured this information anywhere else?"

"I have it all stored on a Global Net site. It's in an encrypted file under my code name. When you open the data-vault, type 3Y-2C and you'll have access. It's the same information you have in the vault."

Frank slid out of the booth and put a dollar on the table. "That covers it and a fifty-cent tip. You can buy next time."

"I'll add to the tip." Jeff dropped two dollars on the table.

Tanner grabbed it up immediately and handed it back to Jeff. "Are you nuts? You give that woman two bucks and she'll be crazy for a week."

"So what?"

"Think! That redhead will remember you in every detail and me as well. Do you want our little meeting to be so outstanding?"

"I don't think so." He stuffed the bills back in his pocket. "Thank you."

"Look, you're in this, whatever it is."

"I understand."

They walked out into the parking lot.

Frank shook Jeff's hand. "You've shown a lot of ability, good stuff, on this story. Keep it up and you'll get that column you want."

"Thanks."

"Be careful."

Tanner walked to his craft. He felt the Paralayne tube in his pocket. "Larry Cross, you sonofabitch!"

Chapter 25
The 747

12:00 PM – Same Day
HANGAR TWENTY FOUR:

*C*ouncilman Larry Cross flashed his ID to the military guard at the side door of the huge hangar housing the top-secret 747 jetliner. The human guard pressed a red button on the built-in console of his security desk and two, well-armed, droid-guards stepped aside.

To the human, Cross said, "I'll be no more than fifteen or twenty minutes. See to it no one else gets in here until I come out—clear?"

"Yes, sir."

Cross glanced at the droid's blank faces as he passed. "Good afternoon, gentlemen." He shook his head and walked between them. The non-human guards did not react.

Cross came into the vast interior of the hangar. He stopped and stared at the giant aircraft. He was aware of the electronic voice behind him. *Security door nine is open,* it echoed twice. With a thick, sealing sound the door closed. The hollow voice echoed that information. *Door nine is secure.*

Silence: an actual sense of atmosphere.

The councilman studied the jetliner a moment longer. The 747 was primitive. It was a simple flying bus, nothing more than a sample of aviation history.

Cross whispered, "A five-hundred year old pile of junk." A skittering chill played along the back of his neck and crawled halfway down his spine. "A hunk of scrap from the past. The key to my future." He mumbled, holding his stare.

A short, bulky-looking man appeared in the forward doorway of the jet. He wore loose, dark coveralls and wiped his hands on an orange cloth. "Mr. Cross?" He stepped onto the top landing of the portable stairs leading up from the concrete floor. The man's face changed from yellow to red in the alternating flash from each of the ten security doors in the outside walls of hangar twenty four. Red alert was a living presence.

Cross answered and started toward the stairs. "Did you expect anyone else?"

* * * *

The man in the doorway is, Charles Tarkin. He works for Steve Palmer deep inside the History Research Commission. Charlie is an electronics wizard who has access to more data than any single member of the United World Council. Any request from an authorized official (Larry Cross specifically) would set Mr. Tarkin into action.

Deceived by Cross, Charlie believes he is involved in interdepartmental security matters. He was told his work is of the highest sensitivity and must be kept secret from his own superiors.

On several occasions, Tarkin's assignment had been to access files from private companies doing business with the government or UWC. He considers it an honor to serve the cause. Larry Cross is, of course, that cause.

* * * *

The councilman climbed the stairs and entered the plane behind Charlie. They went onto the flight deck. "Any problems?"

"No, sir. Not a single glitch in the system."

"Have you finished the recorder?"

"I transferred all the data from the flight recorder into this storage card." He handed Larry what appeared to be a smooth, piece of yellow plastic. It resembled a credit card.

Cross said, "Same code?"

"Just add, back-slash and the numbers, seven four seven to the old entry code." He hesitated before saying, "If you make a mistake entering the sequence, the data will scramble."

Larry examined the card and slipped it into his jacket pocket. "It's just routine data, why a destruct factor?"

Charlie glanced out through the cockpit window as if he suspected an unwanted visitor. "I put your crash program alterations on that card."

"Jesus Charlie. That's dangerous."

"I know it, so I protected your secret operation." He looked out the window again. "Those cards are harder to come by than the data I accessed for you. That one," he pointed at the councilman's jacket pocket, "is classified defective." Larry reached for the card. "No— it's not bad, I logged it as defective and processed it for destruction. As far as HRC knows, the damn thing doesn't exist."

"It's the same one you made for Palmer's people, except for the crash codes, right?"

Mr. Tarkin leaned against the navigation console and gathered a thought. "Okay—it's the same, yes. I did just what you asked me to do."

"Charlie, what the hell is the problem then?" Larry pulled the card from his pocket and turned it over in his fingers.

"The problem—or safety-factor is the letter *E.*" He studied the councilman's face a moment before going on. "The crash command sequence on your card ends with the letter *E.* That character doesn't exist in the card I made for HRC and the plotting people. When they access the crash program without the letter *E,* the secondary program, your sequence, takes over and the plane crashes before the special people can be suspended."

"You put two programs on their card?"

"Exactly. The primary triggers the secondary and wham—mission accomplished!"

"They'll pull the data and find it."

"Not a chance." Charlie laughed and shook his head. "Not on your life—or mine. Twelve seconds after the secondary sequence is activated, the card scrambles." He laughed again—at his own brilliance."

"My card won't destruct?"

"Not at all. Yours doesn't have the primary sequence, just the tiny addition of the *E* character. Nobody else knows that. No *E*—the card goes blank."

Larry turned the card over several more times then looked at it close up. "What made you do it that way?"

Tarkin flushed. He had done a good thing.

* * * *

Cross had convinced him the return of the five key-people to their time was detrimental to present society. He also believed those behind the mission were working against the UWC.

* * * *

When Charlie answered his voice was full of conviction and pride. "Sir, I did it for two reasons. First, to protect you. If somebody got their hands on your card and ran it—your project would be blown wide open." He shuddered visibly. "It might buy you a ticket to Gray plan. Jesus! Just the thought of that makes me sick"

"And the second reason?"

Charlie grinned and felt his ears burn. "To cover my own ass, Councilman. They'd ship me off to the moon on the next available flight." He laughed again, with a vision of *Gray Plan* in his mind.

Cross smiled. "You're the best there is for this work, Charlie. Another bonus is on the way."

"Sir—money is not my motivation."

"I accept that. If it were, you wouldn't be working for me. By the way, thanks to your technical expertise, Nevil Garrett is no longer a threat to global security."

"The digital device doesn't fail."

Larry gripped Tarkin's shoulder. "According to my informant, there isn't enough left to cover the head of a pin." He paused and pointed toward the controls of the big jet. "I want to hear about the recorder and how the crash program damages the aircraft."

Tarkin grinned and pointed to the controls of the flight recorder, which he had reinstalled. "The second half of the tape is blank, Sir."

"Tape?"

"This aircraft is old. All data is recorded on audio tape. It works automatically or can be accessed manually. The device will pick up any and all communication on the flight deck."

"So, if the crew doesn't want to be recorded, they can switch it off, right?"

"You got it. Federal aviation rules, at the time, required flight recordings of each take off and landing and any emergency situation during flight."

"I assume the front part of the tape still has

the take off from Kennedy."

"Yes, but not one word of the gate encounter or anything after."

Cross patted Charlie's shoulder. "Exactly as Fisher and the others requested. That covers your ass."

"Perfectly and yours, sir." Tarkin smiled at his boss and glowed with pride. "Now, when the clone-pilot goes into its emergency program, it'll switch on the recorder and everything from that point will be part of history." He glanced up at Larry Cross and shared his smile.

The councilman nodded. "It's just an unfortunate accident with no survivors." He shook his head in mock sympathy."

Tarkin said, "They'll all die."

Cross squeezed Charlie's shoulder again. "You've done well, extremely well."

Tarkin looked away for a moment then added, "I'm fighting one thing, sir."

"Which is?"

"The clones are nothing. I mean they're just tools we use to get a job done." He stared at the instrument panel. "I can't help but feel sorry for the real people."

Prepared for such an observation, Cross responded. "I've thought about it myself. No, I've been haunted by it." He slipped into the navigator's seat and pretended concern. "It isn't their fault really. In a sense, they're victims of destiny. The main one is Franklin, of course, but the others must die with him to assure the future." He turned to Tarkin. "Our future, Charlie. If Franklin survived the crash, as HRC and Fisher ordered, everything, from that point on would change for the worse."

Charlie shifted his eyes and recalled some distant bit of information from his work with the History Research Commission. "I really don't understand it all, sir, but weren't Franklin and the professor major factors in the society we now enjoy?"

Cross stood and used superiority to his own benefit. "I thought you understood—maybe I was wrong."

"What?"

"Fisher and every other department head want us to believe that bullshit!" He turned his back and glared into the empty cabin of the 747. "Jesus, Tarkin! You have access to more history information than I do. Goddammit, man. Alterations have gotten out of control." He snapped around to face Charlie and leaned toward him. "What we're doing here is putting things in proper order. Don't you see that?"

Charlie studied the councilman's tense expression then looked away. He covered his mouth as if to contain another string of wrong words. After a moment he said, "I'm sorry, Councilman. You're right, of course. It's just the thought of those five—six people really, dying before their time."

"Before *our* time, Mr. Tarkin. Just think about that."

"I see." Charlie faced the glaring eyes of Councilman Cross. "It's just such a complex issue."

A wide grin cut slowly across Larry's face and he nodded. "Forget it. These decisions are difficult for all of us. Those above me share the same emotions."

"I understand, sir."

"Good. Now, explain the crash program."

Pieces of what they had shared sifted through Mr. Tarkin's mind, some of it made sense—most didn't. Charlie had access to a great deal of secret, HRC information. But, he didn't have enough to counter Larry Cross. He explained the sequence of technical events that would set the jetliner on a course of destruction.

Charlie pointed at the on-board *primitive* computer. "When the airplane exits the time gate the destruct program initiates. At that point, a small charge blows the hydraulic lines and cable backup."

Cross nodded and grinned. "Excellent, go on."

"Ten seconds later the right outboard engine tears loose."

Cross said, "That's it! The plane takes a dive and its over."

"Completely." Charlie's voice was shallow.

Cross said, "There's no way Phil can adjust the suspension program before impact?"

"No, sir. By the time the Command Center mission crew realizes what's going on, the jetliner will be scattered over several acres of western Utah." Charlie shuddered and stared across the flight deck.

The councilman said, "What will the investigation boil down to?"

Charlie looked at his hands, then at the dead gauges in front of him. Fetching a quick breath he reached out and touched the cold, blank face of the small computer screen. Without looking up he said, "Metal fatigue."

"A common occurrence?"

"In those days, yes."

Larry Patted Charlie's shoulder. "You're the best."

Tarkin glanced around the cockpit. "Thank you, sir ...." He thought, *God forgive me.*

Chapter 26
DR. Hal JORDAN

12:30 PM
UWC CONFERENCE ROOM:

*L*earning and teaching had always been the fuel of Hal Jordan's life. It was second only to his family. Being a professor of physics at U.C.L.A. meant as much to him as a corporate presidency did to a yuppie of the late nineteen eighties.

Connecting with a special *gifted* student was especially satisfying for Dr. Jordan. Such, was indeed, a rare experience.

He stared at the huge computer screen in the UWC chambers. He shook his head and grinned. Without looking at Chairman Fisher or

Steve Palmer he said, "Gentlemen, there's no way I could ever express what I'm feeling at this moment." He laced his thick fingers and tapped his large knuckles against his forehead. He closed his eyes and whispered, "Thank you God for this opportunity."

The chairman leaned forward and gripped Hal's shoulder. "I'm both impressed and surprised by your reactions Dr. Jordan."

He Looked over his clasped hands. "Why?"

Fisher sat back and studied the professor's relaxed expression. "You've accepted everything we've shown you as if it were academic."

The professor smiled. He met Steve's eyes then turned to Chairman Fisher. "It is. I'm a man of science. Logic plays an important role in the course of these events." He untangled his fingers and gestured toward the big screen. "As a way of relaxing, like others work a crossword puzzle, I play with energy equations. I create worst and best scenarios." He pushed back from the conference table and stood. He paced, studied the floor and punctuated his words with his hands. "I've based energy theories on known absolutes and calculated a power-mass to achieve the speed of light." He paused and smiled. According to everything know. Without some unknown 'X' factor, light speed was out of the question." He stopped and took the back of his chair in both hands. "I knew there was a formula—now I have the key to it."

Palmer stiffened. "Professor, I must re-emphasize a most important point."

"You don't have to, Mr. Palmer. You have my word. I will not alter the course of events." He shook his head and studied the computer screen again. "I will however, be keenly prepared for my very special student, Stephen Russell, when the time comes."

Fisher said, "Eighteen months is a long time to hold your tongue, Hal."

Jordan pulled his chair away from the table and sat down. He smiled and studied the chairman's expression. "If you didn't trust me, you would never have let me know the results of my work with Stephen."

Palmer stood and pointed back toward the big screen. "That information would be dangerous in the wrong hands. We considered not telling you. Chairman Fisher and I discussed convincing deceptions."

"Why did you decide otherwise?"

Fisher held up his hand and nodded to Steve. "Because, you would've eventually seen through them. That's a much more dangerous situation."

Jordan creased his forehead and considered the comment. "How so?"

To Palmer, Fisher said, "It was your suggestion, explain it."

Steve weighed his thoughts. After a moment he began. "There was a chance you'd perceive Russell's developments as out of the ordinary. You might've evaluated his findings against our lies and seen us as a threat. Should those events prove true, there was no way to predict your reactions. The risk of telling you the truth is the lesser of the two."

Jordan responded. "Gentlemen, with me, there are no risks."

Fisher said, "You're human. There *are* risks."

Steve added, "We trust you, but you will be watched."

Jordan said, "By TAs I suppose."

The chairman leaned back and rubbed his chin. "Exactly, Dr. I expect it to be a useless expense, but necessary nonetheless."

Steve cut in. "Given the facts, Hal, and putting yourself in our position, what would you do?"

"The same damn thing."

"Thank you," smiled Fisher, we have to cover all bases."

Jordan leaned back and tapped the edge of the table with his fingers. He listened to the soft, thudding sound as though the rhythm summoned the order of his next comment. "You sure as hell do." He sat up straight and leaned on his elbows. "I know any number of upstanding, honest men in an equal position with me, at the university, who would see this opportunity as a way to hundreds of thousands of dollars in grant money. Not to mention the recognition. I'm not made that way gentlemen."

Steve cleared his throat and asked, "What about the rest of your life, doctor, the things you haven't seen yet?"

"I think not, Steve. Let it rest, at least for now." He turned to Fisher. "Can we get back to it later?"

"Of course, whenever you wish."

"I may not ...."

"Understandable. Anything else?"

"The clones. Either of you please. I'm concerned about the clones."

"Steve answered. "Like our TAs, they're tools, nothing more. They're not human and have no feeling."

"You're sure?"

"Positive. They're plastic copies."

"No feeling?"

"None."

"How'd you manage that? The cloned cell is identical to the parent cell."

Palmer smiled and stepped away from the table. "Correct, Hal. I meant emotional feelings. The cloned cell will be altered before any accelerated growth process begins." He turned to Fisher. "I have to get back to Kathy and the others."

The Chairman said, "Of course. Hal, go with Steve and I'll join you all later this evening for a nice supper."

Jordan said, "Mr. Palmer, I'm interested in more information regarding your cloning process."

"I'm not the right person to answer your questions."

"Who is? I'll talk to him, her, and whoever."

"That would be Dr. Zanster and his department is classified." Steve glanced at Fisher.

The chairman thought a moment. "I don't see any harm in letting Hal and Jerry have a little chat." He grinned. "I think they'd enjoy a meeting-of-the-minds."

Dr Jordan's face lit up. "If I can keep my secret for eighteen months, I'm sure I can be trusted with anything I might learn from Dr. Zanster."

"I know you can, Hal." He waved toward the door. "Show the man to where the others are having lunch. After that, introduce him to Jerry."

"Thank you both for being honest."

Fisher leaned back. "I never really thought anything else would've worked with you."

"Wise decision, Chairman." He thought a moment and added, "The others ... do they know all of this?"

Fisher glanced at Steve and shifted his eyes to Dr. Jordan. "They know what they have to, Hal. I think we have enough complications for the moment." He grinned.

Dr. Jordan said, "I think I would like to have known you in my time."

"Thank you. I wish you could stay with us. Men like you are few and far between."

Steve watched the two of them for a moment then said, "Doctor, if you'll come with me please ...."

Chairman Fisher leaned forward and entered a keyboard command. The giant screen went blank. Staring at it, he muttered, "Dear God, help us ...."

* * * *

When Dr. Jordan and Steve entered the main hallway Hal said, "I have a lot of questions I'd like to ask."

"I'll tell you what I can, Doctor."

"It's mostly natural curiosity. Here we are in the twenty-third century and you people are still accessing computers by keyboard."

Steve chuckled and led Hal through a security scanner about thirty feet in front of a sealed door. "Most of us use a keyboard by choice. Usually we're accessing the mainframe, which is six floors below ground level. While being extremely efficient, TEX, as we call it, is also very sensitive. We can voice-activate any terminal in the headquarters complex."

"We have systems like that in my time."

"Not quite. Tex has special architecture that functions in an organic solution and protein gel. It's a brain really." They stopped at the sealed door. Steve continued. "The computer reads voice prints and responds to whatever emotional condition a user might be in at any given moment." He entered a code number in the door's keypad. "Let's say I have to work on a particularly critical research program."

"And you're hung over."

"Okay, that's a good example."

A solid *snap* sounded as the security door opened.

Hal added, "How does it know?"

"I can't say, but it damn well does. So, I'm feeling rotten when I access the mainframe. Tex reads my state of mind and bio rhythms. If the document I've requested is in high security priority, the computer evaluates my existing mental condition."

"Damn."

The security door sealed behind them with a thick, solid sound. Steve went on. "If Tex doesn't agree with my bio readings—access denied. It's that simple."

"So, you bypass through the keyboard."

"Not a chance. Tex reads everything it needs to know through galvanic response as well."

"Damn. I'm sorry, but to me it's fantastic."

"Tell you what. Later, I'll give you an access code to a basic file. You can sweet-talk the computer, key the code and even use the headset. I'll bet you a hundred to one you can't get in."

Jordan said, "Headset?"

"We don't use them very often, but Tex can be accessed by brain waves."

"Now you're kidding."

"Not for a second." Steve laughed. "Would you like a demonstration?"

"I would love it."

"After lunch, Kathy Simmons and I will take you to the History Research Lab. What you'll experience there could make you one of the most intelligent educators of your time."

A droid looked up from its security desk and spoke. "Good afternoon, Mr. Palmer."

Steve grinned. "Hi, Teefer. Everything under control?"

"Yes, sir." The android pressed a key on the board in front of it and nodded.

Steve said, "Thank you." He and Dr. Jordan turned left, into a narrow corridor, and faced another sealed door marked, HRC-LAB #4 (LEVEL-10 ACCESS ONLY). Steve placed his right thumb and index fingertip against a gray screen flush with the wall.

Dr. Jordan looked back at the security officer.

Clack

Heavy steel slide-bolts released. The door opened with the sound of an air-lock. They were bathed in pulsating, red light. A shrill alarm echoed off the hollow corridor beyond. When Steve touched another opaque screen on the inside wall, the door sealed behind them and the alarm cut off instantly.

Discretely, Hal whispered, "What kind of name is, Teefer?"

Steve laughed. "It's a model, T dash four. We call him, Teefer."

"The guard's a clone then?"

"No. Teefer is among the best of artificial intelligence, he, it, is an android."

"Unbelievable."

"We don't have to feed or pay them. We just maintain and program them."

Hal shook his head and they walked toward the end of the long corridor.

Chapter 27
A PRIVATE PARTY

8:15 PM July 16, 2498
THE NEW STAR CLUB:

$\mathcal{F}$rank Tanner arrived at the *New Star* fifteen minutes early. He approached the doorman when he entered the dim interior. "I'm here to see Mack."

"Mack who?" The android's speech patterns were exceptional. It was an R/5 series, just one level below TA models. R/5 androids were available in male and female form and were created to mix with the general public. They could be custom-programmed for any human service short of homicide (they could be *fixed* for that purpose for the right price).

Tanner said, "General Charles Mackendrick. He's expecting me. I'm Frank Tanner."

The R/5 smiled and shook hands with Frank. The droid said, "I'm Billy Jenkins, pleasure to meet you, sir."

Tanner grinned uneasily and waited for the usual four-pump greeting to end. "Tell Mack I'm here." Frank was always uncomfortable in the presence of androids, male or female. There was something hollow about them. It was a distant darkness in their eyes.

Altering an R/5 basic program was a felony. Several people were serving a lot of time on *Gray Plan* for doing just that.

"He told me to tell you to wait at the bar. The drinks are on his tab."

"Thanks." Frank stepped by the droid and glanced at the back of its neck. The red dot was plain as day. Not only was this R/5 a smiling doorman, it was also a bouncer (a cooler). Should a troublesome patron slip out of line, the bartender (human) would press a button. The R/5, and others like it, would zero in on the unruly customer. If the problem target didn't settle down quickly he was in deep shit. The R/5 coolers *never* lost.

Frank shuddered. He remembered too many

stories about a few coolers getting too hot. Sometimes the cooling put trouble makers on ice for a long time.

The bouncer/cooler programs were legal provided the entertainment establishment had a permit. Those little slips of paper, like the UWC liquor license, were expensive and not casually issued, unless money was no object.

Frank eased his way through a heavy Thursday night crowd and took notice of the beautiful female flexing her virtues on stage. It wasn't a woman. He took a seat at the bar and watched the she-droid slither to the beat of the band.

From behind him a deep male voice asked, "What can I get ya?"

Without turning around, Frank said, "A double Jacobs and no ice."

"Got a card?"

Tanner turned and produced a blue, plastic card with his picture and ID number. He said, "Is she new?"

"Bobbie? Hell no. She's been here seven months."

"She's an R/5, right?"

"R/5-F/P. We got four of her type. We use 'em on weekends mostly."

"She's good."

"Best money can buy." The bartender smiled

and asked, "Are you in the market?"

Frank looked down at his card, "No ... I hear it's great, but, no ... I don't think I could."

The bartender laughed. "I thought the same thing. All of a sudden, one night, I said, piss on it!" He glanced away, at the dancer, then back to Frank. "I went for it." He shook his head and closed his eyes. "I haven't had a real woman since. Sonofabitch, she was great! I mean, like no woman I ever had."

"Not for me ... not yet anyway." Tanner chuckled. "Let's have the Jacobs."

"On the way."

R/5-F droids could be legally programmed for paid sex. Human prostitution was a felony. Minimum sentence: six years at Gray Plan.

Frank turned around again and watched the R/5-F/P work through its dance. He thought of Farrah and looked ahead to what might be a great weekend.

At a table directly in front of the bar four military men, with UWMF (United World Military Force) patches on their uniforms, were pooling money to buy an R/5-F/P for the night. The waitress, a human, took their order.

Frank thought, *Nothing changes as much as it stays the same.*

Behind him, the bartender said, "Here's your poison."

Frank said, "It goes on Mack's tab."

"I know. It's taken care of."

"Thanks." He sipped his drink and glanced at the small inhalers of Paralayne the bar-keep had placed neatly on a fresh napkin. He tipped his drink again. This time to his own reflection in the mirror behind the bar. "Party hardy, Mr. Newspaper. You're on the shore of a sea of shit." He threw back the Jacobs, coughed once and handed the tubes of Paralayne back to the bar-keep. "Keep 'em, compliments of Mack."

* * * *

Ten minutes later a roving R/5-F/P approached and whispered, "Mack's ready. Follow me. I'll take you to him."

"Lead the way." Tanner slugged down the rest of his second drink and thought of the Paralayne tube in his jacket pocket and what it contained.

The female droid smiled. "I'm available later."

"No thanks."

"Too bad. I like the way you look."

"Yeah. Let's find Mack."

The female robot grabbed Tanner's hand and led him through the noisy crowd toward the back of the room.

When they reached the closed door marked private the R/5-F/P said, "They're here." She, *it* blinked at him with deep blue distant eyes.

"Sorry, it's not my thing."

The lady droid smiled and walked off into the crowd.

Frank entered the private room and closed the door.

General Mackendrick and Phil Khrismann were seated at a large table in the center of the room. The lights were as dim as those in the main lounge. A tall blonde entered from a rear door and placed a huge tray of sea food on the table. Mack handed her some money and nodded. It had to be at least a twenty. The woman kissed him on the cheek, whispered in his ear and exited through the same rear door. The general stood and reached out to take Tanner's hand. "Sorry for the delay."

"It's okay," grinned Tanner.

Khrismann didn't get up. He didn't offer his hand.

"Mack said, "Frank, you know Phil."

"I know who he is." They nodded to each other. "As I asked earlier, why the hell is he involved?"

Phil said, "That's the same question I asked about you."

Mack gestured toward a chair. "Phil's in this

because I need him. His department is involved to the teeth." He studied Tanner a moment more. "Sit, Frank. Eat, drink and enjoy. What's happened is heavy. The rest is life and death. Put your ass on the damn chair and listen."

Tanner sat down.

Khrismann sipped a copper-colored drink from a narrow-stemmed glass. "I don't like you, Tanner. Let's make that clear from the start. Your kind makes me want to puke."

"What kind is that, Mr. Khrismann?"

"Dip-shit reporters. That kind." Phil gulped the rest of his drink and re-filled his glass from an iced bottle.

Mackendrick said, "Frank, your ass is on the line and the whole goddamn project is in jeopardy."

Frank leaned back and pretended to take a hit of paralayne from the tube he'd removed from his jacket pocket. He said, "Maybe I had too much Jacobs while you kept me waiting, but I'm at a loss as to what you're talking about, General."

Mack said, "Bull shit!" He pressed a button on the small panel in front of him. He glared at Frank. "Does MAF-SR1-CA1-T/G mean anything to you?"

Khrismann shifted in his chair and chuckled. He took a swallow from his fluted glass.

Tanner said, "Not a damn thing."

The general uncapped a tube of Paralayne

and tapped three drops into his mouth. "Tanner, we have you by the nuts." He screwed the plastic cap onto the tube and grinned.

The blonde returned through the back door. "Sir?"

Mack smiled at her and said, "Jacobs. Make it a bottle."

The woman nodded and left as quickly as she came.

Khrismann leaned back in his chair. A hostile smile crossed his face. He didn't look at Frank, but addressed him absently. "Tanner, you got into Tex and we know it." He sat forward abruptly and glared at the reporter. "You breached global security. If it weren't for Mack's compassion, I'd have your ass up on charges right now!"

Frank said, "Mack's compassion? There's no such thing on this planet."

The blonde returned with an iced bottle of Jacobs. Mackendrick tipped her again and winked. She left the room. He raised both hands and said, "Knock off the horse shit!" He turned to Phil and said, "Keep your mouth shut!" To Tanner he said, "And you stop playing pussy-face! You got the fucking code. I know it. Phil knows it. And you know it!" He downed his own drink, took another hit of Paralayne and stood. He walked away from the table and stared at the wall. "Frank, do you know a man named, Nevil

Garrett by any chance?"

"Never heard of him."

Mack snapped around. "He damn-well knew you!"

"What do you mean, *knew* me?"

Phil leaned forward. "Mr. Garrett has been reduced to tiny fragments of human tissue. We think Larry Cross had him snuffed."

"What the hell are you two talking about?"

Mack said, "Did somebody call you with the code I mentioned?"

Frank recoiled. "I get crap like that all the time."

Mack shook his finger "You entered it and got into Time-Gate. Don't try to shit me, Tanner."

"What the hell is Time-Gate?"

Phil stood and waved his arms toward Frank. Stop the games! You got the code. You accessed Tex and opened the Time-Gate file."

"I don't know time gate from shit-gate."

Khrismann said, "The man's an idiot!"

Mack cut in. "Tanner, you're full of crap. You got into Tex through an informer and you found out about Time-Gate."

"This conversation is over."

Mack shouted, "The hell it is!" He tapped another hit and leaned on the table. "Your informant was Nevil Garrett. Mr. Garrett and his girl friend have been reduced to scraps of bleeding, human flesh. The small, neat house they occupied has become a sixty year supply of tooth picks. Somebody put a fix on them. We think it's Cross."

Phil spoke up without looking at Frank. "Twenty minutes after you got the call, Nevil and his whore met their maker."

"Now *you're* full of shit, Mr. Khrismann."

"Am I?"

Mackendrick cut in. "Tanner you're a tool in this case. We suspect Larry Cross. He set you up. Through Garrett, you got the code. Now we want your cooperation. How did you get the code from Garrett?"

Frank opened the fresh bottle of Jacobs and poured one for himself. "Okay, let's make a bad story worse." He sipped and smacked his lips. "Suppose I did get a code from somebody named Garrett—"

"Suppose your ass."

Mack cut in. "Shut it, Phil. Tell the story, Frank."

Tanner twisted the stem of his glass in his fingers. He studied the smooth legs of his Jacobs as he might those of Farrah. "This Garrett person could've known who I am without my knowing him." Shifting his eyes from the drink to Mackendrick, he took another sip.

Phil rolled his eyes and chuckled. He sat down hard and lifted his glass.

Mack said, "You're well known, Frank."

Phil added, "So is stink on shit."

The general glared at him. "Zip it. We're in a situation here, drop the goddamn pot-shots. Go ahead, Tanner."

"So, I use this mystery-code to crack Tex and I'm into a file called, *Time-Gate.* What am I supposed to do with it?"

Mack came back to the table and leaned toward Tanner. "Stop the shit, Frank. Time Gate's been in the news before."

They're on to it, he thought. *Tell them what you know. Not about TTEC, but the rest.* He downed a swallow of Jacobs and refilled his glass. To Mackendrick he said, "You and your buddy here, have threatened me with *Gray Plan* if I refuse to cooperate, which you can't bring off on that basis alone—"

"Don't push it, Tanner."

Mack waved his hand to silence Khrismann. "I don't make empty threats."

Frank took a large, spiced chunk of seafood from the lavish tray. As he munched, he said, "If you have enough evidence to put me on the moon *without* cooperation, then giving it would be self-incrimination, which I'm not obligated to do."

Mack sat down and stabbed a fork, full of meat, into a bowl of melted garlic-butter. "Tell us what you know and you're off the hook. It's the biggest story of your career."

Frank took another bite and chased it with Jacobs. "I tell you what you assume I know and then I write an article about it?"

"Something like that, yeah."

Phil said, "Look, Tanner. We got your balls in a vise and your neck in a noose. The general's people are tightening the vise and mine are pulling the goddamn rope." He took a small communicator from his shirt pocket and activated the keypad. "Two digits, Mr. Reporter and you'll be in custody before you could stand up."

Tanner said, "I thought this was a private party."

Phil grinned. "It is. Digit one alerts security, who is always near, and digit two puts you on your ass. Here and now!"

Mackendrick blotted his mouth with a napkin, swallowed and said, "Easy, Phil." To Frank he said, "Mr. Tanner, we have a security crisis on our hands, you're involved. Maybe more than you realize." He removed a folded envelope from the inside pocket of his military blouse. As he did, he spoke with a hint of apology. "When the dust settled around the ruins of Mr. Garrett's humble home, our investigators found a thick fire-proof safe." He opened the envelope, took out a blue data-card and a slip of folded yellow paper. "Listen, I'm going to read you a short story." He studied the paper for a moment, glanced at Frank and began.

Tanner, tomorrow afternoon. Use the Sun number, 321-6670. Without conversation, give the following code: MAF-SR/-CA1/T/G and Hang up immediately.

He looked up at Frank and added, "Your work number is on the data-card with a message regarding Time-Gate and a five-hundred year old jetliner full *of* people. The name, Cross and the figure, five-thousand is printed boldly under the message."

Phil grinned at Tanner and said, "By the balls, Mr. Newspaper."

Mack continued. "Another prize in the metal box was five-thousand dollars in cash clipped to a bank deposit slip dated for the next day."

Trying for any defense, Frank said, "If Cross were involved in such a scheme, he'd never put anything like that in writing. He'd be crazy to do that."

Mack handed the paper to Tanner. "The note was written by Garrett. He didn't want to chance forgetting the instructions or the code. He apparently wrote Cross's name and the money figure as an afterthought, maybe in greed, who knows. The handwriting's been checked."

Phil couldn't wait to add his comment. "You're in it, Tanner, up to your lower lip, and so is the Honorable, Councilman Larry Cross." Phil slapped the table. "That son-of-a-bitch *will* go to Gray Plan. Count on it."

Frank sat in silence and shuddered. A wave of gooseflesh crept over him. He studied the paper and read his own number several times. *Garrett was the informant. Garrett was also dead.*

Mackendrick stuffed two large chunks of sea food in his mouth. "Think about it, Frank. The only chance you have is cooperation."

"I think I need a lawyer. A hot-shot from the paper."

Khrismann said, "Go that route and you're on your way to the moon."

"I'm a reporter. I got a crazy tip and I followed it."

Mack said. "A tip about what?"

"The damn jetliner. A red alert and something called, TTEC."

Khrismann and the general glanced at each other. Mack said, "The tip came from Garrett?"

"I can't be sure."

Phil leaned forward and raised his voice. "Listen carefully, Mr. Newspaper. Cross paid Garrett to tip you on the airplane, the alert and TTEC. He knew you'd call Mack, which you did! He knew you'd try to get information on TTEC, which you did! And he Goddamn-well knew you'd contact him. Which you also did!"

Tanner said, "Can you prove it?"

Mack added, "Absolutely." He wiped his mouth and filled his glass. "Councilman Cross wanted you to find out about the Time-Gate and the current situation so he could use it against Fisher. Cross wants to be Chairman at any cost. Having Garrett and his woman killed is just a start."

Tanner smiled. "Is there a gate?"

Mack nodded. "Yes and it's top secret."

Frank said, "TTEC?"

Khrismann answered, "Time Travel Enforcement Commission and I'm in charge of it!"

"I knew it." Frank munched another chunk of fish and emptied his glass. "The seven-forty-seven?"

Again Mack nodded. "That's our situation. The plane slipped through the time gate and brought five-hundred years of history with it."

Frank said, "Harry Fellin was right."

Phil added, "Dead right."

Frank refilled his glass. "Where do I fit in to this situation?"

Mack broke off a large piece of steaming meat and soaked it in hot garlic-butter. "Play along with Cross and bring his ass to the surface."

"What?"

Mackendrick continued. "Investigate the sonofabitch, find out what he's up to. When it's over, you were working for us. The UWC. You'll be off the hook and free to write your biggest story." The General shoved the meat into his mouth and grinned.

Khrismann added, "Please say no, Mr. Newspaper, so I can plant your ass on Gray Plan."

"Up yours."

Mack cut in. "Enough!" He leaned back and sipped from his drink. "Do we have a deal, Frank?"

He looked from one man to the other. "Do I have a choice?"

Mackendrick held up his glass. Khrismann glared. Mack said, "Yes, one ... agree." He laughed.

Frank filled his glass and offered a toast. "To Chairman Fisher. I haven't liked Larry Cross since he was appointed." He took a swallow of Jacobs and stared at the glass. "How much time do I have?"

Mack said, "Less than ninety days."

Phil added, "Make it sixty, Tanner, just to be safe."

Chapter 28
The Unborn Son

UWC COMMAND CENTER
SIX HOURS EARLIER:

$\mathcal{K}$athy Simmons and the Sternfelds selected a corner table in dining area seven. The others, Congressman and Mrs. Franklin, Steve Palmer and Dr. Hal Jordan gathered at a large table with Chairman Fisher and his secretary, Sophy. Their conversation was peppered with lightness and occasional laughter. The atmosphere around Ms. Simmons and the Sternfelds was heavier.

Kathy said, "Linda, I need to know what you're feeling right now."

Michael shook his head and stared at the food on his plate. He grinned to himself for a moment then addressed Ms. Simmons. "What the hell do you think she's feeling? What are we all feeling?"

"Please, Michael, I need her response."

Linda patted the back of her husband's hand and shook her head. She leaned back and wiped her mouth with a napkin. "Forgive me," she grinned and studied the ceiling tiles for a moment. "For the first time since our plane shook, I'm famished." She took a healthy fork full of mashed potatoes and cut herself a slice of rare roast beef. "I've got a baby to feed, thank you. A boy who hasn't been born. A person who's already lived and died!" Linda glared at Kathy. "My little boy, who hasn't formed yet has a name. He's had a wife, kids of his own. He's made a contribution to history. I'm a grandmother and I haven't even broke water! God help me." Linda covered her face and began to cry.

Michael held her. He rocked her in his arms. "She can't handle this. I'm not sure I can either."

"You have to, Michael."

"I can't—"

"You can and you will!" Ms. Simmons removed a container of small, white tablets from the pocket of her lab coat. She whispered, "Take Linda to your room, and give her two of these."

"She'll never take them—"

"Do it, Michael. For the sake of your wife and son. Just do it." Kathy glanced toward Steve Palmer. She caught his attention. To Michael she said, "Wait fifteen minutes. Steve and I will escort you and Dr. Jordan to the lab. You both have a lot to learn."

"What about Linda?"

"She'll sleep like a rock—you'll be educated." She softened her tone. "Michael, your lives depend on our help ... we are not your enemy."

"I'm scared to death."

"So are we."

They looked at each other for a moment.

Steve came to their table. He said, "Is there a problem?"

To Michael, Kathy whispered, "Is there?"

"No. I'm sorry. I'll be waiting for you." To Linda he said, "C'mon, honey, you need some sleep."

Linda mumbled, "Do we have to name him, William?"

"Sweetheart, we already have. We'll call him, Bill."

Linda wiped her eyes and looked at Steve and Kathy. "I didn't mean to be a shit ...."

Kathy smiled and pushed a strand of Linda's hair back from her face. "You're no such thing. You're a very special young woman. Go with Michael and please do what he tells you. We'll see each other tomorrow, okay?"

Linda forced a smile and touched Kathy's hand. "Okay."

Steve said, "Can you handle her, Mike?"

"Yes, we're all right." They left the dining area and were met by a droid-guard in the hall, which guided them to their quarters.

Steve accidentally brushed his face against Kathy's thick, chestnut hair. They looked at each other. Steve said, "Do we have a problem?"

"Nothing I didn't foresee. You'll have to deal with Michael. Linda can't handle any more than she's been given."

"Understandable. Look what they're faced with. How about you?"

"Me?"

"You. You're sensitive—these are people, not TAs."

"I know." She gripped Steve's hand. "I need you, a lot."

"You got it and don't ever forget it."

"The others?"

Steve turned back to the group at the large table. Their voices were softer now, but there was still laughter.

Dr. Jordan glanced toward Steve and Kathy then answered some questions for Chairman Fisher. Looking deep into Kathy's eyes, Steve said, "They're okay." He fetched a breath. "I'm uneasy about all this."

Kathy squeezed his hand again. "So am I."

They let the moment linger, then joined the others at the big table. When they did, they both smiled.

Fisher said, "Everything in order?"

Kathy said, "Absolutely."

Steve nodded. "Completely under control, sir."

"Good," added the chairman. To Congressman Franklin he said, "Alan, for dessert, I'd like to enjoy one of your fine cigars."

Laughing, the congressman responded, "What about the one I gave you?"

"A treasure, sir—I'm saving it for a special occasion."

"Which is?"

"The moment of your safe return."

Laura Franklin whispered, "Amen ...."

* * * *

HRC-LAB (A) ONE HOUR LATER:

*M*ichael, Kathy, Steve and Hal gathered around a main computer terminal. Steve said, "Remember what I told you about Tex, Hal?"

The professor flexed his nimble fingers. "Let me go in through the keyboard first."

Kathy said, "Try a basic menu access for this year."

Steve chuckled. "Great. Enter this command, Hal. Asterisk, backslash, dash 'Y'."

Dr. Jordan entered the code.

Steve continued. "Now key the digits for this year, two-four-nine-eight."

Hal finished the sequence. They all stared at the screen.

Kathy said, "Press enter."

Hal did.

A smooth, synthesized male voice came from the terminal speakers.

Unauthorized entry attempted.
Access denied.

They all laughed.

Steve entered the same code.

Tex responded,

Good evening, Steve.
How can I be of service?

Several choices were displayed numbered from one to six.

Kathy squeezed Hal's shoulder and said. "Okay, Steve's into the mainframe, now you press four."

Dr. Jordan pressed the digit four.

Tex responded,
> *Unauthorized entry attempted.*
> *Access denied.*

A beep sounded. The screen went black.

Hal muttered, "Damn."

Steve said, "Tex knows my touch, Hal. You struck out"

Dr. Jordan smiled. "The damn thing's prejudiced."

The computer responded.

Only against unauthorized touch. Dr. Jordan.

Michael and Hal jumped and stared at the screen.

Scattered chuckles were heard from other research staff busy at their own nearby terminals.

Hal said, "It knows my name!"

Kathy grinned and offered an explanation. "Tex listens. It heard my voice and Steve's, which it knows. When your name was mentioned, Tex sifted through its files and matched existing data with the name."

Michael spoke up. "I'm Michael Sternfeld, do you know me?"

STANDBY

Tex responded.

I know all about you, Michael Sternfeld.
I know about your wife, Linda Sternfeld.
I'm impressed with the accomplishments
of your son, William Sternfeld.

Michael said, "My God ...."
Steve said, "The computer knows all of you and everything you've done or ever will accomplish. Tex knows the flight crew, Captain Ballard and the others, but only as file data."
Kathy said, "Demonstrate the voice system, Steve."
"Love to."
Dr. Jordan thought a moment. "What about them, Captain Ballard and his people and all the others?"
Fumbling with the computer headset, Steve looked at Kathy and nodded.
Kathy said, "They're part of the twenty-third century, Doctor."
Michael added, "They're not going back are they?"

Kathy shook her head. "No, Michael, they're here to stay."

"I can't believe this."

Adjusting the headset, Steve said, "Let's talk with Tex directly and discuss a few historic events."

They did.

Chapter 29
The Tarkin/Blake Solution

Hangar #24:
FIVE HOURS EARLIER:

*C*ouncilman Larry Cross left hangar #24 and spoke with the security officer at the gate. "My assistant will be here in a few minutes. He needs to see Mr. Tarkin on a matter involving the 747. His ID number is 1025C. He has full access to the hangar on my authority. Let him pass without delay."

The guard wrote down the ID number. "Yes, sir."

"When my assistant comes out lock down the hangar until otherwise ordered."

"Got it. Yes, sir."

"Good, call my office if there's any problem."

* * * *

Charles Tarkin heard footsteps on the stairs. "Did you forget something, Larry?" He looked up to see a tall man in the doorway. "Who are you?"

"Councilman Cross sent me. Have you sealed the box?"

"I sealed it before Larry left, he knew that."

"He just likes to be sure."

"Who the hell are you?"

"Your last vision, I guess." The tall man stabbed Mr. Tarkin in the neck with a syringe and pushed the plunger. "Your job's done, Chuck. Enjoy your heart attack."

* * * *

COUNCILMAN CROSS' OFFICE:
ONE HOUR LATER:

*L*arry's com-console lit up on line five. "Yes?"

"Blake just left the coffee shop from his meeting with Tanner."

"Pull him over and bring him here." He thought a moment. "Take him to my private entrance I don't want him seen."

"What about his craft, sir?"

"Get rid of it, he won't need it anymore."

"It's a nice unit."

"Get rid of the damn thing!"

"Okay, will do."

FORTY-FIVE MINUTES LATER:

*J*eff struggled against the two guards holding him. "What the hell's this about, Cross?"

"Take the cuffs off of him."

"I haven't done a damn thing!"

"Did you have a nice lunch with Frank Tanner?"

"What the hell's that got to do with anything?"

Cross nodded to the two droids. "Make Mr. Blake comfortable."

He was jammed into a chair across from Larry's desk. Jeff said, "All this will make a great story in tomorrow's edition of the Sun!"

"Who's going to write it?"

"I am you sonofabitch!"

"I don't think so." Cross nodded to one of the droids.

The droid grabbed Jeff's right hand and broke two of the young man's fingers.

Jeff screamed in pain. "You bastard!"

Cross took two hits from a tube of Paralayne. "I'm not a mean person, Jeff. Now, tell me about your lunch with Tanner."

The swelling in Jeff's broken fingers was immediate and the pain made him sick. "I knew you were involved with the Garrett thing and I'll publish everything I have!"

"I think not, Mr. Blake." Cross nodded to the other droid. It grabbed Jeff's left hand.

"Wait." Cross poured a drink for himself. "What did you and Mr. Tanner share during your lovely lunch?"

"We talked about an unfortunate explosion that accidentally killed two people." He tried not to move the two broken fingers on his right hand. "That's a story, Cross, an' I intend to report it."

"Perhaps not." Larry nodded to the second droid again. It snapped two fingers on Jeff's left hand.

Jeff fell forward in the chair and vomited on his shoes.

Cross filled his glass and took another hit of Paralayne. "I admire your spunk, Mr. Blake but, I'm afraid it's misplaced." Larry stood and walked around his desk to Jeff's chair. He grabbed Blake's hair and pulled his head back. "Listen to me, you simple jerk." He leaned into Jeff's face. "You took pictures at the explosion site and we have them." Cross shoved Jeff's head forward. "You interviewed a neighbor. We have that recording." Cross shook his head. "Unfortunately, that talkative neighbor has had a fatal accident. The poor man lost his life trying to save Nevil and his girlfriend."

"You're a piece of shit, Cross!"

"And you're a major security risk." He slipped his right hand into a tight black leather glove and backhanded Jeff across the face twice. "You gave copies of your pictures and the interview to Tanner didn't you, Mr. Blake?"

"I had lunch with Tanner, that's not a crime." Pain shot up both arms from his broken fingers. "This little torture-story will make great copy and expose your ass for what you really are."

Cross laughed. "You'll never write the story, Jeff. Tanner won't either. You might think I'm dumb. I assure you, I'm not." He took a five-drop hit of Paralayne and shook his head rapidly. "Damn, that's good stuff!"

Jeff tried to get out of the chair. He grabbed the armrests and the pain from his broken fingers bolted through his arms. "Damn it, Cross you'll you'll pay for this."

Larry nodded toward one of the droids. Jeff was yanked back into the chair and held there. Cross nodded again and said, "Let him sit." He waved the droid away.

Jeff pulled in a deep breath and gathered all the strength he could. "Tanner has what I told him, Cross, and he'll nail your ass to the wall!"

Larry rubbed his chin then took a sip of his drink. "There's a flight leaving for Gray Plan in twenty minutes. If I don't hear what I need to by then you'll be on it."

"I don't know what you want to hear. I gave the pictures and the voice recording to your people. I don't have anything else to tell you."

"You're getting on my nerves, Mr. Blake. You gave Tanner copies of the photos and a copy of the voice recording." He finished his drink and poured another. "You've put Mr. Tanner in jeopardy. How do you feel about that?"

"I'm sure Frank can take care of himself. All he has is what I told him." Jeff's broken fingers were throbbing. The pain showed in his eyes.

Cross nodded to one of the droids. "Break both his thumbs."

The droid grabbed Jeff's left hand.

"Wait! Please!" He jerked his hand away from the droid's grip. The pain was like an electric shock. It blurred his vision.

Cross smiled. "Time for a little truth, Jeff?"

"I sent the pictures and voice files to a secure box on the Sun's global server."

Cross sipped from his glass. "How nice of you to be so cooperative. What's the address and file code?" Larry took an electronic pad out of a desk drawer. "The numbers, Mr. Blake, please."

Jeff rested his broken hands in his lap and winced from the pain of movement. "It's, JB~925~D_26B. That's the code." He felt sick again.

"You know I'm going to access that file right now."

"Have at it you bastard."

Cross keyed in the code and the file came up on his screen. "Excellent. You've done well, Jeff." He nodded to one of the droids. "Break his left thumb for good measure."

Jeff screamed as the bone snapped. He passed out.

* * * *

What Cross didn't know was that the file wasn't the one stored in the paper's database. It was saved in a local file on Jeff's PC. It also required the letters JB when accessed. Without those two letters the file would be deleted instead of opening.

* * * *

Cross took two more hits of Paralayne. He looked at Jeff and spoke to the droids. "Put him on the next garbage shuttle to Saturn. Code him out as tainted meat. Nobody will question it."

"What if he wakes up?"

"Make sure he doesn't."

"He's coming around now, sir."

"Didn't you hear what I just said?"

"I heard."

"Then take care of it."

The droid cupped Jeff's chin and grabbed the back of the young man's head. He gave a quick twist and Jeff's neck *snapped.*

Cross took another sip from his drink. "That pretty well does it."

Chapter 30
The Passengers

3:30 PM July 16, 2498
THE MEDICAL WING:
Dr. Gregory Rankin's Office:

"*A*rlene, would you put me through to Fisher on priority red?"

"Right away, Doctor." With her usual efficiency, Rankin's assistant keyed in the doctor's private code.

While waiting for the Chairman, Greg studied the passenger list on his transparent monitor. The key subjects and the cockpit crew had been processed. So far there hadn't been any serious problem. That could change fast.

"Mr. Chairman, thank you for taking my call."

"Is there any problem?"

"My team has brought fifty *select* passengers out of sedation. They're individuals who were traveling alone and their anxiety is more intense than we expected."

"I had an idea this might happen." Fisher pinched the bridge of his nose and thought a moment. "Greg, I'm afraid we have to use the quarantine scenario."

"That's why I called, sir. I need your approval to even consider that option."

"You have my authorization completely. Those people must all be made to believe that they're in 1998 and have been exposed to some toxin."

Dr Rankin stared at the long list of names on his screen. "I suggest we handle them as a group and conduct bogus examinations and treat them with harmless medications."

"Exactly, be creative, Greg. I'm sure you have the imagination to pull it off."

Dr. Rankin took a long breath. "I can, sir and with the help of my staff, we can make it work." He hesitated then asked the profound question. "Mr. Chairman, when do I tell them they're not going home?"

"Honestly, I can't answer that question

right now. We have time on our side. For the moment do what you can to make all those people comfortable. We have the necessary facilities to deal with all their needs. It's in your hands, Greg."

Dr. Rankin took another short breath. "Housing is an issue. Two hundred-twenty odd people cannot be jammed into a common ward."

Fisher thought a moment then chuckled. "It's summer, Greg. The UWC University dorms are empty. Put up our guests in private rooms."

"With outside access?"

"Yes, let them have the run of the campus. It's an excellent idea!"

"They may see things."

"What? Maybe a hover-craft? If they ask, explain it to them."

"It can work."

"Great, make it happen." The Chairman terminated the call. He shouted to Sophy. "Get me a list of all the other passengers on that damn seven-forty-seven!"

Part Three
the human
element

Chapter 31
A Change of Plans

TANNER HAS SECOND THOUGHTS:

*L*ess than a mile from the *New Star*, Frank decided to take route 95 south instead of the express tube. The choice meant sixty miles of manual driving and about twenty minutes for the trip to *Schurz*. Farrah was waiting at his place. Not a good idea.

He called her on his personal cyber-line. He needed time to sort things out. Farrah answered on the third tone.

"Is this the one and only Frank Tanner?"

"It is, Ms. Wonderful. We have a change of plans."

"An' that would be what?"

"Go to your place. I'm headed there now."

"Is there a problem?"

"Not yet. I'll see you in about twenty minutes."

"Okay, Mr. Newspaper, I'll be there."

"Do you have to use that phrase?"

"When I heard Mackendrick say it, I thought it fit quite well." Farrah had a good chuckle.

"You could get yourself spanked for that."

"Are you making a promise?"

"Just get to your place safe and sound."

"There is a problem. I hear it in your voice."

"I don't want to say anything right now. Not on a remote transmission."

"Understood. You want me to shut everything down here?"

"I think that's a wise idea. I'll see you in about fifteen minutes."

"Frank … be careful."

"I always am. Get going."

His thoughts were incomplete. He needed to process what he'd learned from Mackendrick and Khrismann. For some reason, any mention of *Time Gate* seemed dangerous at the moment.

Frank turned off the access ramp to the south bound express tube and drove onto the 95 highway. There would be virtually no traffic to deal with and he would have time to sort through the facts of what he had suspected, and now *knew* existed.

He keyed the vehicle from *auto-standby* to *manual-locked*. A female computer-voice, which he had special ordered to match Farrah's, whispered, *Manual override engaged. Have a good trip.*

Frank smiled at the sound of the voice. He slipped his vehicle into surface flight two and set the control for one hundred ten miles per hour though two hundred was the posted limit. He needed the extra time.

* * * *

The High-speed Interstate Transit System Monorail (HITSM) ran above the north and south bound Interstate Auto Express Tubes (IAET) and paralleled highway 95 all the way to Old Vegas. There they branched into monorails and tubes that spider-webbed the entire United States.

* * * *

Farrah lived in Complex 22000. It was on the northern tip of Walker Lake, outside the town of Schurz. Frank lived in the town of Walker Lake itself, developed two-hundred years ago. Walker Lake was the home of the Nevada Sun. Frank didn't like living in complex communities. He preferred an apartment in the city. The luxury cost twice as much as a complex unit and was usually two or more years in the getting.

Tanner studied the road in front of him and beyond the beams of the vehicle's headlights. He focused his thoughts on the black infinity.

Time Gate. A hole in the universe. It exists. What a discovery. Dear old Harry Fellin thought so too. Dear Harry's dead!

"Jesus!" Frank snapped out of his wonder and remembered the look in Mackendrick's eyes when Mack told him he would have the story of his career.

"Frank, you're an ass." He spoke to the vehicle's interior. "They're not gonna let you publish the details of Time Gate. Not on your life!"

He popped open the center compartment between the front seats and took out his voice recorder. Simultaneously, he keyed the computer in the dashboard console.

Farrah's soft voice asked, *What can I do for you, love?* Despite his sudden fear of impending doom, he grinned at the sultry electronic tones. He keyed V/A *voice activate* and began.

"Transmit to the Sun mainframe through my

code, FT-35 imbedded sequence nine, all of the following verbal data." He switched on his hand-held personal voice recorder and cleared his throat. "Verbal data feed FT-35-nine begin."

Farrah's duplicated voice responded. *Voice line open. Voice Data-send ready.*

Frank transmitted and recorded every detail of his meeting with Khrismann and Mackendrick to the memory of the Sun's master computer. Every word was scrambled and coded and could only be accessed by himself or someone who knew the command sequence. Farrah had that information.

When he finished the data-send Frank said, "Add blue security lockout."

The computer responded. *Data stored. Lockout activated.*

"Thank you, sweetheart. The real you will soon be involved in this shit right up to her lovely, little, round ass."

A lighted sign appeared out of the black void:
EXIT 26 SCHURZ & COMPLEX 22000

Frank drove by and headed to Farrah's place.

Chapter 32
CL-15 the Clone Process

THE GENETIC RESEARCH LAB:
Two hours earlier:

$\mathcal{F}$or the past hour and a half, Jerry Zanster, Science Advisor for the United World Council, had patiently answered questions from Dr. Hal Jordan and Michael Sternfeld. Polite at first, he now seemed irritated, impatient. He looked at Ms. Simmons. "Is there anything more?"

Kathy said, "That rests with Michael."

Young Sternfeld thought a moment. "Is this the work of my son?"

Without emotion, Zanster said, "I don't know your son. The CL-15 process is the result of genetic engineering conducted by a Dr. William Sternfeld less than five-hundred years ago. Dr. Sternfeld made the breakthrough. Others followed his theories and the process became workable with human cells."

Steve and Kathy looked at each other. They shared concern with Zanster's uncharacteristic curtness. Steve said, "Do you realize how Michael might feel about the way you're putting things?"

"Yes, I do. Excuse my directness, but I'm not convinced CL-15 should ever be employed. In my heart, I wish the process had never been developed."

Hal sensed irritation from Steve and Kathy. "Pardon me, Dr. Zanster, but I'm surprised a man of your advanced scientific knowledge would disagree with such a breakthrough."

Jerry responded flatly. "I'm against the way the process is being used." He got off his stool and gestured toward the microscope monitor. "You're looking at a clear-cut scientific fact here. It's fascinating and exciting." He pointed at the monitor, and studied the four people in front of him, he raised his voice. "Have you, Michael or you, Dr. Jordan ever seen or dealt with a cloned animal?"

They shook their heads.

Kathy said, "Where are you going with this, Jerry?" She was getting upset.

"Stay with me and you'll see."

Several of the staff looked up from their work stations.

Dr. Zanster took a ring of small, plastic rectangles from the right pocket of his lab coat. They were all the same size and each a different color.

Kathy said, "This isn't necessary—"

"It is indeed. Follow me."

The four of them walked behind Zanster, Steve pleaded, "Jerry, we know the pressure you're under, but I don't think these people should be exposed to anything further."

"I do." He turned right between a row of lab tables and headed toward the far end of the large laboratory. "Mr. Sternfeld, Dr. Jordan, prepare to get educated."

Kathy said, "Jerry, please."

"I'll be selective, Ms. Simmons."

Steve ordered, "You damn-well better be." He caught Dr. Jordan's grin as the four of them followed the chief science officer.

Zanster stopped at a set of oversized double doors. The words *RESTRICTED ENTRY* in blood red were printed across the doors. He inserted a red plastic card into a slot to the right of the door frame. An electronic lock released. Jerry pulled the door open and stepped aside.

The party walked through. Steve said, "I'm warning you, Jerry."

Zanster stepped ahead of Steve and Kathy. "One more gate," he said, and selected a yellow plastic card.

They were in a shallow, antiseptic-smelling, stark-white corridor. The only contrast was another large, wood door. It was imprinted with the words, *OBSERVATION CELLS.* Jerry inserted the card into another slot. The lock *snapped* open. He stepped in and held the door for the others. They entered a narrow hall and faced three levels of heavily-tinted glass enclosures. They couldn't see into any of the compartments. To the right of each glass square, about twenty-four inches on all sides, was another electronic slot, each in a different color.

Hal thought of the time he and his daughter went to the animal shelter to find a replacement for her dead kitten.

Michael was reminded of the pet store where he and Linda bought Kelsey, their miniature poodle.

Unable to hide her anger or avoid notice by Michael and Hal, Kathy said, "Jerry, you better have a responsible motive here or I promise you a serious reprimand."

Dr. Zanster inserted a green plastic card into the lock-slot of a mid-level enclosure and let the ring hang free. He said, "Chairman Fisher gave me a full briefing on these people and the importance of this mission. I'm supervising the cloning of two-hundred and twenty-three human beings. That number has never been attempted before."

Dr. Jordan said, "Why is there so much tension and anger here?"

Steve said, "You shouldn't be this far in Doctor—"

"Yes he should be, Michael, and the rest have a right." He looked at Jordan, then Sternfeld and continued. "The five of you are going back. The others aren't."

Michael said, "We know that, Doctor."

Jerry grinned without humor. "What do you suppose will take the place of the other passengers on your five-hundred year old jetliner—sandbags?"

Hal said, "Genetic copies."

"Clones, Dr. Jordan—human meat!"

Kathy said, "Jerry—stop this."

Steve shouted. "Anymore, Zanster and I file a full report with Fisher." He reached for the ring of plastic keys.

Jerry grabbed his hand and glared at him.

Dr. Jordan held up his hands and cut in. "Stop! Both of you. Now just calm down." He glanced at Michael who had become pale. Hal lowered his voice and went on. "I, for one, want to know what Dr. Zanster's trying to say, and is damn-well afraid of." To Michael he said, "What about you? If anybody's close to the center of this you are."

Michael mumbled, "Dr. Jordan, I operate a small camera store. Linda and I have a simple life in a simple town. Everything that's happened since we woke up is science fiction— I'm lost."

"Are you afraid to know?"

"No ... dammit, I guess not."

Hal said, "Good. Dr. Zanster, please continue."

The faint sound of a dog's whimper and soft scratching was heard. A muffled cat-cry came from behind a lower glass door. A low, wet, guttural response—distant and painful, drifted into the hallway. It seemed to come from the far end, behind the uppermost panel. Dr. Jordan and Michael turned in that direction to see a red light blinking above the slot-lock.

Steve and Kathy met each other's eyes and shook their heads in disapproval.

Dr. Zanster opened the mid-level compartment.

Michael and Hal grinned from ear to ear.

Chapter 33
The Presence of Danger

FARRAH'S PLACE:

$\mathcal{F}$rank wrote his access code on a slip of paper:

$$FT\text{-}35\text{-}9$$

He handed it to Farrah. "It's new. The one you know is no longer valid. I changed it earlier."

Her hand shook as she studied the letters and numbers.

"Don't even whisper it. Put it in your head and never forget it." He walked across the oval living room to the service bar of the automated kitchen.

Farrah remained on the peach, magnetic sofa. She stared at the paper. "I'm scared to death."

"We'll have to share that, I guess." He poured another Jacobs, and without looking at her, he said, "Don't move your lips either."

"What?"

"Don't mouth the sequence like you do when you read something to yourself."

She got up from the sofa leaving it suspended above the floor. "You've noticed how I do that?"

He slid himself onto a stool that, like all the furniture in the unit, was magnetically suspended. "I've created a mental file of what I call, "Farrah's quirks and warts, they're cute." He held out his iced glass. "Want a sip?"

She nodded and drank from his glass. "I don't have warts." She chuckled and had another sip.

He took the paper from her and shredded it. "Your biggest wart is me." He dropped the bits of paper in the waste disintegrator built into the counter.

She handed back his Jacobs, leaned on his thighs and smiled. "Occasionally you are an ass, but I've never seen you as a wart." She bit his left earlobe playfully and blew into his ear.

An electric tingle crept through Frank's loins as if he had just settled into a hot bath. He touched her forehead with the icy glass. "What else have you put away in one of those secret drawers you have up there?"

"It's all about the Frank Tanner I know and nobody else does."

"Don't say or even dream what I just gave you."

"This is not the office. Can't we be safe here?"

"People like Mackendrick, Cross—and even their damn droids have monitoring devices we couldn't imagine. For all I know, this disintegrator could be wired to re-assemble the code and send it to Tex." He looked beyond Farrah, across the peach and dark blue room, out through the expansive tinted windows into the desert night. "I would give anything to keep you out of this."

"I wouldn't let you." She sat beside him and moved her stool closer. She kissed his cheek. "I had to become part of it sooner or later. Think about it, Mr. Newspaper."

"I hate that."

"I loved it when Mack said it. I could just see you gritting your teeth." She rested her head against his shoulder. A soft flutter came into her voice. "Frank ... I'm afraid."

"Yeah ...." He kissed the top of her head and inhaled the fresh scent of her hair. "You smell nice."

"Better than the *Pay n' Play* droids?"

Frank chuckled. "Than the what?"

"I know about the attractions at the New Star. Don't shit me." She pulled away, slipped off her stool and stood in front of him with her hands planted against her exquisite hips. Her dark blue dressing gown parted at her upper left thigh displaying one long shapely leg. "Did the fake bitch smell good too?"

"I don't know. I didn't get close enough."

"Did the thing look as good as me?"

"Not even close."

"You thought about it didn't you?"

"What?"

"Getting it on."

"Crossed my mind."

"How could you?" She shook her hair back. Her cheeks flushed. She was playing a game. They both knew the rules. The thought excited her.

"How could I what?" Frank filled his glass from the iced bottle of Jacobs.

"Make it with a droid-bitch." Farrah tossed

her hair again, letting long strands fall across the right side of her face. "You're sick." She shifted her hips and let one hand slide down along her left thigh.

"I heard they're better than real women. They'll do anything." He unbuttoned his shirt.

"I'll do anything." She stroked her neck and brushed her hair back over her shoulder.

"Oh yeah. Like what?" Frank threw back his drink and grinned.

"Anything you could ever dream up. More than you can handle." She smiled at him and licked her lips.

"I have a vivid imagination." He pulled his shirt out of his trousers.

"Would you take one?" Farrah moved her right hand slowly over the curve of her substantial breasts.

"A female droid?"

"Yes."

"No."

"Why?" She shifted her weight again, moved like liquid and strummed her left thigh with her long fingers.

"Because I'd rather have you." His breath quickened. He slid off the stool and moved toward Farrah.

"Make love to me now, Frank."

He eased her down onto the dark blue

carpet between the living room and the service counter.

A hot wind danced across the huge tinted glass. It cried a mournful song. It was a tune Frank tried not to hear.

Chapter 34
Trial & Error

THE CLONING LAB – EARLIER:

*M*ichael and Dr. Jordan bent forward, shoulder to shoulder and looked into the mid-level compartment. Michael said, "Linda would love him."

A brown and white beagle pup tried to lick Hal's hand through wire mesh. "Hi there, little guy." Hal stuck two fingers through the wire and let the dog have a good lick.

Jerry Zanster said, "Tandy's four months old. He was cloned yesterday." He glanced at Steve and Kathy to catch their irritated expressions.

Hal stepped away from the cage to give Michael a closer look. To Zanster he said, "Yesterday?"

Jerry nodded. "We can accelerate the growth process to any life-stage. In Tandy's case, science stops here." Dr. Zanster lifted the catch on the wire screen. To Michael he said, "Take him out if you like. He loves attention."

Steve and Kathy were nervous. They had no authority over Dr. Zanster. Cloning and genetic research were his departments. The lab was his. He answered only to Chairman Fisher. However, Steve and Kathy *were* in charge of *Time-Gate* projects. Michael, Jordan and the others were their responsibility. As they saw it, Jerry Zanster was going too far.

Michael played with the puppy.

Hal was filling up with questions. He asked, "Why four months, Doctor?"

Steve cut in. "I'm afraid that's classified."

Jerry shook his head. "Not for these people. We need their cooperation and trust."

"That's enough!" Kathy was angry. "The less they know, the easier it will be for all of us."

Dr. Jordan waved his hand to stop the argument. "On the contrary, Ms. Simmons. Existing circumstances give us a great deal of responsibility. Speaking for myself—"

"Is there a problem here?" Chairman Fisher

stood in the doorway. He nodded at Michael and Hal. "Jerry?"

"It's a question of security, sir. I don't feel it applies in their case." He gestured toward the guests.

Michael put Tandy back in the compartment and hooked the wire gate. Tandy whimpered and pawed the mesh.

Fisher tapped his chin. "Steve, Kathy?"

Palmer cleared his throat. "I think Dr. Zanster's going too far."

"Hal, when I came in you were about to make a point. Please continue."

Dr. Jordan scratched his head and smiled. "Personally, I insist on knowing everything Jerry can tell me."

"And you, Michael?" Fisher cocked his head and listened.

"To be honest, sir," he looked down at the puppy, "I'm pretty well overloaded right now. I'd just as soon let it rest until Linda and I are back where we belong." He pushed a finger through the wire and let Tandy have another lick.

"How far have you gone so far, Jerry?"

"Growth acceleration."

"I don't believe Dr. Jordan is a security risk. Kathy, you, Steve and I can escort Michael to his quarters. That's why I came up here." He nodded to Michael. "Sophy's with Linda now but your wife would rather be with you."

"I'm ready." He rubbed his finger on Tandy's wet nose one last time.

The chairman looked at Jordan again. "The puppy's story is a happy one, Hal." He glanced at the blinking red light on the cell in the far corner. "There are projects in this lab that are unfortunate. Once you've seen them, I promise, you won't forget them for the rest of your life."

"I'll take the bad with the good." He grinned."

Muffled scratching and a murmur came from the far compartment.

Kathy shuddered. "Michael, we can wait for Chairman Fisher in the lab." She glanced at Dr. Zanster with disapproval. Michael left the hall ahead of her and Steve.

Fisher patted Jerry's shoulder. "Dr. Zanster will take you to your quarters when you're through." He looked down at Tandy, the puppy continued to beg for attention. "Someday we may all have a second chance." He stuck two fingers through the wire. The puppy's wet tongue went into immediate action, right in time with its wagging tail. "Welcome back, little friend." He gripped Jerry's arm. "Congratulations, your project grant has been extended. I signed the papers this morning."

Jerry's face lit up.

"Thank you, sir."

They shook hands. Fisher slapped Jerry on the back and smiled. "That was another reason I came up here. I wanted to tell you face to face. You and your people are doing a great job."

"Thank you again, Mr. Chairman." He thought a moment and added, "And thank the council, Cross lost the bid for second seat."

"Sophy keeps telling me the same thing." He nodded at Jordan. "These five people are priority one right now, so let's give them our best."

"Absolutely." Jerry's attitude had turned around in the tick of fifteen seconds.

"Hal, we'll talk tomorrow. Good night gentlemen."

"Tomorrow, Mr. Chairman."

"Good night, sir." Jerry opened the wire screen again and let Tandy out onto the floor.

Hal hunkered down and petted the excited puppy. "What did Fisher mean when he said, *welcome back* to the dog?"

"Since you want to know everything, that's where we'll start. Zanster squatted opposite the Professor and shared Tandy's playful energy. "As I told you, this little pooch was cloned yesterday."

"And you said he's four months old." Tandy stole licks, rubs and heavenly attention from both men as they talked.

"The cloning is really nothing. We do that as general routine." He watched Hal rub the dog's ears and let it lick his face. "Tandy died four months ago."

Hal stopped playing with the dog and stared straight at Jerry. "Died?"

"If I remember correctly, he was about twenty years old. Eighteen at least."

The professor shifted his eyes to Tandy and watched him pawing playfully at Jerry's knee. "This dog was dead?"

"Yes and no." Dr. Zanster changed his position and picked up the puppy. "The original Tandy is in dog heaven. As you can see, the new Tandy is doing just fine." He let the puppy lick his chin.

"I'm sorry, Jerry. I don't see. We haven't gotten into the growth-thing and I'm lost on square one."

"We've been involved in aging research since before my time. Through drugs and genetic research, we've extended the lives of laboratory animals by a factor of eight."

Hal stood. Both knees popped. He scratched his head, as he often did when perplexed, he started pacing the narrow hall. "Wait a second, let me put it together." He turned sharply and faced Jerry. "Something else—you said, *heaven.*"

"I did, yes." Tandy darted away from Dr. Zanster and went after Hal's shoes.

"Excuse me, Dr. I get a clear message that any kind of religious reference is frowned upon."

"Yes again—but not by me. That's another story." He got to his feet. His knees did not pop. "We'll be up all night at this rate."

"I don't give a damn." Hal squeezed his temples and thought hard. Tandy yipped and battled the professor's shoelaces. "Okay, forget the religion-thing for now. Science, in my time, has lengthened human life but not by eight times!"

"Hal, relax." Jerry reached into his lab coat and brought out a treat for Tandy. The puppy gave up Dr. Jordan's shoe and chewed on his prize. "We have a few research animals coming in here you wouldn't recognize."

Hal tilted his head and blinked. "Like?"

Dr. Zanster leaned down with another treat for the dog. "They're Life-forms that evolved from early genetic experiments. The work went wrong because of irresponsibility."

In the moment of quiet, scratching and whimpering could be heard toward the end of the long white corridor.

Jordan listened. He shivered. "There's one of those in there?"

"Yes, a clone. It was supposed to be another *second chance.* It's my error and I live with it every day."

"Get on with Tandy." Hal turned his back to the uppermost cage.

"You want detailed forensics?"

Tandy had sniffed out the source of goodies. Jerry gave him two more and waited for Dr. Jordan to respond.

"No, just plain language, please. I'm a scientist, but not in your area." He leaned against the glass panels then suddenly moved away.

Jerry hooked his thumbs into his belt and rested his back against the opposite wall. "I performed the procedure and CL-fifteen process myself."

"Slow and simple please."

"I took several cell samples from different areas of the original dog then put him to sleep." Zanster cleared his throat.

Hal looked down at the yawning puppy. It let out a contented sigh and rested his head on crossed forepaws. Tandy was tired, safe and happy. "You put him to sleep."

"Yes, the dog was never in any pain."

"Go on." Dr. Jordan remembered the death of his daughter's kitten. He shook his head.

Jerry continued, "I isolated the healthiest cell and froze the others."

"Similar work is being done in my time." Hal paced and listened. He glanced, occasionally, toward the muffled scratching sounds.

"Hal, what I'm going to tell you cannot be known by the Sternfelds."

"I understand."

"Back in 2250 a group of medical doctors and genetic research scientists made an important breakthrough." He tugged on his right earlobe and grinned. "They enhanced the CL-15 cloning process to a higher rate of acceleration."

Dr. Jordan puzzled a moment. "So, Michael an' Linda's unborn child will make all this possible?

"Without William Sternfeld's research we wouldn't be anywhere close to where we are now." Jerry looked down at the puppy. "Just ten years ahead of your time, cell research took a major step forward. In 2008, a privately-funded program made it possible to clone human organs."

Hal bent down to retie the shoe laces that Tandy had pulled loose. "I can see big moral issues being involved with that."

"There were, in your case, will be. However, the research paved the way to save thousands of lives. Despite the political and moral issues, the procedure is common practice in 2498." Dr. Zanster chuckled. "It's become a multi-billion-dollar insurance industry. In a sense, people are paying to live longer."

Dr. Jordan stood. "That cloning process came before William Sternfeld and must've worked in his favor."

"Absolutely. Dr. Sternfeld's work was based on the 2008 breakthrough. He developed the CL-15 process and the rest is history."

Hal glanced toward the blinking red light at the end of the corridor. There hadn't been any sound from that area in several minutes. "I'm thinking about my contribution to all of this."

Dr. Zanster moved away from the wall. "Yes, Stephen Russell. His energy research and development formed the basis of the power-source we now take for granted." He patted Hal's shoulder. "You will help Stephen accomplish what must be done."

Hal drew in a deep breath. "Forgive me for being a bit confused." He gestured toward the contented puppy. "It appears you've managed to extend life and create new life."

"We've managed to eliminate most strains

of virus through advanced medical technology. Aids ceased to exist in 2021. Cancer, of all kinds, was eliminated in 2029." The flashing red light played across Dr. Zanster's face. What's the expected life in the twentieth century--seventy-eight, eighty-five?"

"Roughly, give or take. It depends on the person and many other factors."

"Genetics, right?"

"Yes, definitely." Dr. Jordan felt the sweep of red light. Wet, guttural sounds sent a chill up his spine.

"The life expectancy in twenty-four-ninety-eight is about one-hundred-thirty-to one-hundred-forty-years. Again, it depends on several factors."

"Jerry, would you mind if we went back to your office? I'd like to sit down."

"Sure. I'll order a snack and a bottle of red wine that vintners in 1998 would kill for."

"Great. I do want to come back here, but at the moment, I got the creeps." He looked down at Tandy. "What about him?"

"Let's take him with us."

Hal bent over and picked up the drowsy puppy. "C'mon, little guy. I think you need to get away from here for a while too."

The wood door made an empty, hollow sound when it closed. Hal turned back and thought he heard a painful cry rise as the door slammed shut.

* * * *

A pleasant, young female lab assistant delivered a small tray of various seafood sandwiches and a chilled bottle of a rich red wine to Jerry's private office. She said, "Enjoy your snack, gentlemen."

Dr. Zanster smiled. "Thank you, Paula."

"Jerry, if I understand you correctly, you created Tandy from a cell of the dying dog through the CL-15 process."

"I did just that." He helped himself to a small sea food sandwich. "It's a routine procedure." He took a bite and poured some wine for himself and Dr. Jordan. "It's not an instant result, Hal." He sat back in his desk chair. "The cell was processed in a CL-15 capsule for a period of four minutes. Each minute represents one month of growth."

Hal fetched a sandwich from the tray. "Let me see if I'm following you." He took a bite. "In a period of four minutes the cell from the parent dog became the new puppy?"

"Exactly. A new life, a *second chance.*"

Dr. Jordan scratched Tandy's neck. "That's what Fisher meant when he said, welcome back."

Jerry sipped some wine and thought for a moment. "We're not completely sure yet. However, tests have indicated that, Tandy has retained the complete intellect of the adult dog."

Hal lifted the puppy's chin and looked into its sleepy eyes. "All of it?"

"We believe so."

Hal scratched Tandy behind the ears. "I can't imagine what must be running through his little mind."

"He has at least eighteen years of life he hasn't experienced." Jerry selected another small sandwich.

Hal looked at the puppy, then at Jerry. "From what you said to Ms. Simmons, you're not sure about cloning all the other passengers."

"The number of people to process will require every member of my staff. Each of them will clone and monitor the process of a number of male and female cell cultures." He took another swallow of wine. "It's never been done on such a scale." He hesitated. "We don't want any intellect to be developed from the parent cell to the clone."

Hal sat up straight. "I think I know why."

"I would guess you've been told."

"Our plane isn't going to land safely. However, the Sternfelds, Franklin, Laura and I will make it through some suspension process."

Dr. Zanster rubbed the stubble on his chin. "You will, Hal. It's already a fact."

"You don't want the clones to be aware." Hal shook his head. "Dear, God ... I hope you're right."

Jerry poured a little more wine for both of them. "We have an eighty-five percent chance of success. The odds would be better if we weren't pushing the CL-15 acceleration. That's where we encounter the risk."

Jordan felt Tandy's wet nose poking at his hand. "Hey, guy. You can have it." He let the puppy take the last bite of the small sandwich. To Dr. Zanster he said, "Less acceleration, less risk."

"Exactly. We clone humans for specific purposes." He hesitated. "Let's say we have a young man who's an expert in a useful area involving advanced physics."

Hal nodded. "Like me." He laughed.

"Like you." Jerry grinned. "We get his signed permission, take a cell sample and clone him."

"You get permission?" He stroked the soft fur of Tandy's neck.

"To do otherwise would be considered immoral."

Dr. Jordan nodded. "I'm impressed."

"The clone is assigned elsewhere, often to another country and the two never see each other."

"Excuse me?" Hal rubbed his chin. "The clone is a full adult?"

Dr. Zanster chuckled and selected another sandwich. "I'm truly pleased that we've been able to meet and share such a great time. Dr. Jordan, you're an absolute delight."

Hal grinned. "I'm flattered." He took a sip of wine. "I may have missed something." He cleared his throat. "A full adult, human clone is possible in a short time?"

Jerry smiled, clasped his hands behind his head and leaned back in his chair. "Time is relative, Hal. There's no deadline or reason to force the process. We can take all the time necessary to perfect the resulting clone." He put his feet up on the corner of his desk. "I like to go at the rate of one day for one year of maturity. Thirty days gives us a thirty-year-old clone and so on."

Hal adjusted Tandy on his lap. The pup wagged its tail. "Okay, I get it. The problem is forced acceleration. Am I right?"

Dr. Zanster pulled his feet off the desk and leaned forward. "You're on the money, Hal. That's the danger of cloning the other passengers, the way we have to do it." He poured another glass of wine. "We'll do it—we have to."

"What about the errors, Jerry? Tell me."

Dr. Zanster grabbed another sandwich, bit into it and poured himself a little more wine. "All of our clone projects are conducted with healthy subjects. There's never any question." He took a sip.

"Maybe I shouldn't have asked."

Jerry shook his head. "No, you need to know." He drained his glass.

Hal whispered, "It's between you and me."

"Thank you. However, it's a matter of record."

Dr. Jordan leaned back and petted Tandy. "I'm listening."

Jerry poured another glass of wine and drank two good swallows. "Prior to my success with Tandy I wanted to try the process with a human."

Hal petted the puppy. "The *second chance.* I'm starting to grasp what you had in mind."

Dr. Zanster shook his head. "A dear friend of mine was dying and I wanted to save him." He swallowed another gulp of wine. "I attempted to clone him at the moment of his death." He shook his head. "I should've known better. That was my foolish mistake."

Hal felt Jerry's anguish. "You couldn't save him?"

Dr. Zanster studied the puppy on Hal's lap. "I saved him." His voice cracked. "He got his *second chance.*"

Hal thought of the blinking red light and the sounds he had heard. "He's still with us isn't he?"

"I'm afraid so." Dr. Zanster shuddered and took another drink. "Even if I dispose of my mistake he'll be with me as long as I live."

Hal spoke just above a whisper. "What went wrong?"

"I went wrong." Jerry leaned forward and petted Tandy's head. The dog's tail flipped back and forth. "About eight months ago I jumped the gun and thought I knew enough to perform the *second chance* procedure on human cells." He looked at the pup. "I ordered my friend, John Morgan, moved to my lab. He was dying from an accidental exposure to raycron vapors. It's a toxic fluid used to dissolve rock." He closed his eyes and drew a long breath. "Building new cities ... that was John's total focus."

Hal squeezed Zanster's arm. "You don't need to go into all this."

"Yes, I do." He gripped Hal's hand. "Everybody here agreed, John's exposure was not any kind of *disease* so the process should work. We failed to realize the cells were contaminated and could mutate."

Hal met Zanster's eyes. "I'm sorry."

"The result of what I did to Mr. Morgan confirms my belief in forming a new congregation."

Hal let Jerry's information sift through his racing mind. After a moment he looked up. "You intend to start a church?"

Jerry poured the last of the wine for both of them. "It will be a whole *new* religion. No specific denomination. My guess is, this new faith will spread like a plague and put some sense back into our society."

Hal smiled. "It sounds like a great idea." He lifted his glass. "Here's to your congregation." He took a sip. "Why haven't you done this before now?"

Dr. Zanster sat back, grinned and shook his head. "It took the horror of what I did to John to bring *me* to my senses." He grabbed one of the last two sandwiches off the tray.

"We all make mistakes, Jerry. I'm sure I'll make a few more before I meet my maker."

Dr. Zanster smiled. "You're a delight, Hal. I haven't had such a great conversation with anybody in a long time."

"Thank you, doctor. I assure you, the pleasure is mine. I'd give anything to take you back to the university and let you lecture to a hall full of my students." He took the last sandwich from the tray. "You'd be the most sought after scientist on the planet."

Dr. Zanster chuckled. "If I brought Mr. Morgan along your students would run from the hall in a panic."

Hal finished his sandwich. "I think they'd trample each other just to get your autograph."

"Not after they saw my friend." Jerry cleared his throat. "What happened with John opens the door to the existence of a divine presence."

Dr. Jordan thought a moment, scratched Tandy's neck and smiled. "There's no question of that, Jerry."

"This is basically a Godless society." Jerry's nostrils flared as he spoke.

"No religion at all?" Tandy stirred and sighed again.

"Some—mostly tolerated, plastic bullshit!"

"No churches?"

"Same crap. Leftover buildings serving a make-believe government position of free thinking." Zanster's glare intensified.

There were no windows in Dr. Zanster's office, but Hal felt the presence of monitoring eyes. "Why are you so upset and angry about it?"

"I'm a man of God. That's why!"

"So am I—"

"I know. That's why I'm sharing it with you!" Dr. Zanster relaxed, leaned back, took a long breath.

Not sure of what it was all about, Hal swallowed hard and absently petted Tandy. "I don't see the connection."

"Hal, listen to what I'm about to say. I pray you'll understand. No one in this time does." There was an audible *click* in Dr. Zanster's throat as he continued. "Every human clone we've processed has been healthy and the results have been perfect. They weren't *dying.*" He nodded and pointed toward Tandy. "The parent subject of little Tandy there *was* dying." He drew a short breath. "I cloned him at the moment of death and gave him a second chance—a *second life.*"

"It didn't work with Mr. Morgan." Hal shuddered.

"It worked all right—John has a *second life.* He's a living horror!"

"What went wrong?" Hal shifted in his chair and finished his wine.

Dr Zanster pinched the bridge of his nose and blinked back tears. "My little experiment trapped John's soul between life and death. I can't change that." He shook his head and drew a deep breath. "I suspended my dear friend's soul between heaven and hell!"

"You made an error, Jerry. I'm frightened at the thought of such a thing." Hal shook "What about the other passengers going back on our plane?"

Jerry laughed. "Don't worry about it. I've been instructed to stop the CL-15 process at level eight. They will be nothing more than human shells. No feeling, no intellect."

"You can do that?"

"Starting tomorrow morning I'll be doing just that."

"There's an open issue here, Jerry." Hal leaned forward and disturbed the puppy. "What's going to happen to the people who won't be going back?"

"According to my information they will be placed into communities across the United States and abroad. They will all be well cared for."

Hal sat back. He grinned and nodded. "You're hiding something, doctor. What might that be?"

"Can I trust you, Hal?"

"To the MAX!"

"I'm going to double-clone each of the passengers." He rubbed his chin. "It must be done while I have these new subjects."

Hal sat back, took a breath and stroked the puppy. "This will be your *new* congregation?" He grinned.

Jerry stood. "You approve?"

Hal laughed. "Are you kidding? I think it's

the best thing that could happen."

Dr. Zanster slapped his forehead then gripped the back of his chair. "I've prayed for this opportunity for more than twenty years." He rubbed his eyes. "An accidental incident has made it possible."

Hal petted Tandy. "Maybe it's not an accident."

Dr. Zanster looked at Hal for a moment. "Would you like to meet my friend, John?"

"I think I have to ...."

"Bring the dog. We'll go back to the cages."

Tandy stirred without coming fully awake. The puppy licked Dr. Jordan's hands as he was lifted from the man's lap. Tandy was in a pleasant dream. His mind was full of running and chasing he had not done. He was attracted by odors he had never smelled. He was enveloped in memories born before his own time. Tandy was happy and how didn't matter.

Chapter 35
RECOMBINANT DNA

THE MORGAN EXPERIMENT:

$\mathcal{D}$r. Zanster and Hal Jordan returned to the observation cages with Tandy. Jerry opened the dog's cage and saw a lab worker standing at the opposite end of the corridor. "David."

The lab-man chuckled and looked at Hal and Tandy. "So there you are."

Zanster smiled. "We had him out for a while."

"I figured as much. He has to have a spinal before tomorrow's testing." David took Tandy from Dr. Jordan. "C'mon, pup." Tandy licked the man's face and glanced back at Hal one last time.

Jerry looked at David. "Have you checked Mr. Morgan?"

"Yes. That's the first thing I do every night. I want that experience behind me as soon as possible." The puppy resisted until David gave him a treat.

"I understand. Is he approachable?"

"Mr. Morgan responds to you, Jerry. He barely tolerates the rest of us."

"Thank you." Dr. Zanster held Tandy's compartment open while David put the puppy in and secured the cage.

Hal puzzled. "Why does Tandy need a spinal and tests?"

Jerry stepped away from the wall of cages and glanced toward the blinking, red light. "We monitor amino acids in his spinal fluid as well as cell membrane development." Zanster looked back at Dr. Jordan and thought a moment. "Somehow, the growth-acceleration process thickens the membrane and reduces aging. We don't know why yet, but genetically engineered lower animals and some clones age slower than the parent organism."

Hal looked at Tandy's closed cage. "The puppy will outlive his first life?"

"At least twice that."

"How do you know?"

"Experimental studies at cell level. Today the average dog will live eighteen to twenty years. Not much longer than in your time."

"Right, fourteen, fifteen years is about average."

Dr. Zanster led Hal toward the far end of the narrow hall. "Following recombinant DNA and growth acceleration, your average Golden Retriever will enjoy twenty-five, maybe twenty-eight years."

"Good God!"

"It's a plus for the animals. We hope we can make it work for the human clones." Jerry took his ring of plastic keys from his coat pocket and inserted a blood-red one into the slot below the blinking red light. Zanster pushed a button. A light came on behind the tinted glass. A dark form retreated to the rear of the cage.

Hal caught a quick breath.

"You're sure you want to meet Mr. Morgan?"

"Yes, I'm sure."

"Mr. Morgan, may I present Dr. Hal Jordan." Jerry stepped aside.

Something grotesque, far less than animal or human moved toward the front of the open cage. Through red eyes it studied Dr. Jordan. "Please help me."

Hal gasped and stepped back against the

wall behind him. "Dear Jesus in heaven!" Hal stared at the abomination and shook.

Dr. Zanster slammed the cage door shut and locked it.

"Dear God, Jerry what is that?"

"Mr. Morgan. A half-life, my horrible mistake." He pulled the plastic key from the lock and stared through the tinted glass. "I'm a man of God and yet, I manufacture demons from the bowels of hell." He switched off the interior light and turned away from the cages.

Dr. Jordan wiped his face with a handkerchief and shuddered. "Man of God? You've said things like that earlier. You also told me this is a Godless society. Jerry, I need to know what you're talking about."

Zanster smiled and slipped the plastic keys into his coat pocket. "My father was a minister. He was what they called a *hang-on evangelist.* A few still exist. I'm one of them." He shivered and glanced back at the blinking, red light. "You have to see the accelerator lab. We both need to get out of here."

Hal's frustration bordered anger as he watched Jerry lock the security door to the observation cages. "Doctor Zanster, I'm a teacher, a man of science. I'm also a born and raised Baptist."

Jerry snapped his ring of plastic keys from

the security lock and studied Jordan's face. "I'm aware of that, professor. Otherwise, I wouldn't have mentioned my Christian leanings." He pointed to a side door from the cloning lab. "We'll cut through here."

Not wanting to draw the attention of nearby laboratory personnel Jordan held his questions until he and Jerry entered the corridor. When the door closed behind them, he let loose. "Explain why you're a man of faith in a Godless society." He stiffened and scanned Zanster's face with his dark eyes.

They stopped walking. Jerry leaned against one wall and shook his head. "My father died fifteen years ago." He slipped his hands into the pockets of his lab coat and slowly raised his eyes to Hal's. "My dad went to his death heartbroken and empty." Jerry swallowed. "During the last few years of his life, our society started to fall away from religion. Little by little his followers stopped attending his services. Finally, he was alone in his empty church. It killed him."

A wave of guilt passed through Dr. Jordan as he saw the pain in Jerry's eyes. "How did your mother take it?"

"She passed six months later." Dr. Zanster shuddered and shifted his weight. He looked beyond Hal. His eyes glazed out of focus. For an instant some private memory flashed across his mind and touched his mouth with a gentle smile. "I'm sure they're together now ... wherever they are."

"You don't have to go on, I'm sorry I pressed it."

Dr. Zanster stood up straight and gestured with his hands. "It's okay. I was hoping I could reach you." He focused on Hal and nodded. "When I read your file, I knew we could talk. I want to share these things. I can with you, but not with anyone here." He looked around as if the hall were filled with hostile observers.

"What killed faith?"

Zanster laughed and looked away. "Faith is alive and well. Faith in technology, science and selfishly, in ourselves."

"What about Jesus and God?"

Jerry glanced up at the ceiling and chuckled under his breath. "Old hat—something for the less educated." He stood ridged, pulled the plastic keys from his pocket. "Not one intelligent life form, discovered so far, has any reference or history suggesting a Christ or God influence."

Hal moved his hands back and forth. "You have the *Time-Gate*. Haven't you tried to get the truth?"

Jerry raised his head and let out a long, deep sigh. "A man named Jesus lived and died as the Bible said he did." He pushed away from the wall and started down the long corridor.

Standing in place, Jordan shook his head. "Genesis, Moses, the bush, the Red Sea. What about the tablets?"

Zanster stopped at the end of the hall and inserted one of his keys into the lock to the right of the security door. He turned back to Hal. "Moses, yes and the tablets, yes. We sent TA's. It happened as written." Jerry opened the door.

Right behind him, Hal continued. "The rest?"

Dr. Zanster held the door and let Professor Jordan pass through. "No TA's came back from Genesis, the Red Sea or the bush. We sent three to the encounter Moses had with the burning bush. None returned."

Hal stopped in the forward corridor and looked at Dr. Zanster. "I don't understand."

"We don't either—it's a dead issue." The security door shut and locked behind them.

"You're not curious for Christ's sake?"

Jerry smiled. "For Christ's sake, I am. Unfortunately, no one else gives a damn."

"You still believe?"

"Absolutely. I have a small following." He opened another door. They entered LAB CL/H-9. Dr. Zanster stopped and addressed Hal. "I need to share something with you in utmost confidence."

"Of course."

"I've recorded the names and distribution records of the other passengers. When the time's right, I'll ask them to join my congregation." He grinned and shook his head. "Hal, those people are a Godsend! I believe that. When all this is over, and the dust settles, I'll have a real church. Small, but real."

Dr. Jordan shivered and smiled. "God bless you." He patted Jerry's shoulder.

"Thanks to your time-gate crossing, he already has."

They entered the growth acceleration control room.

Alex Sweigart got up from his station. He nodded. "Doctor Zanster, the first twenty-four are perfect." He glanced at Hal.

Jerry picked up and studied a clipboard. He gestured to Dr. Jordan. "Alex, meet Hal Jordan. He's one of the special five."

Hal took Alex's hand. "Pleasure—what is this place?"

Catching approval from Zanster, Alex smiled and sat down before his controls and meters. "Acceleration, sir. The final phase of the cloning process." He waved toward the thick glass. "Another two dozen CL's are fifty percent cooked. I mean ready." He flushed.

Jerry hooked the clipboard on the end of the console and stared into the chamber. "You're at quarter rate?"

Alex entered a code into the computer, through the keyboard. "Palmer insisted."

Jerry patted Sweigart's shoulder while staring into the foggy chamber. "I agree. There's no rush." He pointed toward the window and looked into Hal's shifting, wide eyes. "Your fellow passengers, Doctor."

Jordan turned to Dr. Zanster. "They're just copies—with no feelings?"

Jerry gripped Sweigart's shoulder. "Not so far as we know."

The voice of the acceleration team-leader filtered through the speakers above Sweigart's control board.

"Pressure stabilized at fourteen psi." White fog drifted away from the first few horizontal containers.

Alex glanced at his meters. "Check. Fourteen and steady. They'll be done in another hour." The leader waved and went about his work.

Dr. Jordan studied the proceedings as well as he could through the shifting fog. "These clones have no minds?"

Alex grinned. "Dumb as a beef steak on the hoof." He pressed the intercom key. "Check eighteen, I'm getting erratic pulse and temperature increase."

The team leader waved again and passed the word.

Alex tapped the face of one of his meters. "Shit!" He hit the intercom key again. "We're into fibrillation on eighteen and over one-ten. Close the nitrogen valve—stat!"

As if watching a team of doctors in an operating room, Hal shifted his eyes from Sweigart's console to the activity in the chamber.

Alex entered a code sequence through his keyboard. "Sonofabitch!" He hit the intercom again. "Forget it! we're flat-line. She's gone. Shut down eighteen."

Dr. Jordan strained to see through the white fog. "What happened?"

Alex grabbed the clipboard. "We lost CL number eighteen. Better luck next time." He drew a red line through the name, Carol Price and the numbers, 18-5/A. He handed the clipboard to Dr. Zanster. "Your department, Jerry."

Zanster picked up a note pad and jotted down the code numbers. "I'll process this one tomorrow. We'll schedule it in next week." He hung up the clipboard and slipped the note into his pocket.

Jordan shook his head slowly. He smiled without humor. "Did one of those people just die here, or am I imagining all this?"

Sweigart glanced at Hal, then focused his

attention on the board.

Jerry, looking tired, eased himself onto a stool next to Alex. "They're not people, Hal. We're making biological copies–that's it."

"You believe that?"

"I have to, or go nuts." Zanster folded his arms and stifled a yawn.

Jordan paced, put his hands on his hips, muttered, looked into the acceleration chamber, then back at Jerry. "They have no brains?"

Unable to hold it, Dr. Zanster yawned. "Every cell the original had."

"Intelligence?"

"For all body functions and enough to take direction. They have no souls, Hal—"

"You're sure?"

"You mean, can I prove it?"

"Exactly!"

"Not specifically, no, I can't."

Frustrated, Dr. Jordan looked into the chamber then at Alex, who was busy with his work, then back at Zanster. "They could be full of knowledge, feelings, memories—even soul!"

"None of the above." Jerry stretched and rubbed his face. "Excuse me. I'm a little dragged right now. I'll get my second wind in a minute."

"Could they have what I said?"

"Not very likely."

"How the hell can you be so sure?"

"Brain scans." Jerry gestured toward the glass. "Those clones exist in a vacuum. I told you. Intelligence, personal memory, emotion—none of it transfers from the parent cell to the copy unless we go to level eight." He rubbed his eyes and yawned again.

"How do they function?"

"Code implant."

"What?"

"We implant a memory code at the base of the skull and send functional messages to the brain. Say sit--they sit."

Dr. Jordan looked at Alex, then into the chamber. He could see shadowy figures moving about. It struck him as a scene from a science fiction movie. "Jesus. They respond like—like monkeys!"

More alert, Dr. Zanster got off the stool. "Pretty much, yeah." He studied Jordan. "The clones are not human. Think back to poor Mr. Morgan—that's a whole different matter. He was human. He had a soul. Be concerned for him—whatever he is now. I made that thing. I manipulated the cell through recombinant DNA."

Hal shivered at the memory.

Jerry's voice quivered. "Mr. Morgan is a real-life horror. He's caught on the edge of hell. I put him there." Dr. Zanster gestured across the expanse of thick glass between the control room and the acceleration chamber. "Those things in there are mindless duplications. Nothing more. They're tools. That's it." He turned away and stroked his chin.

Jordan said, "I didn't mean to upset you. I'm sorry."

"Forget it." He managed a slight smile. "These clones are being mass produced for a reason.

Hal looked away. "I know that. Fisher explained it completely. I just can't help wondering."

"Don't worry about it." Jerry considered his thoughts. "Clones have a positive benefit in our society."

"Which is?"

Zanster's face brightened. He watched Alex program the next sequence of the acceleration process. "We use female clones as surrogate mothers."

Hal sat in a chair near the far end of Mr. Sweigart's console. "You do what?"

Dr. Zanster articulated with his hands as he spoke. "It's incredible." He smiled. "I take the cell of a diseased child, remove the hostile virus, perform gene splicing-recombinant DNA, and implant the healthy, fertile cell into the womb of a female clone." His smile had grown. He nodded excitedly. The baby's born healthy. No disease."

Hal thought a moment, then wrung his hands. "And no mind."

"Wrong." Jerry stood and walked back and forth behind Alex. "That's the mystery. "A clone mother will carry an adjusted, mutated fetus full term. The result is a healthy child. The baby is devoid of the original disease."

Hal crossed his legs and leaned back. A flood of tiredness rushed through him. "I'm one-hundred percent confused."

Jerry walked to a service bar at the back of the room and pressed a button. "Let me break it down." A panel opened and hot coffee filled a plastic cup. "Hal?"

Dr. Jordan nodded.

Jerry pressed the button again. "Intelligence exists on many levels. Animal, insect, plant and artificially." He took the two cups of coffee and crossed the room to Hal. "Alex?"

"I'll pass thanks."

Dr. Zanster looked into the chamber to focus his thoughts. "We've advanced to projecting mental images electronically."

Hal swallowed a gulp of coffee. "Visual mind reading?"

"Yes, three dimensional, and in color."

Dr. Jordan blinked and remembered something he had seen at a high-tech science fair. "They made it happen."

Jerry paced, sipped coffee. "The process works great in law enforcement and mental therapy. Anyway, although intangible, intelligence is hard fact."

Hal sat forward. "And the soul isn't."

"Exactly. Let's call it, the human factor. Something similar exists in other life-forms, but, we'll stick to normal life." Jerry stood behind Alex and watched the acceleration team move about in the chamber. "Despite the, Mr. Morgan problems, recombinant DNA is ninety-eight percent successful at cell level. With lower animals and plants, the desired result carries through full growth." He started pacing again, watching his shoes. "It doesn't matter if growth is accelerated or natural. Except for the cell membrane, as I explained earlier."

Dr. Jordan leaned back and rubbed his neck. "The membrane becomes thicker."

"Only during acceleration, like those." He pointed toward the chamber.

Hal drank more coffee. "And in either case, the final organism is a dumb clone."

"In essence, yes." Jerry dropped his cup into a wall receptacle marked *SOLIDS.* The rush of air startled Hal.

"I wondered why there are no wastebaskets anywhere."

Jerry laughed. "They went out before

churches and organized religion."

Alex turned around. "Amen, Doctor."

"Mr. Sweigart's one of my people." He patted Alex on the back. "Now, once we've cloned cells from a diseased child, and make them healthy, they're placed into a laboratory womb."

"A test tube baby. That's routine, even in the twentieth century."

"It's been well advanced since then." Jerry leaned on the back of the stool. "There's a DNA fragment called *M/W dash two-one-nine-eight.* It was discovered by Doctor, Marlena Westen in the year, 2198. She headed a genetics research team, which became known as, the *M/W Project."* Jerry stepped around in front of the stool. "As far as I'm concerned, *M/W-2198* is the human-factor. The soul."

Dr. Jordan stood up, stretched. "What is the fragment?"

"We don't know for sure. It exists in human stem-cell fluid only. Not in any other living matter."

"What about intelligent mutants?" Hal crossed the room and deposited his cup into the *SOLIDS* door.

Whoosh! The cup was gone. It did not fall, as he expected. It vanished. He stared at the door then looked at Jerry. "Damn!"

Zanster chuckled. "There's a drawback to that system. Whatever you put in there is gone forever.

It's a one-way teleporter."

"Where did the cup go?"

"Into infinity as a tiny cloud of microscopic dust."   Hal jerked his hand away from the panel. "Jesus!"

Alex laughed. "It won't bite, Doctor. That model can't transport tissue—not even an apple core."

Jerry ran his hands through his hair. "Sometime before you go home, I'd be glad to show you the higher ends of that development. Teleportation. We use it for shipping and receiving."

Dr. Jordan stepped away from the service panel altogether. "Travel?"

"That's a little tricky, but it's being done."

"Please, back to the soul, as you put it."

Jerry paced again. "The *M/W* fragment becomes part of the DNA molecule. Once mature, which takes about one-mega second, the molecule encodes a specific blood protein called *LFP.* Life-Force Protein. It has no other definition and we don't know what it is. On one hand it appears to be a random selection. On the other it isn't."

Hal sat down again. "It's late. I'm a bit slow. Please explain."

Dr. Zanster stepped between Hal and Alex and leaned against the end of the console.

"When the mature DNA molecule makes it's move, and that's exactly what it does. It appears to attack protein. Many are encountered. Only one gets encoded. At that instant, what we call, *Embryo-one* forms."

"The new life?"

"Right. At that point, however, I log it as, *the baby.* From then on, I'm a pediatrician following the development of a child."

"In the lab. The test tube?"

Jerry leaned against the stool. "Until the first brain wave—then it goes into the female clone."

Hal rubbed his eyes. "Why not implant the new life in the original mother?" He stared up at the ceiling.

Zanster sat on the stool again. "We've tried—in every case the baby has a more advanced case of the original disease. Something deep in the parent's genetic background reconstitutes the unhealthy process."

Jordan leaned forward and laced his fingers. "What happens to the original baby? The one with the disease?"

Dr. Zanster looked across the control room to Hal. "We kill it of course."

"Jesus!"

"Would it be right to keep it alive?" Jerry stood up straight and ran his hands through his hair.

"I can't believe this."

Dr. Zanster studied him and let his mind go back to previous data. "Cancer and other diseases plague your time."

"Very much so."

"You'll see the end of those horrors, Hal."

"Thank God!"

"Yes, thank God." He nodded toward Alex. "What's scheduled for tomorrow?"

"Dr. Rankin will be supervising additional cloning.

"Great. Make sure he knows about the loss of number eighteen."

"I'll leave a directive for him to replace her."

"Excellent. I'll see you all in the morning."

"Good night, sir."

They left the acceleration control room and entered the main corridor. Dr. Zanster stopped and addressed Hal. "Are you fully aware of what you've learned here tonight?"

"I'm frightened by what I've learned."

Jerry nodded. "Will you be able to live with this knowledge and keep it to yourself?"

"I'm a teacher, Jerry. I share what I know. However, I understand that what I now know cannot be shared in my own time."

"That's going to be very difficult for you. Am I right?"

"Not so much. I can *speculate* can't I?"

"I would imagine you can do just that. Just be sure you project a theory that includes a faith in God."

"You have my absolute promise on that."

"Thank you, Doctor. My dad would be pleased."

Hal grinned. "You mentioned *other life-forms.*"

"Did I say that?"

"Yes, you did."

Zanster paused, thought a moment and smiled. "There is intelligent life beyond our solar system. They are not hostile and have shared a great deal of knowledge. Most of that has been in the area of environmental issues."

Hal shook with excitement. "You've met them?"

"I have and we'll just leave it at that."

"What are they like?"

"They're living creatures, Hal. Just leave it at that."

"You've talked to them?"

"Listen to me. Forget the aliens. Am I clear?"

"So far as I know, they don't exist."

"Good. I never mentioned them."

Hal smiled. "I've had enough for tonight. Take me back to my quarters."

Jerry grinned. "We're both tired."

"Amen to that."

Chapter 36
Growth Acceleration

LAB CL/H-9 7:30 AM July 17, 2498

*C*hairman Fisher and Sophy, came into the laboratory with Steve Palmer and Kathy Simmons. They entered through the environmental lock and met with Dr. Rankin in the main control room. Fisher nodded. "How many so far, Greg?"

Rankin took a clipboard from Alex, the Acceleration Operations Supervisor. "Twenty-four. The rest will be processed over the next thirty to forty-five days." He smiled at the others and addressed Fisher. "We have to go easy, sir."

"I understand, Greg. You won't get any pressure from me. Not with this."

Sophy shivered.

Dr. Rankin put his hand on Alex Sweigart's shoulder. "Al and his people have covered every aspect of mass acceleration through worst and best scenario before a single cell was chambered."

Steve took the clipboard and examined it. "What stage are they at, Alex?"

"Full growth. We're exhausting vapors now. They'll be clear in a minute or so."

Sophy turned her back to the chamber room. She studied a computer monitor which meant nothing to her.

Fisher touched her arm gently, he spoke in a soft voice. "It has to be. Think about something else."

Kathy glanced at the instruments on the master control board then looked through the thick glass into the huge chamber room.

Steve handed the clipboard back to Alex. All eyes but Sophy's watched the proceedings.

The room beyond the window was filled with rolling, white fog.

Dr Rankin was the only one to speak. "It'll clear quickly."

The thick fog vanished and a team of twelve examiners entered the chamber from another environmental lock. They were wearing stark white protective suits with dark face plates. The leader looked toward Alex through the window and nodded.

Alex pressed a key on the control board. "Microns at point zero three, check?"

The leader spoke. His voice filtered through a small speaker on the board. "Zero three. We're clear."

The entry team approached the first row of twelve elevated silver-gray horizontal modules. The last tendrils of white fog dissipated.

The leader's voice came through the console speaker. "We're ready."

Dr. Sweigart nodded. "Go ahead, Gary. Open number one."

Kathy covered her mouth and coughed nervously.

Steve glanced at her then fixed his attention on the activities in the chamber.

Risk was a constant consideration.

The entry-team leader released the pressure seals on module-one.

A *hissing* sound escaped from the chamber into the console speakers.

Alex watched the meters on the main board. "Two point five psi. It's safe Gary."

The leader nodded and opened the module.

An attractive female clone came into view.

Gary touched various parts of the body with sensing instruments. He nodded again. His voice scratched through the control room. "She's fine, great job."

Alex smiled and released a breath. "Excellent." He shook his head and grinned. "Release the others and take them to stage three."

Gary waved. "You got it, boss."

Chairman Fisher nodded and said to Alex, "Good work—damn good."

"Thank you, sir." He logged the results on his clipboard.

Sophy looked away from the computer screen. "Is it over?"

Kathy put her arm around her. "Everything's okay. No monsters this time."

"Thank God."

Steve smiled at Alex and said, "You're a master."

"I try to do my best."

Gary's filtered voice came from the chamber. "The rest are okay, Al. We're ready for phase two and three."

Alex keyed the intercom. "You're in charge. Keep me posted." He faced the others. "We're okay. Everything's under control."

Kathy squeezed Alex's shoulder. "Thanks."

He patted her hand. "Just for you."

Fisher rubbed his chin and watched the team in the chamber. "Thank your people for me, Alex." He looked at the others in the control room. "We're all seeing some history being made here."

They entered the hall and headed toward the main elevators. Kathy spoke above the sound of their footsteps. "Did we let Zanster go too far?"

Fisher glanced back. "Jerry's responsible. I won't attempt to prejudge."

More footfalls echoed off the white walls before Steve spoke. "Franklin and Jordan are the only ones I worry about. We're putting a lot of trust in them."

Fisher stepped forward and pressed an elevator button. "They're good people. I think our trust is well placed. Are there doubts?" He looked at the others.

Steve rubbed the back of his neck. "One or the other—or both, are bound to ask about the rest of the passengers."

Fisher looked at Dr. Rankin. "What do we say?"

"We tell a half-truth."

"Which is?"

Dr. Rankin looked down then at the faces of the others. "They've being distributed. They're becoming part of the twenty-third century."

Kathy walked Sophy into the elevator. "I hope it's that simple."

Greg said, "It won't be."

Fisher held the elevator door. "Is there a problem?"

"Actually, sir there is." He cleared his throat. "We have some two hundred people coming around over the next twenty-four hours who will require constant supervision." He shook his head. "That's the easy part."

Fisher turned to the others. "Go on back to my office, I'll be along shortly." He let the elevator door close. To Dr. Rankin he said, "What's the hard part?"

"Think about it, sir. How do we tell all those people they won't be going home?"

"I've thought about it, Greg." He rubbed his chin. "We don't." Fisher hesitated. "They're under quarantine until this whole mess is sorted out." He smiled. "As I mentioned earlier, they're in Nevada in a government complex and will be returned home as soon as possible." He stepped to the elevator and pressed the button. "That's all they need to know."

Rankin looked frustrated. "They'll want to contact their relatives."

The elevator door opened. Fisher said, "Work out the details, Greg."

"Mr. Chairman, we're talking about over two hundred people."

"You're a smart man, you'll think of something." The elevator door closed.

"I should let them stay asleep." He mumbled and headed back to his office.

Chapter 37
Mackendrick & Cross

A HEATED CONFRONTATION:

General Mackendrick pulled up at the entrance to hangar twenty-four. Before getting out of his X-7 turbo he studied Flower for a long moment. "I've got military business to tend to. Put yourself in program fifteen. That's where we'll start tonight." He smiled. "I've owned four of you and none have been as good as you are at your worst." He kissed the female droid on the cheek and gently bit her neck.

She put her head back against the seat and sighed as she was programmed to do.

"You're the best I've ever had, sir. No one has made me feel like you do." The droid closed her eyes, rocked her head from side to side. "I want you to touch me. Do it now."

Mack grinned and felt hot fever race through his thighs. He fondled the droid's left breast. Her tits were over-sized and came on special order with top-of-the-line models. Flower was the best money could buy.

"I love your hands on me, sir—they feel nice."

"I won't be long, bitch. Keep the thought while I'm gone."

"I love it when you talk to me like that. It makes me shiver an' weak all over."

"Actually, shut yourself down. It's going to be a long day."

Mackendrick left the car and entered hangar twenty-four.

* * * *

Larry Cross appeared in the forward doorway of the 747. Mack started up the steps. "I called you as soon as I got the word."

Mackendrick continued up the metal stairway. He adjusted his hat and stopped two steps below Cross. "What the fuck happened?"

"Tarkin's dead."

"An accident?"

Cross shook his head. "Heart failure."

"That's bullshit, Chuck was in perfect health."

Larry stepped back into the plane. "Come inside."

Mack climbed off the stairs into the area behind the cockpit. "How did you find out?"

Larry gestured through the open door into the flight deck. "Tarkin was found on the floor by security about six this morning. That's when I got the call."

Mack stepped into the cockpit and leaned against the pilot's seat. "What took you over two hours to contact me?"

"I had to secure the scene first and I was twenty minutes away. The medical team got here before me." He sat in the navigator's seat. "I didn't want to contact you until I was sure."

"That was a mistake." He smacked the back of the seat. "Where's Tarkin's body?"

"When I got here the medics confirmed that Chuck had a coronary." Cross rubbed his eyes. "Tarkin was a friend."

"Where's the body?"

"I had the disposal team take it away." He looked up at the general. "We've lost a friend."

"A friend?" Mack walked toward the cockpit door. "Chuck was a *special* engineer. He made things happen that were necessary." He looked out into the first class area of the giant aircraft. "This entire *Time Gate* incident is getting out of control. What the hell else have you not told me?"

"About what?"

"Mr. Tarkin's demise."

"It may be nothing, but the head security officer told me a man flashed ID and used my clearance code to enter hangar twenty four late last night." He stood and leaned against the copilot's seat. "He said Tarkin was in here at that time."

"Nothing?" The general's eyes flared. He paced in front of the open door. "Have you lost your mind?" He raised his voice. "An unknown subject uses your code to access a highly secured area and a few hours later Chuck is found dead."

Larry grinned. "Easy, Mack. I needed to know you weren't involved in this,"

"What are you talking about?"

Larry pulled a bogus program-card out of his pocket. "Tarkin was playing both sides in this whole mess."

Mack took the card. "I don't understand."

Cross chuckled and sat in the navigator's

seat again. "That program card would've caused this huge plane to fail re-entry into 1998. All would be lost. There would be no energy system we now enjoy. The cloning process would be non-existent." He laughed. "You like your female droid? If that program card had gotten inserted into this aircraft's computer system, she would just be a wet dream."

Mack turned the card over in his fingers. "Chuck designed this program. It was made to enable safe passage through the gate."

Cross presented a second card. "This program card is a duplicate of the one Tarkin was paid to design for the safe return of the key-five passengers to 1998." He stood, walked to the front of the cockpit and pointed to the center console on the flight deck. "The master program of this card has been installed into the aircraft's computer."

Mack studied both cards. "Why would Chuck install the destructive program?"

"He was obviously paid more by factions who have their own agenda." Larry put the second card back into his jacket pocket. "The energy system we have in place now and the cloning process is a profitable business. So is our global defense program." Larry grinned with a touch of arrogance. "Consider Congressman Franklin's *Space-Plane* development."

Mack leaned against the pilot's seat again and studied Larry's expressions. "You're saying word of all this has gotten out and in less than forty-eight hours rat-packs are itching to profit in some way?"

Larry shook his head and grinned. "You didn't think it would leak? Mack, wake up! Frank Tanner's onto it in less than twenty four hours. People have been killed. Now, Tarkin's a victim."

Mack said, "I have Tanner under control." He looked back into the first class section. "The key five people have to make it back to 1998. Is that mission in jeopardy?" The general turned to face Cross.

"Not any longer." Larry smiled. "I've replaced and double checked the program myself. I wanted to be sure before I called you. That was another reason for the delay."

General Mackendrick adjusted his hat. "Listen to me, Cross. Hear me clearly." He walked toward the forward door. "If I find out you had anything to do with Tarkin's death—"

"Whoa, hold on here, General. Chuck had a heart attack."

"I believe the man's heart was stopped by the mysterious gentleman who got in here using your ID code." He glared down at Larry. "That breach of security puts you in a bad light."

Cross stood and faced the general. "Chuck

was a friend an' a loyal employee. Why would I want to harm him?"

Mackendrick moved into the cockpit and looked at the console between the two seats. "I have it on good authority that our friend, Chuck had something to do with a recent explosion that killed two people."

Larry sat down on the flight engineer's seat again. "That incident has been investigated. It was ruled an accident."

Mack took a hit of paralayne. "That's bullshit and you know it." He pointed the paralayne tube at Cross. "The dead man was on your payroll and the unfortunate, *Candy Topps* shared your bed on a regular basis."

Larry held up his hands and grinned. "I plead no contest, your honor. I enjoyed Ms. Candy's talents a time or two."

Mack adjusted his hat again. "What about Garrett?"

Larry shook his head. "Nevil was on my staff, he got too arrogant, demanded a raise and I fired his ass."

Mack straightened his uniform blouse. "How convenient. They just happened to be together when Nevil's house blew up."

Larry leaned back and nodded. "I was shocked when I heard about it."

Mackendrick put his Paralayne away,

leaned down and got into Larry's face. "Ms. Topps set Garrett up with a special code and the poor bastard bought into it."

Cross sat back as far as he could. He inhaled the smell of paralayne from Mack's breath. "What the hell are you talking about?"

The general barked his words. "Nevil gave that code to Frank Tanner and it opened the door on *Time gate* and the arrival of this aircraft!"

Cross turned away from Mack's imposing face. "I had nothing to do with any of that."

The general persisted. "I hope not, Larry." Mack hesitated. "Ms. Topps thought she was doing a favor for somebody and she was off the hook." Mackendrick continued. "Poor Ms. Topps didn't realize she had been set up as well."

Larry tried to turn the other way. "I had nothing to do with any of what you're saying."

Mack didn't back off. "Seconds after the call to Tanner—boom-boom! Candy and Mr. Garrett cease to exist!" The general smiled. "My sources tell me that Charles Tarkin may have played a role in the unfortunate accident that blew Mr. Garret and the lovely, Ms. Topps into little pieces of bloody meat." He stepped back.

Larry stood and looked at the general. "I have no knowledge of any of that."

Mackendrick grinned. "I sure hope not." He dropped the grin. "As I started to say earlier, if I find out you were remotely involved, I'll hang you by your balls before the full council." He smiled again. "You'll spend the rest of your life on Gray Plan."

"Think about it, Mack. Why would I or anybody else want to keep the key people from returning to 1998?"

"You know why. Everything those people accomplished would cease to exist."

"That's my point, like I said earlier. It wouldn't be in our best interests."

"You know damn well every advancement the key-five made possible had been challenged by factions that wanted their programs and formulas used instead. They were, and still are, private entities looking to make massive profits."

"That's all outdated and scattered over years before you and I were even thought of."

"I assure you, Mr. Cross, those factors are real and well aware of the opportunity that has surfaced. They do not want our key visitors to survive."

"Mack, you're taking too many hits of Paralayne."

"Am I?" He adjusted his hat again and stepped to the open doorway. "These shadowy elements would need serious inside help to cause the return of this aircraft to 1998 to fail. I hate to think it would be someone we know."

Chapter 38
The Command Center

July 17, 2498 08:55 hrs.

*W*hen Sophy entered Fisher's office from the council chambers he was standing at the window staring into a hot Nevada morning. "They're waiting, Robert. We're late and they're not happy about it."

"Let them wait. This session was set up for yesterday morning and *they* weren't ready." The chairman turned to watch his secretary cross the room to her desk. "I didn't mean to be so damn melancholy last night."

Sophy hefted five red folders and held them to her breast. "It was these files and the wine." She smiled and started back across the office. "One glass of that good red blushes you. Two wets your eyes." She stopped directly in front of him and lowered her voice to an intimate whisper. "Halfway through your third you start telling me all the things I want to hear."

Fisher grinned and kissed her forehead. "You're sure it takes three?"

A parade of images went through her mind. Pictures of mixed events. Memories sorted and filed over years of a non-committed relationship. "Usually. Last night you had four." She brushed her lips against his cheek.

The chairman stepped back and touched the red folders. "I should've had five. One for each of those." He held her close for a moment. That was something rarely done in the office. "The events of the last two days and what will come from those five, *special,* people will impact this world beyond our time."

A shudder worked its way through Sophy. She cleared her throat. "They're waiting."

Fisher pulled away and kissed her forehead again. "Is the global link up?"

"All of them, even Poland. And Iverneskie is bitching as usual."

"That bastard would bitch if you gave him the whole planet."

* * * *

UNITED WORLD COUNCIL CHAMBERS:
Session in progress 09:10 hrs:

*P*hil Khrismann stood before the council and addressed the transmitted image of the Australian President, Davidson Burke. "I assure you, Mr. President, once these five people are in-place, in their own time, security-intensive efforts will have been activated." He tensed for the expected response.

Burke slammed his fist on the table from halfway around the world and spat his response over thirty-six-thousand miles of secret satellite-link. "Your assurance shows a calculated error margin of twenty-two percent! That is a deadly gap, Mr. Khrismann."

Phil glanced at General Mackendrick, then at Fisher. "Mr. Chairman, I'd like the History Research Commission's response please."

Fisher nodded to Kathy Simmons and Steve Palmer.

Kathy keyed her translator. She remained seated as she addressed the council. "A twenty-two percent risk factor is well within acceptable parameters, President Burke. Such a margin is considered safe in any T.A. mission—"

"Without human involvement, yes." His

eyes narrowed. "I've studied the files on your five people, Simmons. Any one of them could have a change of heart. The good Congressman has me worried on that issue." He grinned and leaned back. "Your Dr. Jordan is a man of science. Thanks to you people he now has advanced knowledge. How long will it be before he starts applying what he's learned? Isn't there a chance he'll write a paper and become a risk?"

Jerry Zanster keyed his translator and a request to be heard.

Chairman Fisher turned to Ms. Simmons. "Anything further, Kathy?"

"No sir."

"Thank you." The chairman nodded to Jerry. "Science Officer, Zanster has the floor."

Jerry stood and leaned on the table. He stared at the huge screen, which now divided into nine pictures around a larger image of President Burke, Zanster gathered his thoughts. "Ladies and gentleman, if any of you share President Burke's misgivings, let me ease your minds." He straightened and stepped behind his chair. "We have struck a bargain with Congressman Franklin—"

Burke cut in. "What kind of bargain?"

Fisher interrupted. "Dr. Zanster has the floor. Let him continue."

Jerry leaned on the back of his chair and laced his fingers. "The arrangement is a matter of security and doesn't have to be disclosed here. It's based on project responsibility and that, Mr. Burke, is ours."

The Australian President shook his head in disagreement.

Dr. Zanster went on. "The congressman's life depends on his cooperation. We'll leave it at that." Jerry came around the chair and slipped his hands into the pockets of his lab-coat. "As for Professor Jordan, put your worries to rest. His greatest accomplishment is that which he'll do for us." He leaned on the table again and glared at the image of President Burke. "That, ladies and gentleman was destined before flight two-eighty crossed the time gate. Jordan's work, and the contributions of the other four, cements return to the twentieth century. They must *all* go back."

The picture, on the big screen, shifted to Michael Iverneskie, Poland's president. "My country cannot—will not agree to any human replacement in past-time! Our vote is no!"

Burke cut in without recognition. "Australia votes no!"

Chairman Fisher overrode the speakers. "There is no vote open at this time. All response is invalid."

Larry Cross seized the opportunity, struck his translator and stood. "Representing the people of the United States, our vote concurs—no!" Cross knew the master computer had recorded his protest and aligned him with two other powerful nations. Valid or not, the vote would weigh against Robert Fisher as chairman. It would be logged as an incident of further debate.

Mrs. Noyn Lee Fong, President of China came onto the center screen. "The United Republic of China must agree with America's distinguished representative. Our vote is an emphatic no!"

Unofficially, four out of ten UWC countries were against the United States.

"Mister Cross!" Chairman Fisher's voice silenced the council chambers and drew the collective attention of all member nations. "You, sir are out of order."

That too was recorded by the master computer. It registered negative against Chairman Fisher.

Cross said, "I've spoken for the people I represent—"

Fisher responded. "You've spoken for yourself, sir. And you're damn-well aware of it!"

The statement would be analyzed by Tex as a strike against the chairman as well.

General Mackendrick keyed his translator and requested recognition.

Fisher responded. "The council will be returned to order and General Mackendrick has the floor."

Mack nodded and cleared his throat. "I direct my comments to those dissenting and those considering a formal vote." The huge screen divided into equal images. "I submit the following information for your consideration. At first, I objected to sending these five people back through time. The risk was too great. Not only because of the damage they might do, but because their lives were in danger. The gate is unstable."

Phil Khrismann shot a glance at Mack. *Jesus, Mackendrick,* he thought. *You're digging a hole!* Phil shook his head and stared at his boss. *What the hell are you trying to do?*

Mack continued. He managed a tone of compassion. "We have to deal with the issue of many lives—not just five. Again, the gate isn't stable. It's not safe."

A light smile poked at the corners of Phil's mouth. *Mack—you've been a bull shitter from day-one.*

The general turned his palms up and shrugged. "We can't risk re-entry for ninety-days." He glanced around the chambers. "If you're worried about a leak—forget it. Access what you already know. Go back five-hundred years. Let's say Dr. Jordan wrote a paper on what he learned in our time. Who, in the twentieth century, would believe a single word he wrote?"

Phil's smile broadened. *Mackendrick, you're an asshole-genius. As much as I dislike you, you're all right!*

Mack droned on. "My fellow councilmen—and women, our five key-people will serve us well."

Black African President Mootoo Kahamba spoke up. "There were others on the plane, sir—what of them?"

Mack leaned back and took a hit of paralayne.

The chairman frowned. Nobody else cared.

"The remaining passengers are being cloned for re-entry. The real people are being considered for relocation world-wide. For that we need the council's approval."

Kahamba squinted and rubbed his ebony chin. "Some are black?"

"Three percent."

The African President smiled. "We'll accept them."

Mack nodded. "Thank you."

Iverneskie's image filled the center of the screen. "Are there poles?"

Mack thought a moment. He glanced at Khrismann. "Two, maybe three."

"We'll accept them."

Mexico's President, George Fredrico came onto the center screen. "Nationalities aside, what security risk do we face with these people?"

Mack looked away for a moment to gather his thoughts. "Virtually none. Every subject will be mentally adjusted. If there's a problem, we'll handle it."

England's royal leader Wallace Avery Farrington appeared into center position. "I move for a floor vote. Who will second that?"

Canada's Chancellor, Ivan Kershier made the second.

Khrismann thought, *Mack--you're on a roll.*

Chairman Fisher triggered the world-wide voting grid.

"The floor is open—all votes are final. Please indicate with a yes or no on distribution and return."

In less than a minute the results appeared on the center screen for both issues.

The majority clearly favored approval.

Larry Cross gathered his files and left the chamber.

* * * *

Phil glanced at General Mackendrick. Mack winked. He thought, *Mack, you bastard—you pulled it off! You have more guts than brains.*

Chairman Fisher stood and addressed the heads of nations. "Distinguished council, the approval carries. Secondary countries will be informed. Our project moves forward immediately. This session of the United World Council is adjourned." He keyed in his personal code and looked at Sophy. "We were right from the start."

Sophy nodded and watched the big screen fade to black. "God help us if it turns out otherwise ...."

Hearing Sophy's words, as he passed by, Phil whispered, "Amen."

Fisher stepped around the table to face General Mackendrick. "Your observations made the difference, Mack, thanks. Apparently you've changed your mind."

"Duty, sir. Personal feelings aside. Anyway ... we're committed."

The chairman started to turn away then hesitated. "Is there something else?"

Mackendrick glanced around the room. "Can we talk in your office?"

Fisher leaned forward. "Larry Cross, right?"

Mack nodded.

Khrismann stiffened.

The chairman moved away from the table. "Give me a few minutes then come on in." He left Mackendrick and Phil alone in the chamber.

Phil pushed his chair back and sat on the conference table. "How much do you think Cross knows?"

Mack handed Khrismann a blue folder. "That's what I intend to find out." He coughed. "This is Charles Tarkin's file. Run it through your security terminal. Our friend, Cross used Tarkin. Chuck's now dead. I want you to find out how far it goes."

Phil opened the folder and scanned the first page. "I'll get on it right away."

"Do it yourself. Don't involve anyone else except your girlfriend" Khrismann knitted his eyebrows and stared at the general. "Jennifer?"

"Your shack up, my special assistant."

Hot blood came up the back of Phil's neck and turned his ears bright red. "You're off base, Mackendrick. Keep your crude-thoughts to yourself." He slapped the folder on the table and stood.

"Curb your wounded pride and face facts. Shut the hell up and listen."

Phil clenched his teeth and breathed heavily through his nose. "You piss me off!"

"There's a point to it. Before Jennifer

became my secretary she worked for the engineering department. She was in charge of security clearance. Jen-girl was a level-five. When a prospective employee got passed by our beloved Jennifer, she knew how many hairs that person had on his or her ass. Get the drift?"

Phil unclenched his fists and relaxed his lower jaw. "Couldn't you just say that without personal reference?"

"It wouldn't have the same impact." The general tucked his hat under his right arm and gathered his additional papers. "After you run the file, have dinner with Jen-girl." Mack chuckled. "Before or after you dip your stick, tell Jen what we're up to with the death of Tarkin."

"She doesn't know about Tarkin?"

"Only that he worked with Cross. Let her access the clearance files from your personal terminal. She'll get more on Tarkin in five minutes than I could get in a month." The general started toward the door.

"Why can't she do the same from your office?"

Mackendrick grinned. "Like I said, she trusts you. Tell her it's you're idea. She'll have an orgasm while she does it."

Phil raised his voice as the general walked away. "Mackendrick. You're an unfeeling, coarse sonofabitch!"

Mack turned to face him, still grinning. "I'm also the boss. Get the job done."

Momentary contempt toned Phil's voice. He added a departing comment. "Tell me, Mack, does your synthetic bitch like you?"

The general stopped. "When I push the right buttons the lovely thing loves me." He laughed and headed toward Fisher's office.

Chapter 39
A Question of Trust

THE CHAIRMAN'S OFFICE
Following the meeting:

*F*isher sat at his desk squeezing his eyes shut and pinching the bridge of his nose. "Sophy, get Mackendrick in here and record everything he says."

"Manually?"

"Yes." He looked up at her as she came toward his desk. "When we're finished, copy your notes and file the original in code."

Sophy put her pod on Fisher's desk and took a deep breath. "I'm afraid of this, Robert ...." She began rubbing the chairman's shoulder blades and pressing her thumbs into the back of his stiff neck.

"What are you afraid of?"

"All of it. Especially the cunning, Larry Cross."

A pleasant tingle worked down the chairman's spine. "He's a shit! He always was, always will be."

Sophy let go of Fisher's neck and took up her steno-pod. "He's also dangerous."

The chairman leaned back and smiled. "So am I and he knows it."

She cocked her head and regarded her boss. "I hope to God you're *more* dangerous."

He laughed. "If this *God*, we dare not speak of, exists then a demon like Cross will collect his due." Fisher sat forward and stared at the five files in front of him. "I hope that *God* listens well."

"I'll get Mackendrick."

"Please, I need to hear what he has to say."

* * * *

A few minutes later Fisher sat back and stared at the general. "You're accusing Councilman Cross of planning mass murder."

Sophy's hand shook as she recorded the comment.

Mackendrick closed the red folder and placed it on the desk. "The facts in that file do the accusing." He stood and buttoned his uniform blouse.

Fisher slipped his reading glasses over his nose, leaned forward and opened the red folder. He paged through the file to information regarding Nevil Garrett's death. "Who else beside you and Khrismann know about this?"

Sophy studied Mack's face as he stepped behind the chair he had been sitting in. *He's considering a lie,* she thought.

Mack cleared his throat. The urge to take another shot of paralayne sprung up. He resisted. The first words of his response sounded raw and dry. "Nobody but us. That's it."

Fisher pushed his glasses up over the bridge of his nose. "You're sure?"

Mack brushed a speck of lint off his cap. "Absolutely."

The chairman closed the folder and took off his glasses. "I want a full report as soon as possible. If Cross is doing what you say, I need proof."

"Understood, sir." He straightened and set his hat on his head perfectly.

The chairman studied Mackendrick. "What about Tanner and a missing reporter?"

"Tanner's poking around as he usually does. Phil and I met with him just to feel him out. He isn't buying the death of Garrett and Ms. Topps as an accident." He chuckled. "He thinks Garrett tipped him about the *Time Gate.* Actually, Tanner could be right." *Don't say too much.* "I wouldn't worry about him."

Fisher looked up. "I'm worried about a lot and Frank's not the least of it."

"Yes, sir. I appreciate that."

"Is the disappearance of the young reporter connected to any of this mess?"

"We have unconfirmed information that Jeff met with Tanner before he went missing."

Fisher stood and stepped around his desk. "That sure needs to be clarified as soon as possible."

"It will be, sir. You have my word." *Say something positive and get the hell out of here!* "By next week, we'll have enough against Cross to put him on the moon for the rest of his life."

"I can't say I wouldn't be pleased if you did."

They shook hands.

"One other thing, Mr. Chairman."

"Which is?"

"As hard-ass as I seem." He cleared his throat. "I'm quite concerned about keeping more than two hundred people from returning to their families."

Sophy checked her recorder. *This is not Mackendrick talking.*

Fisher leaned against his desk. "I feel the same way."

Mack continued. "I know they'll be mentally altered, but I would like to think there's a better solution."

The chairman smiled. "There's time, Mack. If we can find an alternative it will be used." He thought a moment. "Watch your back, general."

"I intend to sir." He marched out of the room.

Sophy stood. "How much of all that do you believe."

"A little less than half. Tanner and the missing reporter caused Mack a moment of stress."

"The good general and Khrismann are not alone."

"You're right. Frank Tanner knows more than Mack let on."

"Is he a problem?"

"Let's just wait and see."

Sophy pushed her chair back where it belonged. "I knew Mackendrick was hiding something."

"Did you note it?"

"Of course."

"Excellent. Lunch is on me."

As in justice,
loyalty can be also blind.

* * * *

Beware: malevolence may
be the feeding hand.

Part Four:

* * * *

Damaging Evidence

Chapter 40
The Tarkin File

SATURDAY MORNING
GOVT. COMPLEX-A/15 UNIT 44-B
PHIL KHRISMANN'S QUARTERS:

*J*ennifer squinted at the computer screen and poured about two ounces of *Chalmer's Mint* into her black coffee. "Phil", she yawned, "I think Mr. Tarkin's a victim."

He answered from the kitchen. "That isn't news." He cracked two more eggs into a large mixing bowl. "Tarkin's *function* is the issue, not his motives."

"He was Top-Secret electronics."

Phil shook assorted spices into the bowl. "I'm making omelets that talk back."

"Good--damn ...."

He ground fresh pepper and blended it into the eggs. "Damn what?"

"Charles Tarkin's service record is spotless." Jennifer pushed back from the computer terminal and took a sip of coffee.

Khrismann chuckled as he whisked the eggs to perfection. "If you ran Larry Cross you'd find the same thing. Mr. Great, a model countryman. It's pure bullshit!" He poured the egg mixture into a pre-heated skillet.

Jennifer left the terminal and joined him in the small kitchen. "Then what's the point of running Tarkin?" She slipped her arms around Phil's waist and kissed his neck.

"To prove Tarkin was in Cross' pocket." Phil slid a cover over the eggs. "They've been working together for the past five years."
He tilted his head back, enjoying Jennifer's mouth on his neck. "Excellent!" He shook his head and grinned.

She hugged him. "What's excellent?"

Phil shifted the omelet around the pan. "The eggs, my love—the eggs."

She pulled away and moved around to study his face. "Going after Cross could be dangerous. Mack has said so himself."

His smile turned upside down. "What he's up to is the danger. I'm not worried about him."

Jennifer leaned against the counter. "The whole *Time-Gate* thing scares me."

He rocked the pan from side to side. "Yeah, five more lives are on the line."

Jen glanced at the computer screen in the next room. "Does Tarkin figure into the Garrett killing?"

Phil reduced the heat under the omelet pan. "I believe that's what caused his so-called heart attack."

She sipped some coffee. "Tarkin's profile doesn't indicate any sign of violence."

He removed the glass pan from the stove. "I think Charles *engineered* the explosion that killed Garrett and the lovely Ms. Topps. Somehow, Larry convinced him it was a necessary mission. What I suspect doesn't count. We must have proof." He smiled. "That's where your expertise comes in."

Jennifer shuddered. "Larry orders—Tarkin does."

Phil slipped the perfect omelet onto a plate and divided it in half. "Cross seems to get whatever he wants."

She thought a moment. "Why would a man like Tarkin kill for Larry?"

Phil added more seasoning to the separate

omelet sections. "He believed it was for country and state with a measure of Loyalty." He tasted a bite of his egg dish. "I didn't believe Mackendrick was right until now." Phil shook his head. "I want Cross—I want his ass on the moon!"

Jennifer shuddered and hugged herself against an internal chill. "Tarkin dies, Cross' ass is covered."

Phil's eyes flashed. He swallowed another forkful of omelet. "Like you said, Tarkin's a victim. Larry doesn't want that plane or the five key people returned to 1998." He sipped some coffee. "Cross is the monster here and we're gonna nail his ass."

* * * *

After breakfast, Jennifer returned to the terminal and entered the access code for the Larry Cross files.

Phil finished up the dishes and stacked them in the sanitizer. "Get what you can on the good councilman and the unfortunate, Mr. Tarkin. I'll find a way to use it. It's about time the sonofabitch paid the piper." Phil shook his head. "Jen I just thought of something."

"What?" She turned away from the computer.

"Recent security clearances."

"Exactly. I can start accessing security files immediately."

A warm rush ran through him as he approached Jennifer. "We used to click like that a lot ...."

She nodded then turned to the computer screen. "Three, four times a day," she whispered.

"I'm sorry, Jenny ...."

A tense smile wrinkled her nose. "Don't. Let's just take it from here ... okay?"

"Yeah, I agree ...." Phil kissed the top of her head. "We have enough to deal with right now."

She faced him and blinked rapidly. "You want me to access security files, right?"

"Would you be legal?"

"Yes, working for Mackendrick has advantages."

"Get recent approvals, special clearance. That sort of information."

Jennifer chuckled. "I love you. I'm going in." She keyed a restricted code. The screen displayed:

LOADING FILES

In fewer than five minutes Jennifer had accessed a new security file.

She and Phil stared at the screen he touched her shoulder. "Print it."

Ten seconds later the light-printer stacked up a six page file. The cover page read:

FLIGHT 280
(Time Gate Breach)
EVENT HISTORY:

The first three pages outlined the accidental crossing of flight 280 through the *Time-Gate.* Page four listed the five key people, a brief profile and an authorized return designation.

Priority security clearance had been documented for Commanding General Charles Mackendrick (Chief of Operations), Phillip Khrismann (Gate Coordinator). Councilman Larry Cross had been designated (Project Monitor).

Phil gestured toward the screen. "Ask Tex to define *project monitor.*"

Jennifer brought up a sub-text menu. "The information might be restricted." She entered a numeric code. An instant later the screen changed.

They looked at each other and smiled.

PROJECT MONITOR (Time-Gate breach)
DESIGNATE: COUNCILMAN LARRY CROSS:

FUNCTION:
OBSERVE AND DOCUMENT
ALL PHASES OF
RE-ENTRY OPERATIONS:
(SPECIAL CLEARANCE)
SUPERVISE DATA IMPLANT FOR
AERODYNAMIC STRESS PROGRAM

Jennifer shifted her eyes to the screen. "There's nothing here. Mack's aware of Cross' involvement. There's no unauthorized activity"

Phil began rubbing Jennifer's shoulders. "Run Tarkin through special clearance."

She entered Tarkin's name and a number-code.

The screen changed.

CHARLES TARKIN (Electronics Division)
SECURITY LEVEL: RED/9 (TOP SECRET)
SPECIAL CLEARANCE 7/17/2498:
TEMPORARY AUTHORIZATION:
TIME GATE PROJECT
(RE-ENTRY PROGRAM/FLT. 280)
CLEARANCE LIMITATION:
INSTALL RE-ENTRY DATA AND
TIME-DELAY AERODYNAMIC
STRESS PROGRAM.
CLEARANCE REP: CLC/UWC/594

Phil stepped back from Jennifer and clapped his hands. "There it is!"

She turned to face him. "What is?"

"C.L.C. The clearance rep. It's Cross!"

"Big deal. Tarkin was qualified. Cross would use him in any case. They worked together for years."

Phil spread his arms and paced around the room. "Does Mack know how Tarkin and Cross were involved in this project?"

She watched him and nodded. "Of course he does—"

"Does he know what they might have been up to?"

Jennifer sat back from the computer and shook her head. "I don't know what you mean. Make sense."

He leaned on the desk and stared down at her. "Tarkin altered the stress program! Cross used him to sabotage the re-entry sequence of the aircraft. He wants that plane to go down early and kill all onboard. He had Tarkin believing it was necessary and then had the man eliminated.

"How?"

"I don't know, but I intend to find out." He walked around behind her again and kissed the back of her neck.

She tilted her head back and watched him. "You're the nuttiest man I've ever met."

"And you're the best thing that's ever happened in my life."

She smiled. "What now?"

"I have the chairman's ear and I need to get to him and Mack with this."

"There's still no proof."

"It's on the airplane and we'll find it."

Chapter 41
The General & the Reporter
Round three

THE NEVADA SUN: Monday.
Frank Tanner's office: 9:00 AM

$\mathcal{H}$e stared at his keyboard then entered an equation into a private memory-file $E=mc\ 2$. "Idiot." He called out to his secretary. "Farrah, would you come in here please."

She entered the room carrying her steno-pod. "You called, sir?" Frank looked up from his desk. "Here," he gestured, "come around here." Frank tapped at the figures on the screen. Farrah moved behind him.

"It's the Classic theory of relativity, not altogether correct. So what?"

"Forget the application. You know the equation without thinking, right?"

She blinked at the screen then glanced at Frank. "Right again, so what?"

He turned to face her. "Remember the code I gave you."

"Of course."

"Forget it! This is the code from now on."

Farrah leaned against the counter behind Frank's desk, puzzled. "Why?"

"Because it'll take a hundred years for anyone else to stumble onto."

"Why wouldn't the other code work?"

"Just a hunch. I changed it."

"It's only been in the grid over the weekend. Nobody knows but us."

"All Mack needs is a hunch."

She glared at the screen. "I hate it!"

"What?"

"All this shit." She walked across the room and stared out the window. "Equation, whatever. If I have to access that Goddamn file you'll be dead!"

Frank went to her, wrapped his arms around her from behind. "You're right. And it's necessary." He pushed his face into her soft hair. "I love you more because you care so damn much."

Farrah turned in his arms to face him, and

tapped her pod against his forehead. She grinned and pressed her face into his shoulder. "Why couldn't you be in Energy Control or Space-Farming? I'd gladly work with you in an orbit-lab!"

He held her tighter and drew in her scent. "Thermodynamics and quantum theories are beyond me. Reporting I understand—so do you. That's why we're who we are."

Farrah pulled back, pinched his nose and kissed it. "You're the biggest shit I know, Frank Tanner. Sometimes I wish I didn't love you."

"But you do." He grinned and hugged her again.

The phone rang. Frank let go. "I'll get it." He grabbed the handset. "Tanner here." He waved Farrah toward her reception area. He mouthed the word, *record.* She left his office immediately.

It was General Mackendrick. "Don't you have a sex-a-tarry, Tanner?

"What is it, Mack?"

"I think I caught Cross with his pants down."

"You think?" Frank chuckled and entered the new file code into memory.

Mackendrick's voice filtered through the phone. "Every time I call you, I wonder if this is really a clear link."

"It's safe. I'm listening."

"Khrismann's onto something involving our project. The flight ...."

"Mack, you don't have to talk in codes. The link's safe trust me."

"I've heard that before, Tanner. I have scars on my ass to prove it!"

Frank grinned and watched the computer screen digest his file. A shiver passed through him as he wondered how safe they all *really* were.

From the doorway, Farrah indicated the conversation was in-fact being documented.

"Thanks for the thought. What's Phil stumbled onto?"

"He's a good man, Tanner."

"I'm sure of it--crude, like you—but good at what he does."

"You're Goddamn right. I don't like your attitude, Mister."

"Tough shit. You're stuck with it."

"Did you forget who's running this show?"

"Hell no, Mack—it's you all the way." Frank leaned back in his chair and suppressed a laugh. "I'm all ears."

Farrah slipped her ear-piece in place and got ready to take hand-written notes. She dated the page on her steno-pod.

Mackendrick cleared his throat. "Charles Tarkin died suddenly last week. It was reported as a heart attack. I don't buy it. Tarkin and Cross were up something that involves this gate situation."

Frank keyed his file on recent Cross clearances and related names. He highlighted the name Charles Tarkin. "Who's Tarkin?"

Mack snarled into the phone. "A high security technologist Goddammit!"

Frank smirked. "Yeah, got it. He and your buddy, Cross had a working relationship."

In the other room, at her desk, Farrah covered her mouth and chuckled.

Mack said, "Cross had the same kind of relationship with Nevil Garrett. He didn't come out too well, remember?"

"You think, Mr. Tarkin was killed?"

"I won't say that directly. I'm concerned about the project, Tanner. Find out how the engineer fit in."

Frank brought up specifics on Charles Tarkin and cross-referenced his file with a broad-scope experience file. "The man was a high-level program-development specialist. Why ask me to get information you can access any day of the week?"

"Because, Mr. Newspaper, I don't want anyone to know I'm looking."

Farrah leaned around the doorway to Frank's office and grinned. He winked and answered Mackendrick. "Got it."

Mack went on. "We believe Tarkin had

created an alternate program card for the plane."

"Why?"

"To take the Goddamn thing down early and wipe out the five key-people!"

Frank let the thought seep in. "Tarkin would do this on his own?"

"No—he was just another Garrett."

"Working for Cross and his cause?"

"Exactly."

Frank glanced at Farrah, still in the doorway. "Pull the damn card, Mack. Bring Cross in."

"We pulled it and ran it. It's perfect."

Farrah returned to her desk to monitor the taping.

Frank stared at his screen and shook his head. "What the hell do you want from me?"

Mack cleared his throat and lowered his voice. "There's a second card, Frank—for my money it's in the hands of Larry Cross. He's the key."

"What?"

"His card is a master override program. He can trigger an early crash of the plane no matter how many primary programs we develop."

"Not if he's in custody. Jesus, Mack!"

"Look, I know it sounds crazy. Listen, we have no proof against Cross. We can't just pick him up. He may have others like Tarkin and Garrett on his payroll. We can't be sure. There could be a half-dozen duplicate cards. All it takes is one."

Frank keyed the Tarkin/Cross files again and watched them come up on the screen. "You have close to three months for Christ's sake."

"Right. Remember, I told you to do what you had to in sixty days?"

"How. What am I supposed to do?"

"Put your head to it, Mr. Newspaper. Get to people who knew Tarkin--you can. I can't."

"Bullshit! You own the project!"

"Right. I make a move. Fifty people send out waves. I need you Goddammit!" He coughed. "Work with me, Tanner."

"Tell me how." He looked up to see Farrah walk into his office. She whispered, "I don't like this, I don't like it ...."

"Frank, I'm asking you to find out about Tarkin by the back door."

"Last week you were threatening me with a vacation at Gray Plan. Now you're asking me to become an investigator in a plot that has already cost three lives." He paused. "Not to mention a missing reporter I had lunch with."

"I need you, Tanner. Last week I didn't. Things have changed."

Frank sat back and nodded at Farrah who had the look of fear on her face. "I'll give you this much, Mack. I'll bet you're on the right track. Cross is your man. That sonofabitch is behind the deaths of three people and I just might be his next target."

"I need proof on Cross and you can get it. Are you with me?"

Silence.

"I'm a reporter. I can only go so far."

"Come in from behind. I'll open doors for you. Contact Leo Davis. He worked for Tarkin in the engineering lab as a program specialist. Tell Mr. Davis you know about his creative programming for Tarkin. Play it up. Push him. Tell him you have information about at least three control programs. He'll crack, I know he will. If there's more than one. He'll spill it. I need this--Goddammit! I need you!"

"If I get into this and it falls apart—I'm on Gray Plan. You're the big guys. You have all the high cards. How can I be expected to do what you ask and come out in one piece?"

"If you had a way, a sure way, would you contact Davis?"

Frank looked at the screen. He felt a chill. He thought of space-farming and shuddered. "Will you guarantee immunity if the approach fails?"

"You have my word as a military chief—now get off your ass and do it!"

Frank tensed. "What happened to Jeff Blake?"

"We don't know. Help us nail Cross and we'll find out."

"How do I get to Davis?" Frank let himself fall back in his chair and stared up at the ceiling.

"You're smart."

"Yeah, I'm a real rocket scientist."

"Take down this sequence. Ready?"

"Mack, when this is over—"

"Forget it. Write down the numbers."

"I'm listening."

"Level four, write it as L-4."

"I know the drill."

"Good. Level four, dash two, dash five six, dash nine. Read it back as the code."

"Mackendrick if this falls through—"

"You're protected, Tanner--read it back as the code."

"Right. L4-2-56-9. Okay?"

"Perfect. Access that code on your office terminal within about two hours. Davis will respond. Set up a meet and nail his ass for us." Mackendrick cleared his throat. "Tell, Mr. Davis if he cooperates he's off the hook."

"For us? You're full of shit. You mean for you." He laughed. "I don't think Mr. Davis is off any hook."

"Whatever, Tanner--get it done!"

* * * *

Mackendrick hung up and grinned across his desk at Phil Khrismann. "Click, click, click ... clockwork. Everything greased and running smooth."

"You're clever, Mack, of that there is no doubt. You're also cunning."

"Like an' old Gray fox." The general sat back and took a hit of Paralayne.

Khrismann stood and leaned on Mack's desk. "You can add careless. Not with the project—not with your ass. Not a chance of that."

Mack stretched and laced his fingers behind his head. "I believe we're talking about Mr. Newspaper here."

"Right. Tanner, Davis, and anybody else who happens to be too close to the fire."

"You and Tanner become buddies all of a sudden?"

Phil stepped back and gave his boss a cold smile. "He's a person."

"A Goddamn, pain-in-the-ass, nosey reporter is what he is." Mackendrick stood. "He put his own ass on the line when he stuck his nose in *Time Gate.*"

"And you're pushing him in over his head. He's in deeper now than he'd ever get on his own. If the roof caves in, Tanner gets buried. You're using him."

The general came around his desk and glared at Khrismann. "You bet your ass I am. Think about it. Tanner busted into a top-secret project! If I couldn't use him, I'd have his reporter's ass on the moon. Where the hell's your sense of country, loyalty, all that shit?"

"Don't ever question my loyalty. I wanted Tanner busted the minute we got onto him."

The general sat on the edge of his desk and smiled. "That's the difference between the execution of strategic, military thinking and slam-bam civilian reaction. In time, Mr. Newspaper will get his due. In the meanwhile, he serves a greater purpose—mine!"

"You don't intend to let him off the hook. You never did."

The general chortled. He walked behind his desk and took a bottle of private stock from an oak cabinet. He nodded toward Khrismann.

Phil declined.

Mack poured two fingers of expensive liquor into a short glass. "It's not really all that bad on Gray Plan, if you're smart." He raised his drink to Phil and threw it back in one swallow. He made a face and grinned. "Tanner's smarter than most ... he'll be okay."

"And, Davis?"

Mack poured again. He held the glass up to the window and studied its contents. He turned to Khrismann, gestured with the booze and said, "Davis isn't quite smart enough. He would have a bad time up there."

"Excuse me?"

Mackendrick sat on the edge of his desk.

"C'mon, Phil. Don't tell me you really believe Mr. Davis will be around long enough to win a trip to Gray Plan." He tipped his glass and downed the drink then smiled. "I don't doubt that Leo Davis will be history less than twenty-four hours after Tanner breaks him down."

"Jesus!" Phil sat down and stared at the carpet. "Tanner will face charges?"

"Yup. I've got people on him right now. They're also just two steps behind his sweet little, Ms. Farrah."

Khrismann stiffened. "What happens to her?"

Mack reached across his desk and lifted a green folder from an oak file basket. "There's a female section at Gray Plan. I don't think she'll handle it very well. But then, we don't send people to the moon for a vacation, do we?" He handed the folder to Khrismann. "Take that with you and read it over. You'll enjoy the writing."

"More on Cross?"

Mackendrick shook his head. "Tanner. It's his secret file on our little project." He turned his glass in his hands and laughed. "Every time he makes an entry, my people copy the data into a special section of Tex's memory grid. The document is then sent to my office until I call it up from the light-printer.

Phil dropped the folder on the table. "Okay, Mack." His face flushed. "All due respect." He paced around the room. "Boss or not. You're over the edge here. I won't standby and see Davis and Tanner put in mortal danger so you can nail Cross." He faced the general and continued. "We'll get Cross one way or another, but we won't cause anymore harm to anyone." He slammed his hand down on the folder. "I cannot believe you'd go so far!" He picked up the folder. "Tanner will get what he can from Mr. Davis and report back to us." He leaned toward the general. "It will end there."

Mack took another hit of paralayne. "You have some big balls talking to me like that."

"You're not a bad man. Stop trying to be one." He smiled. "Cut the bullshit."

Mackendrick ran his hands through his hair. "You're right. Absolutely right." He shook Phil's hand. "Let's get the damn job done."

"What about Jennifer and me?" He hesitated. "Are we on some hit list?"

"You know better than that."

"Do I … *really?*"

Chapter 42
Khrismann & Jordan

CONTROL CENTER (Level 6)
ONE HOUR LATER:

a chill crept across the back of Phil's neck when he entered the control center. An image of General Mackendrick's cold smile came to mind. He spotted his guest. "Professor."

Dr. Jordan stepped away from the security desk. "I'm early, it's a habit."

"And a good one." They shook hands.

Kathy Simmons grinned. "Morning."

"I just came from Mack's office." He rolled his eyes. "I've known the man a long time and he still surprises me."

"I know the feeling."

Khrismann looked at Dr. Jordan. He smiled. "Are you ready for the education of your life?"

Kathy said, "I'll leave you two together until after lunch."

The Professor added, "Why not have lunch with us?"

"I'll be with the Sternfelds, they're not quite as strong as you and Congressman Franklin."

"They're young. This whole matter is beyond them." He laughed. "It's past me, but I'm a man of science. On the one hand—I'm scared out of my pants. On the other, I'm so excited, I could scream. As for Franklin, I think he's the strength of our group."

Kathy glanced at Phil. "After lunch then?"

Phil said, "We may be late."

* * * *

Within forty minutes, Dr. Hal Jordan realized the full impact of what had happened to him and the others on flight 280. He sat beside Phil in the master control room and stared at the video screen. "That's the gate?"

Phil stood and walked to the back of the room. He poured two cups of black coffee. "So far as we know."

"Good God-in heaven ...."

Phil laughed. "Perhaps."

"Sorry."

"Don't be. I'm supposed to answer your questions. Ask away, Doctor."

"I can't think of a place to start."

"Close your eyes and point." Phil chuckled and came back to the console. "Here, there's enough whack in this to bring you back to reality."

Jordan Took his cup, held it in both hands and continued to stare at the screen. "I'm not sure I know reality anymore." He sipped the hot brew then looked at Khrismann.

Phil said, "I can almost hear the questions running back and forth across your mind."

Dr. Jordan pointed to the graphic image on the screen. "If the gate is like a funnel and has a constant location, why haven't others slipped through?"

Phil swallowed a gulp of coffee then sat down next to Dr. Jordan. "Watch the tip of the funnel while I back up two screens."

The dim light from the video monitor cast an eerie, glow on the professor's face. "It shifted north by ten degrees."

"Exactly. Keep looking." Phil advanced the image by four screens.

"South by ten. A wagging tail." Jordan turned away from the monitor and stared at Khrismann.

"Surprised, Doctor?"

"Amazed, astonished—both, I guess. A twenty degree shift reduces the opportunity of contact." Dr. Jordan rubbed his face. "Are these graphics accurate?"

Phil sipped his coffee and leaned against the counter. "To the letter."

"The gate is a cone then? Like a light-cone. That's the Stephen Hawking theory." Hal leaned forward and studied the screen.

Khrismann smiled and sat in a chair next to Dr. Jordan. "Mr. Hawking was right. His model of the light cone hasn't been disproved. You know Hawking?" Phil set his coffee aside and pulled up to the keyboard.

"No, I've read him extensively and attended two of his lectures on the no-boundary theory—why are you grinning, Phil?"

Khrismann leaned back in his chair. "Stephen Hawking was right again. His theory is now *classic*."

Dr. Jordan thought deeply and shifted his eyes to a group of men. They were seated around a large work-table. After a moment he turned back to Phil. "The universe is infinite then?"

"According to all calculations and advanced simulations, yes, the universe is endless."

Hal studied the computer screen. He blinked at the time gate graphics. "The boundary singularity never existed."

Phil lifted his cup and took a swallow of coffee. "Our friend, Mr. Hawking never believed it did, but he had to prove his theory would conform to observation."

Dr. Jordan chuckled. "That's the barrier—the theory-killer. Hal met Phil's eyes. "Hawking hasn't done it yet. I mean, in my time—nineteen ninety eight. The boundary singularity is still a factor." He relaxed and smiled. "Stephen will prove it, won't he?"

"That's what I was grinning about, Hal. You've learned something today that is still a few years beyond the greatest minds of your time." He sipped more coffee and set his cup down. "Yes, Hawking will prove his theory agrees with observations."

"How? How does he do it?"

Khrismann looked down at his keyboard and thought a moment. Rubbing his chin he said, "Too much knowledge can be a curse."

"I already know more than any scientist in my time."

"Results, yes. Procedures and methods,

no. Not quite yet."

"Phil, I'm one of the key people—I'm involved in results."

Khrismann studied the men at the work-table. He thought about what they were doing. "See those men, Hal?" He pointed toward the group.

"Yes."

"They're trying to find a way to harness the time gate—put it in a box. Control it."

Hal stared at Phil's people. "What does that have to do with Hawking's theory?"

"It's his theory, Doctor. It must come to maturity through his work. His alone."

Hal turned back. "I don't understand."

"Okay. Let's say someone from five-hundred years ahead of us, right now, popped into this room and gave those men the answer they're searching for."

"Great! It would save a lot of time and trouble—"

"It would upset time, Doctor—and create trouble."

Jordan sat back. "How could that be?"

"Things must take place at the rate of current evolution. It can't be upset."

Hal shook his head again. "My knowing how Stephen Hawking solved boundary-singularity would upset evolution?"

Phil drank more coffee. "In itself, no. If you acted upon that information, yes."

Dr. Jordan laughed. "You think I'd get to Stephen and tell him. Come on. As I said, I already know more—"

"You know what you have to in order to carry out the evolution of events you're involved in. That's the only reason you're going back, you and the others. Don't forget it."

Hal shifted his eyes away from Khrismann and shuddered. "I understand ... I'm sorry for pushing."

Phil cleared his throat and sat up straight. "I didn't mean to raise my voice."

"It's okay."

Phil gripped the Doctor's shoulder. "Seriously, let me show you something."

Hal relaxed.

"The gate shifts." Phil turned to his keyboard and entered a series of numbers. "Look at the screen, Doctor." The graphic of the gate was now shown over a background of a map of the United States.

Dr. Jordan let the information seep in and studied the screen. "The gate acts like a weather pattern."

"Very much so, except it's stronger and more stable over the ocean."

Hal touched the screen. He traced the

outline of the gate as if he could feel its texture. "The gate is some kind of natural storm."

Phil pushed his chair away from the console and crossed his legs. "A storm we can't quite understand. Not yet anyway."

Dr. Jordan tapped the screen with his finger. "I'm sure you've considered the role gravity might have in the gate." He looked at Khrismann.

Phil smiled and sat back. "Doctor, I wish to hell you weren't going home."

"Thanks a whole lot."

"Let me digress for a moment. Earlier we touched on Dr. Hawking's theories regarding the universe and time. You respect his work?"

"Absolutely, He's a bit deep, but what a mind."

"You're a man of faith, right?"

"Born and raised Southern Baptist."

"On May fifteenth 2011, Dr. Hawking states, in an interview in a publication called, *The Clarion* :

I regard the brain as a computer which will stop working when its components fail. There is no heaven or afterlife for broken down computers; that is a fairy story for people afraid of the dark.

"How do you respond to that?"

"No differently than I responded to his 1988 book *A Brief History of Time* it sold 9 million copies, and in it Hawking referenced God metaphorically as the force that could fully explain the creation of the universe. It is, after all, a *theory* and can't be proven by observation. The only observers are *dead* and they aren't talking."

Phil chuckled. "I had a feeling you'd see it like that. It seems, Dr. Hawking believes *God* is the answer to all things *unanswerable."*

"And that would be yet another theory." Hal grinned and pointed to the screen. "The *Time-Gate* can't be answered, you can't see it, but it does exist and you're trying to harness it. With all your advanced science, I don't believe you ever will."

"Perhaps not in my time, but for now, we're able to use it for the good of all."

"Are you sure? From what I've learned, the gate is controlled by a select few and they decide what's good for the *whole."*

"You are an interesting man, Hal."

"Thank you, and so is all of this."

Phil stood and stepped behind his chair. He laughed. "It took some of our best minds and weeks of complicated simulations to come up with a gravity-factor. Of course, that was sometime ago." He slapped the back of the chair.

"You've been exposed to the gate less than an hour and you've calculate the same answer."

Hal nodded. "Your people may have been too close to the forest to see the trees."

"Perhaps, Doctor. How?"

"How, what?"

Khrismann sat down again and leaned toward Dr. Jordan. "How in hell did you see a gravity factor so damn quickly?"

One of the men at the work-table heard Phil's raised voice. He leaned back in his chair and studied Dr. Jordan.

Hal said, "How is really academic. The shape and activity of the gate brings to mind Stephen Hawking's model of a black hole—"

"An imploding star?"

Dr. Jordan took a sip of cool coffee. "Right. According to Hawking's studies, a black hole ain't black—that's a quote."

They both chuckled.

Phil said, "The intense gravity holds in light." He smiled.

"Precisely." Hal used his hands to form a circle in the air. "The event-horizon of the hole—its outer edge or ring—is round. You know that, just let me go on a minute. The whole of it is like a funnel." He tapped the screen again. "Your gate-diagram is shown as a funnel I see it as a mutation of a black hole." He studied the computer image for a long moment, then reached up and ran his finger along the top of the screen. "What's up here could very well be an event horizon. The tip." Jordan pointed to the shifting tail of the gate. "Here, the tail of the funnel might well be the door of space-time reversed." He tapped the screen once more. "The past, Phil. This tail could be a needle-prick hole in the fabric of time itself."

Khrismann smiled and glanced over at the work-table. Three more people were listening intently. "How do you factor in gravity?"

The Professor looked at the screen. "I'm not sure, but I know it's involved ...."

One of the men at the work-table stood and walked toward them. He cleared his throat and addressed Phil. "May I?"

Khrismann nodded. "Of course." To Hal, Phil said, "Doctor, meet George Rainey, he's the head physicist on the Project."

Dr. Jordan stood and held out his hand. "The pleasure is mine, sir."

George Rainey stood four inches over Hal and was a good ten years younger. He grinned then slipped both hands into the pockets of his trousers. "I've been listening to what you and Phil have been talking about. I must commend you on your advanced perceptions. I'm impressed."

Hal smiled and leaned against the console. "Thank you, but I'm afraid I have a lot more to learn."

George pointed toward the computer screen. "Our friend there, the gate, seems to be full of gravity, condensed, focused." He stepped closer and pointed at the large graphic. "The point of its gravitational energy is, as you suggested, at the tail. The hole in the fabric of time."

Dr. Jordan rubbed his chin. "And the top, the widest part of the funnel cone is, in fact, an event horizon?"

George leaned against the console and grinned. "It is, Doctor and it's a wide open door to the future."

Hal shuddered. "You've tried it and failed—right?"

Phil held up his hand to silence George. "We're getting off track."

Hal shook his head. "I know about your probes and the loss."

George said, "We're just three or four equations from the answer."

"Thank you, that's all for now." Phil gestured toward the work table and nodded. The message was understood. Without further words, George left Phil and Hal to themselves.

Professor Jordan said, "Intelligent young man."

"He's one of our best. When all the answers are in, he'll be the biggest contributor."

Hal pinched the bridge of his nose and

squeezed his eyes shut. "You can't send us back now because the gate is unstable, right?"

"Correct. The risks are too great."

Jordan opened his eyes and looked at Khrismann. "Is the gravity-factor higher or lower?"

Phil pulled himself up to the console and keyed a set of sequential numbers. The screen displayed the current status of the gate. "The top of the cone is showing high gravity, the bottom is fragmented and spotty."

Dr. Jordan gripped his chin with his left hand, smiled and held up his right. "It may be dumb, but take this down." He blinked several times and knitted his brow.

Phil grabbed a pad and pen from his desk and stared at Hal. "I'm ready."

"Okay, this may be stupid, just bear with me anyway."

"Let's have it"

Hal chuckled. "I'd give a month's pay to be right on this. When the gate's gravity reduces at the tip of the funnel, it will increase at the event horizon by the exact same degree."

Khrismann wrote down the statement word for word. "Go on."

"The gate is not unstable. It's simply shifting energy and re-stabilizing at the event horizon. The door to the future."

Phil looked up and shook his head. "What?"

"I don't know how, I just know! The top of the gate is the way into tomorrow—the bottom is open to yesterday!"

Khrismann finished his notes, underlined the time and Dr. Jordan's name.

Hal sat back in his chair and let out a long breath. "I don't have any idea what happened. All of a sudden, I saw the answer as if it'd been worked out in advanced calculus."

A slight chill walked up the back of Phil's neck. "I took it all down. We'll run a few simulations."

A sheen of sweat formed on Hal's brow. "Damn, that was strange."

Phil clicked off the image of the gate. "Okay, we're done here. Next stop, the *Time Lab.* You'll get to meet, Dr. Jonathan King and he's excited about meeting you."

Hal said, "The *Time Lab?*"

"It's six floors underground and you'll love it."

"I'm ready."

Chapter 43
A Nice Lunch

DINING AREA 8
COMPLEX LEVEL FOUR I:10 PM:

$\mathcal{K}$athy Simmons ground fresh pepper onto her salad then offered the mill to Michael Sternfeld.

"Thank you," he said, listening to Robert Fisher.

The chairman took a sip of herbal tea and continued what he had been telling Congressman Franklin. "About two-hundred years ago the United States, Russia, England, Poland, Australia, Germany, Ireland, Canada and France joined forces against a rebel faction that had developed in Kuwait. They were strong, but not enough."

Congressman Franklin dabbed his mouth with a paper napkin and sat back from his lobster-noodle soup. "It took the strength of nine nations to deal with rebels?"

Fisher considered the congressman's reaction and squeezed lemon juice into his tea. "Two-hundred years ago, splinter groups had more power than any third-world nation of the twentieth century."

"To what degree?"

"They had nuclear capability and the knowledge to use it." The chairman studied Franklin's eyes. He could feel the congressman sifting through the data.

Alan immediately considered the issue as it might apply to something similar in 1998 and shook his head. "Did they push the button?"

Fisher contemplated his seafood salad. "They did indeed."

Alan shivered. "How was it countered?"

Fisher shook seasoned salt on large chunks of shrimp and crab. "An advanced version of your anti-missile security system stopped them dead, and I mean *dead.*"

The congressman took a breath. "My program was passed?" His wife patted his hand.

"It was approved in October of 1999 and implemented in 2001." Fisher grinned. "That's another reason you and your lovely wife are going back."

"How was my system improved?"

"I don't know all the technical details. It's now called project *Boomerang*. When the rebels launched their nuclear device it was intercepted and returned to the point of origin and detonated. The rebel faction ceased to exist." The chairman smiled. "There hasn't been a hostile conflict since that day."

"What advances were made to my original concept?"

"I can't explain all that, Alan. I'll have Phil give you the details later."

The Sternfelds had been listening intently. Michael spoke up. "A whole country was wiped out?"

Kathy answered. "It was two-hundred years ago. Things have changed since then."

All at once everyone's attention was drawn to the dining room entrance. General Charles Mackendrick had walked into the room. He moved directly to a position between Chairman Fisher and Sophy.

Mack smiled and nodded then leaned over and said something into the chairman's left ear. He straightened and looked at the group.

Fisher turned pale, cleared his throat,

and addressed Sophy. "Locate Khrismann and have him come to my office immediately." Obviously shaken, Fisher pushed away from the table. He paused then whispered something to Sophy. Her eyes widened and she got to her feet instantly.

The general stepped back from the table. He grinned down at the others. "Forgive the interruption. We have government business to attend to." He nodded, smiled and the three of them exited the dining area in a hurry.

Chapter 44
A Dangerous Connection

THE NEVADA SUN 3HRS. EARLIER:

$\mathcal{F}$rank Tanner on his private link with Leo Davis:

"I didn't expect such quick response."

"How in hell did you get my code?"

Farrah nodded to Frank from across the desk. The recorder was rolling and she was taking the conversation by hand.

Frank looked at his computer screen, which displayed Davis' complete work-history and personal data. "Take it easy, Leo, I'm a friendly cont—"

"You're a fucking reporter! There are three people with access to my code and I'm one of them. My wife doesn't know it."

"I didn't know you were married," Frank lied. That information, the names and ages of Davis's two boys were highlighted on the screen. Tanner had decided those facts would work in his favor.

"Look, Tanner, I responded to you because I have to answer my Goddamn communicator. Failure to do so means I'm dead!"

"That could be a near-future reality." Frank heard Davis's teeth click.

"Okay, Mr. Reporter, here's an immediate reality for you. This cute little trick has put your ass in deep shit! Within the hour, I'll have you picked up for breach of security—"

"Excellent, Leo. Then I can tell the enforcement commission what I know about you, Larry Cross—"

The engineer's throat clicked. "Councilman Cross?"

"The very same. I think the commission would also like to hear about one of your most recent projects."

Silence.

Davis's voice dropped to a whisper. "What project?"

Frank glanced at his secretary. She nodded. He continued. "A little destruct-program that was installed in a five-hundred year old jetliner."

Silence.

Tanner waited a moment. "Did you hear me?"

In a low, hoarse voice, Leo said, "Whatever you think you know is also classified. Any connection I have with Councilman Cross is restricted, government business." Word-by-word, Leo's voice climbed in volume. "You and whoever your informant is have just bought a Gray Plan vacation. Have a nice trip!"

"We might run into each other up there. General Mackendrick mentioned the moon and your name in the same breath."

Davis clicked his teeth again. "Mackendrick?"

"Good old Mack himself." Frank lowered his voice for effect. "The general said you and Cross would be crusty old bastards when you came back, if you ever did that is."

"Tanner—I don't know what you're up to, but let me tell you something!" He took a short breath and raised his voice. "Councilman Cross is a highly respected official. He warned me about the kind of shit you're trying pull here."

"You do work for him then?"

"On special projects, yes—I do."

"Like Time Gate and the old 747?"

Silence.

Frank hesitated a second or two, then shot off another round. "There was another little job you and Tarkin did for good old Larry. Wasn't it a secret, electronic detonator that was triggered by numerical sequence?"

"That was an experimental device for military aircraft."

"Well congratulations, Mr. Davis. The experiment worked. The damn thing blew one, Mr. Nevil Garrett and his lady friend into the cosmos."

"Who the hell is Nevil Garrett?"

"He was a Larry Cross employee. An inside informant, like you, Leo."

"Why would Larry kill this guy, Garrett?"

"It seems, Nevil gave me restricted information, Cross wanted me to have. With that done, Garrett was no longer needed. Bang! Larry's ass is covered."

Farrah shivered and adjusted her earphones. *Cross could do the same damn thing to you, Love.* She continued documenting the conversation.

Frank said, "Mackendrick and Khrismann connected Garrett to me through a partly-burned link-number. Jesus—they're clever." Tanner added the last three words to set up another lie.

Leo whispered. "So, your ass is on the line now."

"Right—and so is yours, my friend." He hesitated. "Along with the scrap of paper that brought me in, they found a fragment of your trigger-gadget." Frank let the story hit home.

"Sonofabitch ...."

"That's right. Your friend Cross is a real sonofabitch—a rather dangerous one."

The engineer gulped a breath and spat out his defense. "I had nothing to do with Garrett's death. Not a damn thing!"

"You and Tarkin made the device for Cross—you're an accessory to murder. That could put you on the moon." Frank glanced at Farrah and winked.

She didn't smile or grin, she did shudder.

"I can't believe all this."

Frank hesitated and went for the brass ring. "I'm in the boat with you, Leo." He paused. "We can save each other's butts by working together on this."

"How do we do that?"

So far—so good, thought Tanner. *The little lie worked.* "Listen, my ass is in the soup because I used the information Garrett gave me to get into Tex and the Time Gate file."

"Goddammit, man! You know what they can do to you for that?"

Now I got him. He grinned. "I'm sure it would make Gray Plan a better option. In any case, I have to get to Cross within sixty days and I need your help!"

Silence.

"Leo?"

"I have a family. If this crap goes wrong they'll suffer for it."

I don't have to use the wife an' kids punch. He's doing it himself. "Look at it another way. If everything goes right you'll be the man of the hour."

"How do you imagine that will happen?"

"We work as a team. Where can we meet? It's got to be now and someplace safe."

A moment passed. "You know the Perry place off route ninety-five?"

Frank thought about it. "The old-time café just outside Dayton?"

"That's it."

"We meet there?"

"No. We can't be seen together. Drive exactly three miles past the place. Take a left on the first paved road. You'll go northeast about a mile before you come to a government power station."

"An old solar installation?"

"Yes. It's fenced and marked 'SPS' 3-6-9-0." Leo said the numbers one-at-a-time. "I have access to the building. It's fully computerized. We'll be alone."

Frank nodded toward Farrah. She had taken down the information. "It'll take me forty minutes or so to get there."

"Get moving. I'll be watching for you. What are you driving?"

"A red turbo."

"Figures ... push, Frank. Make it in a half-hour."

"Thanks, Leo."

"Yeah. I hope you're right, Tanner." The link went dead.

Frank looked over at Farrah. "I don't want to hear it."

She removed her headset and plopped her pod and pen hard on Frank's desk. "Well, you're going to!" She stood and hugged herself as if it was winter and the window was open. "This is the second time you've jumped up from your desk and flew off into the night to some secret, shrouded meeting—"

"First of all—it's my job, remember? Secondly, it isn't night—it's morning!"

"You know what I mean."

"Thirdly," he said, ignoring her comment. "Our friend, Mr. Leo Davis is not hostile. As a matter of fact, he's scared shitless. I got that from his tone, you didn't?"

"Yes, I did." She paced, then turned sharply and leaned on the desk. "What if Cross is having him watched? What if he sends a goon or two along to see what he's up to?"

Frank came around his desk and took Farrah in his arms. He held her a moment. He kissed her forehead, her nose then her mouth. He pulled back and smiled wide. "In the last few days, I've come to realize something I never thought would happen."

"You know—sometimes you irritate the shit out of me."

"Good. You're a prize I never knew existed until all this crap hit the fan." He kissed her mouth again. "And whether you know it or not, lady, you make a big difference in my life."

She looked up and widened her eyes. "I care more than you know."

"I'll say it slow, don't react, just listen. I love you, Farrah. I damn well care what happens to my ass, more than ever."

She opened her mouth.

Frank put two fingers against her lips. "Hold the thought. Have Billy bring my turbo up. I'm on my way to Dayton. He kissed her again and left.

Chapter 45
The Time Lab

**THE COMMAND CENTER TWO HOURS LATER
SUB-LEVEL SIX AREA 4 TIME LAB:**

$\mathcal{P}$hil Khrismann and Dr. Hal Jordan checked in at the security station. Phil addressed the female droid on duty. "We need a visitor badge for Dr. Jordan."

The droid smiled. "Welcome, doctor. Please touch the scanner on the counter."

Hal looked at Phil. "I feel like I'm entering a restricted section of NASA."

Khrismann grinned. "In a sense, you are." He pointed to a small rectangle of glass flush-mounted into the counter top. "The scanner reads your prints and brings up a file on you that's already in the data base."

"When did I volunteer that information?"

"You didn't. By the time you and the other key people were revived in the medical wing, our master computer, *Tex,* had recorded everything we needed to know."

"For security reasons of course."

"Exactly. Go ahead, touch the scanner it won't bite." Phil chuckled and touched the scanner himself. To the droid he said, "Notify, Dr. King that his guest has arrived."

"Immediately, sir." She handed Hal a visitor ID badge.

He clipped the badge to the pocket of his shirt. "I have to say, frightened as I was at first, I'm enjoying the most incredible experiences of my life."

Khrismann smiled. "What you will accomplish is outstanding. Sharing additional knowledge with you is well worth the risk."

"Risk?"

"Do you realize the responsibility you'll have when you go home?"

"I've considered the very weight of it and I shake inside to think of the knowledge I won't be able to share with my students. As a teacher, that's going to be a millstone around my neck."

"I'll give you a little help. Share what you

learned here as *theory*. Create exercises for your students. Play the, *what if* game with their young minds.

"I can do that–yes, I *can* do that." Hal's eyes lit up and he grinned from ear-to-ear.

Phil took on a serious expression. "Understand your restrictions." He hesitated. "You can not, at any time, alter the work of your prize student."

"Why would I?"

"You know the result of Russell's extensive development in self-sustaining energy. It would be very tempting to push him along beyond what he'll accomplish, what we both know he will."

"I understand."

"Do you?"

"Yes, I know and I promise you and the council, I will not–I will *not* make that mistake."

"Go with theory, Hal. Nothing more."

A young man came into the security area with a big smile on his face. He approached Dr. Jordan and offered his hand. "I'm Jonathan King." He was full of excited energy. "It's my pleasure, doctor."

They shook hands.

Phil said, "Dr. Jordan, meet Dr. King."

Jordan chuckled. "I'm here on a pass and the pleasure is mine."

King shook his head. "I've looked

forward to meeting you. Your work is outstanding."

"I'm flattered. I hope I won't bore you to death."

Phil's communicator buzzed. "Khrismann here." He turned away from the other two. "I'm on the way." He tucked the device into his coat pocket. "I've been called to Fisher's office immediately." He made a polite smile. "Hal, you're in good hands." He nodded. "Jonathan, escort Dr. Jordan back to his quarters when you're done."

"No problem, it'll be a while."

"Whatever, you two have fun." He walked to the elevators in haste.

* * * *

An hour later Hal Jordan and Jonathan King sat in a massive control station looking at an enormous computer screen. The image displayed a rapidly changing series of light patterns.

Dr. King said, "Again, I'll emphasize, time doesn't exist. It's a myth."

Jordan shook his head. "You've said that and I'm trying to comprehend. Man created the term *time.* The clock on the wall doesn't mean anything. Correct?"

"In terms of hours and minutes, you're right." Jonathan keyed a few numbers. The screen changed. A mass of colored particles crossed the screen in a random fashion creating what could be considered an elaborate modern art painting.

Hal studied the patterns. "What are they?"

"Energy. If time has a name it has to be *energy.* That's what you're looking at."

"Where are those images coming from?"

"Inside the Time Gate." King keyed another screen. "See how the shapes are reversed and changed color?"

"They've turned red."

"Red indicates the gate is closing and becomes unstable." He keyed in another number sequence. The massive screen changed again. It displayed an enormous circle of white and yellow streaks of light. "That is the image of the gate as it was when your plane passed through into 2498." He cleared his throat. "My guess is, one hour later in your encounter would've sent your 747 another five hundred years into the future."

"Time doesn't exist as we know it." Hal shook his head. "How then does anything exist?"

Dr. King held up his hands. "Tick, tick on a clock—no. That's not *time.* We perceive it as such, but that's just a way to track a minute, an hour, a day, a week, whatever."

"What the hell is it then?"

"It's an entity, doctor. Time is a living thing." He leaned back in his chair. "Time is the past, present and the future. It has no substance, no mass and cannot be harnessed as we're trying to make believe it can."

Jordan leaned forward and stared at the huge screen. "What about the gate?"

"We can plot it, monitor its activities and gauge its fluctuations. However, we'll never really harness it."

Hal looked around the vast control room and saw several people at numerous work stations. "Then I have to believe there's a significant reason this lab is in place and operational."

Dr. King smiled. "You and the work of your student, Russell, are part of why this lab exists." He clicked a few more numbers on his keyboard. A new screen displayed curving streaks of bright blue light. "Russell's work captured what you see on the screen."

"I've never seen anything displayed like that."

"No, but Russell wrote a paper on it."

"You mean *will* write the article."

"Yes. He isolated a band of subatomic particles. He realized those particles were emitted by the sun. They spun around the sun, gained gravity and formed a never-ending loop." He looked at Hal. "Steve's theory is that the loop was the formation of time?" Jonathan shook his head.

"I'd love to clap my hands and say that's it. That's the answer."

Hal rubbed his chin. "There is no answer, is there?"

"We haven't found it yet."

"Has Stephen's theory been proven?"

"No, and it hasn't been disproved either."

The imaged changed to a closer view.

Jonathan pointed toward the screen. "You're seeing light bending and that's supposed to be impossible. However it's happening inside the Time Gate right now."

"So, if we accept Russell's theory, we may be looking at the concept of time as we perceive it."

"Based on what we've learned, I would have to agree."

Hal grinned. "If it *is* true, what does it mean? Secondly, what can we do with it?"

"Doctor, those are the very questions that keep this lab busy night and day." He cleared the screen. "Your second question has an easy answer. We're using it on a highly controlled basis. The Time Gate is a tool."

Dr. Jordan sat back from the console. "Like any tool, it can be misused."

"That's the reason for the intense security. The general population knows of the gate as just a rumor and we intend to keep it that way." Jonathan pushed back from the control board and stood. "How about having lunch with me down here instead of going back up?"

"You've read my mind. I'd be pleased to spend more time in your company."

"Excellent. After we eat, I'll show you the light lab."

"I can't believe all of this." Hal stood and looked around the massive laboratory. "Now you tell me there's even more?"

"There's a lot more. After our meal we'll stop by the Botanical Research Center."

They started toward the exit.

Hal said, "A greenhouse?"

"Sort of. We have plants there that are from out of this world. You can try a fresh salad made from a few of them in the dining area."

Chapter 46
COMMAND CENTER

SHUTTLE-PAD 18:

a ground crewman (service droid S-5M) secured the shuttle's passenger door from the outside. He waved to the co-pilot. The shuttle lifted off and headed west-northwest at maximum acceleration.

Mackendrick stepped out of the flight deck and closed the door. He studied the intense faces of Chairman Fisher and Phil Khrismann and grinned. He slipped into a seat, facing them, and secured his harness. He glanced at his watch. "We'll be there in seven minutes."

Automatically, Khrismann checked his own watch. It was a habit he developed as a result of working with the military.

Fisher shaded his eyes and glanced out through his port-side window. He looked back at Mackendrick to see him remove his hat and place it on the seat next to him. Mack was still grinning. "There's something amusing about all this, general?"

Mack sat back and took a hit of Paralayne. "Regarding Davis and Tanner? Hardly, Mr. Chairman, but there is a tickle in the way things are leading to his Honor, Councilman Larry Cross." He capped his Paralayne tube and slipped it into the right pocket of his crisp blouse.

Phil leaned forward and glared at the general. "We put those men on the firing-line, we own the result."

Mack stiffened. "They're pawns in this game, Khrismann, keep that in perspective."

Fisher cut in, demanding and loud. "Knock it off—both of you! Let it rest. I need to work this out. Mack, you said Tanner was all right. Can we trust him?"

Mackendrick sat up straight and cocked his head. "He was okay when he made contact." He hesitated. "Trust is another issue. So far, he's on a leash and he knows it."

"How long before we touch down?"

Mack said, "Five-six minutes."

"Good. I don't want to hear anything from either of you until we know what we're dealing with."

Mackendrick stared at Khrismann. "Yes, sir."

The noise of the shuttle's engines grew louder.

Chapter 47
The Botanic Project

SUBLEVEL SIX AREA 9:

*D*r. Jordan stood inside the entrance looking up. "This is a vast, enclosed rain forest."

Jonathan secured the interior door. "The section we're in is exactly that. It's also a great deal more." He stood beside Hal. "The roof of the enclosure is two hundred ten feet high. The vegetation creates its own atmosphere. Sometimes one or two small storms drench everything behind the glass walls twice a day."

"It looks like a giant terrarium."

"You're right. The glass walls are two panels six inches thick with five inches of air space between them."

Jordan looked left and right then up again. "The weight must be astronomical."

"Actually the weight is quite manageable. The panels are not the kind of glass you have in 1998. I don't know all the technical details. However, you could carry a panel by yourself. It'd be a bit clumsy, but you could pick it up."

"How much of this is there? I guess it's at least fifty feet to my left and about a hundred to the right."

"We're at the southwest corner of this enclosure. It has a ground-mass of sixty acres and it's just one of twelve units."

"Unbelievable." Hal shook his head. "I've never seen plants so huge. Can we go in there?"

"You don't want to. Plants are not the only things living in that terrarium." Dr. King climbed into a vehicle resembling a large golf cart. "C'mon, we'll stop at the green lab on our way to the Light Research Complex."

"You mind telling me what else lives in there?" He gestured toward the glass wall.

"Up ahead, we'll stop there." Jonathan pulled over close to the glass. "There's a small speaker on the wall here. You can't hear through the glass. There are listening, viewing stations about forty feet apart.

Our young research students monitor various activities heard and seen from inside the enclosure." He reached out and tapped on the glass. "Maybe Freddie would like to get a look at you."

"Freddie?"

"It's just a pet name. Nobody's sure what Freddie really is."

They stepped out of the cart and approached the glass wall. Jonathan sat down in front of a small keyboard and transparent computer monitor. "The researchers study any activity and document anything that happens." He keyed a sequence of numbers. "Freddie seems to like electronic wave sounds. This is his favorite."

Hal heard what sounded like a harp playing from inside the terrarium. "There's movement behind that enormous yellow plant." His mouth went dry.

"I believe that's Freddie." Jonathan spoke into a small microphone next to the keyboard. "Hi Freddie, how's your day?"

Hal stepped back from the glass and sat down hard in the cart. He gasped a short breath and whispered, "Dear mother in heaven."

The creature came up to the glass. It was at least six feet four.

What Hal saw was an upright rodent of about two hundred pounds with powerful arms and legs. Instead of paws, Freddie had human-like hands. "Oh my god …."

The creature tapped the glass, nodded and pointed toward Dr. Jordan."

Jonathan spoke into the mike. "Meet Hal Jordan, he's our guest from another time."

"That thing understands you?" Hal climbed out of the cart.

"On one level, I have to say yes, but we can't be sure." He clicked off the mike. "Think of a dog that knows you. It comes time to take him for a walk. You say things to him, call him by name and the dog gets all excited. Does the animal understand English?" He shrugged. "No, but the dog knows what you're saying."

Hal took a step closer to the glass. "Click on the mike."

Jonathan turned it on. "Talk to him."

Hal rubbed his hand across his face. "Hello, Freddie. I'm Hal."

The creature came face-to-face with Dr. Jordan and placed both hands against the glass. Freddie turned his rodent head to Jonathan.

"Its okay, Hal is a friend." He nodded and patted the doctor's arm.

Jordan stayed back from the glass. "I'm pleased to meet you, Freddie."

The rodent nodded and stared into Hal's eyes.

Dr. Jordan stepped back. "This creature *is* intelligent."

Freddie nodded again.

Hal noticed a skittering of movement in the vegetation around the creature's human-like feet. "What's this?"

Freddie reached down and picked up a furry little animal that looked a lot like him. He held it up to the glass and scratched it behind its ears. The little thing barked at Jordan and blinked its jade-green eyes.

Hal smiled through a shaky breath. "That's Freddie's child?"

The creature held the little animal securely, waved at Dr. King and walked away into the clusters of yellow and dark green plants.

Hal sat back into the cart. "What on earth have I just seen?"

Jonathan closed down the little research station. "It isn't from this earth"

"I think I know that. It defies belief, but I just witnessed it with my own eyes an' I heard it."

Dr. King got into the cart and looked at Hal. "Freddie is over a hundred and twenty five years old." He started driving along the long corridor. "This green house project is the result of a deep-space probe that brought back soil and plant samples from a distant planet in alpha galaxy nine. It required four-times the speed of light to launch and return the unmanned probe."

Hal caught a breath. "Beyond the speed of light?"

"It was and has been done since." He turned right into a long, well lighted corridor. "The plants and Freddie emerged from the establishment of what you've just seen."

"Freddie evolved in that jungle?"

"He did, and so did other life-forms."

"Which are?"

"More unbelievable than Freddie and his little offspring."

"Are they intelligent?" Hal hung on as they pulled to a stop.

"We're not sure yet."

"Where are we now?" He watched a security droid approach their cart.

"The Green-Lab, you'll love it. The salad you had for lunch was created here."

"Great. What little creatures will I meet?"

The droid waved them through. Dr. King laughed. "No monsters here, just the best vegetables ever grown."

Chapter 48
Desert Encounter

SOLAR POWER STATION 3690
TWO HOURS EARLIER:

$\mathcal{F}$rank Tanner pulled his red turbo through the open gate and drove behind the block structure of the power station. He parked beside an official-looking green work-craft.

Except for the constant wind, everything seemed dead.

Gritty sand stung his face as he slipped out of his vehicle. He gripped the bill of his cap and clutched the collar of his jacket. He approached the power house door. When he touched the handle the door swung inward.

"Davis, it's Tanner."

Nothing.

Frank closed the door. A thick silence settled in. "Leo?"

A shadow moved behind a stack of old electronic equipment. The muzzle of a laser-gun came out from the dark and pointed directly at him.

"Davis!" Tanner's voice bounced off the interior walls. Frank fell back against the door and shifted his eyes from side-to-side. "You don't need a damn gun."

The working end of the weapon was followed by Leo. "Sorry." He put the gun away. "I'm a little jumpy at this point."

"I can't imagine why." Frank glanced around the spotless, polished room. "This station must go back at least fifty years." He walked toward the unmanned control area. "None of them are huge like this anymore." He pulled a desk chair away from the control board and sat down.

"Tanner, I didn't come out here to discuss old technology."

"Easy, I need an answer or two before we plunge right in." The chair squeaked when Frank turned to face the engineer. "First question. Were the early stations bigger?"

Davis stood at the far end of the control

counter. "Frank, what the fu—"

Tanner waved his hand and shook his head. Pointing to a red light on the main control panel he said, "I'd better take notes on all this. I want my article on power stations to be accurate." He took a pad and pen from his jacket pocket. "Well, were they?" He nodded his head rapidly and wrote a few words on the pad.

Davis wrinkled his brow and watched Frank's head bob up and down. He shifted his eyes around the interior and answered the question. "Some of the early solar stations were three-times this size."

Frank handed him the note. "Did I get the designation of this station right?" He continued to nod.

Davis looked at the note. He read it to himself, he answered, "Yes—everything's correct ...." He raised his eyes from the paper to Tanner, then to the red light. The words on the note read:

We're being monitored!

The message sent a chill through Leo's entire body. *Sonofabitch!* He met Frank's eyes with a frightened stare.

Frank tapped his lips with his index finger and turned his head from side to side. "I'd like to get a closer look at the outside of the building before we get too involved in here."

The note shook in Leo's hand. "Good—let's take a look."

Frank got up and slid the chair back in its place. "Just want to get my facts right. Okay?"

Nervous, Davis answered. "I understand. All this is pretty involved." They walked toward the exit.

* * * *

COMMAND COMPLEX: SECURITY LEVEL-10

"Shit!" Danielle Janning pushed away from her keyboard and entered a three-letter, three-digit code into her communicator.

Her contact responded an instant later.

"TWB946–open."

Danielle said, "Target subjects left the building."

"Data acquired?"

"Nothing, sir. They're aware of surveillance."

"Is tracker-one in place?"

"Yes, sir." Ms. Janning studied her screen. She watched Davis and Frank leave the power station and close the door. She pushed a long lock of blonde hair behind her left ear.

"Activate T-I and power its monitoring and tracking program. I'll supervise from here. Clear your link—you're out."

"Yes, sir." She switched off her communicator and reached for link-termination then hesitated. *Something's wrong with this,* she thought and keyed a command that would monitor and record all audio and the full event-sequence of tracker-one. All event-data would be routed to a security sub-memory grid in the bowels of Tex and held under a code Ms. Janning would create upon termination of the event-sequence.

Should there ever be a question regarding this specific operation, Danielle could account for every detail. She Activated Tracker-1 and put its program into operation.

Chapter 49
The Green Lab

SUBLEVEL SIX AREA 10
EAST SECURITY ENTRANCE:

*D*octors Jordan and King stepped out of the cart. Hal looked back at the enormous wall of glass that housed the *Botanic Project.* "What other creatures live in there besides Freddie?"

"Over the last hundred twenty five years researchers have logged more than eight hundred species of birds and animals that have sprung to life in there."

"That's incredible." Something moved behind a cluster of dark red growth. Hal took a short breath. "There's one."

Jonathan looked. "That's a *Skitter.* It's a creature about the size of an average rabbit. They get their name from being able to climb the big trees right to the top in seconds."

The animal clung to a branch about ten feet off the ground. It peered out at the two men through glowing, amber eyes.

Hal stepped toward the glass. The *Skitter* blinked and shot up the tree out of sight. "It looks harmless."

"They run in packs and attack larger animals with deadly force."

"Freddie's managed to survive."

"Nothing in there has ever harmed Freddie or his offspring." Jonathan gestured toward the Green Lab entrance. "Let's go inside."

* * * *

Once through security, Hal stopped and stared. "These people are all student researchers?"

"They're working on various degrees from the UWC University in Houston, Texas." Jonathan chuckled. "Welcome to the *salad garden.*"

"What?" Hal looked around the many rows of work stations. "I don't see a tomato or a single head of lettuce anywhere."

"The actual produce is grown on vast

environmentally controlled, agricultural compounds in California and throughout the Midwest."

They walked along the main aisle toward the exit. Hal said, "I'm guessing that you've managed to reduce pollution in the environment."

"It's non-existent." Dr. King smiled. "Your 747 created more air contamination in one landing than we've seen in a hundred years."

They stopped by a young researcher. Jonathan tapped her on the shoulder. "Excuse me."

The young girl turned and smiled. "Hello, Doctor."

Jonathan noticed her ID badge. "Hi, Sandy. This is Dr. Hal Jordan, he's my guest."

Hal nodded. "Hi, pleased to meet you."

She studied the professor. "My pleasure."

Dr. King pointed toward Sandy's computer screen. "What are you working on?"

Sandy's big grin lit up her blue eyes. "I've isolated the progress of a new fruit. We've coded it as A.L.-562. That means apple-large."

Hal said, "A large apple?"

"Yes, sir. It grows on a vine." She laughed. "It gets as big as a pumpkin."

Jonathan smiled. "Thank you."

They continued along the aisle. Hal Shook his head. "An apple as big as a pumpkin. I'm amazed. And the damn thing grows on a vine!"

"Right through here." Jonathan keyed a sequence of digits into a keypad to the right of a door marked:

LIGHT LAB – LEVEL 5 CLEARENCE REQUIRED

"Hal, this will interest you much more than the growth of vegetables or fruit."

The security lock clacked open.

Dr. King continued. "Did you enjoy your lunch?"

"It was excellent."

"Your salad was created by those students back there."

Chapter 50
Desert Incident

THE SHUTTLE: 3:00 MINUTES BEFORE TOUCH DOWN:

*C*hairman Fisher squeezed his eyes shut then blinked General Mackendrick into focus. "I'm more than a little upset, Mack. I knew nothing of this Tanner-Davis game of yours."

Mack managed a slight grin and a glance at Phil. "We had to act immediately, sir."

We? Khrismann thought. *You—acted!*

The general continued. "Tanner had already become a threat to security—he's a goddamn reporter. We simply used him as a tool and connected him to Davis—our pipeline to Cross."

Phil glared at Mack and thought, *Drop the 'WE', Goddammit! You made the decisions!*

Fisher looked out the window then studied Mack for a moment. "There are two lives here that don't seem to mean anything to you, I can't quite understand that."

Mackendrick responded. "With all due respect, sir. You pulled me off the Poland situation and threw me into this time gate breach. I acted on my instincts. This gate-crossing has cooked up a pot of poison. Our friend, Larry Cross is after your ass. You know it—we know it."

Phil rubbed the back of his neck.

General Mackendrick went on. "What's happened in the last few days goes beyond the goddamned time gate. We're dealing with subversive activity here. Cross is governmentally destructive. If Tanner and Davis are spent in the process then it's just part of the cost."

The co-pilot entered the cabin and addressed Mack. "We're just over one minute from touch-down, sir. The landing area is secure. Should we go directly in?"

Mack said, "Take us straight in, without delay."

Fisher waited until the co-pilot left and closed the door. "You'd better be right, Mack."

"I am, sir—we'll pay the price if I'm not." Khrismann gritted his teeth.

* * * *

THE POWER STATION: ONE HOUR EARLIER:

$\mathscr{F}$rank and Leo stepped into the late-morning wind and slammed the metal door behind them. They faced the hot sand-blow and ran around to the back of the building.

Davis shoved Frank against the structure and stepped back. "What the fuck is going on, Tanner?"

Frank caught his breath. "The red light—we were being watched, Goddammit! They're tracking our asses."

Davis took another two steps back. "You got me in, now—get me out!"

* * * *

Tracker-one came to life. Its scope lit up and came around to a standing image near the rear of the power station. A message flashed in the scope:

LOCK-ON ENGAGED

Leo slammed his right fist into the palm of his left hand. "I'm dead, Tanner!" The engineer lunged at Frank and grabbed him by the front of his jacket.

TARGET ZERO: HOLD FIRE

* * * *

THE SHUTTLE: LANDING AT SPS-3690
45:00 MINUTES LATER:

*C*hairman Fisher watched the ground crew guide the shuttle-pilot toward the rear of the power station, then looked over at General Mackendrick. "Cross is one cunning sonofabitch, but I can't see him as a killer."

Mack shifted in his seat and glanced out the port-side window. "You will soon enough, sir." He turned to Khrismann. "I want Tanner isolated before he says any more than he has."

Phil stretched his neck to see what was going on below, but couldn't. "Is there a large blue security craft down there?"

Mackendrick leaned to his right and looked

out. "There is."

"Then Mr. Newspaper's under control."

Mack grinned at Khrismann. "He better be."

* * * *

SPS-3690: 40:00 MINUTES EARLIER:

$\mathcal{D}$avis pushed away from Frank and shook his head. "Everything I did was for our country, Tanner!"

Frank pulled his jacket back into shape. "What you did was for Cross."

"Bullshit!"

The tracker-scope picked up Davis' image:

TARGET SIGHTED

Frank pushed away from the building. "Did you alter the 747's re-entry program?"

Davis backed into the open. "Tarkin wrote the program. I did what I was told to do!"

TARGET LOCKED

Tanner moved toward the engineer. Nevil

Garrett did the same thing and he's dead!"

FIRE

Davis looked around and pulled a yellow, plastic card from his jacket pocket. "They'll kill me too—Goddamn you!" He threw the card at Tanner. "That's the original." He made a dash for his vehicle.

Frank caught the card. "Is this it?"

Leo stopped beside his craft. "There's one in the plane—Cross has another altered copy."

Tracker-1 reacted:

Davis' chest exploded a split second before he was slammed against the side of his vehicle.

SELF DESTRUCT:

Tracker-1 became an instant ball of fire.

Frank looked up as a plume of black smoke drifted away from a rocky ledge at least a half-mile to the north. "What the hell?"

Davis's body left a wet red smear on the door of the green vehicle as he slid to the ground.

Tanner stared wide-eyed at Leo's body. He

clutched the yellow card. "Sonofabitch!"

Chapter 51
The Light Lab

SUBLEVEL SIX AERA 12:

$\mathcal{D}$r. Jordan sat beside Jonathan at yet another enormous, complicated looking console. He pointed toward a huge screen. "Let me guess. That's an image of a new galaxy, correct?"

"You're half right. What you see is ancient history. It's actually two galaxies." He clicked a few keys and the images changed to a closer view.

Hal leaned forward. "They're merging."

"Colliding is more like it." Dr. King used a mouse-like device to draw a circle around a section of the image. "A little below and to the left you see a blue tail of light."

"I see it. That's the second galaxy?"

"Yes, it's being absorbed by the larger one." Jonathan sat back. "Those images are more than four hundred fifty light years from Earth."

"How did you get those pictures?"

"We didn't." He keyed back to a full view. "The images you're looking at were released to the public in late April, 2008. They were taken by the Hubble Space Telescope earlier that month."

Hal turned from the screen and looked at Jonathan. "In 2008?" He shook his head. "People in my time will get to see them in just a few years?"

"You've just seen an exclusive preview."

"I'm amazed." He took a breath. "You ... your people, are trusting me with a tremendous amount of information."

"We already know you won't betray any of it." He gripped Hal's arm. "I'm more than pleased to be the one to give you this knowledge. I know you'll put it under the cloak of *theory* and educate many young people with what you've learned. That, doctor is a noble exercise."

Hal grinned. "It might mean the Nobel Prize."

"That, my friend, is something I'm not going to get into."

Jordan nodded toward the image on the

screen. "What does that discovery mean?"

"It's just one of twelve similar events involving colliding galaxies. That one created a cosmic shock wave that spread out over two hundred light years." He chuckled. "The shock was so intense it spawned twenty four black holes. Those devils swallowed an equal number of new suns."

Hal thought a moment. "Are you still monitoring this phenomenon?" He pointed toward the screen again. "There was a rumor that the Hubble telescope required too much maintenance and may have to be shut down."

"An outcry from astronomers prevented that."

"Then you're saying it's still in place?"

"Not hardly. It was replaced in 2120 and again in 2310. The one we're using now was developed a few years ago. It's positioned just outside of our solar system." Dr. King keyed a new image on the screen. "Feast your eyes on a galaxy that formed over one hundred thousand light years ago."

The screen lit up with the blazing light of a million suns and circled counter clockwise. In its center a brilliant red star rotated in the opposite direction. Thousands of small stars appeared at even points all around the outer edges of the image.

Hal drew a long breath. "What is this?"

"From all we can tell, it's a parallel universe."

"There must be life there."

"In my opinion, there has to be."

Dr. Jordan stood and studied the huge image. "This is beyond imagination."

"It's real, Hal. That galaxy exists."

"You say that formation is a hundred thousand light years away?"

"Give or take ten or fifteen hundred light years."

"Can I write a paper on this?"

"If you stick to *theory,* I can't see why not." Dr. King grinned. "Sit down, Hal."

Dr. Jordan eased back into his chair. "Again, I'm overwhelmed."

"In your shoes, I would be too." Jonathan pushed away from the console. "The knowledge you're taking back to 1998 can make you another Einstein. Are you aware of that?"

"Not on that level, no."

"Well it damn well can. You write papers on all of this, everything you've learned here, and it will happen." Jonathan keyed the screen clear.

"I'm no Einstein." Hal stared at the blank screen.

"You are now. I'm encouraging you to write the articles. There will be scientists and physicists around the world calculating your work and be unable to discredit it in any way." He patted Jordan's shoulder. "You will achieve global recognition."

"I'm not sure I can deal with that."

"Believe me, Hal ... you will."

Dr. Jordan pointed toward the blank screen. "Can I see that galaxy again?"

"Absolutely." Jonathan keyed the image back onto the huge display.

"It's changed. The center star is now blue."

"It changes daily. We are reading the progress on a regular basis. Tomorrow it may be green. The galaxy is evolving and we believe life there is as well."

"This is all so unbelievable."

"It's real. It's there and it's happening as we watch."

Hal shook his head. "How can I ever thank you for giving me this wealth of knowledge?"

Dr. King took Hal's right hand in both of his. "It has been my pleasure to meet you and give you a chance to educate many young minds in your time."

"I'm confused, honored and scared to death."

Jonathan smiled. "So am I. Let's get you back up-top."

Chapter 52
The Desert Power Station

ONE HOUR LATER:

$\mathcal{C}$hairman Fisher turned the yellow program card over and over in his fingers. He and Frank Tanner were alone in the blue security vehicle. Fisher had ordered Mackendrick and Khrismann outside. The Chairman laid the card on the table. He studied it for a moment then removed his glasses. "Frank, I'm sure you're well aware of how serious this situation is."

Tanner rested his elbows on the table and rubbed his temples. "About an hour ago the full impact hit home. Seeing Davis splattered against his truck did it."

Fisher sat back. He watched the reporter closely. "You knew about Garrett?"

"I didn't *see* that." He looked up at Fisher. "I saw Leo blown up, Goddammit! I set the man up for Christ's sake."

"You're a tool, Frank. They're using you!"

Tanner stood suddenly. "They? Cross is your man. Pick him up before I get it—or some other sap goes down!"

Fisher slapped the edge of the table. "It's not that simple. After what Mackendrick and you told me, I'm convinced Cross is guilty. The problem is, I don't know why, and at the moment, I have no proof."

Frank gripped the back of his chair and squeezed hard. "Dammit, Fisher. I heard Mack tell you he saw Tarkin and Cross in the airplane!"

"Take it easy. Lower your voice."

"Look, I'm not stupid." He glared at the chairman. "You have a five hundred year old airplane in some hangar somewhere. How did it get here?" He waved his arms. "There had to be people on the damn thing. Where are they?" Frank shook his head. "This involves the *Time Gate*. We both know that." He took a quick breath. "I want the story."

"When the time is right, I'll answer your

questions and you'll have your story." The chairman stood. He picked up the yellow card. "That plane has to be returned to its own time. Now you know more than you should "Tarkin and Cross had every right to be on the jetliner." He held up the card. "Davis told you this program had been altered. There's no proof of that. He also said this was the original." He hesitated. "Cross doesn't want the plane sent back."

Frank leaned forward and shook his head. "Right—the card you have there is clean. The program in the 747 has been changed—Cross has a second copy of the altered card."

Robert Fisher shook his head and looked down at the program-card. "In the time it took for you to tell us your story, we ran this program." He met Frank's eyes. "As you said, it's clean. We also had the card in the plane pulled and run— it's clean too. This is the second time we've had the damn thing checked."

Tanner turned to the window on the right side of the van. He saw Mackendrick and Khrismann walk out of the power station. Mack was waving his arms and shouting something Frank couldn't hear. "There is something wrong, Mr. Fisher ... we both know that."

"Exactly. And it does involve our friend, Larry Cross." Fisher slipped the yellow program-card into his jacket pocket. "We need motive and proof ... that's where you come in."

Frank turned away from the window and stared at Fisher with an agitated expression. "With all due respect, sir—I'm out of the whole mess as of right now!"

Fisher grinned. "Not quite yet, I'm afraid." He keyed the communicator on the table. "Ask the General and Mr. Khrismann to join me in the van."

A filtered voice seemed to come out of the air. "Immediately, sir."

Tanner stared at the chairman. "I'll be the next man out and you know it!"

Fisher held up his hands and smiled. "I have two choices for you. Number one, continue with your investigation to nail Larry Cross."

Frank grabbed the back of his chair again and met Fisher's eyes. "And what's the second?"

The chairman leaned back and drummed his fingers on the table. "Pack your bags for a long stay on Gray Plan."

"You can't—"

"I damn well can—and will ... if you force it."

Frank drove a fist into the back of his chair. "What keeps me off the moon when the shit hits the fan?"

"I do."

"I'm a reporter. I'm after the *Time Gate* story—the one Harry Fellin died for!"

"Continue the investigation. You'll answer to me and me only."

Tanner turned away and gritted his teeth. "What about Mackendrick?"

Fisher relaxed and folded his hands on the table. "The general answers to me. For the duration of this project his orders to you go through me first."

Frank turned back to face the chairman. "I want your promise I'll get the full story."

Fisher pushed away from the table and stood up. "Give me Cross, you'll get Time Gate."

"Your word?"

"You got it."

Mackendrick and Khrismann entered the vehicle. Mack looked at Frank, then at Fisher. "You called for us?"

Fisher gestured toward two empty chairs. "Sit down gentlemen and listen—listen with both ears. Mr. Tanner is in for the full run. As of this minute, he has total amnesty. You get that, Mack?"

The general swallowed a hot, dry lump. "Yes, sir."

"Good. Phil, you will give Tanner every possible cooperation he needs to further his investigation of his honor, the *snake* Councilman

Larry Cross—is that absolutely clear?"

Khrismann caught Frank out of the corner of his eye and shuddered. "I'll do what I can, sir—"

"You'll do hell of a lot more than that, Mr. Khrismann—I'm sure of it."

Phil sank slightly in his seat and shifted his eyes to the chairman. "My full department is at Mr. Tanner's disposal."

Fisher walked around the table and rested his hands on Frank's shoulders. "Our target is Larry Cross. Our fire-power is this young man right here." He gripped Frank's shoulders hard and nodded to the others. "Is that agreed?"

Mackendrick and Khrismann nodded without so much as a sigh.

The chairman stepped back and slipped his hands into his pants pockets. "Gentlemen ... there's a deadly disease in our company and we're going to destroy it together." He looked at Khrismann and smiled. "Phil, alert the shuttle— the four of us are going back to the Command Center."

Frank said, "What about my Turbo?"

Mack glanced at Tanner. "I'll have one of my people take it back to the center. Will that be acceptable, Mr. Newspaper?"

Tanner grinned. "Perfectly."

Chapter 53
Yerington Nevada
One month later

AUGUST 18TH. 2498 7:00 AM

*F*rank Tanner sipped strong coffee. Another air-taxi lifted off. It was the third in the last twenty minutes. He was seated at an outside table not quite twenty-five yards from the main pad. The Yerington launch-port was busy that time of year.

"We're late."

Frank looked up.

Kathy Simmons and Steve Palmer sat down.

Tanner glanced at his watch. "Ten minutes. In my business nothing starts on time." He smiled at Kathy.

Palmer sat back. "We didn't drive out here for chit-chat." He tossed a red folder on the table. "That's the Franklin-file you asked for. I could've sent it over a coded link and saved a lot of time."

Frank picked up the folder. He glanced at Steve and opened the file to the cover page.

Kathy waved to a waiter. To Frank she said, "Everything you need is there."

He nodded and paged through the file. "We have less than a month to nail Cross—"

"We?" Steve laughed, pulled off his sun glasses and leaned on the table. "As I told Kathy on the way out here, our involvement is limited to Fisher's orders—"

Frank slapped the folder shut.

A waiter approached. Kathy shot an irritated glance at Steve, then smiled at the waiter. "Could we have some coffee, please?"

"Right away." The young man left to get a fresh pot.

Kathy glared at Palmer. "Stop being an ass, Steve, Mr. Tanner is not the enemy—Larry Cross is."

Frank grinned and leaned across the table toward Palmer. "Like it or not, we're in this together!"

"I don't like it."

"Tough shit." Frank raised the folder then dropped it on the table. "You didn't like coming out here? That's tough shit too. Like Kathy suggested—don't be an ass."

"You're out of line, Tanner."

"Am I?"

"You bet your ass you are."

"You bet your life, yes, your life."

Steve pushed away from the table and stood. "I don't need your bullshit. We delivered—we're out of it."

Frank sat back, smiled and pulled the folder across the table. "Sit down while you still can."

Steve looked at Kathy.

She nodded and glared at him. "Please sit down."

He swallowed a gulp of pride.

Frank tapped the folder. "Cross is the target not me."

Steve cleared his throat and eased himself back into the chair. "What more do you need?"

"That remains to be seen. In any case, you two are involved."

Kathy nodded.

Steve hesitated. "Through Fisher, of course."

"Yes, through the chairman."

The waiter set a pot of hot coffee on the

460 / Ted Tillotson

table. "Can I get you anything else?"

Frank looked at Kathy and Steve. "No, that's it, thanks." He poured for the three of them. "Tarkin and Garrett were necessary expenditures for our friend, Cross."

Another air-taxi roared in and hovered above the landing pad. Frank stirred sweetener into his coffee. He watched the huge aircraft settle onto the tarmac. For a moment he wished he were among the crush of departing travelers. A part of him wanted out of his current involvement. He saw himself and Farrah chasing some ordinary, mundane story across the continent. Another *deeper* part of him voiced the nagging truth. *You're in for the long-ride, Frank—the whole trip.*

Kathy's voice brought him back. "Cross is a bastard, but a killer?"

Tanner snapped out of his thought. "I was indirectly involved in Garrett's death—I watched Leo Davis get blown to hell! Both men worked for Cross—they both had time gate connections." He shifted his eyes from Kathy to Steve. "So do you."

Steve cut in. "Strictly official—council level."

Frank chuckled with no humor. "Yeah ... think about it, you're involved with me now—"

"Through the chairman—that's it."

Steve smacked the table rattling the cups and saucers.

"Chairman Fisher," Frank said, "is Cross' target—*Time Gate* is the weapon."

"Then *your* ass is on the line—"

Frank laughed. "Don't you see it?" He leaned forward and lowered his voice. "I'm the ammunition—the Goddamn tool to blow the gate-project wide open." He shook his head, catching Kathy's frightened expression. "I'm as safe from Cross as his mother." He grinned and took a swallow of coffee. "I will be ... until the gate is exposed and Congressman Franklin is dead."

Kathy shuddered. "If Franklin dies ... what happens to the others?"

Tanner sat back and held his coffee cup in both hands. "Councilman Cross doesn't give a shit about the others. I don't think he's given a thought to the impact of their loss."

Palmer shook his head. "Sonofabitch."

Frank leaned forward and clinked his cup into its saucer. "The key is here!" He rapped his fingers on the Franklin file. "Something Alan Franklin will accomplish in his future has a bearing on Cross' current position. If he can stop that *something* from happening he'll have an advantage he doesn't have at the moment." Frank hesitated and studied Their faces. "Give it a thought, folks. Mr. Cross intends to alter things as we now know them."

Kathy slumped back in her chair. She spoke as if to herself. "Larry could very well be ... *Chairman Cross.* My God!"

Nodding, and pouring more coffee all around, Frank said, "Exactly. And the rest of us may be something other than what we are now."

Palmer sat straight and gripped the arms of his chair. "What you're saying is impossible."

Frank sipped his coffee. "No it isn't. Not with the reality of the gate."

Kathy looked out across the expanse of the desert valley. It was bowl-shaped, eighty to a hundred fifty miles in diameter. The valley was so alkaline that it was blinding white. It may have been formed by the impact of asteroids eons ago. It was as primal as any place on earth. Its outlines had been muted by the passage of millennia. Kathy saw history in the shimmering heat. She understood history, it was documented—solid.

In the distance, tumbleweeds rolled through an arroyo-scarred section of the valley. They disappeared into a liquid-like thermal mirage rising from the parched desert floor. A face formed. It was the likeness of Larry Cross. The face laughed, then fell away. The future-present reflected in that image. The future-present Frank had just suggested.

"*No—*" Kathy heard her own voice from somewhere far off. "No!" she said again and faced the reporter. "Stop him, Frank."

Steve gripped her hand. "Kathy, for God's sake."

She pulled her hand away. "We've got to stop Cross!"

Frank watched both of them for a moment. "We can. If we work together, I know we can."

Steve leaned toward Frank and glared at him. "You said we're in danger—what about that?"

"Stay together—close to Fisher. Don't let anyone know you've talked to me." Frank pushed away from the table and tucked the Franklin folder under his arm. He Looked at Kathy. "I need something else—"

Palmer shoved his chair back and stood. "No way!"

Kathy Ignored him "What is it?"

Frank pushed his chair under the table and considered his request. "Davis and I were monitored at the power station. I'd like to know how, and by whom."

Steve leaned on the table. "That's above our department and you know it."

Kathy cut him off. "Maybe it isn't. I know some security people. I'll do what I can."

Frank stepped into the bright sunlight. "Thanks." He smiled at Kathy.

Steve slipped on his polar-glasses and stared at the reporter. "We've done enough for you, Tanner. Don't ask for anything more."

Kathy nodded and moved out of the shade. "I'll reach you through Farrah when I know something."

Frank arched his eyebrows. "You know Farrah?"

"Well enough. We'll be in touch."

Palmer took a step away from the table then stopped. He looked at Frank. "You're a security threat. If I live through this mess, I intend to bring you up on charges."

Frank grinned and winked at Kathy. "Get some fiber in your diet, Palmer, you're all bound up."

Kathy's laughter was drowned out by the arrival of another air-taxi.

Part Five

The human element

Chapter 54
Moral Issues

PSYCHOTHERAPY CLINIC
AUGUST 18TH. 2498 9:00 AM:

$\mathcal{D}$octors, Jerry Zanster and Gregory Rankin listened to therapist, Carol Evans. She was finishing an interview with one of the *other* passengers. "Where were you born, Judy?"

The young woman smiled. "Madison, Wisconsin, September fifth, 2473."

"So, you have a birthday coming up."

"I'll be twenty five and I still feel eighteen."

"Are you married?"

"God no–I'm not ready for that commitment yet. I need to finish college first."

"What are you studying?"

Judy leaned forward and rested her elbows on the conference table. "I have a major in computer science and a minor in digital design."

"Are you pleased with the courses you've been taking here?"

"More than that. What I've learned here will help me get my degree a year early."

Doctor Rankin addressed the young woman. "I understand the University of Wisconsin has one of the most advanced programs in your field."

"Absolutely, the professors are tops in their expertise. However, the teachers here are outstanding." She sat back and grinned. "I'm ready for any finals Wisconsin can throw at me."

Dr. Evans signed a form and handed it to Judy. "Give this to Professor Baker so you'll get credit for the interview."

"Thank you." She nodded at the doctors. "I'm grateful to have earned this three month scholarship. Thank you again."

Carol added, "You'll be going home in less than thirty days."

"I'm looking forward to that, but I'll miss all my friends here."

"You can always stay in touch."

"I plan to do just that." The young woman left the room.

Doctor Zanster spoke first. "That young woman is one of the *other* passengers from flight two eighty and completely accepts what we're doing here?"

Rankin jumped in. "There's a lot more to it, Jerry." He looked at Dr. Evans. "Carol, tell him."

"Judy is actually, Ruth Goldberg. She's Jewish, her father is a prominent Orthodox Rabbi in San Diego, California. She was born there in 1972. I gave her an extra year. She deserves it. Ruth never attended any university. She hasn't set foot in Madison, Wisconsin. Ruth is married and has three boys." Carol closed the folder in front of her. "Ruth's family will be devastated by her loss. Judy—Ruth will take up a life in Madison she never had."

Dr. Rankin shook his head. "How many have been processed?"

Carol opened the folder. "Judy makes it one hundred fifteen so far." She looked at the two men. "The drug therapy takes five to seven days to clear specific memory. The implant requires forty eight hours after surgery and under sedation to complete the process." Dr. Evans hesitated. "I take it from there with cognitive processing."

Greg leaned forward. "Who's conducting this procedure?" He rubbed his chin.

Zanster cut in. "Can this be done to my clones and give them artificial memory?"

Dr. Evans held up her hands. "Gentlemen. One at a time, please." She sat back, took a breath. "Dr. Josh Tompkins and his surgical team perform the implant procedure. That answers your question. Greg?"

"Tompkins! He's the monkey surgeon." Rankin threw up his hands. "Christ! Where the hell are we going with this?"

"You just saw Judy. The procedure works."

Zanster raised his voice. "Will it work on a clone?"

"We aren't sure, Jerry." Carol stood and picked up her folder. "Select a clone from the passengers and we'll try, that's all I can tell you."

Dr. Rankin got up. "Can the process be reversed?"

"I doubt it ... why would you want to?"

"I don't know." He leaned on the table and faced Dr. Evans. "We're altering the lives of over two hundred people here. There's a moral issue to consider."

"I agree, doctor." She stepped away from the table and stopped. "Do you believe all these people can be relocated without alteration?"

"I believe they should all go back to their own time with the exception of their memories of being here."

Carol smiled. "It's quite possible. However, that's not the current plan."

Rankin stood up straight and grinned. "You're saying that can be accomplished?"

"We'd have to start over, remove the implants and see what happens." She thought a moment. "The problem is, they're all supposed to be replaced by doctor Zanster's clones. They're set up to perish, Greg. You know that."

He smiled. "Maybe there's a way to change all that."

"Let me know, I'm ready to work it out." Carol left the conference room.

Dr. Zanster paced and wondered. "If what Carol says is true, and I think it just might be, I can create new life for my clones."

"Your clones are headed for destruction."

"Maybe not, Greg." He grinned. "Do you want to see all those people relocated, with different lives, all over the globe?"

Dr. Rankin sat on the edge of the conference table. "That's the plan. I have no say in the matter."

"I think you damn well do and so do I."

"What are you saying?"

"Get Dr. Evans to stop her alteration program on the remaining passengers. I want to implant my clones with artificial memory. They will become my *congregation*."

"What about the other passengers?"

"Dr. Evans can use her process to eliminate their memories of 2498. They'll never know what happened to them."

Rankin shook his head. "The plane is going to crash. What the hell can I do about that?"

Zanster took a deep breath. "Show evidence to Fisher regarding what Dr. Evans has documented. The chairman will listen. He'll understand that the plane doesn't have to crash. All the passengers can be returned safely to 1998."

Rankin looked down at the table. "You might be right on target." He studied Zanster for a moment. "Your gain is having intelligent clones flocking to that compound of yours."

"Yes, it is. Dr. Evans can alter their identities."

Rankin patted Jerry on the shoulder. "I'll work on Carol. I think she'll come around. If she does, we'll have something to take to Fisher." Greg hesitated. "Does he know about the little congregation you have now?"

"He's well aware of my church and chooses to ignore it."

"I'll meet with Tompkins and Carol and then we can take the plan to the chairman privately."

"Thanks, Greg, you won't regret it."

"You do realize it will take an executive order through several departments."

"I understand what's involved and I have a feeling the chairman has already considered this solution on some level."

"Personally, I've been in favor all along. I hope it works out."

"I have faith that it will."

Chapter 55
Seeds of Deception

HISTORY RESEARCH COMMISSION
2 HRS LATER:

*M*s. Simmons closed the door of her office, crossed the room and sat at her elaborate work station. She keyed a numerical code-link and waited for network connection.

* * * *

Seated at his desk, in the east wing of the main Headquarters Complex, Larry Cross studied a section of the Franklin file. He grinned and re-read a specific page. *Thank you, Congressman,* he thought. *You'll never know what a contribution you've made to the future—or should I say, the present?* Cross laughed and turned the special program-card over and over in his fingers.

* * * *

Kathy entered a series of commands that would give her voice-control of the central computer.

Tex responded:

VOICE PRINT ACCEPTED
READY

She hesitated. A shiver ran like a spider across the back of her neck. "Access solar power station security." She rubbed her hands together and drew a slow breath.

AUTHORIZATION CODE
PLEASE

A second chill sent waves of goose-flesh along her arms. Kathy was out of her element. She was crossing a line. A line that could snap and take off her head. She said, "HRC twelve dash five."

CODE ACCEPTED
READY

Cold facts ran through her head. *If I go on, I might be getting my mail at Gray-Plan.* The sting of that reality seeped into the hollow of her bones.

Her fears embraced the meaning of her career. *I'm a research specialist. Not a security investigator.* She gave the next verbal command.

"Open recent security observations for SPS-3690 and trace completed events."

TRACKING:

DO YOU WANT OPERATOR DETAIL?

"Yes—everything."

SEARCHING:

She stiffened and watched the screen. Beads of perspiration broke out on her forehead.

* * * *

Councilman Cross noticed the blinking red light at the bottom right of his computer screen. A message followed:

SECURITY BREACH
POSSIBLE ALERT

The last word blinked rapidly.
"Intercept current probing and feed the information to this terminal."
He sat back and watched the screen.

* * * *

Tension came over Kathy as Tex paged through routine security observations at SPS-3690. After more than forty screens Tex stopped. A message flashed:

SPS-3690 INCIDENT
CODE-9 (CLASSIFIED)

Kathy studied the message for a moment. For lack of a better command, she said, "Access code nine."
Tex responded:

ENTER S/P CODE

She spoke slowly "SPS-3690/CODE-9."

ACCESS DENIED

"Dammit!" Ms. Simmons rubbed the back of her neck again. "Who has access?"
Tex responded:

S/P PERSONNEL ONLY

"List S/P personnel."

COMMISSIONERS?
SECURITY MONITORS?
SECURITY TEAM?
SECTOR MAINTENANCE CREW?
SELECT:

She thought a moment, and made her request. "Commissioners ...."
Tex responded:

TIMOTHY FARRELL (CHAIRMAN)
RYAN LASSER
KHRISTAN PLEASANTS
AVRIL JESSOP
LARRY CROSS (SPECIAL ADVISOR)
BELINDA KRANTZEN (RECORDER)

NIGEL PATTINGTON
TRENTON DELLIS
END LIST

Kathy shuddered. "Cross ... you sonofabitch!"

* * * *

Councilman Cross studied the screen and tapped his tented fingers against his chin. "If I were you, who ever you are, I'd think real hard before I went any further." He typed in a code that would trace the source of the security breach. An instant later he had the answer. A window appeared in the lower right corner of his screen.

HISTORY RESEARCH COMMISSION
TERMINAL 1304
KATHY SIMMONS
RESEARCH SPECIALIST

"Ms. Simmons, you're making a serious mistake." He entered a numerical sequence, which routed his terminal information to a private memory bank.

"Stop now, young lady, or face the consequences."

* * * *

Kathy addressed Tex. "List security monitors." A tremor wormed its way through her voice.

Something hung in the air around her. It was like a presence, a threat. The feeling was heavy.

Tex responded:

S/P SECURITY MONITORS:
DANIELLE JANNING (SUPERVISOR)
WILLIAM JENKINS (SECTOR 1-3-6)
DEBBIE RALSTON (SECTOR 5-7-9)
KARL PEARLMAN (SECTOR 2 & 4)
PRESTON DEVOE (SECTOR 10-12-14)
BRYAN IRONS (SECTOR 11 & 13)
END LIST
NEVADA QUADRANT
ADDITIONAL (Y) (N)

Kathy stared at the screen. "Danielle ... I know her." The name held distant meaning. "Danielle. Yes, Danielle Janning."

Accepting the name as a voice-command, Tex responded:

DANIELLE JANNING:
S/P SECURITY SUPERVISOR
(NEVADA SECTOR)
PRIORITY LEVEL-5

* * * *

Councilman Cross gritted his teeth when Danielle's name came across the screen. "Why is Ms. Simmons interested in power stations, specifically SPS-3690 and Janning?"

He jotted both names, and the power station number, on a pad. He tapped his pen on the desk and continued watching the screen.

* * * *

Kathy coded the information from Tex for private access and sent it to her printer. To the computer she said, "Give me Danielle Janning's access number."

Tex responded:

DANIELLE JANNING:
S/P ACCESS: L-5-840

She keyed her printer. "Thank you, Tex."

YOU'RE WELCOME
MS. SIMMONS
ANYTHING FURTHER?

"No, that's all. Terminal clear." The History Research Commission logo filled the screen. Kathy stared at it. *Danielle Janning,* she thought. "I *do* know you."

* * * *

Councilman Cross paced behind his desk mumbling to himself. "Simmons is after information about the incident at the power station—why?" He stopped at the huge window and squinted into the blazing Nevada afternoon. "Unless she's acting under orders from Fisher, her department has no need to know ...."

He turned away from the window, glanced around the interior of the office, thinking out loud. "Fisher has a complete file on the incident. Why would he have HRC dig into it?" He leaned over his desk and studied the pad on which he had written Danielle and Kathy's names. "You're history, ladies—count on it!"

Chapter 56
To Save a Life

HISTORY RESEARCH COMMISSION
A FEW MOMENTS LATER:

$\mathcal{K}$athy read Danielle's name several times. Suddenly it clicked. She accessed a communications link to solar power security and entered Danielle's number.

An electronic voice answered.

"Enter code and clearance level."

Kathy punched in L-5-840.

"Standby for connection."

Within a few seconds that seemed to last for an hour, Danielle came on the link. "Security supervisor, may I help you?"

Kathy took a breath, then blurted, "Danielle, this is Kathy Simmons."

"Kathy who?"

"Simmons. from HRC."

"HRC? Simmons? I'm sorry, I don't—"

"We worked on a solar research project three years ago, remember?" Bits and pieces of the project broke loose from the corners of Kathy's memory. "We spent nine hours a day together for over six weeks, plotting a T/A program. We laughed about it, went out together and spent a lot of time discussing Steve Palmer."

"Kathy! I'm embarrassed. How could I forget? Three years. Damn!" Danielle sucked in a noisy breath. "How's the *Zephyr Club?* If I'm not mistaken, we had quite a few laughs there—"

"Cipher—it was the *Cipher Club.*"

"Right! They had those new-form male-droids on stage. The ones you could order on trial—"

"Danielle. I don't mean to be curt. We can talk about all that later. I need something from you."

"What is it?"

"Listen carefully and evaluate what I'm asking."

"It sounds heavy."

"It is." She cleared her throat and lowered her voice. "You had an incident at SPS-3690. It was monitored. I need to know how and by whom."

Silence.

"That's classified."

"I know. I'm authorized by Chairman Fisher to investigate the incident."

"I need your code number."

"Three dash five four zero."

Danielle wrote down the code. "Give me a second."

Kathy glanced around her private office looking for what could be the lens of a hidden camera.

Danielle came back on the link. "The code is authorized. What do you need?"

"How and by whom?"

"It was a manned-surveillance request—I did it myself." She thought a moment. "I activated a tracker request."

"By whose order?"

"It came from a top commissioner—"

"Who specifically?"

"Councilman Larry Cross."

"Dammit!" She took quick breath. "Okay, listen carefully. You're in danger—"

"Kathy—"

"I know what happened at the power station."

"Nothing happened—"

"You monitored two men there, right?"

"Yes. One was authorized; the other wasn't. I alerted a security team and the men were taken into custody."

"Danielle, the authorized man was shot to death before security arrived. He worked for Larry Cross. When Cross finds out we've talked—and he will. You'll become a target."

"Kathy, please. The tracker was for surveillance only."

"Just listen. Get to the headquarters complex."

"Then what?"

"Go to Chairman Fisher's chambers and stay as close to Sophy as you can get—"

"Sophy?"

Fisher's secretary—move, Danielle. Move now!"

"Kathy—"

"Cut the link and get to headquarters. I'll meet you there." She clipped the connection and stared at her handset. "We'll get you, Cross! Somehow, we'll put your ass on Gray Plan!"

* * * *

THREE MINUTES EARLIER:

Larry Cross listened to the security pulse on Danielle's private link and fumed. "Sonofabitch!" He punched in a four digit code.

An electronic beep sounded three times. The security pulse on Danielle's link stopped. An instant later, Cross heard Kathy's voice. He grinned without humor. When he'd heard enough, Cross re-secured the link and entered another code. "History, ladies," he said, as he waited.

"This is eight-three-five-one."

"Andrews"

"Yeah."

"Cross here."

"I'm listening."

"There's a silver, K-four Turbo on its way to UWC headquarters. Make sure it doesn't get there."

"What route?"

"Ninety-five north to fifty east. Scan to be sure."

"Time factor?"

"Twenty-thirty minutes, give or take."

"Should I know the subject?"

"That's my concern. Just make it clean."

"I'm on it."

Cross broke connection and returned to his keyboard. He called up the file on SPS-3690.

He changed the date of occurrence and altered the data. Now the file was nothing more than a routine security check. He de-classified the file and sent it to Tex's memory.

"That kills your proof, Ms. Kathy Simmons." He chuckled as he made contact with Danielle's office.

"I'm sorry, sir. Ms. Janning has left for the day."

"I'll catch her tomorrow then."

"Is there a message?"

"Nothing important, thanks."

"You're welcome, sir."

Larry broke the link and grinned. "Enjoy your last drive, Ms. Janning."

Chapter 57
Danielle's Run

NEVADA DESERT
ROUTE FIFTY EAST

*W*hen she accelerated past 240 mph. Danielle shuddered and gripped the wheel harder. *I haven't done anything wrong,* she thought. *Why is this happening?*

The turbo came out of a long, smooth curve and shot forward at 260 mph. *Ten minutes, then I'm safe.*

The vehicle skidded slightly left and little right. Amber dust rose up around her. She pressed the throttle—red digits rose to 270 mph. The road straightened. Danielle pressed harder. 280 mph.

The warning system kicked in:

DANGER

She glanced in the mirror. A distant vehicle closed in rapidly. *They're after me!* She pressed harder.

SHUTDOWN WARNING

The turbo reached 290 mph. "A few minutes more—please!" She spoke to the interior of the vehicle which had become a missile in the desert.

The car behind came up fast.

"No way!" Danielle pushed the accelerator to the floor.

MAXIMUM 300 MPH-SHUTDOWN APPROACHED

"C'mon, K- four!"

The chaser was a security interceptor. It rammed against the turbo's rear bumper.

She held the accelerator to the floor. The car lurched ahead to 305 mph.

SHUTDOWN SEQ. ENGAGED

The interceptor slammed into the turbo harder. It slid to the right.

The interceptor hit again.

The K-4 cut to the left. Danielle corrected—

not enough. The K-4 left the roadbed and dropped into the soft sand.

Danielle twisted the wheel—no good.

The interceptor hit once more then braked.

The turbo flipped end-over-end. It shot into the air like an out of control rocket.

Tinted safety-glass exploded in a storm of jagged splinters and thick dust. Flashes of sun glistened through thousands of tearing shards.

For one, dream-slow, moment, Danielle thought she had flown into space and was now crossing the galaxy at light-speed. She marveled at such intense beauty.

The turbo crashed against a low wall of rock. It spun upward again. Danielle felt herself floating—falling into blackness—nothing.

The interceptor skidded to a stop. Andrews climbed out and walked to the edge of the canyon. He unbuckled his helmet and nodded. "Done." He waited long enough to see a tower of greasy, black smoke rise from below then activated his hand-communicator. "Interceptor three-six zero to central control."

"Go ahead, three-six-zero."

"I just lost a violator on fifty east at Hickison Summit."

"Do you need assistance in pursuit?"

"Negative. The subject went over the rim."

"Med-Vac necessary?"

"Not a chance. I'll standby for the removal-craft."

Andrews chuckled and walked back to his interceptor. He keyed in a code on a second communicator.

"Cross."

"The silver turbo won't reach its destination."

"Was it clean?"

"It was a fatal accident."

"How unfortunate. What caused the crash?"

"Excessive speed. The driver lost control."

"Happens all the time."

"Anything else, sir?"

"Not today, sergeant. Thank you. I'll have a little something put into your account."

"I appreciate that, sir. Andrews clear." The officer began filling out a false report.

* * * *

Councilman Cross closed the link on his console and grinned. He whispered, "Well, Kathy, I'm afraid your meeting with Ms. Janning has been cancelled."

Chapter 58
A Sense of Guilt

NEVADA SUN
TANNER'S OFFICE
TWO HOURS LATER:

$\mathcal{F}$rank jumped when his intercom sounded. He pressed the answer key. "Yes?"

Farrah said, "Mackendrick's on three."

"Got it." He set the Franklin-file aside. "Hello, General."

"Frank, I need you to chase a story."

"Sounds familiar."

"Don't be cute, just listen. You asked Kathy Simmons to find out how and by who?"

"Whom, Mack. I'm listening."

"Danielle Janning is the *whom,* dammit. Our good friend, Cross seems to be the how."

"I think we both knew he would be. Great."

"Not quite. The who's missing. Simmons made contact. She told Janning to get to headquarters on the double. She hasn't been heard from since."

"How long?"

"Two hours plus."

"What can I do?"

"Dammit, Tanner! Have you forgotten how to be a reporter? Talk to your buddies in the Sun's central newsroom. I got word there's been an accident on Hickison Summit."

"I can check it from here."

"Please do. I'll be in my office."

Frank keyed Farrah. "You heard?"

"I did."

"Check enforcement. I'll run stories-in-progress."

"Frank"

"What?"

"Cross killed her."

You may be right."

"He can kill you too."

"Not just yet. He still needs me."

* * * *

Kathy stopped pacing and leaned on the file cabinet near Sophy's work-station. "If Danielle's dead. I caused it."

Sophy came around her desk. "Don't even think it," she said, "We're still not sure anything has happened to her at all."

"I made contact and put Danielle on target!"

Chairman Fisher closed the folder on Kathy's report—the file regarding the security breach of SPS-3690. He mumbled to himself. "I've seen enough." He stood and addressed the two women. "I have everything I need to come down on Cross right now." He glanced out into the fading afternoon sun. Fisher turned away from the window and sat on the corner of his desk. "Kathy, you're not to blame for anything that might've happened to Danielle."

She started pacing again. "Danielle had no idea she was involved in anything wrong."

Fisher said, "That seems to be the way Cross works." To Sophy he said, "Call Mackendrick and see if he's got anything yet."

On the way to her desk, Sophy gripped Kathy's shoulder. "You're not at fault."

She turned to the chairman. "I'm in danger now. So is Steve."

Fisher folded his arms. "We all are." He reached back across his desk and picked up the file. "The entire project is in jeopardy!" He held up the folder. "The facts of your report and what actually happened at the power station clearly define the danger as being great."

Kathy swallowed hard and shuddered. She stepped to the large, leather sofa near the chairman's desk and sat down.

Fisher continued. "This file connects Cross with the killing of Charles Tarkin. Other information leads to Cross in the death of Nevil Garrett and an innocent woman." The chairman waved the folder. "Thanks to Frank Tanner, and you, Ms. Simmons, I can put Councilman Larry Cross in custody. If something *has* happened to Danielle Janning, I'll do just that!"

Kathy blinked away tears. She remembered special times she and Danielle had shared during their six-month friendship. Somehow she knew her friend was gone forever.

Sophy looked up from her desk. "Sir, the general's on four."

Fisher keyed his link-code and picked up the handset. "Go ahead, Mack."

"Are we coded, Mr. Chairman?"

"We are and I'm recording."

"Okay. Danielle Janning is dead. I have positive ID. Her Turbo flew off Hickison Summit at three-hundred per."

"Accident?"

At the sound of the word, Kathy felt a cold chill in the very center of her bones. Tears came.

Fisher gestured toward Sophy. She was already on her way to Kathy.

The general went on. "A security enforcer reported it as an accident, but I think that's pure bullshit."

Fisher lowered his voice and turned toward the window. "Do you have ID on the enforcer?"

"He's with Solar Power Authority."

The chairman heard Kathy's wrenching sobs behind him. He gritted his teeth. Into the link he said, "Bring in the enforcer and pick up Cross—immediately!" He looked around to see Sophy holding Kathy, rocking her. "Mack, put your top Military enforcement team on this. You have full, UWC authority."

"What charge, Mr. Chairman?"

"For now the charge is suspicion of red-security breach."

"Consider it done."

"Pick up Tanner too."

"For what?"

"The sake of his life. You and Phil do it yourselves and bring him here right away."

"You want the enforcer and Cross in isolation?"

"Exactly. Separate holding cells in *Gray Plan* phase one." He looked back at Kathy.

"Get it done, Mack."

"Immediately, sir."

Fisher broke the link and turned to face the two women. "Kathy ...."

She looked up at him through tear-filled, red eyes. "Danielle's dead isn't she?"

The chairman nodded and whispered, "I'm sorry ... so very sorry." "Soph, I want two security agents on Palmer before he leaves the lab today."

Chapter 59
An Act of Treason

TWO HOURS EARLIER:

*A*cting on impulse, Councilman Larry Cross keyed a three digit number on his private link. *Janning's dead,* he thought. *Simmons is next.* He stared out the huge window at the distant mountains. *Get her before Fisher can act.* He drummed his fingers on the desk. *Without actual testimony from Simmons, Fisher won't have a case.*

The connection responded in four beeps.

"This is four-six-five."

"Carter?"

"Hello, Larry."

"I need an A-five-nine immediately."

"A-class droids are expensive. Especially when you waste them like you do."

"How much?"

"Eighteen-thousand."

"You're crazy!"

"I'm a businessman."

"You're a thief."

"Want it or not?"

"One day, Carter, you'll be at my call."

"Until then, councilman, we deal my way. You want a five-nine. I want cash."

"Be at the New Star at seven. I'll have the payment."

"It's a pleasure doing business with you."

"Someday, I'll have you for breakfast."

"Count the cash correctly."

"Seven, the New Star, be on time."

"I'll be early and have a bottle. My treat."

"You're all heart, Carter." Cross broke connection and leaned back in his chair. *Ms. Simmons, your time has come.*

* * * *

COMMAND CENTER
LEVEL FOUR:

Khrismann took a small disc from his chief communications officer. "Thanks, Trevor. Stay locked on that link just in case." Trevor nodded and left Phil's office.

General Mackendrick waited until he and Khrismann were alone. "We got the sonofabitch by the short-hairs."

Phil walked around his desk and sat down. He handed the disc to Mack. "This puts Larry on Gray Plan for the rest of his life." He shook his head. "I never thought he'd go so far."

The general grinned. "He did and he's taking a few others to the moon with him." He secured the disc in its protective case and slipped it into his breast pocket. "Okay. My team picks up Cross. You and your unit get Carter."

Phil shook his head. "When we nail Carter, I think we'll open a pipeline to more crap than we can imagine—"

"Right now, I want Cross. That bastard's been stuck in my craw since the day I met him!"

"What about, the cop connected to Janning?"

Mack adjusted his cap and smiled. "He's in custody. According to my Captain, the guy's already spilled enough about Cross to guarantee a ticket to the moon."

Phil keyed his remote communicator. "Security team one, standby to launch." He slipped the device into his jacket pocket and stood. "Let's get to it."

* * * *

HEADQUARTERS:

Fisher greeted Steve with a firm handshake. Palmer had been escorted to the chairman's office under armed guard. "I'm sorry, Steve." To the three droids he said, "Wait outside."

Steve glanced at Kathy, who was seated beside Sophy on the couch. Kathy's eyes were red, her complexion was ashen. She nodded, forced a weak smile. To Fisher, he said, "What the hell's going on?"

The chairman took off his glasses. "Sit down, Steve, please."

Kathy reached out and took Steve's hand as he sat beside her. He met her eyes, then Fisher's. "We're on the line because of Tanner, right?"

"Cross is the enemy, not Frank. Larry has ordered the death of several people. Danielle Janning is his most recent victim. Before her it was

Nevil Garrett, then Charles Tarkin and Leo Davis."
Fisher wiped his glasses and looked up. "You and
Kathy were next in line."

"Were?"

"Yes. He's being picked up."

"Then we're safe?"

"For the moment. We can't be sure until we
know if Cross has other accomplices."

Steve gently squeezed Kathy's shoulder.
"Sorry about Danielle." She nodded. To Fisher, he
said, "What do we do now?"

The chairman went around his desk and
picked up the Franklin file. "We go to work. There
are two problems to be solved right away." He
tapped the folder. "The first puzzle is in here." He
crossed the room and handed the file to Kathy.
"It's the Franklin file. Everything there is to know
about the congressman is here. Kathy, Alan
Franklin is yours."

Ms. Simmons took the folder and looked up
at Fisher. "I know the file completely, sir."

The chairman held up his hand. "Hang on."
To Sophy he said, "Get Dr. Rankin and tell him to
have the congressman escorted to Kathy's office at
HRC."

Sophy pushed off the couch. "Right away."

Fisher leaned against his desk, thought a
moment then spoke to Simmons. "We need to
know how Franklin's life, or death, as Cross would

have it, fits into the councilman's plan."

"How much do I tell him?"

"Everything you have to. I trust the man completely." He smiled. "We've struck a bargain."

Palmer stood. "You said there were two problems." The chairman walked behind his desk and opened the top drawer. He picked up a yellow, plastic card. "This," he said, coming around to Steve, "is your project."

Palmer took the card and examined it. "This is a program module."

"It's the program that was created to pilot the 747 back to 1998."

Steve looked at the card and shook his head. "I don't understand. Why isn't it in the plane?"

Fisher tapped his chin. "It is, I should say a copy of it is." He leaned against his desk again. "There are at least three cards, Steve. The late, Mr. Tarkin designed them on orders from our friend, Cross."

"Tarkin was supposed to write the re-entry program." He studied the card again. "There's always a backup for any gate program, but not more than one."

Sophy looked up from her desk. "Excuse me, sir. Dr. Rankin wants to escort Congressman Franklin personally."

"Just make sure he does so with two A-fives."

She spoke into the phone.

Fisher went on. "Cross has the third card, maybe more. He also has access to those programs."

"Not if he's locked up."

"Don't kid yourself. If he can order someone's death, he can damn-well have an accomplice activate a computer program."

Palmer chuckled. "Excuse me, sir. Why don't we simply run the cards and cancel any germs in the program?"

"We have—the event-sequences are flawless."

"What do I do?"

Fisher pushed away from his desk and slipped his hands into his pockets. "We need a new program duplicating Tarkin's original instructions."

"Easy enough, I have several people who can do it."

"I want your best on it. I want that person to know exactly what he or she is doing. You tell that programmer to be extremely careful—if there's one questionable sequence in the program, the result will be devastating."

Palmer stared at the chairman for a moment. "I'll supervise the program myself, sir."

"Good."

Kathy stood and rubbed the back of her neck. She looked worn out. "I take it we stay in the Command Center."

Fisher went to her and gave her a fatherly hug. Softly, he said, "Yes, until Cross is in custody and I know you're safe." He held her at arms length and smiled. "Kathy, I care about you and Steve. I'm sorry about Danielle and the others. I wish I could make that different, but I can't. I can however, protect you, Steve and our five special people—and I will."

"Thank you, sir ...."

Fisher stepped away and made a fist with his right hand. "Now, let's undo what Cross has done!"

Steve held the yellow card. "I'll see to this immediately."

The chairman walked the two of them out of his office. He nodded at the security droids. To both Steve and Kathy he said, "You have access to my private number any time, any hour, use it."

Simmons and Palmer walked away with the three droids guarding them.

Fisher re-entered his office and closed the door. He stood for a moment rubbing his chin. "Sometimes, this job requires more than I have to give ...."

Sophy came out from behind her desk. She walked up to him and took both of his hands in hers.

"And sometimes, Robert, you're bigger than the job itself." She smiled. "Today, sir, you are a saint. I don't care how that word strikes you. Today you're a hero. You care, you have heart. That, my dear man, makes you someone very special." Sophy pressed her face against Fisher's chest. "I love you," she whispered.

He held her away then kissed her on the forehead. "Soph ... fix us a stiff drink."

* * * *

AT THAT SAME TIME:

Councilman Cross completed the last step in the sequence that put the 747 re-entry program into Tex's mainframe. The data was hidden under a four-digit code only he could access. "It's done," he smiled.

His office door burst open. General Mackendrick entered grinning. "Hello, Councilman."

Four security droids came in behind the general. They pointed their weapons directly at Larry Cross.

"Mackendrick—what the fuck is this?" He stared at the droids with fear in his eyes.

Mack stepped forward and leaned on Cross's desk. "You're under arrest for an act of treason and four counts of murder."

Cross pushed his chair back and stood. "You're full of shit!"

"You're in custody. Resist and my team will put you in a world of hurt."

Larry backed up, bumped against his chair, stumbled and fell into it. "I want representation!"

Mack laughed. "According to the treason act of 2255, you have no right to council. You're dead meat, Cross and I got you by the nuts."

Two security droids pulled Cross out of his chair and handcuffed him.

He struggled and shouted, "I'll have your ass for this!"

"I've got yours you sonofabitch, you're going to Gray Plan!" He handed a small pointed device to another droid and nodded. "Use it."

The droid moved in behind Cross and pressed the instrument against the man's neck. Larry went limp.

Mackendrick said, "Treason and murder. Think about that as you drift away." He laughed. "Have fun on the moon."

* * * *

SECURITY COMPOUND
ELEVEN EIGHTY ONE

Twenty minutes later, Khrismann's enforcement shuttle landed at the main security pad. Mackendrick's unit was already there. The general stood at the booking counter signing a form. He looked up as Phil and his team brought Carter through the guarded entrance. "Any problems?"

Khrismann grinned. "We didn't even have to stick him."

Carter shot a glance at Mack then looked away. Two of Phil's team took the prisoner into the military lockup. Heavy, electronic doors closed behind them.

Mack handed the forms to the clerk. To Phil he said, "Did Carter say anything?"

"I couldn't shut him up." Khrismann handed a disk to the general. "His every word is crisp and clear. He's asking for immunity."

Mack put the disk in his pocket. "I'll be sure to tell Fisher."

Chapter 60
Sharing the Truth

HISTORY RESEARCH CENTER
THIRTY MINUTES LATER:

*C*ongressman Franklin studied Kathy Simmons's face. "You're hiding something. Be honest with me, I'll be the same with you."

She cleared her throat and looked away. "We have a major security problem and you're involved."

"How so?"

Ms. Simmons leaned back in her chair and held up the congressman's file. "This is you, all of you." She opened the folder. "Everything you've ever done, everything you ever will do is in here."

Franklin nodded. "You have a file on all of us don't you?"

"Yes, but yours is significant. Something you did, or will do, plays an important role in time."

"Your time?"

"Exactly."

Alan stood and leaned on Kathy's desk. He smiled. "What's the security problem?"

"The Time-Gate and a politician named Larry Cross. He's a United World Councilman. And a dangerous one. He's responsible for the deaths of four people. He either has been or soon will be arrested. You and a couple of others, me included, are on his list."

"Why me?" Franklin stepped back. "I'm an unexpected visitor here. How in hell can I fit into the man's plot?"

Kathy pushed away from her desk. "You're a key, congressman, a major link in Cross' plan." She stood and went to the glass wall along the front of her office.

Franklin stared at her for a moment. "Ms. Simmons," he said, in a raspy voice. "I want it all. I need to know."

Kathy looked through the glass partition into the research room. She watched members of her team at work on their computers. "Until today my job was clear-cut. I plot the activities of Time-Agents, they're droids. They perform missions for the good of society—for the good of all. Mr. Cross has been doing things for the good of himself." She turned and faced the Congressman. "Chairman Fisher told me to tell you what I had to." She gestured toward the leather sofa beside her desk. "Sit down, Alan. What I'm going to say might scare you to death." She walked around to the far side of her desk and sat on the edge of it. Nodding and pointing to the couch again she said, "Sit and listen carefully. "

The congressman eased himself onto the sofa. He smiled. "You do have a flair for dramatics."

Kathy grinned. "When you hear what I have to say, you'll wish it was just drama."

Alan glanced around the room making mental notes of odd contrasts. "Some things haven't changed at all."

Kathy sat in a white, gravity-chair across from the congressman. "Crooked officials," she grinned. "No, they haven't changed very much."

Alan leaned back and squeezed the thick, arm of the sofa. "I meant something less troublesome." He patted the sofa cushion beside him. "This couch could've come from a furniture store in 1990. You're sitting in a gravity-chair unheard of in my time." He pointed across the room. "Those filing cabinets. I have five in my office almost exactly the same." He waved in the direction of Kathy's computer terminal. "You have a computer system that makes our most complex Cray look like a video play station. Why the contrasts?"

Kathy smiled. She studied the sofa for a moment then glanced at her computer. "As you said, some things never change." She leaned back in her suspended chair, which adjusted to her new position automatically. "In this century a person can have pretty much whatever he wants. That sofa isn't from 1990. It's less than two years old. I had it made for me because I like the style. My work in history research has its advantages. When I see something from the past that strikes my fancy, I have it re-created." She smiled and adjusted the folder on her lap. "I detect about a hundred questions behind those eyes of yours."

"Closer to a thousand." The congressman relaxed a little.

"I assume mostly political. I'm sorry— governmental questions."

Alan laughed and leaned back. "Governmental-political, both the same, Kathy. Don't be afraid of offending me. I'm a babe-in-the-woods here. Consider me a dirt-dry sponge. I'll soak up anything you can tell me. Just be straight forward."

Flushing slightly, Kathy said, "You're a lot like Dr. Jordan. You're both very special."

Alan shook his head. "We're from two different worlds."

"True, but each of you has a core of honesty. It lends a higher value to the project."

"We're a project are we?"

"You are indeed." Ms. Simmons tapped the folder on her lap. "Before we get into this, I'd be happy to answer whatever questions I can."

Congressman Franklin looked off to the file cabinets, which reminded him of his own office. He glanced again at the super-computer terminal on Kathy's desk. Gathering his thoughts he smiled. "I did win."

"Win?"

"Yes, my missile-defense appropriation got congressional approval." The saying of the words made his mouth dry. He swallowed hard.

"Fisher told you?"

He looked up at the ceiling, shut his eyes for a second and asked, "Has the system ever been called into service?"

"Yes." She hesitated. "The missiles were launched in the year 2203."

The next question escaped Franklin's mouth as a raspy breath. "Under what circumstances?"

"To stop a misguided revolution. I can show you how it was launched and how efficiently it worked."

A shiver crawled up Alan's spine.

Chapter 61
Protective Custody

THE NEVADA SUN
TANNER'S OFFICE:

$\mathcal{W}$hen the call from General Mackendrick came through, Frank took it at Farrah's desk. She handed him the communicator.

"What've we got?"

"Everything we need. A security team will pick you up in ten minutes."

"For what?"

"To save your ass, Mr. Newspaper. Go willingly or go in irons. Either way, you're going."

"Where?"

"Fisher wants you at the Command Center under tight security."

"You got Cross, right?"

"Right."

He glanced at Farrah. "I'm safe then."

Mackendrick chuckled, "Wrong, Frank. Pack a toothbrush and a clean shirt—you ain't goin' home right away."

"Mack, what the hell's going on?"

"Be ready, Tanner. My men are on the way." Mackendrick clicked off.

Frank held the communicator for a moment then turned to Farrah. "They're picking me up. I gotta go to the Command Center. Fisher's orders."

Farrah nodded. "Good ...." A slow chill crawled up her arms.

"I'll be okay."

She shook her head. "You damn well better be." The last two words caught in her throat. "This whole thing is bullshit."

Frank stepped forward and hugged her. "Without you everything would be bullshit."

She pressed her face against his chest. "I don't want to lose you."

"You won't. You're stuck with me, woman— totally stuck."

They pulled apart. Farrah blinked. "I want this whole thing over with." She grinned then pressed close again.

Frank squeezed her, shut his eyes tight. "There's a measure of good in this mess."

Farrah whispered. "I'd like to hear it." She leaned back and looked at him.

He grinned, kissed her on the forehead. "We've gotten a hell of a lot closer since the whole thing started." He kissed her again.

COMMAND CENTER - LEVEL THREE:

When the security party entered Fisher's office they found the chairman standing at his window. He turned slightly. "Dismiss the droids, general." He put his back to the room again and stared out across the Command Complex.

Mackendrick gave the order. "Take the shuttle to security station four and wait there."

The droids marched out of the office in single file.

The chairman reached out to Frank. "Mr. Tanner, thanks for coming." He smiled. "Sorry for the escort."

Frank nodded and shook Fisher's hand.

Mackendrick and Khrismann glanced at each other.

The chairman moved away from his desk and gestured toward the conference room. "Gentlemen, after you." He and Sophy followed.

Mackendrick and Khrismann sat side-by-side.

Frank slipped into a chair on the opposite side of the table and looked around the room.

The atmosphere was tense.

Fisher stood at the head of the table. He leaned on the back of his chair and met Mackendrick's eyes. "Larry Cross has been formally charged with treason and five counts of conspiracy to commit murder." Fisher moved away from his chair. "He will be judged and sentenced by a special UWC civil and governmental panel."

Khrismann and Mack grinned. The general said, "I never trusted that sonofabitch."

Fisher sat down, removed his glasses and rubbed his eyes. "The security enforcer and Mr. Carter were more than willing to cooperate."

Phil pushed back in his chair. "There has to be more than those two in his pocket."

The chairman glanced at Sophy then the others. "Carter has listed two hundred and ten men and women who are on the Cross payroll."

Mack leaned on his elbows and turned to the chairman. "Are any of those people in my department?"

Fisher nodded. "At least a dozen."

Phil said, "How many of my people were dealing with that bastard?"

"Three and they're in custody."

"Sonofabitch!" Khrismann smacked the edge of the table. "Who are they?"

"Mid-level security. They didn't attract too much attention. That's how the Cross organization worked." Fisher turned to Sophy. "Is the HRC file finished?"

"Yes, sir. Cross had six working for him there."

Mack stood, red-faced and fighting mad. "What the hell was Cross trying to do?"

Fisher leaned forward. "Sit down general. Cross was after power." He smiled. "The man wanted my job, but that's the least of it. According to Carter, the Time Gate incident was Cross' golden opportunity. When Larry found out Congressman Franklin was among the passengers on the 747 he was ecstatic."

Mack cut in. "Franklin developed the basis of our ant-missile defense system."

Fisher continued. "Exactly. That put the congressman in Larry's backyard. Eliminate Franklin and the system we now have in place would cease to exist. Using his people and resources, Cross would be in a position to implement his own system."

Phil said, "He proposed that nuclear mess ten years ago and it was defeated by the UWC."

The chairman sat back and nodded. "Franklin's project had already been advanced and had been deployed successfully. The Cross proposal didn't stand a chance."

The general held up his hands. "I'm getting a clear picture here." He stood again. "Cross was after your position and ultimate military control." He hesitated. "I may be wrong, but could Larry actually want a revolution to succeed?"

Fisher tapped the folder in front of him. "With Congressman Franklin's system non-existent, at the time of the revolt, there would've been growing global chaos." He studied the concerned faces. "Larry Cross would have proposed his system during the campaign." He grinned. "Needless to say, the Cross defense system would have been accepted and I would've lost my appointment. Councilman Cross would have become Chairman Cross."

Frank glanced from Phil to Mack then spoke to Fisher. "Where does that leave us?"

"With one less traitor and a vacant seat on the council." He smiled. "That won't be hard to fill."

Frank said, "What about the program. The re-entry card for the 747?"

"We have it under control now."

Frank grinned and slipped the yellow card from his inside pocket. "I think you'd better have this checked out by your best people." He handed the card to the chairman. "Leo Davis gave it to me just before his guts exploded at the power station that's the original program that will plot the airliner safely through the Time Gate." Frank looked at Mackendrick and said. "Mr. Cross is still screwing with you."

Fisher stiffened and leaned forward. "What about the other cards?"

Frank took a breath and felt relief. "They're phony. The program card in the airliner right now has a sub-code that will destroy the plane within the gate." He looked around at the staring faces. "Run a simulation with the program card in the airliner now and then run that one." He pointed to the card Fisher was holding. "That card is the one you want."

"Thank you. Now I want something from you."

"What would that be, sir?"

"Can you preserve world security and still tell an effective story?"

He thought a moment. "I can, with their cooperation."

Phil and Mack moved uneasily in their chairs.

Fisher addressed the general and Khrismann. "I demand your assistance, gentlemen."

Mack said, "Yes, sir. You have it."

Phil glared at Tanner. "I'll do the best I can, sir."

He cleared his throat and added, "What about all the other people working for Cross?"

Chairman Fisher wiped his glasses and slipped them up over his nose. "They're being rounded up as we speak. Now let's move forward and get our five special people home where they belong."

Chapter 62
Justice without Mercy

SEVEN DAYS LATER
UWC CRIMINAL COURT DEPT FIVE:

Security droids lined three of the four walls of the huge Chamber of Justice. Two levels above the floor, the fifteen-member panel sat side by side at a wide curved table. The center and highest chair was empty. The senior justice had not yet entered the chamber.

In the media section, packed with reporters, Frank Tanner nudged Farrah. "This event is going world-wide."

Farrah whispered, "I think Cross will enjoy the attention."

He patted her hand. "After this we go back to covering mundane political crap."

"That pleases me, but remember, fifty of Cross's people are still unaccounted for."

"Not for long. The entire World Council is on their asses."

Behind and above the justice panel, the far wall was a gigantic screen displaying the UWC logo.

In another section, to the left of the media, General Mackendrick pointed toward a secured area where two hundred people were seated. "Twelve of those bastards were in my command." He took a hit of Paralayne. "They look cute in their prison-reds."

"They'll look a lot better in their Gray Plan suits." Phil Khrismann shook his head. "I can't believe three of those sonofabitches worked in my control center."

Kathy Simmons spoke up. "They were good, I'll give them that. The ones in our department were slick as glass."

Steve Palmer slapped the arm of his chair. "We trusted those people. We shared knowledge and worked close together. They were screwing us every day and smiling about it!"

Chairman Fisher and Sophy were seated at a table on the main floor in front of the panel. Sophy fiddled with her steno-pod. "Robert, I'm scared to death."

"You're not as afraid as those folks over there." He nodded toward the section of prisoners. "I have a feeling they'll be getting the full cut of the axe." He smiled. "We're official observers and I'm pleased with that."

"That doesn't make me feel any better."

In another section of the chamber, doctors Jerry Zanster and Greg Rankin waited for the proceedings to begin. Jerry whispered, "How much of my work has been compromised by Cross' accomplices?"

Rankin shook his head. "My question is, how could one man have so much influence in so many critical areas?"

"He recruited the right people. They were smart and they were in the right places."

Therapist Carol Evans, seated behind Doctor Rankin, leaned forward. "I'm appalled by all this. Four of my assistants were involved with Cross. They were working with the relocation program of the passengers. I have no idea how much damage they may have caused." She pointed toward the prisoners. "I hope they get their due."

A door opened to the right of the huge chamber.

Frank Tanner whispered to Farrah. "This is it. Make sure your pod's activated.

"It is. Damn, I'm shaking like a leaf."

"You're not alone."

A young man in a black robe entered the chamber at floor level. "Are the two hundred accused present?"

A member of the justice panel responded. "They are."

The man on the floor continued. "Are the nine international representatives present via global link?"

"They are."

"Let them be shown."

The UWC logo, on the huge screen, dissolved to reveal the images of nine delegates of the United World Council.

"All rise."

The rustling sound of fifteen hundred people filled the chamber.

A door behind the justice panel opened. The senior member appeared, stepped forward and took the center chair.

The man on the floor continued. "The honorable, justice, Karen Wilkinson presides." He nodded toward the panel. "All be seated."

Frank leaned over to Farrah and whispered. "She's a killer judge."

Farrah grinned. "I'm glad it's a woman."

"Those prisoners are on their way to the moon."

Mackendrick poked Khrismann. "This is gonna be good."

Justice Wilkinson addressed the group of prisoners. "All accused stand."

Three and four at a time, the two-hundred prisoners got to their feet. Some were sobbing. Others just stared. They shook in their shackles.

Wilkinson raised her voice. "By the unanimous verdict of the seated panel you have all been found guilty of conspiracy to commit treason." She slammed her gavel hard. The harsh sound echoed through the chamber.

"You have been found guilty of acts of deception within areas of your responsibility. You have violated the trust of your superiors and some of you are guilty of murder."

She slammed her gavel again. "Your crimes are reprehensible. I have no choice but to sentence each and every one of you to fifty years on Gray Plan. Most of you will never return."

The man on the center of the floor addressed the huge screen. "Does the World Council agree?"

One by one each of the nine global representatives keyed the word *affirmative* in his or her language.

The fate of the two hundred prisoners had been sealed.

Mackendrick raised a fist in the air. "Enjoy your stay on the moon you bastards!"

Khrismann slapped the seat in front of him. "That's good, now let's see what Cross gets."

The red-clad prisoners were led out of the chambers by security droids.

Tanner whispered to Farrah. "This is it. Larry is next."

She gripped his hand. "I hope he gets more than they did."

"You can count on it."

The man on the floor faced the panel. "The people present Lawrence Cross for sentencing."

Wilkinson looked at a folder in front of her. "Bring the subject forward."

The door opened where the other prisoners had been ushered through. Two security droids marched Larry Cross to a chair facing the panel. He sat down and grinned.

Frank whispered to Farrah. "This sonofabitch is going to go down hard."

"Good, he deserves whatever he gets."

Wilkinson looked down at the file. "You've been found guilty of treason and conspiracy to commit four counts of murder. Do you understand the seriousness of those convictions?"

"I surely do." Larry grinned.

The judge gestured toward the security droids. "Stand that man up straight."

The droids yanked Cross to his feet. He cracked another smile. "Did I say something wrong?"

Kathy sat back in her seat. "I can't believe this"

Steve said, "The man's on his way to hell and he's taunting the devil."

Justice Wilkinson closed the folder in front of her. "Lawrence Cross, you are hereby sentenced to one hundred years on Gray Plan. You are to have no human contact whatsoever. You will work at hard labor in a specified mineral mine. There you will toil until you can no more. At that point you will live the rest of your days in your cell." She looked out at Cross. "Have you anything to say?"

Cross glanced around the chamber and grinned. "I must commend her honor for the professionally profound way with which she has pronounced my sentence. I assure her honor, and this absurd gathering, I'm not dead yet and my work is far from completion."

Wilkinson slammed down her gavel. "I order Lawrence Cross remanded to Gray Plan level six immediately."

The man on the floor addressed the members of the United World Council. "Do we have an agreement?"

One after the other, each of the nine world representatives posted the words: *ABSOLUTE AGREEMENT.*

General Mackendrick slapped Phil on the back. "Cross is as good as dead."

"What happened to Carter and that security enforcer?"

"They were tried separately." He laughed. "The dumb bastards thought they'd get immunity. Carter is on the moon for twenty five long years. The enforcer was found guilty of murder in the death of Danielle Janning. He'll do life on Gray Plan at level ten."

Phil looked at Mack. "That's a short sentence. He won't make two years. Very few ever have."

Chapter 63
Ultimate Security

ONE HOUR LATER
CHAIRMAN FISHER'S OFFICE:

"*S*ophy, I'll be in the conference room. Bring the others in when they get here please."

He carried a thick blue folder into the room and stood behind his chair at the head of the polished table.

Cross's comments echoed in the chairman's mind.

I'm not dead yet and my work is far from completion.

He put the folder in front of his console and keyed the big screen to life. The massive

747 aircraft came into view. Hangar twenty four was lit up like a stadium during a major event.

Sophy entered the conference room ahead of the others. "Everybody's here, sir."

Fisher turned to the people entering the room "Thank you for coming, please take a seat."

General Mackendrick and Phil Khrismann were followed by Kathy Simmons, Steve Palmer and Frank Tanner.

Frank stopped half way to the table. "That's the plane?"

Mack was first to grab a chair. "That's her, Mr. Newspaper. What'd you expect a hot air balloon?"

Fisher smacked the back of his chair. "As of this minute, I want the hostile attitude toward Mr. Tanner dropped!"

The general nodded. "Just poking a little fun."

"There's no room for *fun* in this matter. Is that clear?"

"Yes, sir ... sorry."

Fisher offered the chair next to his. "Sit, Frank. You're in this event because you have the eyes and ears of the public. So far you've demonstrated responsibility and I respect that."

"Thank you, sir. I have no intention of doing otherwise."

Phil said, "Is that a live picture?"

The chairman sat down and opened the folder. "Yes, that's the interior of hangar twenty four at this very second."

Smaller screens, in each of the four corners of the larger image, appeared and then changed every few seconds.

Chairman Fisher continued. "Immediately following the court session I ordered ultimate security for hangar twenty four."

Mack leaned forward. "We're monitoring the aircraft inside and out continuously?"

"Exactly and every image is being recorded and stored on TEX."

Phil glanced at Fisher. "Excuse me, sir. Are those droids at the foot of the access stairs F-K-512 units?"

"They are indeed and they're programmed at Red-DI-SP."

Mack leaned back. "Destroy instantly, security priority." He looked at Phil. "Nobody's getting near that plane."

Fisher held up his hand. "You all have a clearance code. Memorize it. Here's the sequence. You must say it out loud and clearly. UWC-zero-one-nine-nine-eight. Speak the numbers, do not use digits. My code is the same." He turned to Frank. I'll allow you one visit to the aircraft so you can get your facts straight. That's it, one visit." He nodded at Steve and Kathy. "Yes, you're included in case you need something for HRC." He glanced from face to face. "Understand me completely. Do not aggravate those droids in any way. They will kill you."

Frank said, "Do we have to repeat the code to every guard?"

Sophy held up her hand. "No. The droid at the gate to the hangar is the only one. When you clear him, it, or whatever, none of the others will challenge you."

Fisher said. "You all have the code memorized?"

They nodded.

"Here's the key. Each of you must pronounce the first letter of your last name following the code."

Kathy said, "I'm not sure I want to go near that hangar."

Mack laughed. "Ms. Simmons, you won't be able to stay away from it. The aircraft is primitive, but she's loaded with aviation history. I doubt you or Steve can resist seeing and actually touching the five hundred year old relic."

Frank spoke up. "Mr. Chairman, will I be allowed to get some pictures?"

"Yes, you may take some digital images. I

see no problem with that."

"Thank you."

"Listen, Frank. I'm not trying to tell you how to write your story. However, you might want to call it an *accident of time* with no mention of the passengers."

"I don't know about the passengers, sir."

"Good. We don't have to be concerned about them, do we?"

"Not at all."

"I'll look forward to reading your article."

Mack pointed toward the screen. "Mr. Chairman, may I ask what triggered ultimate security?"

"The last words of Larry Cross did the trick, general."

"The man's an idiot. He was just running off at the mouth."

"Don't be too sure. There are still fifty of his people at large."

"They're running scared and scattered in the wind."

"Are you sure about that?"

"I'd bet on it."

"Don't bet more than you can afford to lose, General."

"I never do, sir."

"Hold that thought."

Phil said, "Cross will never get off Gray Plan. He's as good as dead."

Fisher glanced at Sophy. "Do we have the link?"

She checked her POD. "We're connected."

Fisher cleared the screen and the image of a man seated at a table appeared. "Twelve fifty are you receiving?"

"Perfectly." The man's face was blanked out.

"What is the status now?"

"Four cells have been closed. All members are in custody."

"They were Cross operatives?"

"Affirmative."

"How many are left?"

"One cell remains functional with the last ten of the missing fifty."

"Location?"

"In a mountain cabin East of San Diego, California."

Estimated contact."

"Within the next twenty four hours."

"Can they be taken alive?"

"That depends on the subjects."

"Bring them in alive if you can."

"Deadly force may be required, sir."

"Understood, but alive is for the best."

"My team will do what's necessary, sir."

"You have my full support either way."

"Thank you, Mr. Chairman."

Fisher brought hangar twenty four back on the screen. He looked at the faces of the people seated at the conference table. "Until all of Cross's accomplices are in custody, or dead, we have a major security problem." He opened the blue folder. "The information in this file is a calculated death sentence for every one of the key people on flight 280. Larry's thirst for power and my job is appalling. He was willing to snuff out the lives of innocent people, which he has done, to implement his own agenda."

PART SIX
The Return
Phase one

Chapter 64
Lethal Deception

EIGHT HOURS LATER
UWC PRIVATE HOUSING BLDG 46 UNIT 465:

$\mathcal{P}$hil Khrismann stood on the balcony of his fourth floor apartment. He looked out over the complex. It was bathed in the reddish glow of the setting sun. Many of the windows facing his point of view appeared to be filled with fire.

He studied the yellow card in his right hand. *It's too late. I can't do it.*

A beeping sound came from behind him. He turned to see the red light blinking on his personal console. He walked over to it and picked up. "Khrismann."

"Any problems?"

"Fisher has jacked up security to the MAX!" He tossed the yellow card onto the console table. "We'll have to wait."

"Wait? Listen, Khrismann, there is no wait!"

Phil raised his voice. "I'm telling you it can't be done now!" He sat down in front of his monitor and keyed in the image of the interior of the hangar. "Have you tapped into hangar twenty four?"

"We're well aware of all the security. You have access, Phil. Do your job."

The sun fell further and the blaze filled the apartment. "Listen, you idiot! Cross is a dead man, his plan has failed." He watched the small images change in the four corners of his screen. "There's no way I can get in there and plant the card!"

"Wrong, you'll do it. Here's your incentive."

A woman came on the line. "Are you backing out on Larry?"

Slivers of scarlet and orange spread across the horizon. This day was done. Phil thought, *so am I.* He fought to keep his voice even. "Silvia, be realistic. It's over. UWC is onto you, there's an inside man after your asses right now." He caught a quick breath. "Break up the group and spread out. The Cross plan is finished. Get the hell out while you still can!"

Silvia chuckled. "Tell you what. If that little yellow card you have is not in place by this time tomorrow, and I'm serious, you will be terminated in a way you can't even imagine." She laughed. "The sad part is the card will be placed anyway after you've suffered the most horrific death I can think up."

Phil picked up the card and studied it for a moment. "You know what, Silvia?"

"I can't imagine."

He looked out into a night that was filling with stars. He smiled. "I think I'd love to put this card right where it belongs."

"Now you're making sense. How soon can you do it?"

"As soon as you bend over far enough for me to shove it straight up your ass."

"You're killing yourself, Khrismann!"

"Actually, dear Silvia, I'm killing you"

"You sonofabitch!"

"Enjoy your sentence on Gray Plan, it's possible we might see each other there. Maybe not, they don't let bitches like you mix with the male population."

"Khrismann!"

"Fuck you, Silvia. I'm done with all of this shit!"

ONE HOUR LATER
CHAIRMAN FISHER'S OFFICE:

*S*ophy sat down and activated her steno-pod. "We're recording, sir."

The chairman crossed his hands behind his back and stared out the window into the star-filed sky. "Sophy and I were just about to enjoy an excellent dinner together when you called." He paused. "Now, I have no appetite."

Khrismann leaned forward and put the yellow card on Fisher's desk. "I'm sorry, sir."

"Sorry?" The chairman turned from the window and looked at Phil. "Sorry?" He glared down at the man. "You're the sorriest bastard on the planet!" He picked up the yellow card and studied it. "This little item has bought you a long term on the moon." Fisher tossed the card aside and grabbed the back of his chair with both hands. "If I hadn't increased security at hangar twenty four, you would've gone into the 747 and put that card into the controlling device of that aircraft."

"I decided against it, sir." Phil shifted in his seat. "I'll give you the names of the remaining people who were involved with Cross and where they are."

Fisher turned back to look at the display

of stars through his large office window. "We already have that information. Those vermin are being rounded up as we speak."

Phil shuddered in his chair. "I put myself at the mercy of the court."

The chairman came back to his desk and sat down. "Mercy?" He grinned. "I've known you for twelve years. I trusted you. Actually, I didn't really know you at all." He nodded toward Sophy. "You got everything?"

"Every word, sir."

"Good." He looked at Khrismann for a moment and tapped his pen on the desk. "There is no mercy for the likes of you. Sophy. Call security."

Fisher leaned back and pointed his pen at Phil. "You're on your way to the moon."

Chapter 65
The Return
Phase two
Indoctrination

SEPTEMBER 1st, 2498 8:30am

$\mathcal{F}$or the last several weeks, Kathy Simmons and Steve Palmer had been working closely with the key-five. This morning, Congressman Franklin, Dr. Hal Jordan and Michael Sternfeld met with Kathy and Steve in the HRC Plotting Center.

Steve enlarged the lower, left-quarter of the huge computer screen.

"We'll have full audio and video contact for the first thirty minutes."

Michael stared at the simulation of the 747 and shook his head. "You'll be able to see and hear us?"

Kathy smiled and gestured toward the screen. "We'll see your aircraft just the way it's shown here. Chairman Fisher will be locked onto the plane's radio and PA system."

Dr. Jordan grinned from ear to ear. "So when I panic you'll hear my screams?"

Steve nodded, "If you need to be heard individually, press any stewardess call-button."

Congressman Franklin studied the screen for a moment. "You said, thirty minutes, Steve, why?"

Palmer hesitated, weighing the answer. "Once you cross through you're off the monitor."

Michael turned away abruptly. "Off the monitor!" He walked to the large, glass wall separating the control room from the rest of the plotting center. "And right out of existence."

Steve and Kathy shared a concerned glance. Alan and Hal tensed.

Kathy went to Michael and stood beside him. For a moment they watched the activity in the room beyond. Thirty people were busy at various work-stations. They were calculating, checking and entering blocks of data into the master computer. Tex would sort, code and store the information as a series of special, separate, specific commands.

Ms. Simmons put her hand on Michael's shoulder. "Michael, the entire plotting center is working to get you and Linda, the baby and the others, home safely. The project is under control—"

"Is it?" He stepped away from Kathy and shook his finger at the master plotting-screen. "This high-tech video game is way over my head." He glared at the others. "I don't have the education you do, but I'm not stupid."

Kathy started to say something.

Michael held up his hand and spoke first. "Under control you said."

She nodded.

"What if something goes wrong?"

Dr. Jordan leaned against the counter near Michael. "We all have fears, Mike—"

"I'm asking these people, doctor." He shifted his eyes from Kathy to Steve. "Will either of you answer my question?"

Palmer pushed away from the console. "All right, Michael. There's always a risk."

"Exactly!" He shook his head. "And we're out of your control."

Congressman Franklin stood and approached young Sternfeld. "Mike, you're ranting about a danger that may not exist. You may be overreacting."

"Am I?" He lowered his voice. "Think about it, Alan. Maybe I understand more about this situation than you do." He Looked at Steve and Kathy. "We could be lost out there someplace."

Irritated by Michael's apparent comprehension, Steve blurted, "When your plane clears the gate you're back in your own time and headed for Los Angeles."

Michael clenched a fist and shook it. "And right into nowhere!"

Palmer countered. "That isn't going to happen." He shook his head. "Listen to me carefully. If that had happened none of you would be here right now." He nodded to Kathy.

She pushed between Franklin, Michael and Steve and keyed the computer. In an instant, Michael's file filled the screen. "That's you, Mr. Sternfeld. You see Linda and your happy, healthy baby boy?"

"That's us?"

"Yes, it is. You're not going to get lost anywhere. You're looking at a moment of your future. Stop acting like a child and start learning what we're doing for you."

He looked at Kathy. "I'm sorry."

She hugged the young man. "You and your family are safe."

Palmer cleared the big screen. "You're all

part of history. You will not be lost in the gate." He stood and looked at the others. "Are there any further questions?"

Professor Jordan grinned. "None from me."

Steve nodded toward the congressman. "Alan?"

"Regarding re-entry? None." He smiled. "About our work in the future? I've been educated to a level I never dreamed possible."

Doctor Jordan waved toward the blank screen. "I do have a question."

Steve said, "Which is?"

"I'm under the impression that the other passengers and crew will perish in our programmed return."

Palmer glanced at Kathy. "They will be clones. The real people will be relocated and living new lives in 2498."

"And they're all okay with that?"

"None of them will have any memory of 1998. It's all under control." *That's not quite the actual truth,* he thought.

"I hope you're right."

Michael cut in. "Excuse me. I'm trying to get my head around the tragedy facing the families of more than two hundred people."

Steve spoke up, "Young man, I'm going to assume you can comprehend what I'm about to tell you."

Kathy said, "Be careful what you say."

"It's time these people knew the full score, the truth."

Franklin sat down. "You haven't been honest with us?"

"Listen to me and understand the reality of the situation."

Ms. Simmons protested. "I know where you're going, Steve and I don't think you should."

"I'll answer to Fisher if I have to. Michael hit on an important issue and I'm going to address it. Please, everybody sit down and relax."

Dr. Jordan remained standing. "Whatever it is, we need to hear it."

Steve stood and walked toward the glass wall. "All those people in there are working on alternative programs that may change your re-entry event as it stands now."

The congressman got up and stood behind his chair. "Get to the point, Palmer, I'm not sure I like what you're saying."

"As cordial as we've been with all of you, the bottom line is clear. We want you back in your time for the sake of our existence in 2498. That is the primary goal period."

Michael said, "Even if you cause untold grief to more than two hundred families?"

"You brought it up and I'm giving it to you straight."

Dr. Jordan leaned on the table and looked at Palmer. "For Christ's sake, Steve, spit it out."

"None of you, Laura or Linda will be injured, you know that. The others are considered collateral damage."

Michael said, "That's it, collateral damage?"

"Exactly. We can't send the other passengers and crew back to 1998 with full knowledge that they've been here in the future. The result would be chaos."

Congressman Franklin said, "From all that I've seen and learned here, there must be another way."

Kathy went to the window and pointed toward the busy workers in the other room. "What Steve has revealed to you was not meant for you to know. I put myself at risk to tell you more." She studied the faces of the three men. "There is a program in development to allow you and all the passengers and crew to return to 1998 with a safe landing in Los Angeles. That may not be possible."

Michael said, "Why? With everything I've seen here it should be a snap."

"It's not that easy. We have until the fifteenth of the month until re-entry launch. If it can be done, it will be. If not, the current plan

stands, collateral damage included."
Dr. Jordan said, "I'll pray you can fix it."

Chapter 66
A Change of Command

ONE HOUR LATER
TIME TRAVEL CONTROL UNIT
PROJECT SIMULATION ROOM:

$\mathcal{T}$im Carey, chief supervisor of the
Time Travel Enforcement Commission introduced
General Mackendrick to the head programmer.
"Mack, this is Perry Martin. He'll be running the
simulation and the actual return sequencing."

The general shook Perry's hand. "I hope
you're good at what you do, young man. We've got
a sensitive mission here and not a hell of a lot of
time to get it done."

"I've been involved in the project since the

original breach and I know every aspect of the return sequencing."

"Great, now educate me."

Tim said, "Perry's the best." He stared at Mack.

"Is there a problem?"

"No, no problem. I'm just sick about Khrismann."

"Well, so am I. He screwed up and he's paying for it. You got his job. Now we're both on the line until this damn project is finished." He looked at Perry and waved toward the big screen. "Are we going to shoot the shit here or get something done?"

Tim gestured toward a chair at the massive console. "Take a seat general and Perry will bring you up to speed."

The young programmer keyed the giant screen to life and a detailed image of the 747 came into view. "The aircraft has been linked into TEX and every aspect of the plane has been analyzed and fixed into the master memory. We have absolute control of the airliner."

Mack took a hit of paralayne. "In the last two months, I've come to believe nobody has *absolute* control of anything."

Perry keyed a six-digit sequence. The giant 747 appeared in a fully detailed, virtual duplication.

The aircraft taxied away from Hangar twenty four and onto the main runway. "We're ready for take off, sir." The young programmer was obviously excited.

Mack leaned forward. "You're like a kid playing an expensive video game."

Tim smiled. "It's the most perfectly detailed simulation ever created. Perry and TEX developed the program."

The general stared at the screen. "I'm impressed. Can this be done with our fighters?"

Perry nodded. "Yes, sir, I can program any existing aircraft in the exact same way." He looked at Tim. "Should I bring them in for this run?"

"Go ahead. Let Mack get a feel for the whole thing."

Perry keyed another digital sequence. Two sliver military fighters taxied out ahead of the 747 and stopped.

General Mackendrick smacked the arm of his chair. "Those are F-165 interceptors!" He glared at Tim. "You don't have any authority to use those fighters."

Carey grinned. "It's a simulation, sir. We do need them. Watch the program. I'm sure you'll give us clearance for the fighters."

"We'll see about that."

Perry brought up the audio. The sounds of the three aircraft filled the room. "On your order."

Tim tapped Perry on the shoulder. "Launch the fighters."

"Launching fighters." He typed in a sequence of numbers. The two military fighters shot forward and lifted out of sight. "Altitude thirty thousand and holding at four hundred knots."

Mack stood and waved at the big screen. "Where are they?"

Tim said, "Right where we want them." To Perry he said, "Launch the airliner."

"Throttles forward, sir."

The general watched the 747 roll forward and gain speed. "She's an old bird, but I have to say, she's got some class."

The jetliner lifted off and climbed slowly. Perry said, "Wheels up. I'll take her to thirty thousand."

Mack looked down at Perry's fingers moving across the console. "This kid's flying a 747."

"I'm piloting all three aircraft, sir."

"Sonofabitch!" Mack took another hit of paralayne. "What are the fighters for?"

Tim sat back. "They're monitoring the guidance system of the program on the 747 and the corresponding information from our control information and from TEX."

"Are those fighters manned or programmed?"

"During the actual return operation they will be real live pilots. If there's a fluctuation of more than two percent the event aborts and the 747 returns to base."

"I can't believe all this."

"It's for real, Mack. We've been through this simulation two-hundred times and it hasn't failed."

The general looked at Tim. "It better not."

He smiled. "Do we have your authorization to use the fighters?"

"You got it."

Perry spoke up. "I've accelerated to gate approach."

Mackendrick sat down. "We're there?"

Carey said. "It will take the 747 thirty minutes to reach the Time Gate." He consulted a clipboard on the console table. "The gate shifted two-point-five degrees when it re-stabilized. That created a risk factor of point-zero-four."

"Khrismann told me it could be a factor of ten."

"He was a liar. We all know that now."

"I can't think about that. I worked with that bastard for over twelve years. I trusted his sorry ass."

"Welcome to the club." Tim hesitated. "This Time Gate incident is what triggered all the deception. Phil didn't go bad until this crap happened."

"I disagree, Cross wanted to use the gate to change a few things in his favor. He had Phil in his pocket long before that 747 flew into our time!"

Perry pointed toward the screen. "We're entering the gate at precise longitude and latitude into 1998."

Tim pulled up to the console. "Fighter readout?"

"On the mark, sir."

"Take her in."

The fighters peeled off and shot up to fifty thousand feet. Perry said, "We're inside the gate, all stable."

The images on the screen vibrated.

Tim stood. "Show exit image."

"On track now."

The screen cleared. The simulated 747 soared into a blue sky at thirty thousand feet.

Tim gripped Perry's shoulder. "Great job." He drew a long breath. "I get shaky every time we run this program. It does work. We'll get these people back home in one piece."

Mackendrick sat back and looked at both men. "What about pulling the key-five out of the plane before the programmed crash?" He took another hit of paralayne. "Has all that been worked out?"

Tim sat on the edge of the console table.

"We've done it dozens of times with Time Agents. The process is identical. It won't be a problem."

The general stood, adjusted his blouse and polished the bill of his cap on his sleeve. Smiling at Tim he said. "You'd better be right, Mr. Carey. Lose those five people and what we know today may never exist."

"We'll make it work."

Mack fixed his hat as perfect as always and snapped a salute. "You've got your fighters and you have my support." He looked at Perry. "Young man, you're a genius. Thank you for your impressive demonstration."

"My pleasure, sir."

To Tim, Mack concluded, "We have two weeks. Make it happen."

Chapter 67
Infinite Universe

**1:00 PM
HISTORY RESEARCH COMMISSION
PLOTTING UNIT CONTROL ROOM 5-C:**

Steve Palmer cleared the screen then faced Dr. Jordan. He studied the professor's expression for a moment, grinned and stood up. "This whole project scares the shit out of me."

Hal laughed, leaned back and shook his head. "You're scared? You push the buttons—we take the ride."

Steve crossed his arms and leaned against the console. "I don't. The people at the command center do all the button pushing."

Hal got up, walked to one of the service counters. "I spent quite a bit of time with Phil Khrismann." He pressed the coffee indicator. "Mixing what I already knew with the information I got from Phil, I consider the gate a *mistake.*" He took the cup of hot coffee from the machine and went back to his chair.

"Khrismann has been found guilty of treason and conspiracy to commit murder."

"What are you saying?" Hal sat up straight. "Murder?"

"Phil was involved in a plot to sabotage your return to 1998."

"Why would he do such a thing?"

"He wanted to change things that you and the others will accomplish." Steve sat down. "I'll tell you this much, five people were killed in the process. The threat no longer exists."

Hal sipped some coffee. "I'm not following all of this."

"It was political. Khrismann, and the others involved, had personal agendas." Steve sat back. "Anything Phil told you may have been lies. In any case, the project is safe now and under control."

The professor set his coffee aside. "I liked Phil."

"We all did, for years. This Time Gate

breach brought out the worst in otherwise good people." Steve stood and gestured toward the huge blank screen. "You said the gate is a mistake?"

Hal nodded. "It's an error in universal events. Let's call it an accident of time itself."

Steve came around and leaned on the back of his chair. "I'll entertain that concept, go on."

Hal sipped some coffee and leaned back. "I see the gate as one of millions of pinholes in the fabric of time."

Steve grinned. "That's a rather expansive theory, Doctor."

"Just an educated guess. It's a rough perspective."

"So, there would be thousands of Time Gates throughout our galaxy?"

Dr. Jordan stood up. "Millions." He gestured toward the screen. "Can that computer simulate the stars?"

"What system?"

"Ours--the Milky Way."

Interested in what Hal was leading to, Palmer keyed Tex. An instant later an extensive list of star systems filled the screen. Steve keyed three numbers. "Milky Way comin' up."

Hal said, "How many systems are there?"

A three-dimensional simulation of the Milky Way filled the screen, Steve said, "To date we've

located more than two-hundred-billion galaxies."
He turned away from the screen and smiled at Dr.
Jordan. "Detailed maps of each galaxy have been
recorded in the master memory."

Hal stared at the screen, blinked and said,
"There hasn't been enough time in history for that
much data to be entered in any computer."

Steve nodded. "You're right, Doctor. Ten
years ago, before I became part of the History
Research Commission, I worked with Kathy in
the Science Acquisition Laboratory at DDC, the
Denver Data Center. During a lunch break, I
asked, Tex how many stars there are in the
universe?" He laughed. "The screen cleared
and displayed the message, Sub-systems
locked—return to main menu. I thought I'd
entered an unauthorized code sequence, so I
keyed back to the main menu and forgot about
it."

Jordan grinned. "The computer didn't
forget did it?"

"Not for a second." Steve looked at the
swirling image of the Milky Way and smiled.
"Two years later, while I was on TEX with another
project, my access code flashed on the bottom of
the screen. I keyed Tex to send data. There it
was, a fully organized list of star systems. Each
one had been numbered according to its
distance from our galaxy in a ring-pattern of

three-hundred-sixty degrees."

Hal shook his head. "Two years."

Steve glanced at the screen then looked at Dr. Jordan. "That was eight years ago. Tex is still scanning the universe."

Dr. Jordan leaned forward. "I'm overwhelmed. However, the point I'm trying to make is, by contrast, much simpler." Hal pushed his chair alongside Palmer and pointed at the screen. "Can you enlarge the picture to show the position of the earth?"

Steve keyed another sequence. Instantly the image changed. One more three-digit entry and the earth and the sun were shown in a red circle.

Hal glanced at Steve. "That's the earth and our sun. Now watch." Hal tapped the screen. "We see what appears to be a solid cluster of stars all around our solar system." He was in his own world now—acting as a teacher.

Steve smiled. "I think you're going to show us how deceiving the image really is."

"If I can, yes. Keep the pinholes in mind." He traced his finger across the screen to the center of the galaxy. "It would take thirty-thousand light years to get to the center of our own galaxy." He laughed. "That's academic. The apparent bumper-to-bumper stars are actually so far apart it would take generations to go from one to the other."

Steve said, "Your pinhole theory applies to

all the space in between."

"Exactly—there may be millions of Time Gates throughout the universe."

Palmer leaned back and laced his fingers behind his head. "There are billions."

Dr. Jordan studied the screen. "You know don't you?"

Steve thought a moment. "I'm sorry, Doctor. I was taken by your educated reasoning. I'm afraid I let you work your way through a question I already had the answer to."

Hal shook his head. "I'm a little confused."

Steve stood up. He pointed toward the screen and paced behind his chair. "Your theory is right on target. I posed the question to Tex about a year after my assignment to HRC."

"You needed a massive intelligence to reach such an obvious conclusion?"

"The probability of multiple time gates *does* seem academic in theory. I wanted something more concrete. I based the question to Tex on simple mathematics as it applies to the gate's position."

Hal said, "Longitude and latitude."

"Right, I put those figures over the time-factor between occurrences."

"The gate cycles every ninety days, right?"

Steve leaned against a far counter. "Yes it

does. That's a combination of three thirties to equal ninety. I used those figures in the equation and fed it to Tex." Steve went to the computer and keyed four numbers. "Doctor Jordan, I give you the result."

An instant later the huge screen filled with a circular cluster of tiny dots.

Hal pushed his chair away from the console and stared up at the screen. "It looks like a star system."

Steve leaned on the edge of the console. "It is a system, Doctor, but they're not stars. What you see is about one quarter of the time gates in our galaxy, just twenty five percent."

Hal studied the screen and thought out loud. "If I wrote a paper on these facts and presented it as theory, I could create a new course for the university."

"You are free to do just that. However, this knowledge must be treated as *theory* only." Steve went to the service counter and drew a cup of coffee.

Hal joined him there. "I understand. I've already been briefed in that area."

"It's a serious issue, Hal. The science of your time could never come close to gathering what you've just seen."

Jordan walked back to the console and studied the huge screen. "I'm staring face to face into the reality of a phenomenon beyond the comprehension of any astronomer or physicist in my lifetime." He sat down. "Why have I been given this gift of such great knowledge?"

Steve came back to the console and sat beside Dr. Jordan." That too is a phenomenon."

"What will happen if I put this great knowledge to use?"

Steve leaned back and smiled. "I'm glad I can be the one to tell you."

"Tell me what?"

"When you sort it all out, and you will, your papers, courses and books will make you the Einstein of the twenty first Century."

"What about altering the future?"

"It hasn't happened yet. You won't be altering anything." Steve cleared the big screen and stood. "You'll be contributing to the future. The gates exist, they have since the beginning of the universe."

"This is unbelievable."

"Believe it. Let's get a late lunch."

Chapter 68
The Return
Minus
Fourteen Days

THIRTY MINUTES LATER
HISTORY RESEARCH COMMISSION
PLOTTING UNIT CONTROL ROOM 5-C:

*C*ongressman Franklin, escorted by a security droid, stepped into the room. "I'll have to pass on lunch with you two. It's time I had a chat with my wife."

Steve nodded then addressed Dr. Jordan. "Hal, hang on a minute, please." He walked to the door and stepped into the hall with Alan. "Chairman Fisher would like to see you."

"I must to talk to Laura, it's important."

"Go to Fisher first, please, he's expecting you."

Franklin hesitated. "Is there a problem?"

"None that I know of. Just see the chairman right away." He hesitated. "Fisher needs a favor. He wants to ask you directly."

"You're sure there's nothing wrong."

"Positive." He smiled. "You can have lunch with your wife within twenty minutes."

* * * *

Steve re-entered the control room and walked to the computer console and leaned against the counter. "We have an interesting proposition for you professor." He stepped away from the console. "Hal, would you consider coming back?"

"Coming back?"

Steve went to the glass wall and stared out at the workers beyond. "Yes ... return to the twenty-fifth century." He turned from the window and leaned against the glass. He looked intently at Dr. Jordan. "It can be arranged. You can be of great value here."

A shudder ran through him. He thought about the possibility. He knitted his brow and chuckled. "What can I do here?"

Steve cleared his throat. "Alan's agreed to come back. We can do the same for you. Everything will be explained."

Hal stood up and shook his head. "How is such a thing possible?"

He grinned at Steve. "You're kidding. I don't plan on being on another flight through the Gate."

"That won't be necessary and it would be a lot easier."

Hal took a breath and sat down. "Okay, why and how?"

Steve grinned. "The idea excites you, I can tell."

Dr. Jordan nodded and looked at the huge screen. The images of countless Time Gates and distant galaxies seemed impossible. "Again, why and how?"

"You attend month long conferences every summer. Two weeks of that involve lecturing. The closing two weeks put you in touch with other scientists to share new theories and generally bullshit each other, correct?"

Hal laughed. "You got that right."

"How would you like to spend three months a year lecturing at our major university?"

Jordan studied the big screen again. "Lecturing about what?" The whole concept was raising his heart rate.

Steve leaned forward. "You would be a history, physics professor lecturing young, eager minds. You would have your own office with a research staff at your call."

Dr. Jordan stood and started walking around the room. "What would I tell my wife?"

"You'll be able to figure that out."

Jordan was caught in the idea. His mind was racing. "Three months?"

Steve went to the service counter and drew another cup of coffee. "Remember, you'll only be gone for eight minutes of your time."

"I can't quite understand that." Hal leaned on the massive console and studied the big screen again.

"It's a fact, Hal." Steve walked back to the console and sat down. "Here's the best part." He grinned. "You will have limited access to TEX within your field of expertise."

Hal sat forward again and stared at the screen. "I'll be able to work with this computer?"

Steve took a sip of coffee. "You'll have your own terminal and direct connection from your private office."

Hal smiled. "What's the catch?"

"The extra two months." He hesitated. "You'll

have a seat on the United World Council. You'll be required to report on your lectures and anything you may have learned from TEX." Steve grinned over the rim of his cup. "The opportunity is yours, doctor."

Hal looked around the room. "How can this be done?"

Steve stood and gestured toward the door. "It's a matter of technology." He picked up their coffee cups. "We want you here, doctor."

"Let me give it some thought."

"I'm sure you will. Let's go get a great lunch."

Jordan hesitated. "May I key TEX to clear the screen?"

"Of course. Hit 624-12." He squeezed Hal's shoulder. "That's your personal code."

Dr. Jordan stared at Steve. "My code?"

"It's yours if you decide to come back."

"Sonofabitch!" Jordan keyed the numbers. The giant screen dissolved the view of the universe and faded in the UWC logo. He slapped the console table and shook his head. "Sonofabitch!"

Steve chuckled. "Does that mean you'll agree to come back?"

Hal looked back at the screen and the massive control console. "I don't know." He let out a breath. "I don't know. Good God, I just can't grasp it yet."

Steve held the door open. "You will. I'll enjoy working with you."

Chapter 69
Zanster's Revelation

LATE AFTERNOON
CLONING LAB
DINING HALL:

*D*octors, Hal Jordan and Jerry Zanster had the dining area   to themselves. Neither man had spoken for the last five minutes.

Hal sipped a cup of coffee, trying to remember the faces of the other passengers from flight 280. He met Jerry's eyes. "From now on I'm going to make an extra effort to look at people. I mean *really* look at them." He shook his head. "My God, man. I flew halfway across the country with two hundred some odd souls and I can only remember a few faces outside of our group."

Zanster blotted his mouth with a napkin. "That's human nature."

"You're right and it's sad."

"I remember most of them because I set up their files."

"There are what ... two-hundred-twenty-three including the flight attendants and the cockpit crew?"

"I counseled most them in groups. A lot were handled by Doctor Rankin and Carol Evans."

"Do they know your plan?"

Jerry glanced toward the workers behind the buffet. "I think Rankin suspects. Greg knew my father quite well. He was one of the last to leave his church. I think he'll come back."

"I admire the idea, but I think you're breaking some *grand* rule."

"Once in place my *new* church will survive."

Jordan took a small bite of his pastrami on rye. "You said most of them. How many more do you need?"

"I want them all, Hal. I'm greedy." He laughed. Jerry's first real laugh since they sat down to eat. "I can have my church with a few, maybe a handful, but the more I get the stronger it will be!"

"Not everybody on the plane would've been

Christian, there has to be a wide cross section."

Zanster's face brightened. "Your plane was filled with people of a variety of beliefs. I have Catholics, Protestants of all walks, Buddhists, Indians, Mormons, Jews—a melting pot of faith. That's what my *new* church will be."

"A melting pot?"

"Exactly. When I get them together it will be a religion stronger than any one denomination in history."

Dr. Jordan Felt himself caught in Jerry's excitement. "It's hard to believe they were so willing."

"Not really. Their lives have been altered beyond comprehension." Zanster leaned forward, gesturing with his hands. "One minute a family from upper Sandusky, Ohio was headed for a budget-vacation in San Diego—the next minute they found themselves in the twenty-fifth century." He let out a breath and closed his eyes for a moment.

Hal hesitated. "Something wrong?"

Jerry pushed away from the table. "Give me a minute."

Jordan watched him walk to the buffet.

He came back with two glasses of cold, red wine. "You'll need this."

Hal took the glass. "What's the matter?"

"Reminds me of our late-night session

about eight weeks ago." He sat down and offered his glass in a toast. "Here's to truth and faith."

Hal *clinked* his glass to Jerry's. "I'm not following you."

They both took a sip of wine. Jerry sat back and smiled. "I like you, I trust you and I'm lying to you like a thief." He shook his head. "That's what I am ... a thief." He took another sip of wine.

Dr. Jordan leaned forward and whispered. "What the hell are you talking about?"

"I haven't recruited a single soul from flight 280."

"I don't understand."

"I double-cloned."

"You did what?" He took a gulp of his wine.

"There are now three sets of passengers from your airplane."

Dr. Jordan looked around the room as if someone else might be listening. "You cloned the same people a second time?"

"I told my staff it was an executive order and they were to take the process to level eight."

"Level eight?"

Jerry finished his wine. "I mentioned it to you, but not in any detail. Level eight results in a clone with full cognition." He grinned. "They each know who they are and have no memory of of ever living in 1998."

Hal studied Dr. Zanster. "What about the others?"

Jerry took a bite of his sandwich as if everything he just revealed was a routine practice. "The first clones are level five. They're the ones going back on the plane. everything's in order there."

Hal thought a moment and looked into Jerry's eyes. "What about the *real* passengers?"

"They're safe and sound and still wondering what the hell's going on."

"I thought they were being relocated."

Jerry took another bite of his sandwich. "To date, none have been. That's not my department."

"Why did you do this?"

"That's the main reason for this meeting." He smiled. "I know you've been offered a chance to come back and I need you."

"The real people, Jerry. What about them?"

"All I can tell you is relocation orders have been canceled. Your fellow passengers aren't being sent anywhere."

"I'm getting frustrated here. Why do you need me?"

Jerry took the last bite of his sandwich and wiped his mouth with a paper napkin. "The third set of clones are my congregation. Two hundred twenty three believers. I need you to be a deacon in my new church."

Hal pressed his temples. "I can't believe you've done this."

"Listen to me for a minute. Most of those poor souls felt lost. It wasn't hard to reach them, emotionally I mean. They're glad to have something to take hold of. I suspected it from the start. That's what gave me the idea—those people wanted to come together. They need that strength."

"All of them?"

"Most." He took a folded paper from the pocket of his lab coat. He studied it for a moment. "I have sixty more to interview. At least thirty of those will agree to join us. By the time you're home, doing what you have to, I'll have my congregation completely organized."

"This whole lunch-meeting was set up by you and Steve Palmer to get me to agree to come back here." Hal chuckled. "So Palmer knows about your church?"

"He'll never admit to it."

"Then why did he insist on my seeing you?"

"Do you remember Mr. Morgan?" He looked down and pushed the plate away.

"I'll never forget that—"

"Abomination is the word. It was a gross mutation I created."

"Was?"

"Mr. Morgan died two weeks after you saw him ...."

"Thank God." Dr. Jordan's face stiffened. "I can still hear those sounds—like words, if they were." He shivered. "The thing was pleading. I felt more than I actually heard."

Jerry picked up his napkin and wiped his hands as if to clean away something foul. "David, my assistant, called me. When I got to the cages he was milk-white and shaking. He whispered, 'Mr. Morgan wants you.' I opened the cage and stared. The creature had pushed itself up against the back wall. It stared at me through those insect eyes. I heard strained, rattled breathing. David stood ten feet away shaking his head. I asked, "What is it, Mr. Morgan?"

Dr. Jordan shuddered.

Jerry twisted the napkin as he went on. "Mr. Morgan gathered every ounce of his remaining strength to form words through his serpent-like mouth."

'*I'm dying.*' He said it twice. The sound. God, the sound. It was liquid, choking—awful."

Hal took a breath. "Mr. Morgan was aware?"

"Yes, my monster was trapped intelligence! Everyday of its *damned* existence it thought and felt. It knew what I had done."

"Not you all alone. You had no way of knowing. You didn't intend the result."

"No, I didn't, but it happened! I caught the essence of life—a human soul. I put it into a prison of anguish and horror."

"He couldn't blame you."

"Mr. Morgan forgave me—that poor, painful creature gave me absolution for sending it to hell."

Caught in what Zanster was saying, Dr. Jordan tried to take hold of reality. He needed to hang on to fact. The law of gravity crossed his mind. Quantum mechanics occurred to him. "What you're saying is beyond understanding."

"It gets better, Doctor."

Hal gulped the last swallow of his wine. "I'm listening."

"As he died, Mr. Morgan said, *'The other side exists.'* I could sense the pain he suffered, just to form the words. I hated my knowledge. I despised my own work." He dropped his napkin. *'I know, Doctor,'* Mr. Morgan gurgled, *'I know how you feel.'* Then twice he said, *'Doctor Jordan can give us new faith. Keep Doctor Jordan.'*

Jerry's eyes filled. "That poor, trapped, being heard every word you and I spoke in front of his cage. He felt your strength. Mr. Morgan saw you as a power from the past that we've lost in the present. That's why we met today. That's what Steve Palmer knows. We want you to come back. We need you."

Hal sat straight and stared at Jerry. "I'm a scientist, a teacher—not a savior."

"You're a man of grit. You come from an age of faith and believe in a promise we lost a long time ago. I want you in my church. You're a deacon in yours. I want you as a deacon in mine."

Hal shivered.

Zanster said, "Yes! You can help resurrect faith in the twenty-fifth century."

"You're scaring me to death."

"Good. Tell Palmer you *will* come back. He wants you, I *need* you!" Jerry stood and nodded toward the buffet. "Want another wine?"

"Please, I think I need it."

Jerry picked up the two glasses. "Congressman Franklin's coming back for other reasons. I think yours and mine are a hell of a lot more important."

Hal wrung his hands and stared at the ceiling. "Holy God in heaven."

Jerry chuckled. "My exact thoughts. I'll get more wine."

Chapter 70
Serious Commitments

SEVEN DAYS LATER 8:30 AM
UNITED WORLD COUNCIL SPECIAL SESSION:

*C*hairman Fisher keyed his console. "Ladies and gentlemen of the council, I thank you for your unanimous acceptance of our two new members." He nodded to Congressman Franklin. "Alan, you have the floor."

The congressman stood and faced the representatives of the nine key nations. "As a long-term member of the United States Congress, I will serve this esteemed council with integrity and honesty. It is with great commitment and honor that I shall prove worthy of my appointment to this important position. Thank you."

The Russian representative's image moved to the center of the huge screen. "We are all aware of your accomplishments in national defense and the advances you made possible in space exploration. I'm sad that you'll only be with us for just three months of the year."

Franklin grinned. "In my heart, sir, I'll be here every day." He sat down and took a long, deep breath.

The chairman said, "I ask the council to recognize Doctor Hal Jordan, Professor of Physics at UCLA."

Hal glanced at Kathy Simmons and Steve Palmer. They were both beaming with pride. He stood before the nine images and knew they could see how nervous he was. "Ladies and gentlemen." He cleared his throat. "I'm overwhelmed with the opportunity I've been given, and have accepted. I'm pleased to be a small part of this advanced society." He paused and studied the nine faces. "To learn and work in this intellectual environment is a privilege I could never have imagined."

The French representative filled the center screen. "Doctor Jordan, you're a black man. You'll be teaching a white student who will make a major contribution in technology."

Jordan flinched, but held his composure. "I would never discriminate, sir."

"Wouldn't it be better for you if your student were of your color?"

The question hung in the air for a moment.

Fisher cut in. "I think that issue is inappropriate."

The Italian representative took the center screen. "Let doctor Jordan respond. I think we'd all like to know."

The female representative from China spoke up. "I agree. Can you answer honestly, professor?"

Beads of sweat formed on Hal's forehead. "I already have." He relaxed and smiled. "My student's mind has no color. I don't care if his skin is Asian, Hawaiian, Indian, Mexican, African, Irish-white or emerald green." He took a short breath. "He will get anything and everything I can teach him." He glanced at Kathy, she was smiling. "You already know what I've done." He gestured toward the screen "The question has been answered."

England's representative took the center screen. "Doctor Jordan, We all agreed to pose that question to you to see how you'd respond. It was not meant to be personal."

Hal thought a moment. "Well, I'll tell you

what. It *is* personal and offensive. If five hundred years haven't changed the need for such a question then your society hasn't really learned a whole hell of a lot after all!" Hal sat down.

Chairman Fisher said, "I move to close."

Steve Palmer added, "I second the motion."

Fisher continued, "We have a motion to close. It's been seconded. All in favor respond."

Every member at the conference table keyed their consoles. All lights were green.

Sophy said, "The motion carries."

The chairman slammed his gavel down. "This session is adjourned!"

The giant screen filled with the UWC logo.

Hal felt all eyes on him "I guess I blew it."

Kathy started the applause, the others joined in.

Fisher stood. "That was the best response I've ever heard in this chamber. Welcome to UWC."

Chapter 71
The Last Day

PHASE THREE: DEPARTURE:
THE READY-ROOM
HANGAR 24 9:00 AM:

*K*athy Simmons studied the five chosen faces, the sixth was in Linda's womb. She smiled. "In less than one hour you'll be on your way home." She glanced toward the open door and saw the access-stairs in place against the huge 747. Looking directly at Dr. Hal Jordan. "Any questions?"

He rubbed his forehead. "I'm still concerned about the other passengers, the clones, and what they might really be aware of."

"Believe me, they're not aware of anything."

"I sure hope you're right."

She patted Hal's shoulder. "I'm positive." Kathy took a small envelope from the pocket of her lab coat and handed it to Congressmen Franklin. "This is from Chairman Fisher."

He turned the envelope over several times then tore it open. Alan grinned as he read the handwritten note:

When you're on the other side,

light up one of those cigars.

I'll be smoking mine with you.

God bless,

Robert

Alan folded the note and slipped it into his breast pocket where he had his last three imported cigars. He looked at his wife. "We're going home."

Laura squeezed her husband's hand. "It's about damn time."

Dr. Jordan picked up his duffle bag and looked at the Sternfelds. "It's been a long three

Months for all of us."

Michael put his arm around Linda. "Professor, it's been a lifetime."

A security droid appeared at the doorway. "We're ready."

Kathy nodded. "Thank you." She smiled at the group. "I'll get you seated." She gestured toward the giant aircraft. "Shall we?"

* * * *

THREE HOURS EARLIER
UWC CONFERENCE CHAMBER:

*C*hairman Fisher stood before the huge screen watching the activity in hangar twenty four. He turned around and addressed Steve Palmer and General Mackendrick. "You two will be in the control center for the entire event?"

Steve leaned on the conference table. "Yes, sir, we'll be monitoring every aspect of the mission."

Mack sat back. "I'm in charge of the military escort up to gate entry."

The chairman looked back at the screen. "They're your best?"

"Absolutely, I've assigned two of the same

pilots who brought the 747 in back in July."

Fisher walked to his seat at the head of the table. He stood behind his chair. "Greg, I need to hear from you."

Dr. Rankin cleared his throat. "As of yesterday afternoon, our team had completed all of the brain scans. The results were perfect." He consulted a folder on the table in front of him. "Even the few children have no memory of where they've been for the last three months."

The chairman addressed Dr. Carol Evans. "Ms. Evans, your input is most important."

"My team supports Doctor Rankin's findings. "All the passengers, including the cockpit crew, will have no memory of the last three months."

"Thank you." Fisher gestured toward the big screen and spoke to Steve Palmer. "That massive aircraft is going to be taking off soon. Is the new program in place and running?"

"It is, and it's been tested to the MAX." He glanced at the open folder in front of him. "At precisely one minute, thirty seconds into the gate, flight 280 slips back into 1998."

Fisher walked away from his chair and stared at the image of the 747 on the giant screen. "I want audio communication with the aircraft as it approaches the gate."

Mack spoke up. "That's already been arranged, sir."

The chairman leaned on a far corner of the table. "Ms. Simmons, I had no intention of ignoring you. You're close to our key-five, well, six actually." He grinned. "You'll be getting them on the plane. I'm sure Franklin and Jordan will have questions." He pointed toward the screen. "I think it's a good idea to keep what we've learned here confidential until I can address them in flight."

"I have no problem with that, sir."

"Thank you." He gestured toward the group. "Let's get these people back where they belong."

Chapter 72
The Return
Phase Four

TIME GATE OPERATIONS CENTER
LAUNCH CONTROL – STATION ONE:

Steve Palmer watched the screen as Tex tracked the aircraft toward the Gate. He glanced at General Mackendrick. "We're on the mark—thirty seconds down-range and counting."

Mack swallowed a gulp of black coffee. "How long before entry?"

Thirty minutes then it's out of our hands."

Mack lifted his cup in a toast. "And out of our hair for good."

"That remains to be seen."

* * * *

25:00 DOWN-RANGE: RE-ENTRY

Vibration

$\mathcal{T}$he voice of the chairman came over the jetliner's P/A system.

"This is Chairman Fisher I'm in the Operations Center where we are tracking your flight. I wanted to speak to all of you myself. In Just five more minutes your plane will begin re-entry into the Gate."

Congressman Franklin held both of Laura's trembling hands. "Everything's going to be all right." He thought he knew what the Chairman was about to say.

Linda clung to Michael with all the strength she had. "Michael, I'm frightened.

"I am too, honey."

In coach, Dr. Jordan swallowed the last of another scotch. "Good God in heaven." He gripped Carol Hollinger's arm. "It'll be okay, sweetheart."

Chairman Fisher continued in a comforting tone. "Each of you has an important mission which must be completed. At this time it is my responsibility to inform you." He hesitated. "There has been a change in the program."

Carol Hollinger turned and looked at Hal.

"Professor Jordan, Why did you slap me?"

Alan whispered, "I had a feeling he'd change the plan."

"To what, honey?"

"Listen." He smiled and patted Laura's arm.

Fisher spoke in a soft voice. "Your plane will exit the Gate without damage and you'll be on your way to a routine, safe landing in Los Angeles."

Dr. Jordan hugged Carol. "I knew it!"

"In addition," Fisher continued, "your flight crew and fellow passengers are not clones. They're in an altered state for now."

Alan kissed his wife. "I had a hunch ... all along. I had a hunch and I was damn right." He shouted at the first class section. "God bless you, Fisher!"

The chairman concluded. "When your aircraft slips back into 1998 it will be as if you never encountered the Time Gate at all. You five are the only ones in your time who know where you've been." He chuckled. "One more little detail that only Hal might really understand. You've been gone a mere eight minutes. Enjoy your flight." He cleared his throat. "It's been my pleasure to have met each of you, God bless."

* * * *

More turbulence.

A billion stars.

Linda held her husband's right hand . "It's beautiful, Michael. My God, It's beautiful!"

He shook his head. "I can't believe what I'm thinking. I see you and me with grandchildren from the loins of our son who hasn't been born."

The baby moved under Michael's hand.

The light intensified.

A billion suns.

All sound faded away.

Dense silence.

Dr. Jordan felt himself floating, as if rising up through deep, warm water. He sucked a short breath. "We're crossing over."

He squeezed Carol's tiny hand. The child smiled and uttered a soft sigh.

Jordan tried to turn toward Carol. He could not. He felt numb, heavy. He had no breath, no voice.

The interior of the aircraft blurred.

Gray.

Hal thought of Mr. Morgan. The horrible, genetic mistake. He heard its miserable cry for help.

Jordan moved his lips to form one soundless name: Virginia.

Starstorm

Epilogue

**ONE YEAR LATER
JULY 15 1:00 PM 1999
AN UPSCALE HOTEL LOUNGE
DIAMOND BAR, ORANGE CO, CA:**

$\mathcal{D}$r. Hal Jordan approached a corner booth with a big smile on his face. "Alan, it's so great to see you."

Congressman Franklin stood. The two men didn't shake hands, they hugged.

Alan said, "Damn, you look great!" He gestured toward the table. "Sit. We'll order something. They told me two o'clock for the car."

Hal slipped into the booth. "I got the same message last night."

Alan sat back and beamed. "This is so great. We could work out our schedules together." He waved toward a waitress. "Congress is out for the next few months and you're between semesters at the university."

A young waitress approached the table. "Lunch, gentlemen?"

Alan said, "I'd like a glass of Brunello di Montalcino with the Brie-and apple appetizer."

The waitress smiled. "The Brunello is only available by the bottle."

"Good." He looked at Hal. "Share the bottle?"

"What the hell, we're not driving."

"Your lunch, sir?"

"I'll have the apple thing." Hal laughed.

Alan grinned at the waitress. "Uncork it for us and let it breathe a bit."

"I'll have your order up in a few minutes."

Alan said, "What'd they tell you?"

"I got an E-mail last Friday. I wasn't sure about it. The message came to my computer at the university. It was very short and it came from UWC service dot net." He looked around the room. "I didn't question it. I opened the message immediately. It was straight forward. It said, meet you here at 1:00 PM this date."

Alan leaned forward. "I got the same message." He grinned and shook his head. "I'm telling you, I've never been so excited about anything in all my political life."

"Nor have I, it's the anniversary of our crossing and it's time to return.

The waitress arrived with their lunch. "The wine has taken its breath. Would you like me to pour?"

Hal held up his glass. "By all means, dear lady."

* * * *

Alan took a bite of cheese and a slice of fresh apple. Has anything been different for you this past year?"

Hal took a sip of his wine. "My papers on time theories have been published in scientific journals world wide."

"That's exciting. It stirs the pot."

"How about you?"

Alan smiled. "I've proposed a bill that lowers the cost of energy production. It doesn't alter anything. It just cuts the expense of what we're already doing."

* * * *

A young man, dressed in a finely tailored Italian suit approached the table. "Excuse me. Are you two gentlemen, Congressman, Alan Franklin and Professor, Hal Jordan?"

Alan spoke for the both of them. "We are."

The young man smiled. "I'm Roger Callis, your escort to John Wayne Airport. We have a car waiting at the hotel entrance." He checked his watch. "It's one forty. Finish your lunch. I'll meet you out front." Roger smiled and left.

Alan leaned forward. "He's one of them, I'd bet on it."

"You'd win. I've had two time agents in my classes all year." He grinned. They showed up at every lecture I gave off campus. One was an attractive female and she fit in perfectly." Hal drank some wine. "Both of them were top students. Everything they did was perfect. I actually enjoyed having them around."

Alan said, "I had the same combination in my office in Washington. They out shined any interns I've ever worked with." He picked up a gift-wrapped package off the seat.

Hal chuckled. "You return bearing gifts?"

"It's a box of imported cigars. Fisher will be delighted."

Dr. Jordan spread some cheese on a slice of apple. "Have you heard from the Sternfelds?"

"Laura keeps in touch with them. Bless her heart, she spent the weekend at their place when Linda had the baby."

"I got a card from Michael with a picture of little William—*little,* hell. He came into the world at nine point six pounds."

"Did Virginia see the card?"

"I told her they were a couple I'd met on a boring flight last July."

They both laughed.

* * * *

2499 ONE WEEK LATER
THE NEW FAITH CONGREGATIONAL CHURCH:

$\mathcal{T}$he Reverend, Dr. Jerry Zanster stood before more than three hundred of his believers. "It swells my heart to address you this evening." He waved out to the packed sanctuary and smiled. "We may have to expand our facility."

Soft laughter whispered through the crowd.

"Over the last year we've come together here twice a week and joined in prayer." Jerry glanced toward Dr. Jordan who was seated to the left of the pulpit. "Tonight we shall enjoy a three-fold answer to those heartfelt prayers." He gestured to Hal. "I give you the deacon of our New Faith Congregation. Professor, Hal Jordan."

Seated to the right of Reverend Zanster, Congressman Franklin and Chairman Robert Fisher started the rising round of applause.

Dr. Jordan stepped to the lectern and raised his hands. "It is with utmost honor that I humbly serve as deacon to this body of faithful. I'm overwhelmed at what Reverend Zanster has accomplished in a single year." He paused and looked at the smiling faces. "This is an emotional moment for me." He took a soft breath. "A year ago, I saw most of you, but I failed to *see* any of you." Hal's voice wavered. "You have my solemn word; I *will* see and get to know each and every one of you." His voice dropped to a near whisper. "I thank you for accepting me into this church ... thank you."

Over the second burst of applause Reverend Zanster leaned into the microphone. "Our second *revelation* this evening, if I may use that word, comes from the twenty-member delegation we sent to Northern Ireland. They have successfully started a New Faith Congregation in a small village." He raised both arms and shouted. "They have a building and one hundred twenty members!"

The sanctuary filled with applause.

Reverend Zanster bent toward the microphone again. "I've saved the best for last." He looked to his right and nodded at the chairman. "I'm most proud to present the Chairman of the United World Council, Robert Fisher."

Applause was polite and sparse.

He gripped the edges of the lectern and nodded toward the gathering. "Most of you have no idea what the UWC is or who I am." He hesitated, measuring his words. "I represent a government the majority of you have never heard of. It's been a government that has allowed the experience you're sharing here tonight, and one you had in another time, to crumble and fall away." He turned to the pulpit. "The reverend Zanster has turned all that around. Because of him and the genius of his work you *are* here." He cleared his throat. "It is hereby decreed that the New Faith Congregational Church will function and exist within our present society. This church may be established in, and grow within the borders of any nation on this planet." He raised his voice. "The full council concurs."

The applause was deafening. The congregation stood and cheered for several minutes.

When the roar settled down Reverend

Zanster held up a large, gold cross his father had left him. "We've made great strides. Our church has been recognized. Thank you for being here. We'll meet again on Sunday ... God Bless you all."

Dr. Jordan gave Jerry a hug. "I can't believe all this."

"You're part of it. If not for you and the other key people, none of this would've existed."

Congressman Franklin patted Hal's shoulder. "Someone wants to speak with you."

Jordan looked down into the beaming face of Carol Hollinger. "Oh my God!" He swept the child up in his arms. "I'm so glad to see you." He hugged the little girl and rocked her. "Are you okay?"

"I'm fine. Everything is so nice here. I have a lot of new friends an' school is just perfect."

Hal thought a moment. "What about your parents?" He studied her innocent face. "Are they here?"

"Of course, silly. They're waiting for me out front."

Hal looked at Jerry.

The reverend smiled. "I managed a little something extra to make up for Mr. Morgan."

"How did you do it?"

"We'll have breakfast tomorrow, I'll explain it."

Hal put Carol down and brushed a lock of hair from her face. "I've missed you."

She took his big hand in both of her tiny ones. "Thank you for coming back, Professor." She stepped away then turned back. "I forgive you for slapping me." Carol grinned and left the church.

About the author

Ted Tillotson Lives with his family and eight rescued feline friends in Central California.

To contact the author go to:

Http://www.tedtillotsondragonlairbooks.com